SOMEONE LIKE YOU

BECKY ALEXANDER

Storm
PUBLISHING

This is a work of fiction. Names, characters, business, events and incidents are the products of the author's imagination. Any resemblance to actual persons, living or dead, or actual events is purely coincidental.

Permission to quote from *Poison* by Liselot Vekemans, granted by Nick Hern Books.
www.nickhernbooks.co.uk

To request permissions, contact the publisher at rights@stormpublishing.co

Ebook ISBN: 978-1-80508-321-4
Paperback ISBN: 978-1-80508-323-8

Cover design: Henry Steadman
Cover images: Shutterstock

Published by Storm Publishing.
For further information, visit:
www.stormpublishing.co

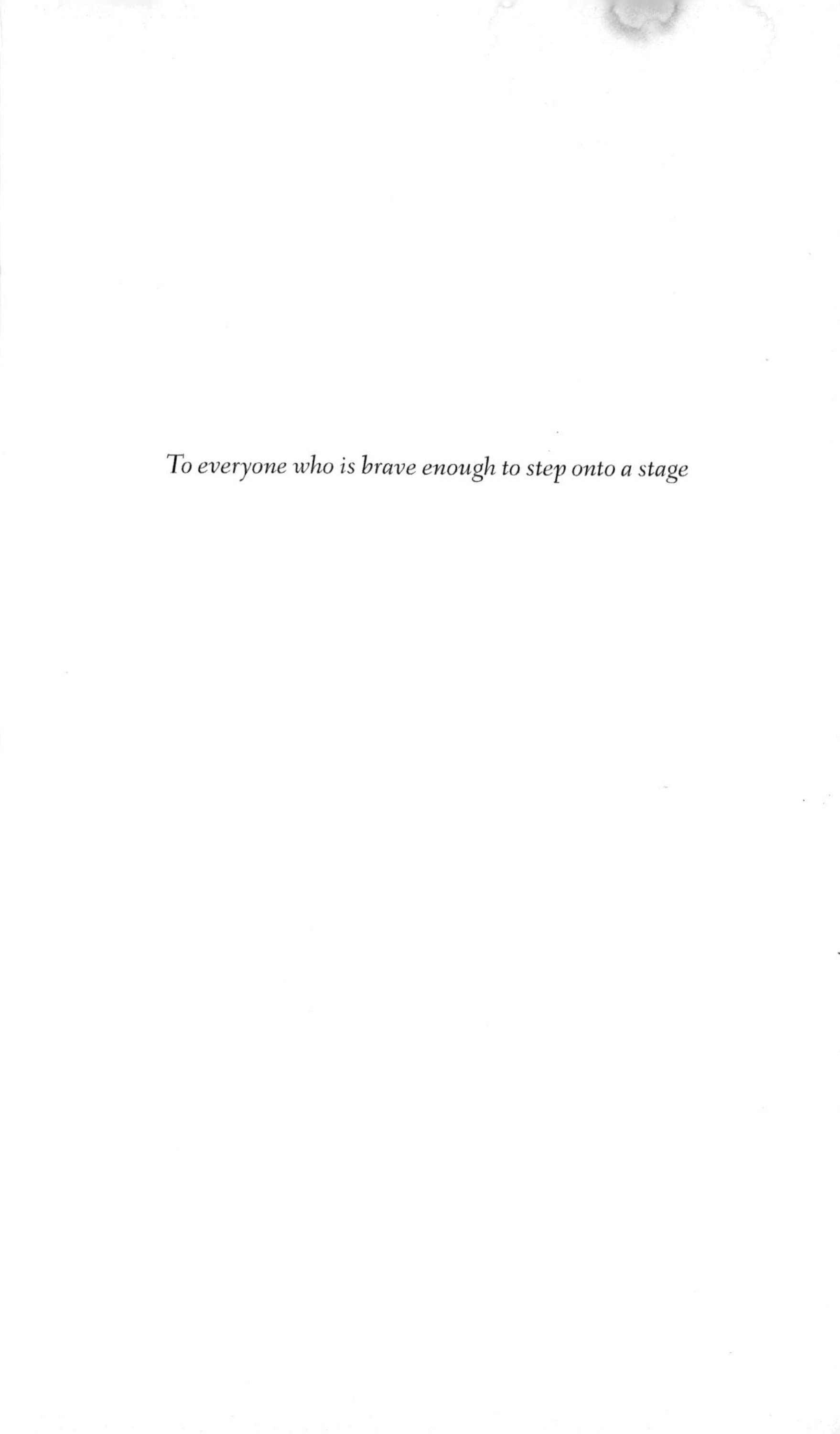

To everyone who is brave enough to step onto a stage

‘Who soars too near the sun, with golden wings, melts them.’

W. Shakespeare

FIVE-MINUTE CALL

Standing on an empty stage, just you and the ghost light, before you are revealed to the audience, is both the best, and the most terrifying, place to be. It has taken so many years to get to this moment. And, at last, it's mine.

I can hear the audience taking their seats, asking to get past, talking about whether there's time to get a drink before the show starts. Not long now. Adrenalin makes my breath shallow, tight. I exhale, slowly, counting to ten, as we have been trained to do before every performance. I have waited *so long* for this.

I start the play standing behind a mesh screen in complete darkness. The audience don't know I'm there. They won't see me until the lights kick in, sending them into blackout and me into blazing white light. I can see the dark outline of Olivia waiting at the side of the stage, pulling at the sleeves of her raincoat while looking down at the floor. We both know that most of the people here tonight have come to see her, and that many expect her to fail. I shake my arms to release the tension in my shoulders and neck. I smooth down my tight red dress, though it doesn't need it.

A play doesn't exist until the audience watches it. Without

the audience, we are just people messing around, playing make-believe. It's the reaction of the audience that brings a play to life and makes it mean something. You feed off the energy – if the audience love the show, it drives you on to give your best performance, and if they don't, well, then you are screwed.

People like Olivia have no idea what it takes for someone like me to make it. I have worked *so* hard to get here, and I've done it on my own. If she screws this up, messes up her lines *again*, then, well, that's on her. This is *my* time to make it.

Who wouldn't kill for a chance like this?

ACT 1

ONE

Did I know how it was all going to turn out? Not that Friday night back in February when I went to the casting. It had been over two years since I graduated from the Royal Academy of Dramatic Art – RADA – and the elation of our final showcase felt a lifetime ago. Yet another batch of graduates had left since then, yet more actors released into the world, all chasing the same few parts.

It was almost 7pm when I walked out of the tube station, and turned left, away from the tourists and shoppers blocking the pavements, clearly not in a rush to get anywhere. I leaned against a wall, changed into my lucky red shoes and checked my phone – the casting was just a short walk past Liberty department store and the Palladium Theatre, its gaudy lights reflected on the rain-soaked pavement. The Liberty flower stall framing the front door looked beautiful, as ever. Steel buckets full of tasteful pale green hydrangeas, lilies, white ranunculus and snowdrops, all displayed to coordinate and tell the wealthy customers that spring was on the way, and all was well in their gilded world. To be able to spend money like that, on something so pointless, and not even worry if your bank card would work. They had no idea.

A man ran across the road towards me, keeping the rain off his hair with a folder. As we passed, he turned briefly to look at me – checking me out? As if I'd be interested in someone that old. I glanced back and saw him disappear through the stage door of the Palladium. Soho is like that, full of doors and alleyways that you only really notice if you work in the acting business. Two years of dead-end castings had helped me get to know that about London, if nothing else. Each casting email arrived full of promise and potential, each a life-changing opportunity to be in a well-paid commercial, a play by an award-winning playwright, or a Netflix series pilot, but first you had to find the casting room down a side street, which led to an office on the third or fourth floor of a tired Soho building that wasn't fit for much else. I wondered if people working in the posh design studios or at their laptops in coffee shops had any idea what was going on upstairs, where rooms were rented by the hour.

Poland Street wasn't far, just along Carnaby Street. Lyrics lit in neon high above the street: *Is this the real life? Is this just fantasy?* It made perfect sense for this part of London, where actors mixed with models, designers, musicians and producers. If you wanted to make it in showbiz, then you would find yourself in the casting rooms of Soho at some point.

Just past 7 now. Where the hell was this casting? I *hate* being late. It was hard enough to get a casting, without pissing off the director or your agent by missing your slot. Elle had gone a bit quiet on me recently, sending fewer opportunities my way. I couldn't blow this one before I even got there. Where was 22A? My phone said close, but there were hardly any numbers above the shops. The rain, harder now, was soaking through my leggings onto my thighs. Great, now I looked a mess as well as being late. A shabby black door, set back from the pavement next to a

Korean grill place, a plastic panel of entry buttons. Studio 1, 22A. What a relief! A pile of *Resident* magazines lay tied in plastic on the step, edges starting to crinkle in the rain; I pulled out a copy to take with me in case I had to wait. Anything to help kill time.

A crackle as I pressed the button, and I leaned forward towards the speaker grate: 'Jemima Evans, for the play casting?' I heard a faint click as the door released and I stepped inside. The sound of the cars swishing past on the rain-drenched road stopped as the heavy door shut behind me.

I made my way up at least four flights of stained carpet, past unmarked doors leading to who knows where. Elle had sent through the Spotlight brief for this play, but it had been pretty vague. They wanted to audition women with a playing age 21–30, which hardly narrowed it down – that would include pretty much any actress who'd just finished drama school and plenty who were already trying to make it. There was no physical description on the brief, because they can't do that in case they seem racist, but we all knew they always had a particular look in mind. Would everyone at the casting look like me, with pale skin, red hair? I knew my hair was one of the reasons I'd been chosen for RADA – I stood out, looked unusual, 'quirky'. That was what they wanted there – people who looked different, that they knew an audience would want to watch, to stare at. Drama school was the home of the freak in many ways, though they didn't say that out loud at the interview. Everyone on my course had something a bit otherworldly about them – a striking bone structure, shaved head, or massive eyes that made you want to stare back at them. The identikits from my school would never have got in, with their ironed blonde hair and bland faces. RADA didn't want them – what was special about them?

'What did you say your name was?' the young guy sitting at the standard-issue Ikea desk asked when I walked in. He didn't look up.

'Jemima Evans.'

We were right up in the roof, and the vaulted ceiling had been opened and exposed to make the room feel as large and light as possible. Lime-green seating edged the walls, empty. There was no-one else in the room. That was odd; there were normally loads of actors at these castings. Bored, everyone waiting their turn, and never enough seats.

'Fill in these forms.' No smile. He passed me a plastic clipboard, his thin, white arms covered in tattoos from the wrists up to his T-shirt sleeves – thorns and dark purple roses. 'There's a page of script, too, underneath.' How much pain do you go through to get your arms to look like that? I imagined my finger tracing the rose briars.

'Take a seat,' he said in a way that implied, *Please move away from me.*

The paperwork was the usual stuff: your name, agent, measurements, height. I turned to the script.

'Which character am I meant to read?' I asked desk boy. The script had two characters, Woman A and Woman B.

'You choose.'

The scene seemed to be an argument between the two women. They each had the same number of lines. I wondered what the other actors had chosen.

'Is anyone else going to be reading it with me, do you know?' I asked.

He shrugged, and put his earbuds in. *End of chat.* I felt a weariness sink over me; the trek across London was probably yet another waste of time. I'd left the coffee van early, so that meant fewer wages, and Ben had been a total dick about it. Below on the street, people had real jobs to do, places to go, perhaps dinner out with friends or a date with cocktails. I didn't even know what this job would pay – if I even got it. *Pull yourself together, Jem. This is what actors want, to be at castings. This is the job.* I tried to read the words, make sense of them. How could I bring this to life without any prep time? Why hadn't Elle sent this to me before? She was a crap agent.

'In you go,' said desk boy, indicating the door behind him. No-one had come out, which surprised me. Usually at these things there is a constant stream of people being seen – one in, one out. So, they weren't seeing anyone before me? I felt a surge of optimism. Maybe I *did* have a chance with this one, after all, if they weren't seeing many people. The odds in my favour. I left my stuff and pushed open the door.

That's when it got weird.

TWO

I walked into the casting room and found myself completely alone. The room, like nearly every other casting room I'd been in, was painted a harsh, bright white, lit by unflattering ceiling spotlights. The walls were empty, except for a black, one-way viewing window that filled most of the far wall. It was like one of those interrogation rooms in a police procedural – I imagined cops behind the mirror with their arms crossed, watching me, waiting for the bad guy to crumble and reveal everything. The crowded, rainy streets of Soho felt far away.

'Thank you for coming, Jemima. If you could stand in the centre of the room.' A voice from behind the viewing window.

The last casting room I'd been in had been packed: a camera on a tripod, casting director, producer and client, sitting close together on fold-up chairs. That was the normal set-up – not enough space for everyone who needed to be in the room, having booked the cheapest they could get.

'About here OK?' I asked, choosing a spot roughly in the centre of the room, facing the window. I stepped gently from left to right, trying to shift some of my nervous energy, trying to ground myself, as trained. 'Hello in there!' I tried to sound confident, relaxed, build a rapport.

'Do you consent to us filming you?' A voice, female, echoed around the room.

'Yes, that's fine!' I felt nerves start to rise. I took a deep breath. *You can do this, Jem.* 'Do you want me to read the script? I don't know it off by heart. I just got it. Sorry.'

No reply. Were they getting the camera ready? A few more seconds passed.

'So, can you tell me more about the play? Is it one that I might know?' I asked the blank window. I could hear a soft buzz from somewhere high in the ceiling. And then her voice again.

'It's called *Poison*. It's about two women who haven't seen each other in a long time. Read Woman A.'

I looked down at the sheet of paper in my hand, rolled my shoulders back and checked that my feet were placed evenly apart. *Woman A. OK, bring it on*! There were no stage directions to give me a sense of time or place; it seemed to be just two women speaking directly to each other, in the same room. Perhaps I could imagine a waiting room of some kind, like at a hospital, or maybe they have just bumped into each other, in a café or a park or somewhere.

Looking back, I think my competitive instinct kicked in. If there was a part to be won, then I wanted it. I could worry about whether the play was any good if I got it. Chances are that I wouldn't, so why not just go with the experience and see what happened? I'd be back outside in the rain soon enough. And if I did get it... no more coffee van, no more blank CV, I could tell my friends from drama school I was working at last... I started to read.

'I'm finding this difficult. I mean sitting here together, waiting. Having to sit here... waiting. And not having seen you for years. And not having any idea how you are. And you not having any idea how I am. And not knowing what to say.'

Should I move about, walk across the room? I felt a bit lost in the space. I was obviously meant to speak to woman B, but without anyone real to look at, I wasn't sure if I sounded genuine.

Then the voice behind the mirror replied, softly: 'So, you don't think I've changed?'

I replied, looking at the blank window with my own reflection looking back at me, 'Not really'.

The voice responded: 'Not at all?'

My line: 'You've got older'.

'Yeah, what do you expect... I'm glad to see you. On the way here I kept thinking: How will she look? How will she look now? And I couldn't stop thinking about the first time I ever saw you.'

It was quite good stuff. There was something about her voice behind the window, sort of warm, but firm – sexy, even? I wondered what she looked like. I replied with my line. 'That was years ago.'

Her line: 'I couldn't get it out of my head. I hope you're glad to see me, too.'

The script told me that there was a pause. I could have done with a chair in the room, to sit down, mix it up a bit.

She spoke. 'Do you know what I find strange? You and me, here together, after all this time.'

Did I know her voice from somewhere? There was something really familiar about it. Must have heard her on TV or somewhere. She was probably an actress brought in to read the lines.

'Jemima. I've been waiting for you.'

That felt strange, her saying my name like that. It threw me. I looked at my next line. *Take a breath, focus.* That line wasn't here in the script. I turned the page. Blank. Was she doing improv?

The voice continued. 'I've seen you around. At home. At work. Getting on with your life.'

I thought of me at work at the coffee van, or sitting out on the deck of Seagrass, drinking wine. *That's so odd.* What was I meant to say to that? The lines on the script didn't match. Was I missing a page?

'I'm sorry, I don't have these lines,' I said.

'I've wanted to meet you properly, for ages.' Her voice, calm, echoing around the blank room.

I focused on the window, trying to see in. 'Have we met? I feel I know your voice?'

She didn't reply. I waited for what felt like an age. 'Do you want me to do the lines again? I think I've got it now, so I can try and read it off-page, and, you know, make it sound more real?' Messios had taught us that you have to show you are flexible, ready to try new things, build a relationship with the director so they know you are easy to work with. That you'd be happy to do what they asked of you.

'That's enough. Thank you, Jemima. You can go.'

I could see a shadow of movement behind the glass. Was she leaving? Was that it? That wasn't good. Was there more than one person behind the window? It was impossible to know.

'OK, thank you. Thank you for asking me in!' Too chirpy, eager.

I paused by the door, half expecting someone to say something. How long had I been in there? Not even ten minutes. *Another waste of time.*

I was surprised to see that desk boy wasn't in his chair. The reception room was silent. All I could hear was the faint vibration of traffic from the street, many floors below. Were they not seeing any other actors at all? That was so odd – maybe I *was* in with a chance. I picked up my coat and placed the script in its place. The way she'd said my name, it was as if she *knew* me. I went down the stairs more quickly than I'd come up and I felt oddly relieved when I stepped out onto rainy Poland Street again, and joined the pavements full of people.

I texted my agent, Elle.

> Went well!! Fingers crossed. Thanks for the opportunity. Let me know if you hear. J xxx

I glanced into the window of a bar as I walked towards the station and a man sitting inside caught my eye, smiled. I could smile back, go in for a drink, he'd buy, of course. I could do with something to steady my nerves after that casting. I could hear her voice, repeating her lines in my head. '*I've seen you around...*' She knew me from somewhere, surely, but why hadn't she said? It crossed my mind that maybe whoever it was might walk past any moment, I might see her. I could sit in the window. Perhaps they had more actors to see. I knew one thing – it was out of my control.

But this moment wasn't. I walked into the bar.

THREE

It had taken forever to get to sleep, despite the gentle rocking of Seagrass and the dull sound of rain on the roof. Another stupid waste of time audition. Wasted money home on an Uber, and now a hangover, too. My eyes were almost level with the surface of the canal, framed in the small circular window. No-one could see in from this side of the boat, so I didn't bother to pull the curtain across anymore. The water changed every day and that soothed me; sometimes it was emerald green with algae, but today the canal was inky black and blue, the surface broken by pieces of brown weed floating past. Less than seven feet deep here in the boatyard; probably best not to think about what might be at the bottom of it.

I texted Sancha.

> Just up. Audition done, bit strange. Can I call you? X

I stared at the phone, willing her to call. Usually this was a good time, Polly would be in bed.

Nothing. Probably out having an actual life.

I really needed coffee. Seagrass's galley was tiny, with just enough kit for one person, which suited me just fine. There was no way I was inviting anyone on here – it was no place to impress a pickup. That guy in the bar had wanted me to go back to his hotel, and that might have been warmer, at least, for sure. I spooned some of Ben's coffee into the cafetière; he didn't seem to notice if I took a bag home from the van now and then. It was good stuff, expensive. It had been a long time since I'd had instant; RADA had taught me that instant was a big no – even on a student budget, 'real' coffee was non-negotiable. It was all about acting the part.

The casting script repeated in my head. *So, you don't think I've changed? Not really. On the way here I kept thinking: How will she look? How will she look now?*

Sipping my coffee, I tried to make sense of it. Why were the characters in the script meeting again? What had kept them apart? It was good writing. I googled the lines and found the play, *Poison*, was by Lot Vekemans, a Dutch writer. I guessed it meant that there was poison between the characters or that something or someone had poisoned them – or was the poison to come? A two-hander, it would be intense to play it and challenging to learn the lines. I could do it, I felt sure about that. *Who was I kidding?* The casting was too short, which was never a good sign. No point thinking about the script, trying to make it work, if I was never going to do it.

When I first signed with Elle, I'd always ask her if there had been any feedback after a casting. We'd been used to that at drama school; we'd do a scene, give it everything and then turn to look at Messios. He would always have notes, criticism or occasionally, a nod, if we'd done something well enough. Out in the real world, it seemed like no-one had time to give feedback; they didn't get paid for that.

Early Saturday morning was dead around St Pancras station. The tourists were not out yet and the office workers were home for the weekend. I stepped out onto the tiny deck, pulling the galley doors behind me to trap any warmth inside Seagrass. I loved the smell of the fresh, damp air.

There is no way that woman could have known me; she must have been trying to get me to act in some way, a drama game of some kind. And I'd acted like an idiot, hadn't known what to say. I should have done improv – impressed her, somehow.

I leaned back against Seagrass and drank my coffee. Trains passed overhead. I liked to imagine all the people leaving London as the lines split like arteries away from the heart. It cost something like a million pounds to live in one of the Gasholders flats right opposite me. I guessed they worked for Google or one of the other new buildings shooting up around St Pancras. Sometimes you could hear the sound of kids playing, if the wind was in the right direction. Their perfect little lives in their designer flats.

My phone lit up. Sancha!

Strange how?

Just me in there. No other actors. Didn't meet the director either. Bit creepy. Shall I call?

She didn't like me just calling in case Jon was around, expecting her full attention; it felt like I had to ask first.

Sorry. Chaos here. That does sound a bit odd, but maybe good?

Maybe.

It would be so much easier to talk about this. I wished she didn't live so far away.

Getting a casting at all is great! Be proud of that. Onwards and upwards, babe. Got to go, S x

I threw my phone down on the bench.

Who else could I talk it through with? I hadn't heard from Elle. She had strict boundaries about working weekends. I felt my mood sinking. I needed to eat. Get out of here. Jeans, boots, big coat, hat to cover my frizzy hair. No point in make up – no-one here cared what I looked like.

Along the wet canal path, over the bridge and towards Central St Martins College, which dominated the far side of Granary Square. When the students did their end-of-degree shows, the courtyard became a vast catwalk, and light projections onto the building served as a theatrical backdrop – I loved watching that, like a West End show, but free. In summer, fountains filled the courtyard, and families brought their kids on day trips to play in them, but today they were lifeless. Ben's coffee van was just above the green plastic steps where office workers and students sat to eat their lunch. It was all a bit fake around here, but I felt at home with that.

I could see Ben in the van, orange beanie on his head, serving a man. No-one waiting. I wasn't in the mood for his clichéd, irritating lines, trying to be sympathetic. 'Oh, your turn will come, you are *so* talented...' That could wait 'til Monday when I was getting paid to listen to him.

I set off towards Camden. Just under the bridge, two small tents had set up camp. Cheap and so thin, and this close to the canal path, anyone could walk past and steal from them, just slice through the flimsy walls to reveal the person inside. A pair of tired walking boots parked outside. A plastic tub, hoping for change. Richer people than me walked past here; they could give them something. I didn't have any spare.

As I was reaching the far end of the tunnel, I felt my pocket vibrate. By the time I got it out, the call had gone to voicemail: one message. From Elle. Oh my god!

'Move over!' A cyclist cut across me, making me jump back against the wall.

I swore at him, then pressed playback.

'Jemima! It's Elle. So. They want to see you again. The *Poison* thing? I'll email over details and the script. Give me a call when you get this message. Well done – you must have made quite an impression.'

My hands shook as I pressed to hear the message again. After all this time... after all the rejections. They wanted me for a callback? They wanted to see me again. I let out a huge exhale. *About time!*

FOUR

Elle told me to get to the Arcola Theatre on Monday for 5pm, which didn't give me much time to prepare the script she had sent. Her guess was someone had pulled out – it was all so last minute. She didn't know how many other actors were in the running still, and if there'd be others at the recall. This was the furthest I'd got since she'd signed me.

'It's Sheridan Productions. They've won loads of awards, BAFTAs, things like that. So, worth being seen by them, whatever the outcome. You might even meet Rebecca Sheridan.' Elle had briefed me, sounded almost optimistic.

I knew who Sheridan Productions were. Everybody did. Neema had got a job with them straight out of RADA, of course she had. She got cast in a play straight after graduation, had told us all about it on the WhatsApp group. Loads of them had gone to see it, even though most people couldn't stand her. They had swarmed around her, chasing the success story, hoping her luck would rub off on them. This was a small play by Sheridan Productions standards, Elle had explained, but who cared? My turn was well overdue.

I bailed on Ben for work, saying I couldn't come in, needed

to prepare. He wasn't pleased, Monday being his busiest day. I would be £80 down, but I needed to at least try and learn the lines, and give my hair some attention. There were so many times someone had said to my mother – me right next to her, in a shop, in the school playground at pick-up – 'I bet she has a temper to go with it,' or my favourite, 'Oh she'll hate it now, but she'll love it when she's older.' Why did adults think that kids couldn't hear that stuff?

Make up. Without mascara, my eyes disappeared into my face so I applied a thick flick of black eyeliner and two coats of Max Factor Masterpiece – the name appealed in the shop. I pulled out the darkest red lipstick I had. The woman I'd taken it from was too drunk to notice. Her bag was right there in the toilets as she was chatting to a mate; it was just wide open. I love its ribbed gold case, with its in-built light that came on when you pressed the tiny nipple at the bottom. These cost £28 at SpaceNK, I'd checked. I carefully followed the shape of my lips, watching them change from pale pink skin, to dark, blood red, as I painted from top to bottom.

Dalston felt like a different world to flash, shiny St Pancras. The smell of rotisserie kebab meat mixed with the traffic fumes on Kingsland High Street and the tables outside bars were rammed, people buying time before having to go home to their partners, their kids, their awful housemates.

I sent a selfie to Sancha.

Back here again!!

When we were students we'd come to Dalston to get costumes from the charity shops; Sancha could make anything look good – she had shown me what to look out for, what labels to pick out. She bought me my first cashmere sweater – it felt so classy, so much softer than any I'd owned before. It had a massive hole in the armpit but that fit in with the drama school vibe.

Tucked away behind the main road, the Arcola didn't much look like a theatre; there weren't any posters outside advertising upcoming shows, no bright lights or anything, just an old warehouse with red doors, parted to reveal the glass entrance inside, but it was a start.

The email from Elle had told me to ask for Ed, assistant producer for Sheridan Productions. I checked my phone. I was right on time. *Perfect.* This felt good! I walked up to the glass door and it slid smoothly to the right, revealing a concrete and brick entrance with a ticket counter on the right. Piles of leaflets and programmes were scattered across, advertising all the plays I wasn't in. Lights just ahead, so I walked towards them, passing a couple of bar tables that hadn't been cleared properly. There were two plates and a copy of *The Stage* on the nearest one, and a wine glass, half full, just left there. I was tempted to take a swig.

'Hello? Am I in the right place?' I called out. It was a huge space, with floor-to-ceiling windows along one side, a bar to my right. Red fairy lights flickered across the bottles.

Overhead lights stuttered on, and a short guy, made wider with a padded jacket, appeared by the side of the bar.

'Jemima?' he barked.

'Yes. Hi! Just got here. The door was open. I'm Jemima. Jem.'

'I saw your name on the call sheet. It's been a while.'

I blinked. Of all the people... You had to be kidding me. *Ed.*

'They're nearly ready for you.' It was coming back to me now, and that hair... floppy, greasy, but without doubt, intentional. Ed put his folder down on the bar and walked behind it, helped himself to a whisky. Showing me he belonged here. And I didn't.

'Um... how are you?' I asked, because that felt like the right thing to say. Would he have any part in the decision-making here? I didn't remember him producing at RADA, it was more the lighting side of things, wasn't it? I walked towards him. He looked tired, twitchy, his eyes a bit red, but otherwise the same.

He drained his glass, and placed it on the bar. Gold pinkie ring. Posh boy. Or trying to be posh. A small part of me could relate to that.

'You know. Busy. I haven't stopped since college.'

Good for him.

Ed's phone buzzed. 'We're downstairs. Follow me.'

'This is a great place!' I said, brightly, not feeling it.

'You not been here before?'

I followed him down concrete steps, holding the handrail. Would it have hurt them to put some lights on down here?

I could have come here before. Maybe I should have... The WhatsApp group was always saying who was in plays, telling us about other people's successes. After a while I got sick of it all, all the showing off, the opening nights. I tried to remember what they'd all been talking about.

'I think someone in my class was in a play here. It was about apes who were really humans, or something like that? Apparently it was brilliant!'

Plus, they could afford to go to all the plays. I couldn't.

'Ah, yes, Nama, was it, or some Indian name like that. You had much work? Not seen you in anything'. That comment did not help my building nerves.

We continued along the dark corridor, which must have been taking us under the bar if I had my sense of direction right. It was freezing down here. The whole theatre building was far larger than I imagined from outside.

'Here we are.' Ed pushed an unmarked door open and held it for me, filling the space with his large belly, so I had to squeeze past him. 'You're looking good, Jemima.' He smiled at me. His whisky breath stank. 'Break a leg.'

I found myself standing at the side of a vast, open stage. Overhead, scaffolding hung with lamps, sending hot beams of yellow light down onto me. As my eyes adjusted, I could make out banks of red, folded-up seats on two sides. Behind me, my enormous shadow loomed on the exposed brick wall. I walked to the centre and dropped my bag and coat on the floor. Did I just stand there, and wait?

'Thank you for coming in, Jemima.' Somewhere up high, a woman's voice spoke down to me. Was it the woman from the Soho casting? I couldn't quite tell.

'Hi,' I replied. I sounded lost, small, in the cavernous space. *You are going to need to project, Jem.*

'Apologies for the short notice. We were very pleased with your first audition. Did you get the script we sent to your agent?'

No, it didn't sound like the same voice. Friendlier, for a start. 'That's OK, I got the script, thanks.' I shaded my eyes with my hand, looking up, trying to see who was talking.

'I'm Sarah Monroe, director. I've been given a brief for you to follow today, and we will film it, if that's OK with you. I'm sure Ed gave you the permissions forms. Ultimately, the decision about who gets the part will be with our Executive Producer.'

He hadn't. And Executive Producer? That had to be Rebecca Sheridan. I felt slightly disappointed that she wasn't here, but this was all very promising. I was in the room anyway, which meant something.

I wanted to ask Sarah to turn the lights down; I could feel burning heat on my face and sweat prickling under my armpits. Was it that hot in here, or was it nerves? It felt more comfortable to look down at the floor.

'Let's start! It's a very physical, demanding play. It will be just two actors on the stage so the audience will be watching everything that you do. We need to see if you can keep the audience's attention. I have a list of movements that the producer would like you to do – I will call them out and you do them. Is that clear?'

Sarah sounded about my age. Possibly older. An expensive London accent that reminded me of the students at college who'd gone to private school – they spoke with a confidence that whatever happened to them in life, they would be OK, that they would be listened to. It was very different from the people I went to school with. That accent was the first voice I learned to do when I started at drama school. I rolled my shoulders back to try and shift a little of the tension that I could feel creeping into my body.

'Can you take off your sweatshirt?'

I was relieved to take it off, and instantly felt cooler. I knew my top was a bit see-through but there was nothing I could do about that now.

'And your shoes.' Whenever we'd done movement work at college, we'd done it barefoot to be able to move more freely. I should have thought of that. I took them off, awkwardly, and threw them next to my bag. There was now a little pile of me on the floor.

'Walk slowly to the front of the stage. Slowly.' I did that, easing my shoulders back again.

'Turn around.' OK, no problem.

'Now, Jemima, we want you to shake. Shake as if electrocuted.'

A little out there, but we had done something like this at RADA; you move from stillness to a shake, as if electricity is powering you from the base of your feet, up through your spine, activating your limbs, and then out of your head. I started to move, with small pulsing actions. The pulse moved into my legs, then my hips and pelvis, then out to my arms and hands. I felt adrenaline start to surge through me, and I let myself release into the movement until I was shaking every part of my body.

'More.' I heard the voice from above me, a little firmer.

I increased the intensity of the shaking until I could feel the blood beating behind my eyes. My neck jerked back and forwards. My arms swung up, around, down, as if controlled by someone else. I felt nausea rise in my throat.

'Stop.'

I stood still. Blood pounded in my head. I tried to calm my breathing and heart rate as the movement subsided.

'Collapse onto the floor.'

I fell to the floor, letting my body crumple as if pushed by someone much stronger than me. I rested my cheek on the floor, with my arms bent above my head, and waited for the next instruction. It felt good to get my breath back and I gulped in some air, along with some dust from the floor that I could see swirling around my face.

'Crawl.'

I pulled my right hand back towards my waist, and then pushed myself up a little, keeping my body in a low crawl position. I slid the left side of my body forward, and then my right, keeping as low to the floor as possible. I glanced to the left and right, as a lizard might. Dust and grit stuck to my hands. Just ahead of me, I could imagine a theatre packed with faces, watching me crawl.

'Roll onto your back.'

I rolled slowly onto my back as instructed, and pushed back a little with my feet and hands to create some space between me and the floor. As I pushed away, I arched my back, and lifted my knees a little, which meant I could push back more easily. I let my body relax into a dead pose, and waited for the next instruction.

'Caress yourself.'

OK, a little weird. I took my hands to the top of my head, and stroked slowly down the front of my face and onto my neck. We'd been trained to leave inhibitions outside the studio. It wasn't you anymore when you walked into the rehearsal space; you were just a vessel for the character, for the part you needed to play. I could do this.

My hands continued down over my shoulders, and I let my fingers spread, moving down over my clavicles and onto my breasts. I paused a while, knowing that was where the eyes in the theatre would want to be. Was the camera focused on my breasts? Is this what they wanted to watch? My hands followed over the contours of my body, and down onto my stomach. I pushed my hands between my legs, and parted them slightly. I took my hands slowly inside my thighs, then rolled onto my side. I lay there like a foetus, waiting to see what would be the next command. Was this going to be in the play?

'Ed,' the voice said calmly. I wasn't sure if it was Sarah or not; it felt like it was coming from somewhere above or behind me.

And then Ed was next to me; he must have been waiting in the wings somewhere. He knelt down next to me then reached across my body and took my wrists. His grip became firmer. Then he pulled my arms back above my head with some force. I was on my back, with him holding my wrists, when he lowered himself onto me, his heavy, fat body on mine and his face alongside my neck. His smell made me gag as he exhaled onto my face. Was this a test? Was I meant to push him away? Was I meant to show that I could handle intimacy with a man, with a stranger, another actor?

Ed shifted his weight and then pushed a knee between my legs, forcing them apart. I realised that even if I wanted to, I would struggle to push him off me. Blood rushed to my face, burning. My lungs working hard to get enough oxygen in under the weight of his body. I felt the beginning of a panic attack coming on, rising through my body. Ed's forearm was slightly across my neck. 'Get off me,' I exhaled into his ear. My voice sounded restricted, laboured.

'Ed.' Her voice up there, like calling a dog.

Slowly, Ed pushed himself away, his bloodshot eyes looking right at me. Then he smirked. The asshole smirked. He rolled onto his side, heavy, unsteady, and then he was up and standing, brushing down his clothes.

I quickly pushed myself up to sitting and brushed off my arms and stomach. I felt covered in dirt.

'Thank you, Jemima.' Sarah spoke, and I looked up to where she was sitting. I could make out a figure, and I think someone just behind. 'Please do the monologue we sent through.'

Words came out of me, but breathless, agitated. I said the monologue that they'd sent me, but it was like watching myself from far away. Disconnected, not sure if I was saying it right, whisky and sour breath still in my nostrils. I could still feel where Ed had gripped my wrists.

'That's the recording finished, thank you. We have what we need.'

I pulled on my shoes, and scooped up the rest of my things. 'Do you need anything else?'

'That's all. We have the recording.'

'Thank you,' I managed to say, though it felt all wrong, unbalanced. I looked around me, trying to find the door.

'Time to go, Jemima. I'll show you out.' Ed said, from somewhere nearby. I didn't want him anywhere near me.

'Fuck you,' I muttered, and pushed past him, found the door.

Ed caught up with me by the stairs to the bar. 'Calm down. You must be used to that kind of thing from RADA. You used to love all that, you actors. They wanted to surprise you, catch you out. I just did what they told me. That's Rebecca's style.'

The outside world was just a few steps away. I could be back on Seagrass in an hour. Give Sancha a call, tell her about this audition. We'd laugh about it. And then, next day, I'd be back at the coffee van, watching others leading their successful lives. *Pull yourself together, Jemima.* I tried to breathe calmly. Ed was hovering nearby. I did need this job.

'It's all acting, right?' I managed to say, avoiding his eye. I could hear voices somewhere along the corridor, or through a door somewhere. *More actors?*

'Have you got anyone else booked in now?' I asked Ed, walking slowly towards the exit, keeping it as casual as I could, acting relaxed.

'Not many, as far as I know.' That was helpful. Maybe he could be helpful to me. I stopped and looked at him. He looked rough, much fatter than I remembered, red face. How much whisky was he getting through?

'Do you know when the play is due to start? When they might make a decision?' I asked.

'Meant to have rehearsals starting next week. They are freaking out about it.'

'Has someone pulled out, then?'

Ed shrugged. 'They don't tell me that stuff.' He looked at me. 'What are you doing later? There's a party that some of the Arcola people are going to. Not far from here. It's actually a big deal – Rebecca's house.' He smiled, tipped forward a little, too close. He made my skin crawl. I hate drunks.

'I can just go to that? I don't know them.'

'Sure. If you're with me.'

I had nothing planned for tonight. No-one was waiting for me back at home. Rebecca's house... For real? Rebecca Sheridan's actual house? It was insane that he was inviting me, surely there was a guest list or something. But, if people from the

Arcola were going, it could be an amazing opportunity. But I did not want to encourage this asshole in any way.

'What's the address? Not sure I can make it. Got another casting,' I lied. Maybe he would tell Sarah that, make me seem more desirable.

Ed grabbed my phone, started typing in his details. His hands, large and sweaty, on the keys. I would need to clean that. 'Excellent. Let's meet first. Catch up properly...' He leered at me. No chance.

'Ah, maybe. If it doesn't run over, you know how castings are. I'll see you there, hopefully.' I had the address. That's all I wanted from him.

FIVE

BEFORE

'They'll stop soon,' said Mark from the top bunk. It was so dark in our bedroom, no streetlight coming in around the edges of the blind so it must have been really, really late.

Mum screamed something at Dad; it sounded as if they were both underwater, the words muffled. And then a door slammed, and she shouted again, louder. Dad's voice sounded really angry. He didn't sound like that in the day, when he was asking us about how our day had been at school, or when we curled up watching TV together. The fight had been about him coming back late, and then it was about other stuff. Some words made their way up the stairs: *selfish, yourself, hate, loser*. I pulled the duvet up around my ears which helped to muffle out the sounds, but I could still hear them shouting. My heart rate was too fast for me to sleep.

'Try and go to sleep, Gemma,' whispered Mark. 'You'll be tired for school.'

'Can't sleep.' I replied. I wasn't sure why we were whispering as there was no way they could hear us anyway.

'If she didn't shout at him, he might not go out so much,' Mark muttered.

The voices got even louder, clearer; they must have moved to the bottom of the stairs. Our room was at the top.

'Will they split up?'

Mark didn't reply straight away. 'Lots of parents split up.'

That was true. I knew Alex's parents were divorced and she had gone to live with her dad. She didn't go to our school anymore. The idea of moving to a different house made me scared. I liked our room, with all our stuff around us. With Mark here with me. Would we be split up?

Then the front door slammed. That usually meant quiet. Where did Dad go? It was really late and it was so dark out there – would he be OK? Mum sounded like she'd gone to the kitchen, her crying far away.

'Tell me the story.'

The bunk creaked above me as Mark rolled over, and he started to tell me about the family of five children who lived in Australia, in the giant house, and the hot chocolate they had before bed, with cream on top, and they all slept in one giant room, all in a row, and that they would have pancakes for breakfast, and the garden that was always sunny, and I must have fallen asleep.

Dad wasn't around when we got up. And he wasn't back when we got in from school. Teatime came and went, and Mark put some fishfingers in for us two and Mum stayed in her room.

It felt all wrong going to bed with no adults around, so we watched *Friends*, one episode after the other, wondering if Dad would come back. I was almost asleep when she came in.

'So you expect me to clean up that mess?' Her voice was slurry, slow.

Mark moved me gently off his lap, and walked through to the kitchen. She followed him in. I could hear them arguing, grill pan banging into the sink, taps running, voices raised. I tried to focus on the screen in front of me – the smiling actors, the funny American clothes, all happiness and jokes.

And then a bang, and Mark cried out. I rushed in, and saw her, hitting him, hard, with the metal tray, and then, clang, it was on the floor, and she was using her fists, her arms, pushing him on to the floor, pushing him against the cupboards. And she was kicking him. I am sure I cried out, shouted for her to stop, I'm sure I did, but there was whooshing in my head, and I couldn't hear anything clearly.

His face, blood on his hair. Why was he bleeding?

'Stop!' I shouted, but she kept kicking him, his arms trying to shield his face.

I tried to pull at her, to catch her arm, but she was much stronger than me.

'Go out... Gemma, get out!' Mark was trying to talk to me.

I should have done more. Instead, I ran – did as I was told – while he took the blows for both of us that night.

SIX

NOW

Albion Square was one of those dream London squares that you only see in Disney films and rom-coms. Every house was perfect, as if a child had drawn it – glossy front doors with sash windows either side. I remember walking past houses like this on our way to school, and Mark asking me to pick: 'What's your favourite? Where would you live?' I liked the brightly coloured doors, the oranges, reds and purples. He chose black or navy, as if to remind me that he was the grown-up one.

It was a real square too, with an iron-fenced garden in the centre, clearly labelled 'RESIDENTS ONLY'. No vans here, just expensive clean cars parked neatly in diagonal rows.

You could hear the party from across the garden – loud drum and bass. The house must have cost millions – marble front steps and those trees in pots on either side. I had never been inside a house like this; even if I just stayed long enough to look around, it would be worth coming.

'Darling, can I help you?' A man standing guard at the door checked me out. I knew my H&M dress looked cheap, but it was the best I had. *Best smile, Jem. Act confident, as if you belong here.*

'Ed invited me, from the Arcola.' He looked at me slowly, taking in my bare legs. He had an iPad in his hand. A guest list?

'Don't know an Ed.' He went to check his iPad and then smiled. 'You can come in though. If you get bored, come and talk to me. I'm getting lonely out here.'

Right. I gave him my best smile and fake giggle, and walked past him.

I found myself in a vast hallway, larger than I'd have guessed from the outside, people everywhere, shouting to be heard. More people sitting on the stairs, people trying to work their way up past them. No-one looked at me as I pushed through – the party must have started hours ago, it was so packed! One more person didn't even register. A room on the left, a rack of coats and bags on the floor around it. I squeezed my coat onto a hook, and left the bottle of wine I'd bought on the floor – it wasn't that sort of party. I could take it home later.

It was like walking into a film set. The walls were covered in framed posters of plays, many with black signatures of the cast. *A Midsummer Night's Dream* at Oxford University. A play at the Pinter Theatre. Photographs, too: a black-and-white of students, I think, sitting on some grand steps. Another group of friends laughing, a ball or wedding. A cast list for *Cabaret*. It was like walking through Rebecca's life, her history. So many productions, so many successes. Friends, cast members, all so close. That was the sort of life I wanted.

I followed the music into a huge open-plan kitchen, which must have been the whole width of the house, and such high ceilings! The people all beautifully lit, laughing, so happy to be here, looking exactly as if they spent their whole lives in places like this. More had spilled out into the garden beyond, lit with strings of white lights hung high across their gorgeous heads. I couldn't see Ed anywhere, and that suited me just fine.

'Champagne?'

I took a saucer from the tray offered to me. A little slopped over the edge. What was wrong with normal glasses? A tall woman wearing a low-cut jumpsuit with thin silver straps reached for a glass, her breast barely covered as she leaned forward. She had mesmerising green eyes, massive.

'Do I know you?' she asked. I must have been staring.

'Sorry. I don't think so.'

'Cute dress. Balenciaga?'

Was she kidding me? I nodded.

'Nice boots,' I replied. They were nice boots. Lots of cut-out bits, with studs on them, her thin legs soaring out of them.

'Thanks. Alaia. So painful though. I don't think I'll wear them again. So, what brings you here? How do you know Rebecca?'

'I'm an actor.'

'Oh, another one. This party is full of them.' She glanced over my shoulder, clearly now looking for an excuse to move on.

'I'm about to be in a play for her.' Shit. Why had I said that? What if that got back to Rebecca?

She looked back at me. 'Oh right. Well done, you.'

'How do you know Rebecca then? Are you in the business too? Not an actor though,' I smiled, trying to show how relaxed and fun I was.

She laughed, showing her perfect, whitened teeth. 'Oh, no, darling. I was at Oxford with her. A little while ago now though.' She laughed at this. 'With Jonny over there.' She looked over to where people were dancing, as if I could possibly pick out who Jonny was. I followed her gaze, to where she clearly would rather be, and then, there he was – Ed, talking to a group of men in the corner. Their voices loud, so pleased with themselves for being here. He looked awful, red, sweaty; he'd clearly kept on drinking since I'd seen him.

'Do you know, you look so like a friend of ours from then.' She was looking at me carefully, perhaps a little sadly. 'Weird really.'

People always said that to me. It's the red hair – we tend to be grouped together. I smiled, unsure what to say.

'I'm Anisha. So lovely to meet you.' She did an awkward head bob like an air kiss, but miles away, and turned away, left me to it. She hadn't bothered to ask my name. I reached for another drink.

The music kicked up a gear and the room roared its approval. A DJ's head bobbing in the far corner, one of the few Black people in a room full of white. Did the guests really like this music, or did they just want to pretend that they did? Maybe it helped them pretend that they were not just spoilt, rich people in cushy theatre, television and media jobs. I had no doubt that on another night they would be gushing about how much they loved choral music in a fancy old building – whatever was needed to fit in with the other rich people. I wanted to stay clear of Ed so made my way in the opposite direction. The chances of me knowing anyone here were pretty slim, but you never know. Maybe I should have told Elle I was coming, she knew people. How do others handle this stuff – networking? I had no idea.

Might as well go out in the garden, see if I could meet important people. How would I know what Sarah or Rebecca looked like? I tried to look purposeful, as if I was trying to find someone, or that someone was waiting for me.

'Jemima? How funny to see you here.' I turned. Neema. Out of all the people at RADA she would be the one here. I leaned in to kiss her cheek.

'You look amazing, Neema! How great to see you.' An astonishingly handsome man hovered by her side.

'Are you working on anything at the moment?' She smiled, head cocked. I hated that question.

'A play. Can't say much about it at the moment, though.'

'Oh right, that's amazing! You've been so quiet on the

group. I wasn't sure if you were still in the business. So pleased for you. Let us know and we can all come and watch!'

The idea filled me with horror. I knew what I was meant to say next.

'How about you?'

'Oh my god! It's been so intense! So busy.' She smiled at the man. 'I've been a nightmare to live with, haven't I? I'm filming a new Netflix at the moment – all very hush-hush.' Of course she was.

'I can't wait to see it!' I beamed at her. 'I am meeting my director. So sorry. Let me know when it airs, won't you?'

'I will. Amazing to see you!' They walked out into the garden, so I didn't. I couldn't stay near the bar, and I didn't want to see Ed. Back in the hallway then.

It felt even busier than before, and everyone was in little, cosy groups. I could see people on the stairs so made my way there. Might as well look around up here, check out the house, see some of the rooms. It was just as crowded upstairs; two women sitting on the top stair, kissing, blocking my way. I pushed past. Conversation was louder here, further away from the music.

'Excuse me, have you seen Sarah?' I asked a couple blocking a doorway. He, at least, looked at me, and indicated towards a room along the landing.

'Jemima! Over here.' *Ed. Great.* I thought I'd left him downstairs. 'I thought I saw you. Then I lost you!' He kissed me, his lips slobbery against my cheek. 'Great dress,' Ed slurred, looking down my top briefly. 'What a party, yeah? Everyone's here.'

'Thanks for inviting me. So kind of you.' I threw him a mega-watt smile. We were surrounded by people. *Get what you can from him, and move on.*

'You met Sarah yet? We were talking about you!' He clearly assumed I knew what she looked like.

'Not yet!'

'Come in here. It's got the best view of the garden.' *A bedroom? Please let it be full of people.* He pushed open the door, and I was relieved to see it was more like a library, with people sitting around on sofas, the music more chilled than downstairs. Like some sort of private member's club, not that I'd been in one of those, but I'd seem them on Insta.

'The VIP room. Do you know him, over there? He won a BAFTA.' Ed waved at a man across the room sitting on a velvet sofa, who glanced up at the word BAFTA, then turned back to the woman he was talking to. Unfazed by being ignored, Ed carried on.

'There's Sarah. Come on.' Ed snaked his arm around my waist, pressing against me. I could feel the heat from his body; being so close to him again made my skin crawl. Did he think I was *into* him? That I was here because of him?

'Sarah! I've found Jemima!' A woman with sharp bobbed hair looked round. About my height. Grey silk shirt, tucked into jeans. Effortlessly expensive-looking. Ed kissed me again. God, he smelt bad, so sweaty.

'Hello again.' She held out her hand, and took mine, shaking it, thick silver bangles falling down her arm.

'Lovely to meet you. Properly, I mean. Thanks for the casting earlier. I was so pleased to be called in.'

'Thank Rebecca for that. You were her choice.'

I felt a rush of anxiety. Was she telling me that I wasn't her choice, too? *Come on, Jemima. Make polite conversation.* 'Ed invited me to the party.'

'Oh, I bet he did.' She smiled, though it didn't reach her eyes. 'Ed, darling. Can you get me an ashtray?'

Ed looked pissed off at that, and then smiled. 'Course! Leave you two girls to chat.'

'Girls... honestly.' So Sarah thought Ed was a dick, too. I warmed to her.

'So, you must be excited about the play. The script looks so good.' I was pleased with that line, sounded intelligent, relaxed. Not desperate.

'Excited... Well, more stressed at this point, to be honest. Look, we haven't made our casting decisions yet... sorry.'

'No, of course not! It's a party. That's work. Don't worry at all, I am completely fine about it. You choose who will be just right for you. I just wanted to say hi. Ed suggested I say hi.' That felt like something Sancha would say. Breezy, confident.

'Yes, well. I don't think I should talk about work right now. It would be unprofessional of me. I don't want to sound awful, but you know...' Sarah's voice trailed off.

I thought it was worth one more question. 'Is Rebecca here? I haven't seen her yet?' Quite good, I thought, as if I knew her.

'It is her house...' A smile started to form on Sarah's face, then she softened. 'Garden, I think. Not seen her for a while.' She took a sip of her drink. Was it water? Or vodka.

'Oh yes, lovely. I might head out there. I just wanted to say thank you, say hi and all that. I mean, I've got a couple of other things going on, that I'm thinking about. But your play looks great.' *Liar.*

'No need to thank me, really, Jemima. Just relax. It's nice to meet you. Maybe we will work together. Who knows?' She smiled and started to turn away from me.

'I've just seen one of my friends, from college. RADA. The play is so...' But Sarah was now joining two women standing by the fireplace.

I needed air. If she had wanted me for the part, she'd have said, right? Been friendlier, encouraging? It clearly wasn't going to be mine. Suddenly I felt very alone, surrounded by people who didn't know me, who didn't give a shit about me.

I made my way along the landing, which was so crowded, no space for me. People not moving for me, as I tried to edge through. It would be a relief to get outside, breathe properly.

But when would I get this chance again? I should see if I

could spot Rebecca, talk to her. Maybe she would like me. Maybe I could get Ed to show me who Rebecca is, point her out to me. Where was he?

I could see people making their way into another room, and followed them, where it opened out to a balcony with lights overhead, a table of drinks, even busier here, so crowded, clearly the place to be, the bodies so tightly packed together that you couldn't even feel the night air. People laughing, faces lit by the moonlight. The garden, trees, beyond.

I stood at the edge, trying to take it all in, to decide what to do next, and then spotted Ed, laughing. He was right in the corner of the balcony, the furthest point from the house, and I could see he seemed to be pushing against a man. The man, much taller, had his hand on Ed's chest, his arm muscles showing, trying to make space between them. Their faces uncomfortably close together. Ed's face, so red, the other man's calmer, more focused, doing all the talking. He pushed Ed away. Clearly someone else didn't think much of Ed either. I pushed my way over to him. I needed him to show me who Rebecca was. He could do that for me.

'Jemima!' He reached past a woman, who scowled at him, and grabbed my arm, pulling me towards him.

'This is Freddie!' Freddie stared at me, as drunk as Ed. Eyes not focusing; had he taken something?

'Me and Jemima had a lot of fun at RADA. Didn't we?' Ed leered towards me, snaked his arm around my waist. The man, Freddie, looked at me in a way I didn't like.

'You know what they say about actresses, right?' Ed said. Freddie laughed.

Ed leaned against me, almost falling on me, trying to steady himself.

'You seen Rebecca?' I shouted, pulling back, trying to make space between us.

'Work, work, work with you, isn't it?' He lifted his drink to my mouth, slopping it in the glass, spilling it on my face.

I pulled my head back – god knows what was in that. 'I've got a drink, thanks.' I could see people near us, staring. Freddie reached for a bottle of something, trying to top up Ed's glass.

'Hey, look at us, all close together again.' Ed smirked at me, and the memory of him in the casting room flashed into my brain. I pulled away from him, bumping into Freddie.

'Careful, love. Stay classy.'

'Hey, come here!' Ed tried to pull me back towards him, taking a slug from his glass at the same time.

No chance. I moved away, towards the balcony edge. I could hear Neema in the garden below, chatting, laughing. I leaned on the balcony edge, looked down, her handsome man next to her. She looked amazing; the soft lights suited her face.

And right next to her... Tall, bare shoulders, dark hair. Was that her? Rebecca? A crowd nearby, listening to her. Attentive. At the heart of things. Of course, Neema would know who she is; she knew all the right people. It was so effortless for her. Me not included, as ever.

Behind me, shouting. Ed – was he shouting at someone? A man shouting back. So much noise up here, so many bodies, tightly packed in together. Could this balcony even hold us all? It was hard to know where to stand, where to move to. I felt constricted, my chest tight, panic rising, blurry and too hot, even though I was outside, it didn't feel like it.

I needed to get out of here, fast. I forced my way to the top of the stairs, pushing my way down. I needed air. The front door stood wide open just ahead, people packing out the hallway. I wanted to get my coat and leave. No-one here wanted to talk to me, and it wasn't going to help me being here, not tonight. The industry felt like a closed shop, as per usual, a clique that wasn't in any hurry to let me in. The music was so loud, throbbing in my head, as I made my way to the coats, and I realised the couple in front of me had stopped talking, and were looking towards the kitchen, worried expressions on their faces. The doorman was pushing his way through, his mouth moving, but I couldn't hear what he was saying above the drum and bass.

And then we heard the screaming.

The couple looking at each other – confused, scared? People pushed past me, making their way towards the kitchen, not caring if they banged against me. Pressed against the wall, I felt the edge of a framed poster against the back of my head. A glass smashed on the tiled floor, crystal clear. A woman screamed, so high and sharp above the music.

I felt drawn towards the kitchen, following the crowd. Anisha was just standing there, her face, frozen in horror, drained for a moment of its beauty. A waiter barged past, shouting into his mobile phone. We streamed out onto the terrace, white lights and lanterns gently bobbing in the breeze above us. There, I could see what had caused the screaming.

Ed lay face-down on the edge of the terrace, his left arm at an impossible angle. A slow, dark pool of blood spread around his head, shining brightly against the whiteness of the limestone. He was eerily still, as if sleeping, a little oasis of calm surrounded by screaming, distraught faces. Their perfect evening, ruined.

SEVEN

It's amazing how you can function on no sleep if you have to. I wasn't sure what time I got back to Seagrass, but St Pancras was deserted.

I remember looking at my sodden, grimy shoes, hoping they would clean up OK. It was freezing on Seagrass and the duvet felt damp as I pulled it up around my ears. The boat rocked gently, but I lay there, awake for hours, drifting in and out of thoughts, waiting for the alcohol in my bloodstream to dissolve and let my body sink into sleep. I heard the first trains crawl into the station over the bridge. Who was on those early trains? People going to work early shifts, ready to look after the city workers who would still be asleep in their warm beds right now.

I couldn't get the image of Ed out of my head. The way his blood had spread towards his left arm, bent and broken. I remember wondering if it would reach his fingers, and flow between them, filling his palms. We had all just stood there, watching. If this was TV, someone would jump forward, tear their shirt into strips, save the life of a total stranger, who would later thank them, smiling from a safe, clean hospital bed. 'Who is he?' a man had asked, just in front of me. His neighbour shook his head. 'Ambulance is coming. Don't move him!' someone shouted.

People were looking up and pointing, towards the top of the house. Faces up there, leaning over, looking down at us. Looking at me? No, looking at Ed's body. The flash of a phone camera.

I remember my coat was on the floor, people stepping on it, not caring. Hanging above it, a black coat, velvety, expensive. I glanced around. No-one was looking. I followed two women out of the front door, as if part of their group, pulling on the coat as I walked fast down the steps.

I remember walking along the canal back here to Seagrass. It was dark, quiet. I knew somewhere in my mind that the canal at night wasn't safe, but I kept walking, trying to process it all. What would happen next? Would Ed be OK? He didn't look OK – the blood... so still. If he died, would police want to talk to me? I thought of the people on the balcony; who had seen what happened? The police had loads of people to talk to. I knew nobody, was a nobody. Would they link me to working with him? Would Sarah say anything? Or Neema? The same thoughts went round and round in my head, all night.

My phone buzzed. Ben.

> Are you working today? From 7 would be AMAZING!!

Just over an hour until 7. I felt sick with exhaustion. I couldn't think of work right now.

What if this whole thing meant the play wouldn't happen, or would get delayed? This had happened in Rebecca's house. They might not choose me anyway... I lay there, feeling swamped in despair. How could this be happening to me?

With no chance of sleep now, I opened a news app. Would the accident be on the news? If Ed had died, then yes, maybe. Five deaths in a house fire in the north. A story about a miliary cadet found dead – twenty-one years old, the unnamed woman was found in her room at the base on Wednesday. Nothing about Ed.

I lay there, thinking. Was a death in London even news? And if it was, how long did it take for journalists to get the story, talk to police, check facts, write about it? I wanted to search for 'death in Albion Square', to find out more. But what if someone, the police perhaps, wanted to check my phone one day? Should I even be searching for that? It would show I was interested, too interested. And someone might want to know why.

Some part of me felt sorry for Ed, but also... no. He'd acted like a creep during the audition, and he'd enjoyed it, too.

I rolled onto my back and stared at the ceiling. I reached up and touched the roof of Seagrass with the flat of my hand. My fingers traced the edges of the wood panels where they locked together, creating a solid, safe roof. I thought of my brother, Mark, and him being here, not so long ago.

My phone buzzed.

Are you coming in?

For goodness' sake, he'd be knocking on the door at this rate. If I went to work, I could get paid, get coffee, eat something, and it would all look normal, if anyone ever asked. If I didn't go in, I'd have to come up with a reason. No time for a shower, but I didn't expect anyone to get close enough to notice. Jeans, black sweatshirt, hair scraped back, scarf tied round.

The black coat was on the table where I'd left it; I'd have to get rid of it. What was I thinking? I was cold, my stupid dress too thin, or was it shock? Astrakhan – the soft, knotted wool was so glamorous, inky and warm. It had been wrong to take it, and I couldn't exactly wear it to the Arcola theatre. It would be sod's law that the owner would be someone who worked there, or recognised it from a friend. A real shame, it was so gorgeous.

Ben's silver airstream van sparkled in the early morning

light, and there were three people waiting to be served as I opened the door at the side and stepped inside.

'You're late. Can you do a flat white?' Ben turned away from me, and got to work on the sandwich grill, while I poured milk ready for steaming.

'Sorry, I was slow getting up today.'

'Here you go. That's £6.80. Thanks, mate. See you tomorrow.' Ben glanced round at me. 'I need to know if you are coming in.'

I leaned over the counter to take the next person's order. She was perfectly made up, hair blow-dried, at what, seven in the morning? I should have put make up on – a little mascara would have helped me look more normal.

We worked our way through the queue for about twenty minutes before we spoke much again. I downed two espressos which helped a lot; the confusion of the night started to clear.

What would Rebecca do? Someone getting hurt at her party, the mess, the ambulance, all of it. I wish I'd met her. Would blood clean up from her terrace? Did it stain? *Get a grip, Jem.*

'So, late night, then?' Ben was looking at me.

'Yep. Reading scripts.'

'You got it?'

'Not sure. You know how they go. They see so many people.'

He nodded, satisfied with the lines he'd heard me say loads of times before. I handed a coffee to one of the regulars; our guess was he was a journalist at the *Guardian*, or a lecturer. He wore the same jacket day in, day out, tried to look younger than he was. I needed to keep Ben on side, keep this job, at least for the time being.

'Thanks for letting me go to auditions. You're very understanding.'

'Yep. Something like that.' Ben turned to me, and leaned on the counter. 'When are you likely to hear?'

'Don't know... they might still be deciding, or seeing some more people today. I'm not sure.'

'Well, let me know. So, I can get cover for you here if I need to.'

We worked our way through the commuters, and by 10 the customers looked scruffier, as students replaced the software and media types. The lack of sleep started to kick in and I was finding it harder to concentrate, had messed up a couple of orders.

'Ben, do you mind if I head off soon?' I would be leaving him to do the clear up.

He looked a bit irritated, but agreed. 'Get some rest, yeah? See you tomorrow.'

It was just a short walk through the fountains and sliding glass doors into the internal courtyard of Central St Martins College. Two students were playing ping-pong, and the sound echoed around the cavernous concrete space. I waited until one of the hot-desk computers was free. I had to click through the boring information about the university and their latest art show, before I could search for 'London news', and there it was. Right in front of me. *The Hackney Citizen.*

Drama at showbiz party in Hackney

Police and emergency services were called to the £3 million luxury home of Rebecca Sheridan on Albion Square last night, following reports of an accident. Ed Everett, 30, from Shoreditch, is in intensive care following a fall.

Eye-witnesses report that Everett fell from a balcony onto the garden terrace. Ambulance crew attended the scene. Hackney Police report that they are investigating.

Rebecca Sheridan was not available for comment. Her PR company have issued the following statement: 'We are supporting the police in their enquiries and wish a speedy and full recovery for Ed, who is a talented and much valued member of our team.'

I read through the piece twice, trying to take it in. He was alive, had survived the fall. There had been so much blood... my stomach churned at the memory of it, his body lying there broken. But he was alive.

I clicked on the link to Sheridan Productions. It was a very impressive website, with photographs of famous West End musicals and plays on the banner at the top; it would be a dream to be in any of them. The opening bars of a musical boomed out and I scrabbled to turn off the volume. I mouthed 'sorry' at the student sitting next to me. I read the home page:

Sheridan Productions is a West End, Broadway, TV and Film production company responsible for many of the most successful theatre productions in the USA and UK. We are very proud that our talented team have won 4 Olivier Awards, 3 Tonys and 1 BAFTA this year. Rebecca Sheridan started her eponymous company in 2002 with her ground-breaking production of Electra. *Since then, Rebecca has won 'Producer of the Year' at* The Stage *Awards numerous times.*

So many plays listed, most I hadn't seen. *Jerusalem*... I'd seen that one. It had won loads of awards. School trip in the sixth form. Everyone else had loved it, but I'd sat there thinking that the jokes felt too real, too recognisable, as if people I knew were being laughed at.

So, the party was in the news. The local paper at the moment, but it would make it into *Metro* and the *Evening Standard* soon enough. Probably the nationals, too, because of the Rebecca Sheridan connection. God, it was going to be everywhere.

Just hours before, Ed had laid on top of me, pressing down onto me, breathing onto my neck. And now he was in hospital somewhere. The police surely wouldn't be interested in an accident; just an idiot at a party who'd drunk too much, had taken drugs, too, probably? He would be easy paperwork, just another man who'd got carried away hanging out with the beautiful people.

I could see Ben across the square, closing up. Like clockwork, he was taking his end of morning rush break, getting more milk, heading into a nearby restaurant to use their toilets.

My phone vibrated. My agent! Elle was ringing me.

'Hi!'

'Jemima. Morning. Well, it's good news. I think we should meet.'

'They want me for the play?'

'Looks very promising. There's been an incident though. Look, come and meet me this evening? I've got an incredibly busy day, but let's have a drink tonight. I'll talk you through it.'

EIGHT

The last place I wanted to be that evening was on a balcony. Elle had suggested we meet at the roof bar of Sea Containers, near her office. Elle hadn't said much on the phone, but the fact that she wanted to meet in person was good, surely? It must mean I'd got the play.

The Sea Containers bar looked intimidatingly expensive on the website; dark, moody lighting, velvet seating and enormous chandeliers that looked like dandelion clocks before you blow them away. What was I supposed to wear? Black dress would do. I really needed some better clothes. Just as I left Seagrass I pulled on the Astrakhan coat – classy, perfect to see Elle.

Emerging from Blackfriars station at rush hour, I could see skyscrapers all around me. In each tiny window, people were working at their boring desk jobs, sending the last few emails of the day. Sea Containers was just a short walk away, and I'd passed it many times on my way to the National Theatre. Not that I went to many plays there, but the bars were good.

Like so much of London, Sea Containers had changed

purpose over the years. It used to be a publishing office with framed magazine covers on the walls, but they couldn't afford London rents anymore. It was now an expensive hotel, with a red phone box outside, for the perfect Insta selfie. Sancha would have walked in, as if right at home; she always looked the part, wherever she went. Confident, able to afford any bar, shop or hotel. Which she could now, of course.

Act like you're staying here, Jem, as if you are acting at the Globe, perhaps in a ground-breaking Shakespeare play, Ophelia maybe, or something at the National. Pretend that your assistant had booked the room, the theatre is picking up the bill, pleased that I was staying so close by so I could get to rehearsals easily. It probably *was* full of actors staying here, resting before a show. I walked into the spacious lobby which screamed expense and luxury. I found the lift to the roof bar, and got whisked up.

'Do you have a reservation?' A woman with ironed hair and a black suit stepped towards me holding an iPad. Balearic dance music pulsed behind her; so much laughter, noise.

'I'm here to meet Elle? Elle Lobina?'

She looked surprised, then said, 'Follow me.'

She walked purposefully through the bar with me following behind, a budget version in my cheap black dress and shoes. I saw a flash of lipstick-red soles as she walked across the black lacquer floor; were they *real* Christian Louboutins? What was she being paid to work here? We passed through the cocktail crowd, framed by a backdrop of glittering London lights shining through the huge windows.

'Ms Lobina is out on the balcony.' She indicated outside, and the door swished closed behind me, the noise of the bar had gone, replaced with the sound of distant sirens. Before me, the whole of London stretched out. My stomach lurched – the terrace floor was glass, and I could see straight down to the river.

Elle stood right at the far end, looking towards St Paul's

Cathedral. She was wearing a thin, white coat that rippled gently in the wind. Her white-blonde cropped hair stood out against the night sky. She watched me walk towards her, my left hand gripping the edge of the banister – the further I got from the door, the further away from safety I felt.

'Jemima. Isn't it amazing?' Elle gestured across the river. 'I never get tired of coming out here. You can see for miles, especially on a clear night like tonight.'

Did she not feel the cold? It was freezing out here. I could feel the wind blowing gusts along the balcony, my hair whipping across my face. Shit – the balcony was moving. I gripped the banister more tightly. 'Beautiful.'

'It wakes me up. Energises me. Up here the air isn't so polluted. It hasn't been through the lungs of millions of people. There are no car fumes, no smoke. No stale air pumped out of buildings. It's one of the few places in London you can actually breathe.'

Elle took a sip from a glass of red wine. Should I have bought a drink on my way in? Ordered one? In the movies, agents took their clients out for lunch in places with white tablecloths and paid; I'd sort of expected a bit of that tonight – a table at least.

'So, Jemima. It looks as if the Arcola wants you. They want you to start on *Poison* as soon as possible.'

Oh. My. God. They wanted me. 'That's brilliant!'

'They emailed to ask about your availability, and you are free, but I said I would talk to you first.'

I wanted to shout 'YES!' at the top of my voice, out to the river and to anyone out there in London who might be able to hear. Adrenaline flooded through my body. Elle was still talking and I realised I had lost the thread of what she was saying. *They wanted me!*

'There isn't a great deal of money in it, but you need to get something on your CV. It's an odd play for Sheridan, and a very short run, but if it goes well, they might want to extend it or transfer it to one of their larger theatres.'

I was going to work as an actress, a professional, paid actress, at long last. 'That's amazing. Thank you. I wasn't sure how it had gone. I mean, they said they weren't seeing many people, but I wasn't sure...' Ed, lying on top of me, appeared in my head. I shook the thought away.

'Well, that's right. I don't think they did see many people. The casting director did seem very into you.' Elle looked at me as if to say she was surprised herself, then changed her mind. 'Did you meet the director? And was Rebecca there?'

'I met Sarah. The director.'

Elle nodded. 'OK. Well, doing a Sheridan Productions play is amazing. A great opportunity for you. If you're happy to take the job, which I assume you are, then I'll get the contract organised.'

Elle took a sip from her wine and looked at me carefully, as if choosing her next words. 'So, this is what you wanted. The big break! I rather like these moments of my job. You take someone on, but you never quite know... and well, here we are.'

Rumour was that Elle had wanted to be an actor. It can't have worked out for her. The wind had picked up and I could feel the cold on every part of my skin, but it felt amazing! Pure, intense excitement and happiness, like I could do *anything*. So alive!

This is what I had trained for. All those years at school when I went to drama club and auditioned for plays, when it was clear that the other kids didn't really want me to be there. Applying for RADA seemed like a fantasy, something other people did. I had been right all along. I *did* have talent. This is what I was meant to do.

'I'll take it. Definitely.' I tried to sound calm, professional, but I knew I sounded more like a big kid.

Elle nodded, smiled. 'That's great, Jemima. I know you have

worked hard to get here. You are really talented. That's why I signed you...' Her words hung in the air. Why did I feel there was a 'but' coming?

'I've got my reservations about this job. I can't quite put my finger on it.' She looked at me carefully. 'It's all been very rushed, and although you are very good... don't take this the wrong way, but I was surprised they didn't want to see more of my actors when they sent through the briefing. They said they'd seen you at RADA, so wanted you.'

'Who had seen me?'

'Not sure they actually told me. It was all a bit of a rush.'

'Maybe they didn't have time to go through a long casting process?' RADA was the most competitive drama school to get into. Maybe they hadn't needed to see anyone else? Surely Elle knew that. She was meant to be on my side.

'Very possible. Time was clearly a factor. Listen... did you hear about the party?' She took a sip from her drink. Ah, so this was why we were here. And outside, not near anyone else. What was I meant to say as a response? I slowly shook my head.

'It was very sad. Just last night. It was at Rebecca Sheridan's house. A young man fell and is in hospital. Apparently, Sheridan Productions are in a total PR mess dealing with it all. I'm just letting you know as it is bound to come up.'

'That is really sad.'

Elle nodded. 'Thing is, he worked at the Arcola.'

'Oh...'

She looked at me. 'I imagine Rebecca Sheridan will stay clear of the theatre for a while. Which, in some ways, is a blessing. Jemima, as your agent, I feel I should pre-warn you. She's quite the character. You have to be at your absolute A-game working with Rebecca. Stay on the right side of her.'

'Yes, of course.' What did she mean by that? Of course I would be at my best.

Elle looked at me carefully. 'Good. Oh, theatre is *such* a funny business.'

'Thanks, Elle. Thanks so much. Should I go now?' God, I sounded like a kid talking to a teacher. Elle put down her glass and reached towards me, as if to hug me, and then awkwardly rubbed my arm. She wasn't really the hugging type.

'So glad you could come and see me. I'm pleased for you. It's a shame about the party, and all that situation, but that shouldn't impact on you. I just thought you should know. I'll send over the contract.' That was my cue to go – I was dismissed.

The noise and warmth of the bar hit me as I stepped back inside. I badly needed a drink, but I didn't want to stay here. I wanted to walk, get my head together and get a beer, not one of these over-priced cocktails. The door woman glanced at me as I walked past her towards the lift. *Yes, lady, remember this face.*

NINE

I left Sea Containers, turned left and walked fast. I knew exactly where to go. I knew the South Bank long before I moved to London. Anyone who loves films knows it – the tree-lined promenade, the street performers and 60s concrete architecture are familiar even if you have never actually been to London. Spies meet on iron benches to discuss top secret plans. Couples stroll along on awkward dates, pausing to lean on a railing overlooking the river when they get to a key point in the script. Hugh Grant runs to catch up with Andie MacDowell to apologise for falling in love with her, and they deliver their cheesy lines about not noticing the rain. I get a buzz walking along here day or night; it makes me feel as if I am a character in a film, that something exciting is about to happen. And at last, something exciting *is* happening to me. I'm no longer the reject, the one who didn't get the part. I'm in. I'm going to be a professional, paid actress.

White lights shine in the tree branches above my head, creating a runway, a catwalk, making everyone who walks here feel special. It's just a few minutes to the National Theatre that dominates the South Bank, its brutal concrete hiding the magic that happens inside. School took us to the National when I was sixteen and that was my first trip to London. It wasn't exactly what I was expecting – no bright lights, no West End glamour – but once inside, I loved it. The wide, open spaces with concrete staircases disappearing above our heads, images of future shows projected onto the walls. The bookshop full of books just about theatre! The people walking around looked so cool – amazing clothes, so stylish, so rich, nothing like the people I knew back home. There was a sense that anything could happen here, a creative energy where you could be anything you wanted to be. We weren't allowed to take our coats with us inside the theatre, something to do with the air conditioning, so we lined up to put them in the cloakroom; I remember worrying about whether I had to pay for that. The Olivier, so large, and you could see right up into the roof where all the lighting rigs were on show. The play was a bit extra; all the characters in *Peter Pan* were played by adults, and although it sort of made sense at the end as they were looking back at their lost childhood, I thought real kids would have made more sense. Seeing adults whizzing around on ropes trying to fly, shouting out '*Wheeeee*' made us laugh, and not in a good way. We were a tough crowd. But I left that day with a new purpose. I could have done that play and I could see how it could be better.

Back then we wouldn't have been allowed to go in the Understudy bar, even though at home pubs were happy to have us. I've spent more time in the Understudy than in any of the actual theatres. You can always get somewhere to sit as most out-of-towners visiting the theatre miss it and head straight into the main building; the Understudy is tacked on to the corner like an after-thought, which it probably was.

I've always thought it was a stupid name for a bar that was mostly full of drama students and out-of-work actors. You could tell who we were – when the plays started and the audience left to take their seats, we were the ones left behind. If you timed it right, you could even help yourself to a half-finished bottle of wine. We did it all the time.

'We're broke students, Jem. They can help us out.' Sancha thought it was so funny. The bar staff gave us clean glasses; they were between-jobs actors or students like us. I wish Sancha was with me now to celebrate. She should be. Mark should be here, too; he would have been the one to get the drinks in, making a toast to me, for my first proper, professional job.

An old couple were blocking the bar, taking ages reading the gin menu; would they really be able to tell the difference? I leaned across them. 'Hi, glass of Champagne please?'

The woman behind the bar looked about my age, buzzcut, great eyes. I watched her peel off the gold foil, untwist the metal cage.

A man wrapped in a thick grey sweater, way too thick for in here, was standing just along from me. 'Celebrating something?'

'There you go.' Buzzcut girl handed me the glass. I tapped my card on the machine, tried not to look at the cost.

'Cheers,' the man said. I smiled but didn't say anything. Didn't owe him an explanation.

My favourite place to sit was in the window. I could see another couple in raincoats heading there too, but they were not moving at London speed and I got there first. I slung my jacket and bag on top of one stool and sat on the other so I could tuck myself into the corner and keep space around me. The woman shot me a look and they turned back to try and find somewhere else to sit; I could hear her complaining at her husband about being too slow. I felt a bit sorry for him, but, hey, I needed this.

Well, well done, Jemima. You did it. I took a long sip of the Champagne and felt my shoulders relax. It had a dry, buttery flavour, much nicer than the cheap Prosecco we used to buy at the end of a show. I rang Sancha. No answer.

Someone had left a programme on the shelf, and I flicked through it, straight to the headshots of the cast. *Look at them all, staring out at you, living the dream.* The most famous actors first, half a page each. Oh, she was in *everything*. I turned to the pages where I was more likely to know someone. This one had red hair, looked like me in a way. I studied her face; why had she been cast for this play, and not me? Her debut. Elle hadn't even sent me for this play.

And Arjun! From the year above. Handsome, looked much better in his headshot than I remembered – playing a refugee. London born and bred, but playing a refugee – same old cliché. He hadn't been great in *Othello*. Cast all wrong as Iago. Messed up his lines, too. I wonder how many lines he has in this? I sent a screenshot to Sancha.

Look at this! Guess where I am! The Understudy! I got the part!

Too many exclamation points; the alcohol was kicking in. Bit desperate.

I tried to find Arjun on Instagram, see if he followed me. No. I sent him a message.

Yay, Arjun, look at you in the National!!!! Star!!! Can't wait to see you.

He would have no idea if I saw him or not. Or maybe I should get a rush ticket? See him afterwards at the stage door.

My phone buzzed in my hand. Sancha!

I picked up.

'What the hell? You're in the Understudy! I miss that place! Hang on, just putting Polly down. If I shut the door, we won't hear her. Hang on.'

I watched Sancha walk across her massive landing. She had shown me around her Hamptons house via FaceTime before; it was all open-plan white, everywhere gleaming, sun-drenched. It was insane. Worth marrying boring Jon for, no question.

'OK, I'm all yours. Is it just as disgusting in there as I remember? Show me!'

I held up my phone to show her the bar. 'Looks the same, doesn't it? Listen, I got the part! The play at the Arcola.'

'You're kidding me. That is amazing news! You so deserve it, kiddo. I'm so proud of you. Tell me everything.'

'It's called *Poison* by Lot Vekemans. Do you know it?'

'Nope, never heard of it, but that doesn't mean anything. I know nothing these days. Love the title. I'll google it.'

'Rehearsals start soon. Last minute, I think. Not sure why. I guess someone pulled out.'

'Thanks, darling.' I heard Jon in the background.

'Hi, Jon!' I shouted. Sancha sipped from a tiny espresso cup he'd just handed her.

'Doesn't matter. A part is a part. God, I need this so much – we had an exhausting night with Polly.' She drained her coffee. 'So, tell me interesting things... when does it all start? I'm so jealous! I would love to be there right now. It's so boring out here in the winter – there is literally *nothing* to do.'

I knew that wasn't strictly true – her Insta posts were full of brunches with glamorous friends and hikes with Polly in a papoose. I should have asked about my goddaughter. But me first.

'I don't have the start date yet, but Elle is sending me the contract, so soon I hope. How's that beautiful daughter of yours?'

'You need to get that contract ASAP. Tie them down. Polly is amazing, cute, adorable... but god, it's relentless. Jon keeps telling me to get a nanny in, and I am seriously tempted.'

I had come to the end of my drink – if Sancha was here, one of us, probably her, would have gone to the bar, while the other saved the seats. 'I wish you were here with me. It's a bit tragic celebrating on my own.'

She held out her espresso cup as if to toast me. 'I wish I

could be there with you. Maybe I could fly over for opening night?'

'Do it! That would be perfect. I'd love you to be there.'

'I can't imagine Jon would let me though.'

My guess was it suited Jon just the way things were; he did the work stuff and Sancha did the baby stuff. It didn't leave much time for acting. When she'd left London, she had been full of promises of flying back all the time, and of coming to see us all in plays, when we made it. She hadn't been back once.

'Listen, Jem, I need to go. I can hear Polly. That girl can project! I wish I could just appear in the Understudy next to you and buy us a bottle. I'm proud of you, Jem. You know that, right?'

'Yes, yes, go! Go and look after that gorgeous girl. Love you. Bye.' I pressed end call, and Sancha disappeared, leaving me with an empty glass, looking out over the grey concrete outside. I wanted her to be here, sitting on the stool next to me so we could celebrate late into the night, talk things through properly. Tell her about the party. About Ed. I looked towards the bar and tried to work out how long it would take me to get there, order a drink and get back; was there time to do it before someone nabbed my seat? I badly wanted another drink, something cheaper would do.

'Off the phone, then?' Grey sweater man was walking towards me. A woman to my left glanced at him as he walked past. He was reasonable looking, I guess. Hair too long in my opinion. Must think he's younger than he is.

I held up my phone. 'Yep, finished.'

'And your drink, I see. Can I buy you another?' He was standing quite close now; any closer and he would be invading my personal space. Mid-thirties? Oh, why the hell not. Save me losing my spot.

'Sure, yes thank you.' Talking to him was better than sitting here on my own. He returned quickly holding two glasses of Champagne.

'Here you go. So, my guess is you are celebrating.' I moved my coat off the stool. He sat down, pulling the stool out slightly so he could tuck his long legs under the ledge, and then peeled off his sweater, showing a couple of inches of thickset belly as he did so, before pulling down his shirt to cover it again.

'I got a part in a play. Thanks for the drink.'

'That's great! Congratulations.' He clinked my glass. 'So, what's the role then? Is it here, at the National?' He smiled at me, and took a sip of his Champagne. The glass looked small in his large hands; I was pretty sure he would be happier drinking a beer.

'No. I wish. Well, maybe one day. No, it's at a small theatre in East London. Nothing flash.'

'Worth buying a glass of Champagne for though.' He smiled at me again. 'And you know what they say: No such thing as a small part.' I resisted the urge to do an eye roll at him; I'd heard that line my whole life.

'I'm happy about it.'

'Good to hear. So, is it the Arcola?' *Shit, he knew the Arcola.*

'Yes. How do you know it? It's pretty small.'

'I'm a director. I haven't worked there, but I've seen many plays there. It's a great space. Greg Trelawney.' He held out his hand to shake mine.

A director, really? Was I meant to be impressed? An actress sitting alone in a theatre bar was just waiting for a director to come along and chat to her, wasn't she? It was the perfect line, whether it was true or not. Well, I was happy to play along; I had nowhere else to be.

'What have you directed, then?' My second glass of fizz was taking effect.

'Oh, all sorts of things. I was involved in *War Horse* here. Did you see it?' I'd seen one of the giant horse puppets behind the scenes when we did our school tour. That was a few years ago, and I wondered if he always opened with that.

'No, I haven't seen it.'

'Oh, OK, fair enough.' His face fell a little.

I took a long sip; maybe I should have lied, been nicer. 'I'm Jemima. Not sure I said. What are you working on next, then?' If he was for real, then this could be interesting. All the times me and Sancha had sat here and not once met anyone useful. I couldn't wait to tell her.

'We are workshopping a couple of projects. One here, with any luck, and then something of my own. I will need actors for it. You should send me your Spotlight link.'

I stifled a groan. Half the men I'd met in the acting world were working on something of their own, trying to get a film or television screenplay off the ground. So many idiots out there who put a casting call online and get women to audition for them, only for there not to be a project at all, just a creepy way of getting women into their flats.

'Maybe... I've heard that line before.'

His clothes, to be fair, looked expensive. He looked like he *could* be the real deal. He had that 'I'm posh but trying not to be' vibe that lots of the guys at RADA had. Trying to shrug off their private school background, though they'd bring it back asap if needed. There was no way I was his type. Maybe that was the point for him?

'Ah, sorry. Didn't mean to sound like a dick.' He ran his hand across his forehead. 'I'm nervous. Sorry. Trying to make a good impression. And failing.' I was surprised. Nervous?

'Look. I hope it goes well for you. Thanks for the drink. That was nice.'

'And that sounds like you want to end this conversation.' He looked slightly hurt. 'Sorry, I just thought that with you being an actress, sorry, an actor, you might be interested. I'm sorry if I sounded like an idiot.' He sounded like he meant it.

'Oh, well... I mean, anyone sitting in here could say, "Oh, I'm a director". It's got to be wall-to-wall with writers and directors and producers in here.'

'I could say that about actresses, too.'

He had a point. My fizz was nearly finished. Maybe I should give him a chance? 'Wouldn't you rather be drinking beer?' I asked. I could get a round in, beer would be cheaper.

'Well, yes, to be honest. But you said you were celebrating and I can be flexible. I can drink beer any time, but it's not every day I'm going to drink with you, am I?' It was another cheesy line.

Oh, what the hell. 'You must drink Champagne all the time at opening nights, and awards and things? It must be pretty usual for you, being such a top director?'

He smiled at me. 'Yes, I have been to some glamorous parties and opening nights, but as you know, those things can be dire.'

The last party I'd been to flashed into my head. I drained my glass. 'You probably go to more than me.'

'Do you want to get something to eat, Jemima? I know I need to eat.'

The Understudy had street food, loaded fries and things, coming out from a hatch behind us. I hadn't eaten for hours.

'Sure, why not.' I felt a bit unsteady. I definitely needed food.

'Where do you want to go?' Greg asked, standing up.

'Oh. Not here?'

'God, no. We can do better than this.' He grinned at me. 'Come on, let's get out and see what the city has to offer.'

Why not?

We walked past street food trucks, lining the riverbank; each one would have been fine for me, but Greg seemed to want to keep walking, and talking. We were heading towards Blackfriars station so it was sort of on my way. Well, that's what I told myself.

'It's all terrible pizza and doughnuts along here. My place isn't far away, if you're cold? It's behind the Tate Modern if you can make it that far without freezing to death. You aren't exactly dressed for the weather, are you?'

'I'm fine.'

Did I actually want to go to his flat with him? He didn't really do it for me. If we went out, maybe he would pay for dinner. There were places behind the Tate, weren't there? Borough Market and posh places there. *What are you doing, Jem?* We were about ten minutes from the station and my way home, so I had a little time to think. Decisions, decisions.

'Do you know this part of London?' he asked, glancing at me as we walked, river shiny black on our left.

OK, let's do small talk while I decide. I told him I had been a student in London. That prompted him to tell me, in quite a lot of detail, about a student showcase he'd been involved with. My head was starting to clear in the cold air. My thoughts were on rotation like this:

It's stupid going to a flat with a man I don't know. Who does that?

But maybe he's a huge deal, really influential and could help me.

Yeah, right.

Going back to Seagrass when I should be out celebrating seems sad.

I miss Sancha. I should have made more effort with the other RADA people. Made more

than one friend.

Decision made. He was a director – well, probably – and he might be useful. Know people, the right people. And he seemed nice enough.

It might have been the alcohol or the white lights in the trees overhead, or that I'd finally, at last, got a real acting job, but as we got to Blackfriars station I kept on walking alongside Greg. Just before we reached the looming structure of Tate Modern, I followed him between an avenue of silver birch trees, each lit with spotlights.

'It's just through here. Not far now.' We walked past an Italian café. So, he wasn't focused on food.

'This looks good?' I stopped walking.

'Oh, no, I can do better than that.' Greg pulled out a credit card – no, a pass. 'Here we are.' We were in front of NEO Bankside – it towered above us, a block made from steel, glass and wealth.

'You live here?' I asked, not managing to hide my surprise. OK, maybe I'd made the right call.

'Yes, when I'm in London. It's easy to get to everywhere, handy for the National.' Greg held the card near a security panel and the door released silently. We stepped inside a spacious foyer with polished marble floor, and a woman behind a concierge desk, which made me feel better somehow, safer. I had walked past the NEO building many times, but I had never been inside. I had never expected to either; it was a place for hedge-fund managers, bankers, rich people who had made their money in ways I didn't really understand.

A silent lift, which opened straight into a vast apartment with incredible views reaching far across the River Thames, St Paul's, the Millennium bridge and beyond. It was breathtaking. The open-plan space was a triangle, with glass on two sides, giving the impression that the room was floating high above the city. *Wow. Act cool, Jemima.*

'Lights.' Soft mood lighting flicked on at the sound of Greg's voice. He threw his bag on the long, designer sofa. It didn't look very comfortable.

'I'll get the fire going. Warm you up.' It was like a hotel room; the sofas had perfectly placed cushions that didn't look as if they ever moved. The coffee table had a neat stack of design magazines on it, surely never read. There were no empty coffee cups, or old newspapers or half-eaten breakfast, which is what I knew was on the table in Seagrass.

'There. It isn't real, of course. They wouldn't allow it in here, but it does the job.' A fire that looked real to me flickered into life in a large white cube that filled most of the one wall that wasn't glass.

'Champagne? I'll call down and ask Monique to order dinner.'

'So, being a director clearly pays far better than being an actor...'

Sancha had once told me not to talk about money with rich people; I regretted it as soon as the words came out. Her advice to me was always act like you totally belong with the rich people, that an apartment like this was normal to you. I had seen where she had used to stay with her Dad: tiny, old furniture, stacked with boxes. She hadn't come from money. Though it was all real for her now. She'd always been a good actress.

'Depends on the director, depends on the actor.' Greg smiled at me, and went to the fridge. I followed him, not sure what to do with myself, and when he opened the fridge I could see that there was barely any food in it, just rows of wine bottles, beers and a container of green juice in the fridge door. Did he really live like this?

'Here, you open it.' He passed me a bottle of Nyetimber and indicated where the glasses were kept on a rack above the kitchen island. He made a call while I filled two glasses.

Wasn't this exactly what I'd wanted when I'd moved to London? To hang out with directors, to be in expensive flats and drink expensive wine? No-one from my hometown had even moved to London, as far as I knew. When I got into college it felt like when Charlie found the golden ticket in his chocolate, or when Harry got his invite offering him a place at Hogwarts.

To some of the people on my drama course, this life was their normal, but it definitely wasn't to me. I made a silent toast to myself. This day was turning out well.

'I hope pasta is OK? Padella do the best pasta and it's more relaxing eating it here than being in the restaurant.'

'Sounds great.' I walked over to the window, and took a large gulp. I could look down across London. Life was changing for the better, at last.

'You get used to the view after a while.' Greg joined me.

'I'm not sure I could ever get used to that view. It's amazing. Like the whole world is before you.'

'I guess it is, Jemima.' Greg put his glass on the table near him and turned to face me. He reached forward and ran his hand around the side of my face, tucking my hair behind my ear. He took the glass out of my hand and placed it beside his, then kissed me, roughly, firmly.

'This OK?' he asked me, quietly. I nodded.

His hand moved down my back, and he pulled me closer towards him, and he kissed me again. I found myself pulling him closer, and taking my hands to his face, and kissing him in return. I felt warmth rise through my body, not unpleasant. The edge of the glass table pressed against the back of my legs, keeping me focused, alert. All around us, the night sky of London glittered, forming a backdrop to the scene playing out inside the expensive apartment.

We ate the pasta later, wrapped in a cashmere blanket on Greg's ridiculous sofa, the cushions left on the floor where they had fallen. It felt all wrong to try and bring up work now. It would make me look desperate. I felt I should act like I didn't need his help. I'd just got a job, right? I was on the way up. So, why was I here? Well, it was better than being on Seagrass for a night anyway.

Greg put down his plate, looked pleased with himself, and

then pulled me once again towards the bed, and it was OK. I'd had better sex, and worse. Much worse.

The sky turned to a fake, artificial orange around the flat as night turned into morning. Greg's breathing became heavier beside me, holding me tightly against him. When I knew he was asleep, I pulled on my clothes and sat there, thinking. He was nice enough – a bit too grateful even, that I'd slept with him. But someone like him, who lived in a place like this, would never really want me, would he? We were from totally different worlds.

I sat there for a while. What was the plan? Wake up together? Go get brunch together like a cute couple? Chat through opportunities for future work? *Get real, Jem.* I picked up one of the magazines. I could leave my number, let him get in touch with me. Maybe he really did need an actor for his new project. What would Sancha do? She would never do this. She didn't need to. She had Jon and everything.

Time to go. *Back to where you belong, Jem.* He didn't notice when I left.

ACT 2

TEN

Ten days. That was how long we were given to rehearse *Poison*. The script Elle emailed over was insane – pages and pages of duologue, just me and one other. It was so rambling, so confusing to follow – if I had dropped all the pages on the floor, I would have struggled to put them all back in the right order. The money wasn't life-changing, but it was good. Better than good. I could drop my shifts at the coffee van, eat better, go out a bit more. At long last.

'First rehearsal tonight.' Sancha was in her beautiful kitchen, light streaming in as she made coffee. 'Are you off-book?'

'No, nowhere near. Lines won't go in.'

'It'll go in when you start marking.'

'I know... it's just been a while.'

She moved around making breakfast, yoghurt, fresh berries, some protein powder. I'd eaten a stale bagel. I needed to buy some fruit – improve my immune system.

'Sanch, I've got news.'

'More news?'

I had wanted to tell her the second I found out, but it had

still been night for her, so I had to wait. I had counted down the hours until it felt like a reasonable time.

'It's Olivia Goldsmith. The other actor.' I couldn't quite bring myself to say 'co-star' yet.

She turned into the camera, put her bowl down. 'You're kidding!'

I couldn't help but enjoy the moment. 'I know!'

'Wow! She's huge! Why is she doing that play?' I could have been irritated at the implication that somehow the play wasn't quite good enough but decided to ride it out.

'She wants to do more theatre, apparently. Elle was surprised, too.'

'Wow. Olivia Goldsmith. That's impressive, Jem. It's all coming together for you!'

'I know. I was beginning to think it wouldn't...'

'You should talk to Neema. She was on *Dragonhunter*, too. She'll know her.'

Neema was the last person I'd just pick up the phone and call. Though it would be an interesting thing to tell her. No, it might jinx it in some way.

'Yeah, thanks. Might do. You know what she's like.'

'Oh, she's not that bad. It's all about contacts, Jem. Can't ignore that.'

'OK. I am listening. Just not sure about Neema.'

'Can't get my head around actual Olivia Goldsmith! Jem, this is *huge* for you. Maybe you'll meet her mum!' Olivia's mother was an even bigger star, had been in so many incredible films. Nepotism was so normal in this business. 'It will get massive coverage. It's such a great opportunity for you. When you told me about the play, I thought, well, that's great, she's waited ages, but it's quite a niche play, quite small, but this is *massive*.'

'You should come. Meet her.' That was a bit cocky of me – I hadn't even met her myself yet.

'Oh my god, I should! Ha. Can you imagine?'

I *could* imagine. The selfies, the way they'd get on, Sancha charming her with her usual effortless chat.

'Ah, Jon's calling me. Let me know how it goes and what she's like. Love you!'

I'd been told to head to the Arcola bar for the first read-through, and it looked pretty much as I remembered it – the string of red lights flickering against the spirits bottles. Bar tables had been pushed back against the edges of the room to make space for a circle of chairs in the centre. I was first, unfashionably on time. Should I leave, come back in five minutes?

'Jemima. Right on time. Good start.' Sarah walked in behind me, looking just the same as at the party. Sleek hair. Red lips. Black clothes. 'I know it's all been very last-minute for you. So pleased you were available.' We both knew that I'd been available.

Act confident, Jem. 'Thanks for giving me the part! I was so pleased, too. The play looks excellent – I love the script.' *Oh god,* I was gushing again.

Sarah nodded, glanced at her phone. I chose the chair nearest to me and dumped my bag on the floor next to it.

'Just us three today. Oh, the joys of a two-hander,' Sarah replied, sitting down, seeming to choose a chair as far from me as possible. 'Olivia will be here any minute, hopefully'. She glanced at the door. 'We'll do a straight read-through today and then as I have you both here, we can work out the rehearsal schedule for the next week.'

'Does Rebecca tend to come to rehearsals?'

She looked up at me, surprised. 'No, goodness. She doesn't have time. She might come to dress, but not to read-throughs.' She paused a moment. 'Were you expecting her?'

'I thought she might have been at the castings?'

'The castings?' I could have sworn she frowned a little, just before she leaned into her bag to remove a thick notebook. I noticed she didn't answer.

'We don't have long, is that right?'

'It's the way it is, Jemima. No, we don't have long, but with your training, I am sure you will be just fine.' Sarah glanced at her phone. Was she expecting a message? From Olivia?

It was a pretty low-cost way to put on a play; just two actors, one director and, I guessed, the in-house team to handle staging, costumes, whatever else was needed. Surely Olivia would be getting paid more than me. Double? More? I had no idea. And yet she was now fifteen minutes late.

Sarah glanced up from her phone. 'I was looking at your Spotlight profile. You haven't done much work since you graduated, have you?'

'It wasn't that long ago, since I graduated,' I replied, quickly. 'I did some travel, wrote some things. It's been a hugely productive time.'

She nodded, not looking convinced. The door banged, and our conversation was cut mercifully short.

I recognised Olivia Goldsmith at once. Huge brown eyes in a tiny, heart-shaped face and the most incredible cheekbones. She looked just the same as she did in the Agatha Christie thing I'd watched her in at Christmas. Flawless make up, as if done by a professional. Maybe it *had* been done by a professional. Was that normal for rehearsals?

'So sorry I'm late! I hate being late! God, we're in the middle of nowhere!' She kissed Sarah, shrugged off a huge white padded coat, revealing a stick-thin frame, then threw herself down on the chair next to me. 'Hi! I'm Olivia!' That famous, dazzling smile. 'I've heard such amazing things about you, Jemima! They sent me your show reel from drama school.'

'Thanks! I've seen loads of your work, too – the Agatha Christie was great!' I sounded like a fan. *Act cool.*

'Oh, thanks. I loved doing that. Such a great cast. Made a change from the usual shit I get asked to do.' She shone her beam on me, showing her perfectly aligned, bleached white teeth, perfect pink lips. 'You'll have to tell me all about RADA some time. Now, *that's* where you will find the real actors. It's a good job you know what you're doing – one of us will need to.' She laughed, looking over at Sarah to share the joke.

Sarah didn't respond, instead passing us each a plastic-bound script, keeping one for herself. I already had a copy in my bag, covered in notes, but I took the one she gave me anyway.

'So, who's going to be the one to bring it up, then?' Olivia said, brightly.

'Bring what up?' Sarah said.

'The man at Rebecca's party. Everyone's been talking about it. He worked here, didn't he? Just so disturbing. Do we know what happened?'

I shifted in my chair, looked down at my hands.

Sarah opened her script. 'It was so sad. Ed. Yes, he worked here for a while. Apparently he will be OK, though I don't know the latest. Alcohol problems – he did have a reputation for it. Incredibly sad.'

I leaned forward, put my hand on my face. My brain scrambled to decide what to say. Should I mention that he had been in my audition to Olivia? That I had been at the party? I mean, I hardly knew him, why talk about him more than I needed to?

Olivia filled in the awkward silence. 'Apparently there was blood everywhere, he fell into the garden, right in front of everyone! Complete chaos as everyone was so out of it, so drunk. Someone said they were all freaking out that the police would start searching people for drugs. Rebecca wanted everyone out of her house...'

'I'm sure Jemima doesn't need to hear all the gory details.' Sarah was right, I didn't. Olivia didn't know that I had seen him myself, lying there, soaked in blood. I glanced at Sarah. We had both been at the party. I wondered what she had made of it all.

'Right, you've got the scripts, so let's get started. As you know the schedule for this is stupidly tight so we can't sit here gossiping. If we get an update, I'll let you both know. Might as well start with scene one and see where we get to.' Was that the subject of Ed dealt with? I felt myself breathe out slowly.

My name was typed at the top: Woman B: Jemima Evans. Olivia was Woman A the much larger part, but it gave me a thrill to see my name right there on the script. This was real... it was happening.

Sarah sat up straight and planted her feet squarely in front of her. 'So, just to get you in the zone... The play opens with you two in a waiting room. The audience don't know where or why. You are waiting for someone, a caretaker, perhaps. You haven't seen each other for years. It's awkward, you don't know how to talk to each other.' Sarah glanced at me. 'Later, we will find out why you are there, what's brought you back together, but for now, focus on the awkwardness between you.' She turned to look at Olivia and nodded.

'Ah! Me first. OK, let's do this!' she said, flicking back her hair. 'You haven't changed a bit,' she said her line a little too theatrically.

'Oh, well, don't look too closely.' I replied. I felt excited; here I was, reading an actual play with Olivia Goldsmith. I felt an overwhelming urge to take a photo of us, to share it with everyone, especially the RADA WhatsApp group.

'I only got this the day before yesterday.' Olivia said, and mimed taking a letter out of her pocket like the stage directions told her to.

'I didn't know if you'd get it in time.' I replied.

'I meant to phone to tell you I was coming. But I'm not much of a phoner.'

'No, I've noticed.'

We read through the first scene, and slowly our voices changed to match the gentle cadence of the script. The two women knew each other intimately, and the sense of loss was clear in the script. I found myself feeling moved by Lot Vekemans' words. We came to the part that I'd first read at the first casting in Soho:

'Having to sit here... waiting.

'And not having seen you for years.

'And not having any idea how you are.

'And you not having any idea how I am.

'And not knowing what to say.'

It took me right back to when it was just me in that room, with the woman behind the one-way window. With a jolt, it became clear. That voice back then wasn't Sarah. Listening to Sarah describe the scene to us now, it wasn't her at the casting that night. Who, then? Rebecca? I promised myself that I would ask Sarah again later.

The scene then shifted towards Olivia's character and I found myself watching her long, pale neck, and her exquisite face. She pushed her hand slowly through her hair, and glanced briefly to see if we were both watching. Which we were. You didn't need to be the best actress in the world if you looked like that.

'Oh, Sarah, it's such an earnest play, isn't it?' Olivia held up the script.

'It is what it is. Rebecca loves it.' Sarah replied. Was it Rebecca behind that window? It must have been her, the one who'd seen me at RADA, so it must have been her calling me in for the casting. She had wanted *me*.

Olivia sighed. 'The lines are very repetitive. I was reading it last night, and the pages sort of blur together. It's going to be a nightmare to get it in the right order.'

'Well, that's what rehearsals are for.' Sarah smiled, though the smile didn't quite reach her eyes.

'Once we start blocking it will sink in,' I added, trying to sound reassuring.

'Well, with all your RADA training, Jemima, it's easier for you. In TV if we screw up, we just do it again.' Olivia turned her mega-watt smile towards me.

I wanted to say to her, 'You just need to get on and learn it. Do the work. Read it over and over again until you know it inside out. Record the lines on your phone so you can practice it back at yourself. Put in the hours.' But I didn't. Instead I said, 'We've got time. It will be OK. We're a team. It will be really good...' I smiled back at her.

I'm sure Olivia had been told that it would be OK all her life, and for someone with her looks, it probably *had* always been OK. Famous parents, great school, great friendships, dazzling opportunities... And it probably *would* be OK for her. This play would be good – it had to be. I would do everything in my power for it to be amazing.

ELEVEN
BEFORE

Dad was long gone by the time I started at secondary school. His job had taken him to Edinburgh, and he had a girlfriend there now, so didn't come down to visit us as much anymore. It was a long way to Scotland from Bristol, though we said to Mum that we didn't mind getting the train. She said the cost of the tickets was insane so we would have to wait for Dad to pay for them, and it was his choice he'd moved up there anyway.

Mark was the one who got into the school, and I just followed as a younger sibling, given a place regardless. He was clever, passed the tests – he was always the brains of the family. Mum took all the credit, told everyone about it, but we both knew he had done it despite her, not with her help. It was perfect for him, but it was the wrong place for me.

'What are you wearing?' That was Sophie.

'Charity shop.' Kate. They were our class captains, voted in by our form. A stupid job that made them feel important, popular. It was non-uniform day, so we got to wear our own clothes, instead of the black skirt and jacket we usually wore. Most people loved it, the chance to wear their own clothes, but I hated it. I walked past the bike racks quickly, but I could hear Sophie and Kate behind me. I knew my jeans were a bit too short, and needed a wash, but I'd rolled them up at the bottom, which I'd thought looked OK. I hadn't had much choice; it was too cold for my denim skirt on its own and I only had black school tights. There was nothing wrong with my blue jumper, it was from Zara, but they were right – it was second-hand. *Act like you don't care, Gemma.* Lesson one. I learned a lot about acting at that school – try to blend in, don't get noticed.

The drama block was just ahead and the door was open, and Ms Tatham would be in there, getting ready for our drama lesson. Once inside, I knew I had two hours, two whole hours, before I would have to face the outside world.

I didn't mind working in the fish and chip shop. I could walk there after school, didn't have to go home to her, they paid me in cash, and I could eat the leftover fish and chicken at the end of the shift. Dinner sorted.

'Oh my god, do you *work* here?'

Sophie, from school, and two boys, behind her.

'Hi. Yes. What can I get you?'

Sophie was wearing dance kit – pale pink ballet tights, and a long grey sweatshirt, hair tied up.

'God, no, can't eat this shit... We saw you, through the window!' She laughed and wrinkled her nose at me. The boys took their cue from her, grinning. I recognized one from our year – he was OK usually.

'Nothing wrong with working here,' I said, more defiant than I felt. I looked around. It was early, so my manager Sam was in the back, preparing for the rush.

Sophie smiled. 'You know, greasy food gives you acne.'

I felt my hand go to my chin, trying to cover the spots there. There was no point putting on cover-up for work, it just melted.

'Leave it, Sophie.' The boy I recognized – Liam? He was in the other English class.

Sophie didn't like that. Scowled at him, adjusted her shoulder bag.

Sam came out from the back. 'Hello. Can I get anyone, anything?' He looked at Sophie, the boys and at me.

'I wouldn't eat this shit,' Sophie mumbled as they left, banging the door behind her.

'Do you know them?' Sam asked.

'No.'

It was dark by the time I left work. It was a ten-minute walk home, and of course it was raining. I didn't have a coat with me but if I walked fast, I wouldn't get too wet.

'Hey.'

Sophie.

I carried on walking up the hill, cars passing, sending muddy water up onto the pavement.

'Don't ignore me.' Sophie grabbed my arm, pulled me back. Her friend Kate was just behind her. Sophie grabbed my rucksack, which fell to the ground. It would get dirty there, I remember thinking. Kate pushed me, made me stagger back.

'You disrespected me.' Sophie spat out, her face crumpled. She'd changed out of her dance kit, I noticed. I hadn't said anything to disrespect her. But Liam had. And she hadn't liked that.

Kate picked up my rucksack and stepped back, zipping it open.

'Give that back!' I shouted. A car sloshed past, sending more spray towards us. Why didn't they stop and help me? My wages were in the front pocket – Sam had just paid me for the week, in cash from the till. I needed that money. They wouldn't actually take it, would they? I tried to grab the bag back from her.

I watched as Kate tipped the contents onto the wet pavement, my school jumper, pens, school pass, all on the ground. I felt such rage, such pure rage – how dare they treat me like this!

'Leave it alone!' I screamed.

Sophie looked around her. On the far side of the road, a man walked his dog.

I lunged at Kate, pushing her, and grabbed my bag as I stumbled forward. My hand broke my fall, the cold, wet pavement... gravel cutting into my palm. But I had it back.

'Let's go,' I heard Sophie say.

I bent down and picked up my stuff, all wet, dirty from the ground – stuffed it back inside. I reached into the front pocket and was so relieved to feel that my money was still there, tucked in safely, that I began to cry.

'You're late,' my mum said when I walked in, soaked through. I walked to the kitchen, wanting to find something to clean my bag with, get rid of the dirt.

'Busy night.'

'So, did he pay you? We're running short.' She steps forward, expectant.

'Mum, I need it. I need to get some clothes for sixth form.'

'Hand it over.'

Can't she see that I'm soaked from the rain, that I've been out all day, I'm exhausted from school, from work, and she isn't even asking how I am, or if I want a hot drink, or if she can care for me? I look at Mum, her hair scraped back, she looks exhausted too, but her eyes are unfocused. She's been drinking, I know that, and if I give her my money, it won't be spent on food, that's for sure.

'I haven't got paid yet,' I lie. Other people might have mums they can tell about their day, about the girls at school who hate them, about how the teacher said today that I was really good in drama, and that I can't wait to leave that school and get on with my life. Leave it all behind and show them that I'm worth more than they think. But I don't have one of those mums. She looks sad, like she needed that money, and she probably does. But that's not my problem. I need it more. I need it to help me escape one day.

'You OK, Gem?' Mark walks into the kitchen. His smile lifts my spirits.

'Bad day,' I said as we walk up the stairs together.

'Tell me.'

Mark got his place at college in Brighton, and was excited to go, although I knew he was trying not to show it when he talked to me about it. He knew I was dreading him leaving.

'Gemma, just finish this year, and then you can get out, too.' The thought of just me and Mum in the house, and having to go to school every day... Mum didn't drink as much when Mark was around – he was taller than her now, did most of the shopping and stuff, took charge of things. I was as tall as her now, too, but it didn't seem to work in quite the same way. I was always just 'too tall for a girl' or 'your hair is greasy, why don't you wash it more', even though she'd always used up all the hot water by the time I got in from the fish shop.

When she was out, I relaxed, watched TV. I watched everything: comedies, seeing how the actors paused before delivering their killer lines, waiting for the laughter. Thrillers, old Bond films, Agatha Christie, *Silent Witness*, period dramas, Disney films, *Brooklyn Nine-Nine*... there was always something to watch, to keep me company, to learn from.

Mark waited to leave until the last possible day before term started, and said I could go and visit at the weekends, to escape Mum if I needed, though we both knew that wasn't very practical. He had a room in college, and it looked tiny on the website, just a bed, wardrobe and desk along one wall, barely space for a sleeping bag on the floor.

I tried to make it easier for him. 'You are never going to get a boyfriend if you've got me sleeping on the floor.'

'I can't be out shagging every night. Come to stay. You'll love Brighton. Full of actor wannabes.'

'Maybe. You settle in, then we'll see.'

The night he left I slept with his big winter sweatshirt over the top of me. The thought of just me and Mum in that house, no Mark, no Dad, made me feel empty, alone. Staring at the bottom of Mark's bunk bed, I reached out to place my hand on the familiar wooden bars above me.

Mark never really lived with us again. He got bar work in Brighton, said he needed the money. I counted down the days until he was due to visit, and I loved those rare trips back. Mum had a new boyfriend, so was out a lot of the time. That suited me.

After he graduated, Mark moved to London for work. It was the happiest I have ever known him. He met Daniel at a festival, and they were perfect together. Daniel was a bit older, good-looking if you like that sort of face, seemed pathetically into Mark, and had loads of money. Mark told me about him, of course, he told me everything. But he never told Mum. Was it because he didn't think she'd accept that he was gay, or just that he wanted to protect this beautiful, precious part of his life from her? She wouldn't hear any of his news from me, that was for sure.

Clapping, whooping, the faces of the audience before me. The noise, overwhelming. Feet stamping on the gym floor. We had got through it, not perfect, but we had got through our final school drama performance. The examiner in the front row writing in her folder, grading us. I had to admit to myself, it felt amazing. Standing right there, in the middle of the stage, the audience showing how much they had loved it! And they had loved me! I took my bow alongside Will – Benedick to my Beatrice. We'd got through the lines, and better than that, had made people laugh in the right places, had got the language across. It had been a nightmare to get through the scenes in rehearsal, but we'd done it. What was the examiner writing in the folder? What grade was she giving me?

It almost didn't matter – I loved the feeling, standing there, so alive, my heart rate fast, blood pounding, in time with the clapping around me. It felt right – like this was exactly what I was meant to be doing. I was good at this!

Moments later I was at the side of the stage, everyone in my class talking, excited, wanting to get backstage, start celebrating.

'Don't push, Gemma. Jeez. Careful.' Claudia just in front of me.

'Sorry, it's everyone behind me.'

She turned and looked at me, a look of sheer hatred on her face. 'You think you're so special, don't you?'

Will next to me, pushing past. 'You were great, Claudia.' He leaned in to hug her, blocking my way past.

'Let's get out of these costumes and get to mine.' Claudia and Will were swept along towards the changing rooms, where girls and boys split into two groups, into their own spaces. My spot was in the corner, my bag on the bench, shoes under, and coat hanging above on the peg. We'd been changing in this room since Year 7 drama lessons and this was my last time in here, school nearly over.

The sound of laughing, happiness, relief that we'd got through the play, was all around me. I stepped out of my heavy brocade dress that had seen many years of plays at this school – dark mossy green, with a gold corset. I put it on the laundry pile, ready for collection. I opened my bag to get out my jeans and T-shirt.

What the hell? They were covered in dark purple liquid. It smelt like fruit. Smoothie? My jeans, sweatshirt and T-shirt covered in thick, purple gunk. Laughing behind me. My blood rushed to my head, a ringing sound in my ears. Standing there in my underwear, I felt cold, vulnerable. What was I meant to go home in?

I rummaged in my bag, trying to wipe the liquid off my T-shirt. I'd brought my best one, ready for an after-show party if one was happening, if I got invited. Pulled it over my head, felt the stickiness on my arms. I heard the click of a camera phone. I spun around.

'Oh no! What happened, Gemma?' Claudia was standing in the door. And Sophie, just behind her.

Had Sophie done this? Poured this mess into my bag while I was on stage?

'Did you take a photo?' Sophie asked Claudia.

My heart was pounding.

'Claud, you coming?' Will, and others, three or four of them – standing by the door.

Act like it doesn't matter.

I pull on my jeans, feeling sick, the wetness against my thighs all sticky.

'Oh, Gemma! You are a mess.' Sophie, again. I didn't want to turn, to look at her.

Then they were all leaving, talking about the party, arranging rides. I waited for them all to leave, then sat there alone, shaking.

TWELVE

NOW

Mentally drained, I was desperate to go home at the end of the read-through with Sarah and Olivia. It took us over four slow hours to get through the play. The actual run time in front of an audience would be more like seventy minutes – it took so long because Olivia constantly needed breaks to go outside for a cigarette, get a drink, walk around the room. She seemed oblivious to Sarah's growing irritation each time. It didn't bode well for the rehearsals which were going to be all-day sessions. Sarah didn't have much to say to me when Olivia was out of the room; she filled the time checking her work emails and making calls. One, to a school office, seemed to be about making a payment. I tried to look busy studying the script, not listening.

I was on my way to the train station when Olivia called after me. She caught up and walked with me to the end of the road.

'I'm starving. Shall we go and eat?' It was late and really, I wanted to collapse on my bed, but it was actual Olivia Goldsmith. Asking me to go out with her.

'Sure! Aren't you tired?' I asked her.

'Exhausted! But we need to eat. My shout – I know a great

Vietnamese place near here. Should still be open.'

If I went home, I could let my brain empty, shower, call Sancha to update her on how the rehearsals were going. She'd understand completely – we'd trained with people like Olivia. But if I said no, she might not ask again. *Sancha would say yes. Neema would say yes.*

'Right, where's this place? I hope it's good.' I smile my warmest smile at her.

The restaurant was pretty empty, a bored looking woman behind the plasticky counter, just two tables occupied. I wasn't sure what half the things on the menu were, so I just said, 'Sounds perfect!' when Olivia ordered. Large bowls of noodle soup arrived really quickly, and I had to say, Olivia chose well – the steamy tang of chilli, lime and ginger was exactly what my body craved, and I ate the first mouthful quickly, burning the roof of my mouth.

'It's so good, isn't it?' Olivia fished out a cube of tofu expertly with her chopsticks, and popped it into her beautiful mouth. I noticed the two men sitting across the room staring at her.

Was I meant to eat the vegetables and noodles first, or drink the soupy bit? The waiter had given us chopsticks and a chunky white china spoon. I put down my spoon and copied Olivia, trying to pick up a piece of tofu with the chopsticks. It landed back in the bowl, slopping the soup onto the table.

Olivia pulled out a generous handful of paper napkins and passed them to me. 'Oh, it's so messy. That's the joy of it! You know, this is so like this place I went to in Vietnam. I've been craving the food ever since. All the food there was amazing. The banh mi, fresh seafood... I loved it all. Sorry, I'm rambling on. I do that. So, tell me all about *you*, Jemima. I do love that name. You don't come across it very often, do you? I had a friend called Jem at Oxford; lovely girl from the valleys. Tell me, what do you make of Sarah?' She fished out a long noodle, and sucked it in, expertly. 'She's got an amazing reputation, but I find her so... closed.'

Which part of that was I meant to respond to? I didn't know anything about Vietnam. Hadn't been anywhere like that I could just mention. That casual privilege of someone who'd travelled all over, could afford flights, no idea that some people couldn't. Better stick to work.

'I don't know yet. She doesn't give much away.'

'No, that's true, she doesn't, does she? You should see her when she's had a few drinks, though.'

I thought of Sarah at the party, calm, immaculate. 'What do you mean?'

'Oh, just she isn't always so controlled. So uptight. She'll be an absolute pussycat with you though. She needs you to be on side.'

'Really? She barely talks to me when you aren't there. There's a strong chance I only got the part because I was available at short notice.'

'Not what I heard. Apparently Rebecca suggested you. And casting is always Rebecca's shout, whatever Sarah might think. It's her style to be aloof; the director in charge, at all times. We, the humble pawns, there to be bossed around.'

'I *think* Rebecca was at my casting, but Sarah hasn't confirmed that. Have you met Rebecca?'

'Oh, god yes, over the years. Terrifying. I didn't do a casting for this one – they rang me. Now, if we are talking Rebecca already, we need wine.' She called over to the waiter, and then pointed to a bottle on the short menu.

'It'll be dire, but I need a drink, don't you?' Olivia whispered to me. 'First, I'm dying to know. What was RADA like? I had to pull out of my audition for work, but I already had my Oxford place so it really didn't matter.'

Wow. How many boasts had she got in there? I didn't especially want to tell her about my drama school; she probably knew half the people from when I was there. I needed to steer the conversation back to Rebecca and Sarah. I watched the waiter fill our glasses.

'Oh, it was intense, good training. You would have fit in perfectly. I'm sure you did loads of acting at Oxford?'

'Some. I spent more time working though, than actually being at Oxford. It doesn't matter – as long as you can put Oxford on your CV, nobody cares how much studying you actually do.'

Olivia glanced out of the window for a moment, and I was struck by her perfect profile. Chin just held slightly up, her hand against her throat. I found my hand reaching to my own throat, unconsciously mirroring her, and put it down quickly. She turned slowly and looked at me, more serious than before. 'Jemima. Listen, I really need to talk to you about this play. The read-through has freaked me out. It's so difficult. And I think the press are going to be all over us. That guy almost dying thing doesn't help.' She looked at me with her big eyes. 'I've already been door-stepped by some journalist asking if I knew him.'

'Have you? At the theatre?'

'No, at home. They're always hovering about, trying to get a shitty picture of me.'

'That sounds horrible.'

She nodded. 'The journalist said the guy was at Oxford with me, but I have no memory of him. He was probably just fishing, trying to find a story.'

'They are probably approaching everyone they can think of, to try and get reactions.' I doubted a journalist would be interested in me, but maybe saying that would make her feel better. *Would* they want to talk to me? No, I wasn't famous.

'Maybe. I hope you're right. Sarah told me to ignore anyone who asked.' Olivia fished out some noodles, stirred them around, let them slide back into the bowl.

'Excuse me, are you Olivia Goldsmith?' One of the men

sitting across the room walked over, while his friend watched, leaning back in his chair. Olivia glanced at me. 'You were great in that thing at Christmas.'

'*And Then There Were None*?' she replied, quietly.

'Yes, that. You looked great.' He shifted his weight onto one leg, trying to look relaxed, casual.

'Thank you so much. That's really kind.' I watched her slowly tuck her hair behind her ear. I found myself doing the same.

'Can I get a selfie?' He held out his phone.

'Oh, sorry, I don't really do that,' she said, looking at me. Was I meant to do something?

'Oh right.' He walked back to his table and we all heard him say 'Bitch' to his friend, who laughed.

'How's your wine, Jemima?' Olivia asked.

'What a dick. Do you get that a lot?'

'All the time. Didn't expect it round here.' She took a long sip of wine. 'You see, this is the problem. People aren't interested in Sarah and Rebecca, though they actually *knew* the guy. They want the person from the TV. *I'm* the one people recognise. Even though I didn't know him, they can make up a story about *anything*, and they will if they have nothing else to write about.' She drained her glass. I was amazed she was telling me any of this. Maybe she didn't have anyone else to tell. 'I'm ready to leave. Ready when you are. I'll pay.' We left the half-eaten bowls of noodles.

We got into the habit of eating lunch together during rehearsals. Olivia mostly smoked and talked. That's how she was so thin. Sometimes I got a word in: 'Why did you choose to do *Poison*? I bet you get lots of offers to do TV?'

'I do,' Olivia told me, 'but it's always the same roles. Blonde. Posh. Stupid. I need to move away from that stuff, I need to do theatre. Not go abroad for filming so much, too. And Rebecca... she rang and asked. If she asks you to do something, you do it.' She ground her cigarette onto the pavement, littered with her previous cigarettes.

'Is she likely to come to rehearsals?'

Olivia lit another cigarette. She got through about a pack a day. That wouldn't be helping her breathing, her voice control. 'At some point. It had better be good when she does. She's cancelled stuff before.'

I stared at her. 'She won't pull it, will she?' It was unthinkable.

'Who knows with Rebecca? If the play is terrible, it won't look good on her and her brand, so she could pull it, or delay it, I suppose. She won't want to lose money, but she won't put her name to crap either.' Was Olivia just being dramatic? It made no sense.

'They won't cancel it. They're already selling tickets,' I said. 'And I'm replacing someone, right? So they want it to happen.'

'Hasn't stopped them in the past. They just move it, say it's illness or something.' She sucked on her cigarette. She'd get nasty little lines around her mouth if she did that. Like my mother had.

'Do you know who dropped out?' I asked.

Olivia shook her head. 'Whoever it was probably got a better offer. More money. Happens.'

'Well, we'd better be really good, then.' I needed this play to work. I was doing everything I could; it wasn't going to be me who was the weak link.

Olivia looked at the ground in front of her. 'I hate Act One. It's so repetitive. How are we meant to know which bit comes next? So much of this play is them saying the same thing over and over – I'm going to get lost, I know I am. It's really freaking me out.'

We'd started work on the blocking, working out where you

were going to stand or sit as we said each line. You visualize the scenes, the 'room' you are in, the setting, the time of day or whatever, so it gets stuck in your head when you are on the stage. If you are meant to feel tired, sit down or lean against something. If you are meant to feel energised, passionate, use larger movements, move more, take your acting up to a seven out of ten. If you have a line you really want the audience to focus on, move towards the front of the stage so you know all the attention is on you. Your muscle memory takes over and the lines come as you move into position each time. *Stand here, and I say this line. Stand there, say that.* It was the only way we could cope with the endless classical stuff we had to do at college. Much of the time I didn't even understand the words I was saying, but my memory took over and I was able to speak them.

'It will come together, Olivia. We just have to keep rehearsing. Don't panic.'

She nodded at me, and I noticed her hands were shaking. Far too much nicotine. 'It's so much harder than I was expecting. I should have gone for a different play. Something with more people in it. Fewer lines...'

In *Poison*, the two women move around the stage and there is a shift in mood through the play, as they move from awkwardness, to anger, and on to the final resolution. Within each scene, you show how their relationship changes. There is hurt, affection, regret, anger. It could be amazing, with the right actors. Sancha and me could have done it, it would have been brilliant if we had been doing it together. I liked Olivia, but I wasn't sure she'd be able to pull it off.

'How worried are you, Olivia? I mean, it *is* a challenging play, but I'm sure Sarah and Rebecca think we can do it.' When we had left for lunch, I didn't think Sarah had looked very confident at all, but it wouldn't help to tell Olivia that.

'*Really* worried. I'm not used to learning this many lines in one go, and I really don't want to look bad. I didn't know it would be like this... Thing is, if the play is shit, the critics won't write about the play, will they? It will be about the actors. And, no offence, but it will be me that gets everything that's coming.'

No offence taken. I knew that no one knew me. Well, not yet anyway. 'Do you think critics will even come to see this? It's such a little play.'

'Hell yes. It's a Rebecca play. It's like a three-line whip. And with me in it. Of course they will all come.'

Hadn't she thought about this before taking it on? I realised that I hadn't. I was so desperate to get a part, I hadn't thought about the possibility that it could go badly. What if we got terrible reviews? Would I not get cast ever again? For the first time, I felt worried.

'Listen, Olivia. It *has* to be good. We are committed to it now. We just have to put the work in.' She nodded, and I was suddenly struck by the fact that she looked very young. She was genuinely scared. *Oh god, she is going to screw this up for both of us, isn't she?*

I took a deep breath, tried to let my feelings of panic die down. 'Look, let's go back in and run it again. It might be better than you think.'

I followed her inside, past the posters advertising the play, her name large at the top, mine smaller below.

This *had* to work.

Three days later and rehearsals were not going well. Olivia looked exhausted and was regularly coming in late. Sarah, on the other hand, was coming in early, furiously adding notes to the script, giving Olivia more instructions at each run-through, which I could see was just winding her up and confusing her. At lunchtime on that Thursday she wasn't back at two, and Sarah was losing it.

'Where the hell is she?'

'Don't know. Gone to get cigarettes?'

'Abi could have got them.'

'I can call her?'

She shook her head.

'Sarah, is there an understudy? Someone who can cover for either of us?' Surely, they were bringing someone in to be ready, just in case. In case Olivia couldn't do it one night.

'It's such a short run. We should be fine. Why? Are you planning on getting ill?'

'But... it's normal to have an understudy.'

'Not Rebecca's plan. This is all about Olivia. If she can't go on, we postpone a night. The audience is paying to see her.' I tried not to let my feelings on that point show. 'If you can't go on, well, we feel fairly confident you won't be planning to miss any shows. I could bring in an understudy, but I doubt that will help Olivia – Rebecca says it will confuse her. Just stay healthy, alright?'

I nodded. I would do anything not to miss a performance. We all knew that.

A rustle of papers over on my right.

'I could cover Jemima.' It was Abiola, the production assistant for the Arcola.

Sarah turned to where Abiola was sitting on the floor, a pile of papers around her, ready to prompt, take notes, get coffee, anything that Sarah or Olivia needed.

Her voice was hesitant, as if surprised she now had our attention.

'I know the lines. Only in an emergency, of course.'

'Oh right. Remind me, where did you train, Abi?' Sarah asked.

I looked over at Abi, as if seeing her for the first time.

'Bristol Old Vic.'

'Why didn't I know that?' Sarah replied.

Bristol Old Vic was extremely hard to get into. That meant Abiola was good. What was she doing here working as a production assistant?

'Send me over your Spotlight. Thanks, Abiola. I don't think it will come to that. But I'm impressed you offered. Advocating for yourself. Well done.' Sarah smiled over at Abi.

I felt I needed to say something. 'Sarah? Look, this might be a stupid idea. But what about swapping the parts? Mine is much smaller, easier.'

Sarah looked at me as if I was absurd. She shook her head. 'It will confuse her.'

'Will it? It's easier – my lines are always in response. It would be easier for Olivia, I mean. We could try it? Have a go at Act One? There are much fewer words.' I felt my heart rate speed up. It was by far the better part, and it would mean that I could drive the dialogue. If Olivia messed up, I could get us back on track more easily. *I should have suggested it earlier, we could have wasted less time.* I'd have to work really hard to get the new lines in my head, but that didn't scare me. What scared me was this play going wrong, or being cancelled, and my big chance blowing up in my face. I had nothing to lose. 'Why not ask her?'

Sarah looked at me, considering. 'Could you do it? Learn the lines?'

'I already know them.' A lie, but it seemed to work. I sort of knew them. I could learn them though, put everything I had into it. I wasn't scared of the work. I glanced over at Abiola. There were plenty of actors out there, just waiting for a chance. I didn't want to ruin mine.

'If Olivia says no, doesn't matter. It will be fine.'

Sarah leaned back in her chair, stared up at the ceiling for a few seconds. Then looked at me, and then Abiola. 'I'll talk to her.'

THIRTEEN

Olivia's agent had agreed to the switch by the time we got to rehearsals the next day. Olivia bounced into the studio on time, well, just ten minutes later than me and Sarah, and with a card-board tray of coffees for the three of us. Sarah took a coffee, smiled at Olivia and we both waited to hear what Olivia would say.

'We'll try it and if it doesn't work, we will go back. Nothing lost.' Sarah took a sip of her coffee; impressive – mine was still scalding hot. 'It should make it easier for you. Jemima thought...'

'This was your idea?' Olivia turned towards me and I saw the smile slip from her face, just for a moment.

'It's just an idea. We can try it.' I realised there wasn't a coffee for Abiola.

'Do you know my lines?' Olivia asked me.

'I think so...' I'd been up most of the night learning them.

Olivia threw her head back, exhaled loudly. 'Well, let's get on with it, then.'

The remaining rehearsals fell into a pattern, starting each day around 9, and continuing late into the evening. We worked through the weekend. I went over the lines at night, and fell asleep with them swimming through my mind. They started to go in, to take shape. Soon, it felt as though those lines had always been mine. My voice suited the rhythm of them, absorbing Woman A. I read up more on Lot Vekemans: older than me when she wrote the play. *Poison* was usually done by a man and a woman, not two women. I wondered who had made the switch, Sarah or Rebecca? I liked that it was two women. It felt right.

Sancha was amazed when I told her about switching parts.

'Wow. And Olivia was OK with that?'

'Yes, fine. No-one knew who was doing each part anyway, so it doesn't matter.'

'It's the bigger part though, right? Amazing, Jem! They must really rate you.'

Ben from the coffee van texted a few times to ask how rehearsals were going, and did I want any shifts. As if I had time or energy to make coffee.

A small part of me regretted not leaving my number for Greg. Maybe I could have invited him. It would be good to know a director. But he hadn't tried to get in touch, so that said it all really. My instincts told me that he met women all the time. He wasn't going to be interested in someone like me. And I didn't have time right now for men, anyway. I had to get this play right.

Alongside rehearsals, we had appointments for costume fittings, I was sent for a haircut, and a photographer came in to take rehearsal photos. The schedule was relentless, reminding me of the week running up to our RADA finals show– a combination of exhaustion, nerves and rare moments of excitement. Could this actually be good?

I got outside to get air as much as possible, walking laps of the theatre block and along Dalston high street. Olivia didn't join me for lunch so often now, and I was grateful for that. We spent all day together, shouting into each other's faces, holding each other, breathing the same stale air of the rehearsal room. We needed space for at least some part of the day.

At the end of one rehearsal, I overheard Sarah on the phone. Sounded like someone was coming to watch. Rebecca? No-one had mentioned anything. Dress rehearsal was in two days. Maybe she would come to that.

That night I googled Sheridan Productions and Rebecca again. I wanted to be as prepared as possible for when we met. The internet was full of photos of Sheridan plays, awards, past successes. Names from RADA popped up all the time, on past cast lists, in press reviews, people from the years above me. I could hardly believe I would soon be joining them! People would soon be searching for *me*! Rebecca herself seemed to avoid the spotlight. I had to scroll back over a year to find any photos of her. It was usually someone from the cast, famous actors, who collected the awards and got all the press coverage.

But there was one photo that got used a lot in articles about the company. In this one, her face slightly obscured by a shadow, sideways to the camera, laughing. Or talking to someone? I couldn't see. Confident, yes, definitely, and I think tall, usually dressed in black. If you didn't know who she was, you probably wouldn't pick her out as the most important person, but there *was* something about her. She looked expensive, powerful. Used to attention. A confidence I recognised from some of the lecturers at RADA. Rebecca was perhaps late thirties? Hard to tell. Long, dark hair, styled perfectly. There was something about her – a presence. Would I ever look like that? Feel like that?

Sarah didn't get many mentions. Not a big name in Sheridan Productions, clearly; a lot of assistant director credits, and mostly smaller projects, regional theatres. I turned over in my canal boat bunk – solo directing a play at the Arcola would be a big deal for Sarah. And with Olivia in the cast, that was a very big deal. So, it wasn't just me that had a lot riding on this play being a success.

There was lots online about Olivia doing the play – in *The Stage*, *The Guardian* arts pages. The rehearsal pictures weren't being used yet, but the papers were still running news that she was moving to theatre, trying something different from TV.

I typed my own name. Nothing.

A boat chugged slowly past my window, diesel fumes making their way into my space. It smelt disgusting.

Weirdly, nothing on Ed came up. We hadn't talked about him at rehearsals for a while, either. I typed in Rebecca Sheridan, London Party, expecting some article somewhere about Ed, the one I'd seen in the Hackney paper. There was no mention of it at all in the search results. The story seemed to have gone away. Old news already.

Olivia was making progress with her new lines, which was a relief all round. She was more confident with the later scenes, which were easier to act – she just had to follow my cues, my longer speeches. At one point Olivia leaves the stage – it's my longest monologue – and at the start of rehearsals she would take the chance to grab her script and flick through it to find her next lines. We were now at the point where I could see her waiting at the side of the rehearsal area, watching me, ready to come back on, ready to say her lines. It was going in. Sometimes she messed up but was able to pick it up, which was key. Improv really. As long as the key plot lines were said, we could work with that. There was a sense of relief between Sarah and me – this was going to work.

While I ate my sandwich, alone, I thought about sending out some invites. Elle, my agent, said she was coming. Perhaps I should invite the RADA alumni, have them all there, watching me up on stage with Olivia Goldsmith? Wow, that would be delicious. Neema's face! I could get comps for them all, they could all sit in a long row, applauding me, then meet me in the bar afterwards, tell me how good I was. They'd all come – the chance to see something with Olivia in it was a draw, even if I wasn't. I'd ask at the box office – surely I got some comps? It was all starting to get very real.

With just a few rehearsals to go, it was now time to get the play inside the actual theatre, with the set built and ready for us. It was the first time I'd been back down there since the casting, with Ed, and it gave me the creeps. Still quiet, eerie with shadows everywhere, no windows down here, no fresh air.

Sarah was sitting in the centre of the front row, waiting for us. Right in front of her was where Ed had laid on top of me, pressing himself down onto my chest, my arms. Was it hot in here? My skin felt cold, clammy.

Sarah held up her phone as we walked in, as if we could see what was on the screen from across the room.

'Olivia! Morning. Exciting news. I have a date for the press conference. They want to do it Wednesday, to be able to get it in the *Evening Standard* that weekend.'

'Oh god, really? Rebecca said she'd try and avoid one,' Olivia replied, walking towards her.

'I know, I know. We sent out the press release and photos and Rebecca thought that would be enough. But the office is getting so many calls about the play that she thinks this will be the best way to control the interest.'

I felt like the others were midway through a conversation that I'd missed. Olivia hadn't mentioned she'd been speaking to Rebecca. 'Do you usually do press launches? Is that normal?' I walked forward to join them. Sarah glanced at me, as if she'd forgotten I was there.

'We don't tend to do them for the Arcola, but Rebecca thinks this will be best, to try and manage the press interest. Get our message out, control the narrative.'

Olivia let out a loud sigh. 'Jesus, Sarah. You know this is a bad idea. They'll just ask about that guy at her party. Try and get some gory story out of it. They have no interest in the play itself'.

'Do we know how he is?' I asked.

Sarah put her phone down, shifted in her seat. 'Not sure.'

'What does that mean?' Olivia asked.

Sarah looked at her. 'Calm down. It means nothing. He's fine. Not for us to worry about.'

I couldn't help but think that a press conference could be brilliant for me getting my name out there. Maybe it would be in *The Stage*. Maybe a photo of me would be in *The Stage*.

Sarah continued. 'We can keep the launch short, and do it here. Most of the hacks won't bother coming this far from Soho. If you feel you can't handle a question, then let me take it. Rebecca's talking about sending Jonas.'

'Can we get Jonas? That would be amazing. He can handle anything...' Olivia turned to look at me, as if for backup. 'I'm not doing it unless Jonas does it, too.' I had no idea who she was talking about.

'Leave it with me.' Sarah looked tired. 'Now we really need to focus on the actual play.'

I could see the rows of seating behind her, where the audience would sit in about a week's time. I could imagine the seats filled with people in the darkness, waiting for the play to start. Waiting to see Olivia, the famous one from the TV, but also me, the new face, in her debut play. My bio was in the programme, along with a new headshot that had cost me £400, way more than I had, but Elle had insisted on it. 'Think of it as an investment in your future. Your old shots need updating.' Elle must have emailed the headshots to Abiola. I wasn't sure about it – too serious? – I would have chosen a different one, but no-one asked me. Too late now.

Yes, we did need to focus, to get this play nailed, to get

amazing reviews, get my name out there. I was so ready for it. Maybe there would be directors in the audience, casting agents, too, looking for actors to appear in their own plays, to book *me*. It was getting so close now, I could almost taste the success.

'I feel like we're sleepwalking into a nightmare. The play isn't ready and Rebecca is inviting press in!' Olivia's voice was so shrill, it cut through my thoughts.

'A little over-dramatic,' Sarah muttered, not looking up.

I walked across to pick up my script, although I knew the lines already. It gave me a chance to look away from Sarah and Olivia, and let out the breath that I suddenly realised I had been holding. 'We've got a lot to do. What do you want us to do next, Sarah?'

FOURTEEN

Holding the press launch in the Arcola bar rather than in the theatre was probably not the best idea, but Jonas had said it would make it more relaxed, informal. Jonas had warned us that there was more interest than expected, and as I walked upstairs from the rehearsal room, I could hear the room buzzing. I hoped it wasn't the sound of a baying crowd. Abiola was standing by the door, clipboard in hand, and rubbed my arm kindly. 'There's so much interest! Break a leg!' It might have been Ed's role if he'd still been working here. The thought made my skin crawl.

Sarah and Jonas were sitting at a long table set up in front of the bar, facing a packed room. So much for being too far from Soho. Jonas was holding court with the journalists in the front row. Considering he had only flown in from New York yesterday, he was very loud, confident, his energy infecting the room. Olivia and Sarah were all over him from the moment he arrived – clearly, he was someone they needed to impress, to get on side. It had been embarrassing to watch Sarah – it wasn't her natural style.

Jonas' confident New York drawl made him stand out in a room of Londoners. Tanned and glowing with health, the hacks, by contrast, were a jumble sale of black padded jackets and crumpled office wear.

My entrance pretty much went unnoticed. One woman glanced at me as I walked in, but most of the journalists carried on talking – they weren't here for me. I noticed her look me up and down; I was glad my Max Mara jumpsuit was getting some love. I'd got it down the road in one of those shops where rich women sold their cast-offs. Too expensive to give to charity, they wanted cash back. I took it into the changing room, the woman busy with someone emptying out Selfridges bags. Yes, I looked good, expensive, like I was a serious actor. Perfect for the press. I stuffed my leggings and top into my bag and put my hoodie over the top of the jumpsuit. I was outside just moments later. The shop could afford it more than I could.

I took my seat at the table. The plan was for Jonas to welcome everyone, introduce the team, talk about the play, and then invite a few questions. It was just after 7 when he stood up, six-foot-something towering over me and Sarah. With the people standing at the back of the room, there must have been what – over seventy, eighty people there? Abiola watched from near the door, ready to give the nod to Jonas. The plan was for Olivia to make an entrance.

'Grab a chair, everyone! There's some space towards the back. We're going to start any minute. Hi, Matt, amazing to see you.' Jonas didn't need a mic to get the attention of the room. I recognised the man he waved at from *The Stage* in the front row; he had also been at the RADA end-of-term showcase. This was good news – he had mentioned me in his write-up. He clearly had high status in the room; you could see a little cluster of fellow hacks leaning in towards him, wanting to be seen to know him. And he knew who I was! I straightened my back, lifted my chin, Olivia-style, showed my best profile. I tried to catch his eye, but he wasn't looking in my direction. A moment of doubt crept in – *would he remember me?*

Jonas raised his hands and addressed the room. 'Thank you so much everyone for coming to hear about our play! And for coming out to Dalston on this rainy night. London, huh? OK, right! I am really excited to introduce you to two *very* special women.' Was he about to introduce me and Sarah? No. He held his arm out to the door. 'First, the star of our play, Olivia Goldsmith!'

Everyone turned in the direction he was indicating, including me, and Olivia swept in, looking amazing. She wore very skinny black jeans, a thin, almost not-there top and a floaty kimono jacket. High-heeled boots made her legs look coltish long. She looked so confident, make up immaculate, and very different from this morning when she had lost it with me over the final scene run-through – that meltdown had ended in tears.

'Hello, hello! Sorry to keep you all waiting.' She waved expansively, embraced Jonas, and then me, kissing me on both cheeks, then Sarah, as if she hadn't seen us for weeks. Olivia pulled out her chair slowly, hovering before she sat down, knowing that everyone in the room was watching her. I saw men on the front row smile; she made a great impression.

'And, although she needs no introduction, our incredible producer, Rebecca Sheridan.' I turned to look.

And it was her. The face from the photographs. Even taller than I had imagined. Younger, too. That expensive, glowing look about her that some people had, so much better-looking than her photos, which couldn't really show the confidence she had, the presence she radiated when she walked into that room. It was as if a spotlight had fallen on her, and the noise of the room ebbed away for a moment, her effortless charisma drawing all the energy and focus towards her.

And then I saw that she was looking straight at me; looking at *me* as she walked towards the table, and then she looked away, took the seat at the centre of the table, between Olivia and Jonas. I could smell her perfume – strong, whatever it was. I could almost *feel* her, just along from me. I tried hard to look ahead.

Jonas sat down. 'Let's start! From left to right, we have Sarah Monroe, our director; you will know her from many productions across various London theatres.' Sarah nodded at the crowd, smile. Polite applause. They didn't know who she was.

'I now have the *incredible* pleasure of introducing you to Jemima Evans, in her debut with us here at the Arcola, who is fresh from RADA, which I believe, has quite the gilded reputation with you Brits?' There were a few laughs from the crowd, who had clearly warmed to Jonas. 'Fellow alumni include some pretty good actors, I think? Let me see.' Jonas looked down at a sheet of paper on the table as if gathering his thoughts, but he was just doing it for dramatic effect – he knew what he was saying.

'Ah, Mark Rylance. Helen Mirren. Gemma Arterton. Jessie Buckley. Maxine Peake.' He paused for recognition between each name. 'Oh, too many to mention. And quite a few are known over in the States, too, going over there and stealing our Oscars! So, we think we have discovered a rising star of the future.' I could feel the heat rising in my body, my heart racing – he was talking about *me*, in front of all these people! I glanced at Matt to see if he was watching me, if he had remembered me. He did! He was smiling at me!

'And now, a very familiar face to those of you in the business.' He looked out at the room, checking he had all the attention. Was he a trained actor? 'Rebecca Sheridan. Who needs no introduction other than as the best theatre impresario this country has *ever* produced. I should call her an "empressario".' He smiled at her. Rebecca tilted her head slightly, and smiled back. 'And my boss.' The hacks loved that, laughing, and a few hearty claps.

'And last, but by no means least, you all know the amazingly talented Olivia Goldsmith, who, I think we can all agree, looks incredible this evening.' There was a small whoop from someone near the back. I hadn't got whooping.

'Olivia Goldsmith has had an *incredible* twelve months. I am sure you all saw the Agatha Christie on prime-time BBC while enjoying a glass of whisky at Christmas? It has taken months of scheduling and negotiating for us to get Olivia, and we are delighted she can join the Sheridan team for this production of *Poison*. We are incredibly fortunate to have her.' Jonas looked at the audience and beamed. I could see Matt turn and whisper to a woman next to him, a colleague?

'And, I have news for you all. As news is what you came for, am I right? *Poison* is heading towards being one of the most successful plays the Arcola has ever staged. We are looking at a complete sell-out for the entire run. We have a hit on our hands, ladies and gentlemen.' Olivia and I glanced at each other. This was the first we'd heard about it.

'Don't panic. If you are here today, there is a ticket with your name on it.' He beamed again, waited a few moments before continuing. 'I warn you though – you mustn't sell them on eBay!' Jonas laughed at his own joke, but you could see the effect it had on the people in the room; it was a hot ticket and they were now enthusiastic to see it. They felt they were going to see something special. I had no idea if Jonas was just doing an amazing spin job, or if it really had sold out – I hadn't thought to find out.

Jonas spent the next ten minutes talking about the playwright, why Sheridan Productions had chosen this play, its contemporary relevance, all stuff he hoped would form the bulk of any press coverage that would follow. It filled the time beautifully.

'So, we have just a few minutes left for questions before we wrap this up. Abiola over here has a mic, so just put your hand up, and she will get to you as quickly as she can. Any questions for our incredible team here?'

Hands shot up and before Abi had reached him with the microphone, a man in the middle somewhere shouted out, 'Hi, yes, James Harrow from *Today News*. I have a question for Olivia. How are you going to find doing a live play after doing television? Are you nervous?'

Olivia laughed and leaned over. 'I'm utterly terrified! Isn't that the thrill of live theatre? You never quite know how it is going to go! But we have been working incredibly hard and Jemima is *so* talented. It really is going to be a terrific play. You should come.' She beamed at the man.

He smiled, then continued. 'Will your mother be coming to watch you?'

The crowd laughed along, enjoying the celebrity mention.

'I hope so! Though she is incredibly busy.'

It occurred to me that Olivia never mentioned her mother when we were rehearsing or having lunch. Perhaps that was a comparison she didn't want to bring up.

The journalist continued. 'Apparently you have a reputation for not knowing your lines on set. Do you have a good prompter all lined up?' I felt Olivia tense near me.

Jonas replied before Olivia could. 'Television is a very different beast to live theatre. Any more questions over there, Abi darling?'

Abi passed the mic to a man sitting at the end of a row.

'Olivia. Did you know Ed Everett? The man who fell at Ms Sheridan's house party? How's he doing?'

Olivia glanced at Jonas and then Rebecca, who looked faintly amused. I could see Olivia's neck had flushed pink; she put her hand up to cover it, just like she had in the restaurant. She leaned forward. 'Ed worked here at the Arcola as an assistant producer. Everyone adores him. It was a terrible accident, but his close family tell us he is doing just fine. Sadly, I didn't know him very well. He was here before my time.' Perfect, just as Jonas had prepared her to say.

Abi tried to take the mic from the man, but he held on tight. 'Olivia, apparently you did know him. You were students together? At Oxford University?'

I felt Olivia move slightly beside me. 'I'm afraid I didn't. Oxford is a big place. Did you go? If you did, you'd know what I mean.' She smiled at him, and turned her head towards Jonas.

The journalist wasn't thrown by that comment: 'Ha, no, not me. More school of life. Olivia – another question...' I could see Abi look at Jonas, as if he could help her get the mic from this man. 'Apparently you both studied English there, at the same time? Surely you went to some of the same classes and lectures?'

'Oh, I was barely ever there. I was a terrible student. I was so busy working on *Dragonhunter*, as I am sure you know.' A few voices murmured at the mention of *Dragonhunter*, but most people were quiet, waiting to hear what was said next.

'Thank you. Do we have any questions for the rest of the panel?' Jonas boomed next to me, right in my ear. The journalist smiled and wrote something down. Obviously, no-one would have questions for me, the unknown on the panel.

A hand went up. 'Rebecca. It must have been a shock one of your employees having such a bad accident at your home...' A tall woman, standing now, no mic needed. Rebecca indicated with a slight wave of her hand to Jonas that she would take the question.

Rebecca paused, looked at the woman, and I realised she was waiting for the room to be perfectly quiet before she spoke. 'I was devastated. But I don't wish to discuss Ed tonight, out of respect for him and his family. He would want us to focus on this wonderful play, on the team that has worked so hard to make it happen.' She held the woman's gaze. The woman sat down.

Now Matt from *The Stage* spoke. Quiet, confident that

people would listen to him, whether using a mic or not. 'Rebecca. We don't often see you at play launches. You must feel very passionate about this one.'

Complete silence in the room. Rebecca leaned back, away from the mic, knowing she didn't need it – we were all listening.

'Once I discovered *Poison*, I *had* to put it on. It's a play about love in all its messy, devastating forms. It's about wanting someone, something, yet not being able to have it. It is an incredibly powerful play that moved me, spoke to me, when I first read it. Anyone who has ever loved will love this play.' She smiled. 'Does that answer your question, Matthew?' And then, so quickly that I am not sure if I imagined it or not, Rebecca looked at me, and then looked away.

Matt was about to say something else, but Jonas spoke loudly, looking over his head. 'Any other questions?' Matt shook his head and wrote something in his notebook.

A voice from near the back of the room, signalling for the mic. Abi walking towards the upstretched hand. 'How does Jemima Evans feel about her debut role? What are you most excited about?' He knew how to project his voice, strong, confident. A question for me!

I leaned forward. 'I'm excited to be working with Olivia Goldsmith who has been a joy to rehearse with. And I have to thank Sarah Monroe for her incredible direction.' Sarah glanced at me, surprised. 'I've been waiting for a role like this since leaving RADA, where I had the great fortune to train with such talented people from the best teachers in the business. And I am really looking forward to when we open. It's an exciting play that I think will challenge and move people, and make you think differently about love. And yes, I know everyone will be jealous that I get to work with Olivia every day.' The hacks laughed. That had gone so much better than I had rehearsed in my head. I sat back, pleased.

Jonas smiled at me, with raised eyebrows. 'Well, thank you,

Jemima. Beautiful answer.' He raised his arms. 'Well, it's getting late, and I'm sure you all have homes to get to, or at least a decent bar. So I think that draws things to a close. If you want to wait a moment, my glamorous assistant, Abi, has more press info and can make sure you have everything you need. Thank you all so much for coming.'

At this, Olivia pushed back her chair and walked towards the door. Rebecca was immediately behind her. I saw a couple of journalists get up, perhaps hoping to follow them, but Abi stepped neatly into position by the door, leaving space for Olivia and Rebecca and no-one else. As they reached the door, I saw Rebecca place her hand on Olivia's waist, as if to guide her through. Sort of old-fashioned. I stood up, ready to follow them.

'Great job, Jemima. You said all the right things. Good girl.' Jonas patted my shoulder.

'Thanks.' I wanted to catch up with the others, meet Rebecca at last. Would we go for drinks? Talk about what Rebecca thought of the play? I wanted to know if it really was her who chose me, and maybe find out why. There felt like unfinished business between us. I was past Abi and almost at the stairs down to the rehearsal room when the man from the *Today News* grabbed my arm.

'Hey, Jemima. Great to meet you. James. Great answer back there.'

'Hi. Thank you.' I moved towards the stairs. He followed me, grabbed my arm again. Rougher this time.

'I won't keep you long. I need to ask you – did you know Ed?' He was now in front of me, blocking the stairs. I could hear people behind me, filling the corridor. I tried to pull my arm away.

'I didn't know him. I only met him once. Can you let go, please?' I looked around for Abi and Jonas.

'Everyone's gone very quiet about him. Were you at the party?' He looked younger than I first realised; his beard made him look older, which was probably intentional. 'People from here must have gone, but no one from the Arcola is saying anything.' He had a similar nervous energy that Ed had at the party. I stood back firmly, released my arm. I could still feel where he had gripped me. 'What's Olivia like to work with?' He tried a different approach.

'No. Sorry, can't help you.' I turned and walked down the steps, anger rising. He'd picked on me, chosen me, because he thought I'd be the one most likely to talk, to give something away, to say the wrong thing. Because I was the least important person at the press launch, the one most likely not to be surrounded and shielded by PR people. Olivia hadn't been stopped by a hack, just me.

Everyone had just left me on my own. Where was Jonas when I needed him? Or Sarah? Olivia was the one they had protected, not me. I rushed downstairs and into the rehearsal room, expecting to see Rebecca and Olivia, but it was empty. Were they in a dressing room? I couldn't see any lights on down the corridor, no voices. They must have gone somewhere without me.

FIFTEEN

Opening night arrived in a panic of late-night technical rehearsals and growing tension. Olivia had been short with me since the press conference, or maybe it was me irritated with her. I'd asked where she'd gone after the conference and she'd mumbled something about Rebecca.

'I'd have liked to come along. To meet Rebecca.' I'd run that line over and over in my head that night, trying to work out why they hadn't included me.

Had Sarah gone too, or gone home to her kids? No-one said anything. I could imagine Rebecca and Olivia sitting in a cosy bar somewhere, sharing industry stories, catching up on things, talking about how the rehearsals were going, planning their next project, whether I was any good or not... What had been said?

My irritation at not being invited ate away at me, made worse by getting a text from Sancha saying she wasn't coming over for the opening, though she would have loved to. Jon was busy, so couldn't look after Polly.

> Maybe later in the run. I'd love to be there, you know I would. Let me know if it gets extended.

Jonas was in the rehearsal room when I got in at 9. We had a very long day ahead of us. He looked focused with his laptop open at a table in the bar – the jet lag and time difference were clearly working in his favour.

'Good morning, Jemima! How are you feeling today? Pumped?'

'I feel like I need coffee.'

Jonas laughed. 'You should try matcha tea and lemon. Much better for your vocal cords. And you'd get a good dose of vitamin C. We'll be screwed if you get ill.'

When we were at college, Sancha used to bring in huge bags of oranges every day in the run up to a show 'to help us ward off evil germs'. I should've bought oranges for everyone. I really couldn't get ill. I felt sure that Rebecca and Jonas wouldn't forgive me if I was the one to mess this up. Abiola could have stood in if she really had to, but I *had* to do every show. Who knew who could be watching?

'Just one coffee, promise. You're in early.' I knew he didn't like my coffee habit; he'd commented two days running on how my disposable cups were choking the planet.

'Most effective part of the day, before you lot get in. I can work through my New York correspondence.'

'Jonas. Here already.' Sarah appeared in the doorway, large notebook in hand.

'Good morning, Sarah. Girls, before Olivia comes in, quick word. Rebecca is very concerned about the social media situation around *Poison*. Have you seen the comments about Olivia out there? Nasty trolling. Rebecca has been in touch with Olivia and her agent, but I wanted to remind you both, stay clear of social, and don't talk to any journalists. If anyone tries to contact you, put them straight on to me.' Jonas looked at me. 'I hope that's clear.'

'Yes, of course.' The last time someone had said that phrase to me, I was at school.

'Has Olivia said anything about the comments to you? I'm worried. I can't have her lose focus,' Sarah asked Jonas. She glanced along the row of seats as if deciding where to sit. 'Jonas. While it is just us, I have to say something to you. Your presence here isn't helping Olivia's stress levels. I don't think she has the head space to take in more notes. From either of us. Maybe today you need to let us get on with it.'

Jonas leaned back in his chair. 'Rebecca wants me to sit in. We all have reputations riding on this, Sarah. It needs to be right.'

I made myself look like I wasn't listening, rummaging in my bag.

'We need total calm today, Jonas. You give too many notes. It's confusing her. And, it seems I need to remind you...' Sarah hadn't taken in enough air before she spoke. 'It's my job to direct.'

'Look, Sarah honey, there really is no need to stress about it. I often represent Rebecca at her plays. Think of me as an extra pair of eyes, a help.' He leaned towards her. 'A heads-up for you, though. You really threw Rebecca when you switched the parts. The decision was hers to make. Not yours.'

'You know why we did that. Olivia couldn't handle the Act One monologues.'

'It was just a case of asking permission. Basic good manners.' Jonas raised his hands, as if to say, *I'm the reasonable one here.*

At that moment, Olivia walked in, wearing large dark glasses, hair tied back.

'Hi, Liv.'

'Jemima.'

'Amazing. Here we all are, ready to start.' Jonas smiled, as if the dispute with Sarah had never happened.

Sarah walked over to Olivia. 'Let's make this our best ever run-through, and then we can focus on the lighting. Jack has said it isn't quite right yet. Is that OK with you both?' She looked from Olivia to me, managing to avoid eye contact with Jonas. 'Did you sleep OK?' Sarah asked Olivia gently. Moved as if to touch her, then seemed to think better of it.

'No, not really. No, Sarah, I barely slept. I had a hideous night. But let's get on with it.' Olivia removed her glasses; she looked exhausted.

'Let's run through from the start, and then do the lighting check,' Jonas said, irritating Sarah.

The opening was the scene Olivia disliked the most. Yesterday she had missed out a whole chunk of lines about her child, meaning anyone watching the play would have no clue what was going on. Sarah had just looked at me, a look of panic on her face.

We took our places, sitting side by side on a minimalist bench. Up close, I could see that Olivia's eyes were bloodshot. Had she been crying? She also badly needed a shower.

'You OK?' I whispered. She looked at me, and I could see that her pupils were tiny, surrounded by tiny red spider lines. 'Did you sleep at all?'

'No, not really.'

'We've got this.' I whispered to her. She looked up at me, tried to smile and blinked slowly, and I could see that her eyes were slow to focus. Had she taken something? Sleeping tablets? We just had one more run through – *please, god, let her get this right.*

'Ready when you are,' Sarah prompted, turning to the scene in her script.

We took a break mid-morning while the lighting team did tests on the stage, and I went outside to get some air. Olivia had been awful. Really awful. She forgot two key lines and messed up the cue for me to come back on to the stage, meaning Sarah made us start the scene again. Jonas began filming us on his phone at one point, which freaked out Olivia. We all needed a break from each other.

Leaning against the wall, I checked my messages. Elle was coming to the opening. So that was one person anyway.

Mark would have loved it. No way was I inviting Mum. She had never shown any interest in my acting, hadn't gone to the school plays just a few minutes' walk from her house so no way she'd get on a train to London. Whatever.

Ben from the coffee van? I could invite him and I knew he'd come. He'd turn up to anything if I asked. He'd find something good to say about the play, too, even if it was terrible. My finger hovered over his number. No, not opening night. He'd read far too much into it. It would look really sad if I didn't invite anyone though. My fingers hovered over the RADA WhatsApp group. They'd come, wouldn't they? But they'd be here to see Olivia, not me. And what if it was awful? No. I closed the app.

Instead, I typed in Olivia's name and loads of photos came up; she did look amazing dressed up – this one at an awards event, the BAFTAs! Wow, she looked stunning. Beautiful smile. Amazing low-cut dress, beautiful skin. She looked so different from how she appeared in rehearsals. I smiled at the thought that I knew her better than any of these photographers, any of the people tweeting about her. She was a star, right? She could do a play. It would be OK.

More photos, Olivia walking a tiny dog, long skinny legs poking out the bottom of a huge coat. Such a cliché. Some of her with her mum in *Tatler*. Wow, they had great genes. Both so good-looking. Were they close? It was impossible to tell from a photograph, so clearly posing. I searched for her online and there, right under the official Arcola post saying she was in *Poison*, there were loads of comments saying she couldn't act.

Hundreds of them. Surely not all real? Bots? One saying she was a whore, what he'd do to her. David3670 only had three followers, so obviously a bot. That Olivia *was* poison. No talent.

Bulimic. Oh my god, that was from a woman. Lots of followers, too. The replies to that got toxic fast, that Olivia had shagged her way into *Dragonhunter*. Stupid stuff really, easy to ignore. Jealousy. But then it wasn't about me. There were a lot of them... had she been reading all this?

I scrolled down. I felt a rush as I clicked on a *Today News* piece by James Harrow. That guy from the press launch! What had he said about us? A photo of Olivia in her *Dragonhunter* costume, blood-spattered face from a fight scene. I clicked on it, like thousands of others already had.

Drama in theatreland

Olivia Goldsmith performs in Poison at the Arcola. Can she make the transfer from TV to stage?

Rumours of tension at the London theatre indicate that Dragonhunter *star Olivia Goldsmith is struggling with the demands of this challenging play. Opening night will show if the star, once rumoured to date Josh Michales, will dazzle or die.*

What the hell? What tension? A photo of the Arcola theatre. What if Olivia thought it was me that had talked to him? How did the press know rehearsals had been difficult? Had they? Not really, no more than rehearsals usually were, I supposed. But we had switched the scripts. Who knew about that? Scrolling down. More stories, mostly repeating the same stuff, fodder for clickbait sites, cut and pasted, spreading everywhere.

So much coverage of Olivia over the past year or so. I paused on one image. Olivia looking radiant in a pale, pink dress covered in sequins. What caught my eye though was a wave of dark hair in the background. I enlarged the photo. Standing very close, within touching distance of Olivia... was that Rebecca? Her face was mostly hidden, but the profile looked just like hers. I scrolled down to find out where and when it had been taken. Another image from the same party showed Christmas lights, so a couple of months ago? Olivia had never mentioned that. But then, she hadn't said much about how well she knew Rebecca.

'Hey, how's it going out here?' I turned to see Sarah, standing by the door.

'Oh, hi. Do you want me back in?'

'We've got five minutes. Probably longer. Olivia isn't back yet. Heaven knows where she's gone.' Sarah leaned against the wall next to me.

It was the first time Sarah and I had been on our own for a while. I slid my phone into my bag. She noticed, and turned to me. 'You don't have to go in yet. We'll just be hanging around if we go in. Jonas will be in there.' Sarah raised her eyebrows.

I chose my words carefully. 'You haven't worked with him before?'

'No. Can you tell? We've been in meetings together. But not worked together like this. Last play I worked on, Rebecca came along a few times, but usually they leave me to it.'

She pulled a pack of cigarettes out of her bag. 'I'm not going to offer you one, sorry. Mess with your voice.' Fine by me.

I watched her exhale, her face relax. 'Jonas only started working for Rebecca about eighteen months ago and now he seems involved in everything.'

'He was good at the press night.' I wasn't sure what else to say.

'Oh, sure. That really helped. Only seems to have brought more negative press on us.' She exhaled. 'I must be stressed. I'm getting through these...' She attempted a weak smile. 'Can't do it at home.' Sarah took another pull. 'I'd get a lecture on killing myself.'

'Your kids?'

She nodded. 'Teenagers.' She blew smoke away from me, and looked directly at me. 'Jemima, for what it's worth, I think you're being amazing. It's not easy, this play, and you are doing a really great job. I can't say that too much in front of Olivia.'

'Oh, thanks. Well, acting is what I've always wanted to do...' It was the first time I felt she'd said anything positive to me.

'I meant with the Ed situation and everything, Olivia... it's a lot.'

'Thanks. It is a strange situation—'

'I probably shouldn't have taken this play on, but here we are.'

'Why did you take it?' I asked. Sarah smiled at me.

'You don't say no to Rebecca.'

'Have you done lots with Rebecca before?' I was being nosy, but she still had plenty of cigarette to smoke.

'A few things over the years. In some ways she has been good for me...' I felt Sarah wanted to say more, to say that in other ways she hadn't been good for her, but she stopped there, and threw her half-finished cigarette on the pavement. 'Let's go in, Ms Evans. No rest for the wicked.'

As we walked down the corridor back to the rehearsal room, I added, 'I don't feel I know her yet. She left so quickly after the press conference.'

'Oh, that's very Rebecca. Went out with Olivia, but not us. We need to know our place, Jemima.'

I didn't know what to say to that. Not just me who felt like the outsider, then.

One hour to go before curtain up. Olivia wasn't in the rehearsal room when I arrived, so I could see that we wouldn't be starting the vocal warm-up as scheduled.

'Hi. No Olivia yet. You seen her?' Sarah asked.

'No. Must be in her dressing room.'

'She knows the call time.' Sarah looked at her phone, as if expecting a message.

'I'll go and look.' I might as well do something, rather than sit here. The door to my dressing room was open as I walked past; I'd definitely closed it earlier. I stepped in and saw Abiola inside.

'Oh, hi! You've got flowers.' She stood aside to reveal an enormous bunch of purple hydrangeas and alliums, bright red roses and lime-green foliage. The flowers were reflected in the mirror, making the bunch look twice as large. So gaudy. Flashy. I loved them.

'Wow. Thanks, Abi.' She squeezed past me and left. A thick white card was clipped to one of the hydrangea stems.

You're going to be amazing!! Love you. Wish I was there.
S xxxx

Aw. I wished Sancha was here, too. The flowers were great, but she should have been here. There was a little pile of cards, mostly from the crew. One from RADA! Ha. Maybe I'd make it onto their alumni website at last.

I sat down and studied my face in the part of the mirror that wasn't blocked with flowers – this was all starting to feel so real. I had visualised this moment for so long – the well-wishers, cards around the mirror, flowers, good luck messages. It felt *so* good.

I heard a door slam in the corridor, and footsteps go past my room quickly. Must be Olivia. A few moments later, Jonas knocked on my door and walked in, filling the space.

'Flowers? Don't they know it's bad luck to send flowers before a performance?'

'Oh right.' I felt my positive energy slide away. What was I meant to say to that? 'Is Olivia ready?' I asked.

Jonas shook his head. 'I'm sending make up in to you now.

You might as well get ready. We will do the warm-up when Olivia is ready.'

'She OK?'

Jonas beamed at me. 'She's fine! Focus on you.'

Dusty, the make up artist, arrived soon after, with a large black folding box that would have looked at home on a building site, all smiles and enthusiasm. With my hair tied back, Dusty applied thick foundation then contoured my cheeks and jawline; my face changed to become more defined, stronger, like I'd put on a mask. The harsh, bright lights that the lighting director had planned meant we needed strong make up. I watched in the mirror as he brushed dark powder into my eyebrows, making them defined, fuller, then carefully added false eyelashes so my eyes looked more prominent. Finally, using a thin, pointed brush, Dusty painted my mouth with blood-red lipstick. It would look almost natural when I was drowned in bright lights, but I liked what I saw in the mirror – an exaggerated, better version of myself, someone you couldn't ignore, someone you wanted to look at, stare at. Fierce. Brave. I loved it.

About half an hour to go before we were due on stage. *Breathe, Jem*. No point staying in my room, letting nerves build. I walked along the corridor, my robe over my costume, just in case anything spilled on it. I knocked on Olivia's door – maybe she was in there, knew what was happening, getting her make up done? Or maybe she'd gone upstairs, and I needed to get up there, too.

I heard a faint mumble come from inside. I pushed the door open. 'Olivia?'

I saw her, slumped in front of the mirror, the top of her head reflected back at me.

'Oh my god, Olivia. You OK?'

She flinched at the sound of my voice. 'Don't feel right...'

'What's wrong? You look out of it.' I tried to lift Olivia's shoulders, help her sit up, but she felt heavy, leaden. In the mirror, her eyes struggled to focus. 'I'll get Sarah.'

'No. Not Sarah. Just need water.'

A bottle of Evian was just along the shelf, why couldn't she reach it? A crunch as I stepped on something on the floor. It looked like the contents of her bag had spilled out, sunglasses, lip balm, tampons. I held the bottle of water out to her, and she leaned forward and took a small sip. Cigarette packets on the ledge, a sandwich, unopened. A pile of unopened cards.

'What's going on, Olivia?'

'Meant to make me calm. Get some rest. Jonas had them...'

Jonas had given her something?

'Have some more water.'

Olivia tried to sit up, unsteadily. 'No. Feel sick.'

I could feel anger rising, panic. I couldn't believe this was happening, right now, before the play opened. 'What the hell, Olivia? We're on in a minute!'

'Don't. Don't shout.' She steadied herself, and looked at herself in the mirror. The difference between us was striking – me with my full stage make up, and Olivia, pale, almost green, washed out.

'You can't be like this! We go on soon... do we need to cancel? Postpone? The audience will be coming in...' I could feel blind panic rising through me, waves of confusion and anger. Why was this happening?

'Stop shouting! You're hurting me...' Oliva pushed away from me, tried to put her head down on the ledge.

'You need to sort yourself out. Oh my god.' I looked at Olivia with horror.

I had to get out.

The hallway felt dark and narrow, closing in on me, air clammy, so close. Soon the audience would be taking their seats, including all those critics, my agent, Rebecca, and who knows who else, and if they wanted to cancel the play, they needed to do it now.

Why was this happening to me? My hand on the wall, keeping me steady as I made my way upstairs, legs wanting to buckle beneath me. I stumbled to the rehearsal room, where Sarah sat alone, scrolling through her phone.

'Sarah! Something's wrong with Olivia. She can't do the play. She's completely out of it.'

'What?' With a panicked look on her face, Sarah stood up.

'She's in her room...' I managed to say, as she hurried out. Should I call Elle? Ask her what I was meant to do? Or should I just wait here, and wait to be told? I thought of Sancha's flowers in my dressing room, and my hopes for this, my big break. My first professional part. I could hear voices, and realised that the audience were being let into the auditorium, somewhere overhead. People would be in the bar, excited, talking about us. What was I thinking? I couldn't sit here. Someone might see me. Down the stairs again, faster this time, back inside my dressing room. I slammed the door. I swept my arm across the shelf, bright flowers scattering, water dripping across my dressing table, petals falling onto the grey concrete floor.

A loud knock on the door, and Sarah was inside the room. 'Jemima. Listen to me. You need to get ready. Olivia will go on. We might be a bit late starting, but she'll be OK.'

She leaned forward and placed her hand on my arm; I realised it was trembling, or was it me? Looking in the mirror I could see streaks in my make up – when had I started crying? I could see flowers on the floor, under my feet.

'Jemima. You need to focus. We took a chance on you, and now you have to show us that we were right. We'll deal with Olivia. So, sort out your face and be ready.'

'She can't do it.'

'Jonas is with her...' Sarah paused, then added, 'Don't talk to *anyone* about this. Abi will call you when we're ready. We'll say it's a technical issue.'

I could hear footsteps outside in the corridor, coming and going from Olivia's room. Voices, loud. I stayed where I was, out of the way. I wiped my face to smooth out the foundation and to erase the pale rivers that had formed under my eyes.

My call from Abiola came nearly half an hour after we were due to go on. The audience would be impatient, irritated to be kept waiting. 'How is she?' I asked as I followed Abi along the corridor, our feet sounding loud, discordant, on the concrete floor.

'She's ready,' she replied, not looking at me.

I exhale, slowly, counting to ten, as we had been trained to do before any performance. I had waited *so long* for this. I had to focus, get it right.

The audience don't know I'm there. They won't see me until the lights kick in, sending them into blackout and me into blazing white light. I can see Olivia waiting at the side of the stage, pulling at the sleeves of her raincoat while looking down at the floor. She looks all wrong, tense, frightened. How *dare* she mess this up for me.

I shake my arms to release the tension, the anger in my shoulders and neck. I smooth down my tight red dress, though it doesn't need it.

No-one is going to take this away from me. I am on the stage and the audience are here, waiting for the play to start. I'd spent years training for this moment, had overcome every obstacle in my way. People like Olivia have no idea what it takes for someone like me to make it here, to be on this stage. I have worked *so* hard to get here. This *has* to work.

SIXTEEN

The reviews were online by the morning, first in *The Evening Standard*, with their piece posted just after midnight. The rest followed quickly: *Time Out*, *The Stage*... Everyone wanted to get the first shot at maximum clickbait.

I was dead to the world on Seagrass when my phone started pinging. It had taken hours to fall asleep, my mind reliving scenes from the play. The lines that had gone wrong. Olivia's face in the dressing room mirror before the play started. Her vacant eyes.

The overwhelming relief when the play ended and we'd got through it. Olivia missing out a chunk of dialogue, leaving me staring at her, willing her to say something, anything. Me, trying to get us back on track. *Horrific*.

Then polite, awkward applause, us standing there, smiles fixed on. Me leaving the theatre as soon as possible, not wanting to see Sarah, Jonas or Olivia. To get home, back here to Seagrass, with my stuff around me, safe, far away from anyone else.

Early morning light was streaming through the porthole onto my face, making it even harder to ignore the messages arriving on my phone. Elle's assistant, sending me links to the reviews as they appeared. And another one. No chance of sleep now. I sat up in bed and clicked on the first link.

The Evening Standard review already had sixty-four comments under it. How had so many people read it already? A photo of her, that's why. Olivia's name and *Dragonhunter* were tagged so that's how they'd all found it.

FIRST NIGHT / THEATRE
Review: *Poison*, The Arcola, E8
Star casting leaves a bitter taste
2 stars

The minimalist, contemporary setting of the Arcola suits the premise of Lot Vekemans' play Poison, *about two women lost in their own world of passion, loss and love.*

But when you find yourself looking at the set, you know something isn't right. This demanding, two-person play is a challenge for even the most experienced actors, and sadly, Olivia Goldsmith, star of Dragonhunter *and* And Then There Were None, *and well-known London socialite, was not up to the role. Jemima Evans shows moments of brilliance, and is one to watch but cannot carry the play alone. Sheridan Productions have a rare flop on their hands.*
Anna Rosalia, The Evening Standard, 12.05am.

Oh my god.

The next link was to *The Review*. My hands trembled as I waited for it to load.

***Poison* – play lacks sting**
Reviewed by Harry Hitchin
Our rating: **

Director Sarah Monroe gives us a contemporary take on Lot Vekemans' sparse play, casting two women as the couple examining their lost love. The concept could work well in more experienced hands, but the play felt unpolished and lacked the vital spark that could make us care about the characters.
The only saving grace in this production is rising star Jemima Evans. Evans brought passion and warmth to her role, outshining Olivia Goldsmith who seemed exposed on the stark stage.

They thought I was the 'saving grace'? And *The Review* had thought I showed 'moments of brilliance'? They liked me! I clicked on the next one. It was written by Matt Shelton, who had been at the press launch.

The Stage
***Poison* review at The Arcola, Dalston – 'A tale of two performances'**
by Matt Shelton

Poison, *in the right hands, is a powerful play about love, loss, and how communication is everything in a relationship. The decision to make the couple two women has the potential to bring a freshness to the play, to highlight contemporary discussions around fertility, gender stereotyping and lack of family support for same-sex couples.*
Dragonhunter *star Olivia Goldsmith recently switched parts in the challenging duologue, yet even with the smaller role her performance lacked the conviction to make the play speak to us. The sparse staging at the Arcola left nowhere to hide for the actress, more used to the multiple-retake culture of television. Jemima Evans carried the play; the audience only truly relaxed when she was on stage alone – one to watch.*

I felt my blood run cold and then hot. What a weird sensation, my arms trembling – was it shock? 'One to watch.' 'Passion and warmth.' 'Rising star.' 'Saving grace.' The critics had liked, no *loved*, me.

I sat up, and pulled the duvet around me. I read the three reviews again. The reviews were a disaster for Olivia, but I had escaped unharmed. No, better than that; they'd all said that I was *good*. I took a deep breath, and tried to calm my rising excitement. Olivia must be freaking out about this, but from my point of view it was OK. The photos were mostly of Olivia, but *The Review* one had me in it. I looked good. Lit well, the PR photos were good – my cheekbones looked amazing.

I texted Elle.

I'm awake. Shall I call you

She called me straight back.

'Jem. Well, I have to say, well done. Did you see *The Review* one?'

'I know. I can't believe it.'

'Enjoy the moment. But listen to me. You need to be very careful. This won't stay in the theatre pages. Sooner, rather than later, the gossip pages are going to want to do pieces on this, and how Olivia can't cut it outside of her TV roles. They will want to get hold of you, to get some sort of quote out of you. Do not talk to *anyone* about this. And stay off social media.'

I lay there for a while after the call. Was Olivia on the phone to her agent? How was she taking the reviews? If I knew her at all, she would be taking them very badly. Very badly indeed.

I felt a wave of exhaustion come over me; how much sleep had I actually got? We'd have to do it all again tonight. I could tell from the audience's faces that the play hadn't gone well. Some were smiling at me, but most in the front row were talking, whispering, judging. Olivia had lost her way for a whole scene in the second act, but I'd managed to get the script back on track. If anything, she'd tried too hard to get the audience on side, and her acting was exaggerated, too earnest. No subtlety. If she'd done it like she had in the early rehearsals, more naturally, it would have worked much better. My finger hovered over her number. Best not to... wait until later. I'd see her in the theatre.

My phone buzzed. Ben.

> You were great. What a star. So proud.
> Coffee??

Had he been at the play or read the reviews? I needed a decent coffee more than anything, but I didn't want to go over to the van. Elle had told me not to talk to anyone – my plan was to stay here as long as possible. Another message from him.

> Have you seen Metro this morning? They loved
> you!!

There were always stacks of *Metro*s inside St Pancras station; I'd had no idea they were at the play last night, too. That prompted my interest.

> No. Not seen. Just woke up.

> They loved you!! You looked amazing on stage.

Then another message.

> Not good on your co-star. Come and get coffee
> and tell me ALL ABOUT IT!!

How many *Metro*s were now being read on trains and tubes, all across London during the rush hour commute? Thousands? Tens of thousands? Maybe I should call Olivia. No – I was probably the last person she wanted to hear from right now. What if I only made it worse? The critics had liked me, after all.

> Got to rehearse today. Sorry. Can you take a pic of it and send it to me pls xx

He replied with a thumbs up.

Who else had seen the reviews? I forwarded the reviews to Sancha; she would be asleep, but I had to share them with someone. I could get my old teacher Ms Tatham's email from school, send them to her – she'd love it – maybe I should even send her a ticket? Yes, she'd like that.

Maybe I'd get something in the local paper, and those girls from my old school would see it, see that I was working with Olivia Goldsmith.

The Stage was passed round the students religiously the day it came out at RADA so I was certain my teachers would see the reviews at some point. And my classmates... I could imagine them reading it now: 'moments of brilliance...'

I turned to lie on my back, staring up at the ceiling. A surge of adrenaline bubbled up, and filled my body with a warmth I hadn't felt in a long time. I'd done it. I'd actually done it – me, Gemma Evans, had got in a play and got reviewed in the papers. Yes, the play wasn't great, but the critics thought I was talented. Whatever happened next, no one could take this moment away from me.

SEVENTEEN

BEFORE

'It sounds crazy. I bet you fit right in!'

Mark was smiling at me, coffee mug in hand, listening carefully to all my stories from my drama school audition.

At the audition, we had all been told to act like our favourite zoo animal (me: flamingo), and then played a game where we threw an imaginary ball at each other, and caught it or ducked, and you could already see who shone out, who was ultra-confident, by the way they stood, shoulders relaxed, legs wide apart. 'Bring it on!' one tall man shouted at the start of the zoo game, and everyone laughed and I saw one of the tutors write something down. Everyone liked him, he brought something to the room. He'd started the monologues, too – fearless. Easy, masculine confidence. I needed to be more like that.

Then it was my turn. I almost ran away, right there and then, I felt so sick.

'I would have run except I knew you'd be so disappointed in me, Mark. I could hear you in my head: "You don't walk out of an audition at RADA. Stay the hell where you are and just get on with it. You are as good as anyone, anyone there".'

'Too right!' Mark laughed.

If Mark could have seen the people in this room, he might have felt like I did though. They all had poise, confidence, such an air about them. Most seemed to be from London, and the two girls opposite me knew each other from some drama course they had just done in the summer. They were smiling and chatting and when one finished her monologue, her friend actually got up and hugged her, in front of everyone.

When it was my turn, I put my script on the floor beside my chair. My hand was shaking. I knew I needed to stand up, but my legs felt weak, pathetic.

The scene was from *People, Places & Things*, a play which Ms Tatham, my drama teacher from school, had given me. She'd helped me learn the main role, Emma, in lunch-breaks and after class. I knew the lines, knew how to say them. I understood the character of Emma – I doubt anyone else in the room that day had as much idea what someone like her is really like. How it feels when you're running out of options and the life you want is out of reach. Trying to keep hold of yourself when alcohol takes away your looks, intelligence, everything that made you special. I'd seen it happen in my own home. It didn't need much imagination from me to bring this character to life.

I stood up and walked slowly to the centre of the circle. Where was I meant to face? Looking at the tutors? Or should I try and engage with the other candidates, as they were the audience too?

'Thank you. In your own time.' The teacher spoke, and looked at me, waiting for me to start. She hadn't prompted anyone else. Maybe I wasn't what they expected when they invited me for the audition.

The script flowed out of me and suddenly I wasn't there in the room anymore. I was back in our kitchen at home, listening to Mum. She was so angry. I'd just got in from school and I'd put my rucksack on the floor near the door and it was in the way, it made her kick it. Mark had annoyed her earlier, apparently, and she was getting louder, shouting now, angry with us both for something that I didn't really understand, not just the rucksack. Her voice was slurring, sour. Her eyes tired, red.

She pushed past me then, screaming, my arm banged against the doorframe, hard. She was screaming that we didn't understand what it was like for her, and she was right. I did know how it felt to feel sad, lonely, frightened, though. I guessed it wasn't the same, me being twelve and scared of my mum.

My monologue ended and I realised the room was quiet and still, like after a storm had passed. The girl in front of me, with black hair, was nodding, and looked moved, sad. Complete calm in the room, and then one of the teachers, the one who didn't say much, spoke.

'Thank you, Gemma. Good.'

I walked back to my chair, noticing that the eyes followed me, seeing me differently now. OK, so I wasn't posh, rich and confident like the others in the room, but I knew I could act. But was it really acting, when all I was doing was remembering and copying what I'd seen all my life?

Mark was watching me intently, as I told him all about it, and that we'd hear in a few weeks when they'd made their decisions. They had over a thousand applicants and would take sixteen.

'I've got a good feeling about this, Gem. They'd be lucky to have you.'

EIGHTEEN

NOW

I killed time on the train to the Arcola scrolling through online stories. #OliviaGoldsmith was trending. Considering how many people were actually in the theatre last night, a lot more people seemed to have strong opinions on the play and Olivia.

#OliviaGoldsmith So overrated. Hated her in Dragonhunter.

This is the problem with celebrity castings. Just hire actors who can ACT!!! #OliviaGoldsmith

Blow-up doll would be more talented. More useful too. #OliviaGoldsmith

Some comments were positive, but mostly they were cruel, dissecting her other work, commenting on her looks. Did Olivia have someone checking her feed, a PA or someone at her agency, or was she somewhere on her own, reading this shit? By the time I got to Dalston, I was feeling sorry for her. I heard the crowd outside the theatre before I saw them. A group of twenty or thirty people were crowding the pavement, spilling onto the road. One man turned to look at me, then look away. I heard one woman shout, 'It's not her.'

If they were here for Olivia, then I had nothing to hide. *Chin up, walk confidently.* The crowd parted slightly and I walked straight into the main entrance, completely ignored. I wasn't interesting to them. An unknown. Screw them.

Lights were on in the rehearsal room, but no-one was in yet. I was on time, a little late if anything. I expected everyone to be in by now – Olivia, Sarah, probably Jonas, too. Especially after the dire reviews, surely Sarah had notes for us, wanted to run through the second act again, get Olivia back up to speed? I rang Sarah. Her voicemail told me to leave a message. Perhaps they couldn't get in with the hacks outside, had gone round the back, or were just held up? If Olivia wasn't planning to come in or was trying to get past the crowds outside, would we even have a run-through? Had they all decided to can it, and had forgotten to tell me? I was spiralling.

They might all just be in their rooms, getting ready, waiting for me. I walked down to the dressing room area, and tried Olivia's door. No reply. Why hadn't one of them called me? Angry now, I rang Olivia. Where the hell were they all? Having a meeting somewhere, that I wasn't invited to?

'Hi! It's Olivia! Please leave me a message. Byeee.'

Odd. I rang Olivia again. I could hear ringing.

The sound of Olivia's voice again, asking me to leave a message, coming from her dressing room. She must be in there. I pushed the door.

'Olivia? You OK? You in there?'

The dressing room was empty, but I could see a phone light up on the dressing table as it waited for me to leave a message. The screensaver, a photograph of Olivia with a young girl, blonde, about four? Huge smile. So cute. A very young version of Olivia.

I realised with a jolt that it was her child, surely it was – she had never mentioned a child, but they looked so alike, it must be hers. The sound of running water from the bathroom.

'Olivia?' No reply.

I waited a few moments, but she didn't come out of the bathroom. Should I leave? Was this overstepping somehow, me being in here? I knocked on the bathroom door, then gently pushed, but it was blocked by something on the other side.

'Olivia – are you OK in there?' I pushed the door a little more. A moan from inside. I tried to push more, to get inside, and saw Olivia sitting on the floor, strands of damp hair covered her cheek, her skin waxy, grey. She tried to look at me, but her eyes wouldn't focus.

'S'ok. I'm OK.'

Next to the Aesop hand soap and Kate Spade make up bag were two brown plastic pill bottles.

'Shit, Olivia! What have you taken?' *Has Jonas given her something again? She never eats... How much has she taken?*

Olivia shook her head slowly. 'I'm fine.' Her voice sounded thick, swollen.

'If you need to, we can scrap tonight.' This was insane. She couldn't carry on like this, in this state. What was in the bottles? *This was a nightmare.*

'And give the trolls something else to write about?' She shook her head. Olivia paused, and looked at me again. 'Or do you want me not to go on? You another person who thinks I can't do this?'

I leaned against the wall. 'No, that's not it.' I tried to sound calm.

'Press loved you,' Olivia slurred, trying to stand up.

I needed to answer Olivia very carefully. 'It's early days in the run. If we need to take a break, we can say there are technical issues or something. Rehearse more. We'll get better. Rebecca will sort it out.'

Olivia pushed past me, and sat at her dressing table. I watched her, in the mirror, her enormous, beautiful eyes, bloodshot.

'No, she won't. You have no idea.' What did she mean by that?

'They come to see me. It's *me* people are paying to see. Not you. Press were always going to have it in for me.'

Quietly I replied. 'They come to see me, too.'

Olivia looked at me in the mirror. 'Don't kid yourself.' She studied her face for a moment. 'You need to leave.'

I desperately tried to think of something to say, to make things right between us, but she clearly didn't want me there.

'I need to get ready.' Olivia looked at the door.

'Can I help you in any way?' I needed this play to work so badly. *Please don't mess this up for me, Olivia.*

'All this. This shit... the Ed things online... I didn't know him! I mean, he was here a few times, but I hardly spoke to him. But you! You *did* know him!'

I felt the floor tilt, and my legs go cold. I could see my face in the mirror, calm, but I knew I wasn't calm.

'Ed? Why do you think that? My audition... he was at my audition, yes.'

'And before! Abi told me. You were both at RADA.'

I shook my head. 'Not really. Different year, different course.'

'I'm the one getting all this shit, because I'm famous. Should have been you,' she slurred.

I staggered back, found the door frame, held on, my heart racing. She turned away from me, reached for her glass.

'Get out.'

Dismissed, I left, closing the door behind me.

NINETEEN

The energy of the audience was palpable. Buzzing, excited, smug that they had got tickets for the play everyone was talking about. The audience felt as if they were owed something memorable, something that they could go home and tell people about the next day, something they could tweet about, especially if they agreed with the bad reviews, if Olivia really was like they all said. We hadn't rehearsed; I had no idea if Olivia could do the play, what state she was in. It all felt unreal, as if it was slipping away from me. My big break had arrived, but now was going wrong, all wrong, and through no fault of my own.

A play like this was nothing to Olivia, really – she had a TV career, fame, success. She would bounce back from this, however dire the reviews. But me... if it went wrong tonight and the play was pulled, what would I do next? Would I work again?

Sarah appeared at my side. 'Good. You're all ready.' Red lipstick in place, smile fixed. She looked in control.

'She can't do it, Sarah.'

'Let's hope she can. We'll find out in precisely ten minutes.'

'I'm not sure I can do it...'

'Don't you dare. You need to hold it together. Olivia will follow you. Listen – Rebecca is in.' She glanced out at the audience; the auditorium was packed. 'It needs to be good. We don't want her to cancel us. Just do your best. Abi can prompt Olivia if needed. Break a leg, Jemima.'

Somehow, we got through it. The applause was muted at first, then rose again, as if the audience had made a collective decision to be charitable to the two actors on stage who had somehow got through the play, but I knew the difference between an audience who loved a play, and an audience who were being polite.

So many awkward moments like that at RADA – people applauding me, though they didn't like me, and I knew exactly how that felt. We stood there, holding hands, Olivia's hand, cold in mine, smiles fixed on our faces. A man on the front row turned to the woman next to him, half stood up, ready to go, and she pushed him down, with a familiar, firm touch of his leg. And then Olivia was gone from my side, leaving me there on my own, exposed. We usually waited for the stage to go dark before exiting, together, stage right. Everyone watching would have known what it meant – she couldn't wait to get out of there.

I could hear the rumble overhead of the audience making their way out of the theatre. The voices were too low to make out individual comments, but I knew what they were saying to each other. *It was awful... no talent... well, that was embarrassing... did you see...*

Olivia had missed lines, leaving awkward pauses that anyone could tell were not meant to be there. Abi had prompted her at one point in scene two, and was rewarded with a scowl that surely everyone in the audience saw.

Jonas had told us to go up to the bar after the play: 'We need to show confidence. Come up when you're ready.' I imagined him up there now, talking to the most important people in the room, those he knew in the industry, diluting their comments, helping them reframe their thoughts. Sarah would be doing her best, too; she had a career to salvage, couldn't distance herself from the play just yet. Rebecca, too, talking to the key people: investors, trustees, maybe other producers, directors, people who mattered.

I wiped off the sweaty make up and steeled myself to go up, put on a smile. Pulled on my jumpsuit. A large part of me wanted to flee, go home to Seagrass, curl up and rest, but this was my chance to talk to Rebecca. Find out what she thought of me, and my performance; the reviews of me had been good, hadn't they?

But I couldn't forget the memory of Olivia in her dressing room, the way she looked at me. She *hated* me. Hated that I had got good reviews, and that she hadn't.

That was it, wasn't it? She was jealous of *me*. Everyone up there wanted to see her – not me. If I went up there, really they would be looking over my shoulder, waiting for Olivia to enter, to take the floor.

I knew Olivia would be in her room, getting ready, just a few steps along the corridor. Would she go to the party? Should I go to her – talk to her? Would it do any good?

I hovered in my doorway, trying to decide what to do, staring at the concrete floor, dusty, my red shoes, old and cheap.

This should all be perfect for me. I should be up at the party, hearing praise from everyone, having a drink, enjoying my success. But they were there for Olivia, not me. For Rebecca, Jonas... not someone like me. I didn't belong here. I never had.

'Olivia!' Her unmistakable voice. It was Rebecca, shouting.

I stepped back inside my room, pulled the door towards me, just leaving a tiny chink of light.

'Olivia?' Footsteps in the corridor.

I tried to steady my breathing. Do I go out, talk to her, say I'm on my way? Footsteps outside, not sure which direction. Towards Olivia's dressing room, or someone leaving? Then quiet outside.

You can do this, Jem. Go upstairs, take your moment. If Olivia isn't there, the focus is on you, right? That's even better! Just own this. A drink will help. Just go up there and act like everything is normal, going well.

I couldn't, just couldn't.

Moments later I was outside in the night air, a few people hanging around, the soft rain no deterrent. I guess they were hoping that Olivia would come out and sign their programme or agree to a selfie. Idiots. Olivia wouldn't be out there tonight.

'Jemima!' Loud, behind me.

Damn. Who was that? A journalist? I quickened my pace, heading in the direction of the station, wishing I'd done up my coat first, as the rain started to soak into the front of my T-shirt. Louder this time, shouting my name, the sound of footsteps behind me.

'Jemima! Wait. It's me.' Turning, I saw him.

'I saw the play. You were brilliant.' Greg, eyes alive, huge smile, looking really pleased to see me. He stepped forward, as if about to hug me.

'You saw it?' I tried to gather my thoughts, get a grip.

'Yes. Sorry, I should have got in touch. A friend had a spare ticket. It's quite the sensation, isn't it?'

'Not for the right reasons.'

'I saw the reviews. They all loved you.'

I could see people watching us, perhaps recognising me now, wondering if I was worth talking to, even though I wasn't Olivia Goldsmith.

'You got time for a drink?' Greg asked.

'Sorry... I'm not feeling great.'

He reached out and touched my arm. 'You didn't leave your number. So, I guess you aren't interested. But I was curious to see you. Is that OK? Too much?'

That made me smile a little.

'Did you like it?' I asked.

'You were amazing! Honestly. Best thing in it.'

'There were only two of us.' I smiled more widely now.

'You were the best. Come on, what do you need? I can give you a ride? Hungry?'

I shook my head. 'I'm fine to get the train, thank you. It's quicker anyway.'

'You said you live in St Pancras.' Had I told him that? I didn't remember. 'That's going to take at least an hour. Let's eat. I bet you didn't eat before the play. No actors I know ever eat before going on.' He was right, I hadn't eaten.

'I am hungry, yes...' I realised I felt almost seasick – hunger, tiredness, anxiety, had all combined, and I realised I felt exhausted, and yes, starving.

'Anywhere decent round here?' He looked around us, at the men sitting outside the Dalston hookah cafes, sheltering from the drizzle under canopies, and the rotating kebab meat in the window of the Garden Grill opposite. He looked completely out of his depth, and I found myself smiling at the posh boy far away from his London comfort zone. Greg rubbed his hand over his hair, raindrops flicking off it.

'We can go somewhere else, it's OK,' I said.

'Thank heavens. You choose.'

My mind went blank. Was I meant to choose something smart, somewhere in Islington, or somewhere like that? I doubted very much that we went to the same sort of places.

Greg jumped to the rescue. 'Or we can go to mine. It won't take long this time of night. I can order that pasta again.'

'Your place? Again?'

'Ah, sorry! I know that sounds like a pickup line. It really is so close though. It's only about twenty minutes. And you know the food is good.' He looked at me, sheepishly.

I hardly knew Greg, but he was here. Here for me. He'd come to see the play, had stood out in the rain for me. And he'd loved the play, and me in it. I didn't feel like going back to Seagrass just now, to be alone with my thoughts. I glanced back at the theatre. My agent might be in there, with Rebecca, Jonas, Sarah. I couldn't face any of it. Olivia.

I nodded.

Greg spoke quickly into his phone. He wrapped his arm around me and in what felt like just moments, a black car crossed the line of traffic silently and stopped alongside us.

'That was quick,' I said as I slid into the back seat. Greg passed me a bottle of water from the compartment next to his seat. 'Or do you want something stronger? We have vodka, I think.' The car pulled into traffic and glided away silently, leaving the Arcola far behind. 'Sorry, confession time. It's my usual car. This is John.' The man driving, older, face serious, nodded at me in the rearview mirror.

'You have a driver?'

'Not always. But it's useful in London.'

Did he think he was Big from *Sex and the City*? I turned to him. 'Did you have this planned?'

Greg laughed. 'No! I'm not that smooth. I didn't really expect to see you. I thought about getting in touch, I could have left a message at the theatre, but I was sure you were swamped with rehearsals... boundaries and all that... really, I should have got in touch earlier.'

Greg pulled out a beer from the compartment between the seats, was about to take a swig, then held it out to me. I took it, took a long gulp, and another. As we drove effortlessly through late-night London life, I felt the alcohol take effect. This was just what I needed. I could tell Sarah and Jonas the next day that a friend had come to see me, I couldn't make it to the drinks. A director friend. It was a perfect excuse. Maybe I could have taken Greg to the bar with me, played it all differently, he might have known people. Been useful. *No.* The thought of facing them all after that was too much.

'OK, this is more relaxing than the train.'

'You're welcome. Any time.' He smiled at me. 'Now. You didn't tell me you were *that* good. I loved watching you... couldn't take my eyes off you. And I promise, I don't say that to all the actresses.'

'I'm not sure I believe that.'

'Believe it. I've sat through some dire stuff in my time, but that... well, you were great. The audience saw that, too. You could feel the room relax when you were on. Olivia struggled though. I can see why the reviewers went for her.'

'I can't believe it... she was so much better in rehearsals.' I exhaled loudly. I had been holding so much tension in my body.

'She did seem out of her depth.'

'I really wanted this play to work, Greg. You know? I wanted it to be so good.' I drank more of my beer. 'I did everything I could... I tried to help her.'

Greg leaned across and looked at me seriously. 'You'll survive this, Jemima. You were amazing. Don't forget that.'

I could see the lights of Tate Modern looming in the distance, and knew we would be at his soon. Did I want to be with Greg, to sleep with him again? I knew I didn't want to be on my own, alone with my thoughts. There was something about him that felt safe, familiar, even. Like a big brother, looking out for me, but better than that, a rich, successful one, who had life sorted. Greg would probably be horrified if he could hear my thoughts. I leaned across and kissed him lightly on the side of his face.

TWENTY

I woke to see Greg standing beside the bed, wrapped in a towel, water droplets on his shoulders. I had slept deeply for the first time in weeks; my bed in Seagrass had nothing on Greg's expensive mattress and pillows, and here, high above the rest of London, I felt a million miles away from the play, the stress, Olivia, the bad reviews. There was a soft greyness to the morning light coming in through the vast windows, casting a tasteful shadow across the room. Greg had his phone in his hand, turning to me, his brow creased. He looked worried.

'Morning.'

He sat on the bed next to me. I leaned forward to give him a kiss, but his attention was on the phone in front of him. He turned to me, his face serious.

'I'm really sorry, Jemima. There has been some bad, awful news. I'm so sorry. It's about Olivia.'

I suddenly felt cold, ice cold, felt the blood drain from my face, my arms.

'They found her last night. At the theatre. It's all over the news. On the BBC. Her agent has put out a statement.'

'Olivia?' I heard myself say.

Greg nodded, and looked at me, concerned. 'She was found dead in her dressing room. Overdose, they seem to be saying. I'm so sorry, Jemima. You must have been close.' He looked at his phone again. 'So young. What a waste.'

I tried to breathe. Breathe out. I felt the room go into slow motion around me. Greg's mouth was moving, but what was he saying?

'Jemima? Do you want me to call anyone for you? Any family or anything?'

I shook my head. 'No, that can't be right. She was OK. I saw her yesterday. Last night.'

Greg pulled me into a hug and held me; he smelled of warmth, citrus. Water from his neck touched my face, but I stayed there, trying to relax, trying to think. An image of Olivia looking at me, so angry. Trying to get her up from the floor in her bathroom. Later, eyes blurry, trying to get through her lines. Losing her place on stage as she forgot where she was meant to be, looking at me to help her. The worried look on Abiola's face, standing in the wings, ready to prompt. The audience clapping, but faces knowing. Olivia trying to face them, to take a bow. Her beautiful golden hair. Eating her noodles, picking out the tofu with expert precision. The photo of the young girl on her phone.

'What are they saying about her?' I pulled away from Greg's arms.

'Let me get you some breakfast, some coffee.'

I grabbed his phone. The news was using the beautiful photo of Olivia at the BAFTAs.

I scrolled down. More photos. The same news, almost the same lines, copy and pasted. The bad reviews of the play, coming up in the feed. I didn't click on those, kept scrolling. Drug-taking. Someone saying she took drugs. Horrid picture of her looking out of it, coming out of a nightclub. Caught out, looking rough, looking like anyone would at the end of a night out. Any normal person wouldn't get their picture taken though.

Greg took his phone from me, gently. 'You don't need to read that.' He looked at me kindly. 'Did you know she had a daughter?'

I shook my head. I'd seen the photo, but Olivia had never mentioned her. I didn't know how to react, how to act in this situation.

What was Rebecca doing right now? Were they all at the theatre, talking it through? No, they wouldn't be there, and she'd stay clear, surely. I thought of Rebecca's voice in the corridor last night. *Did she see Olivia? Talk to her?*

'Look. Stay here as long as you like. I'll get you a coffee. Or I can get John to drive you home. Whatever you need right now, just say.'

'You're kind, thanks. I'm so sorry to bring this to you. I'd better get home.'

I stood up, wanted my clothes right away, to cover up, escape. This apartment, this calm, quiet space where no-one knew where I was, felt like a really good place to be right now, but Greg would want me out of there. We barely knew each other. I reached down to pick up my clothes, which looked crumpled and tired on the glossy floor. I didn't fit in here.

'You're shaking. Listen. Don't rush. Let me get you something to eat before you go.'

Greg walked over to the kitchen, and I watched him while I pulled on my clothes. I needed a shower, but more than that, I needed to leave; he didn't need to be involved in this. I was an imposition.

'Jemima. I think your phone is ringing. Do you want it? Shall I just leave it?' I'd left my bag on the kitchen counter when we'd got in last night. I nodded, and he handed it to me. Two missed calls from Elle, and a text message from her:

You OK? You must have heard. Call me. Play cancelled.

About an hour later Greg and I were speeding our way out of London, John expertly navigating the Hammersmith flyover. Greg had decided everything. With *Poison* cancelled, and the press looking for stories about anything to do with Olivia, he had suggested we take a few days away at his place down in Cornwall. 'It's the weekend. Do me good to get away... it's fine... honestly.'

We'd stopped near St Pancras station for me to collect clothes. Greg probably assumed I lived in one of the smart flats and I let him think that, walking behind a building and down onto the canal path. I knew I could never bring Greg onto Seagrass – the tiny table, cheap laminate flooring peeling at the edges, my few belongings... it was a world away from his perfect, wealthy existence. I stuffed clothes into a bag, locked the door and walked away without a backward glance.

The traffic heading out of town was light compared to the other direction, where frustrated drivers stared motionless as we sped past.

'You'll feel better if you eat something. It's a long way to Porthcurno.' Greg passed me a white cardboard box. 'John got breakfast while we were waiting. Want one?' The smell of fresh pastry filled the car as I opened the box. I chose an almond cake, studded with fresh blueberries. I ate, staring out of the window, tasting nothing.

'I should call Elle back.'

'Yes.'

I reached for my phone – it was almost out of charge. 'I forgot my charger...'

'You can plug it in here. But, you know. Maybe it's a good

idea to take a break, a proper break, for a few days, until the media storm has died down. It won't do you any good to read endless stories about Olivia.'

I nodded, pressed call. Elle's number rang for a few seconds, then went to the agency answer message. 'Can't get through.'

'Probably swamped. Or screening calls. The press might be trying to talk to them about you.'

'Oh god, why?'

'I might be wrong. Sorry, didn't mean to add stress. Maybe they just want some sort of statement from you about Olivia. Elle will be dealing with all of that.' I nodded. I couldn't believe this was happening. It was midday – I should be heading to the theatre. But it was over. Cancelled.

'I should speak to her. Do you think I should go back?' A horrific thought jumped into my head. 'Greg. What if the police want to talk to me?'

'No. I doubt it. It was an overdose, wasn't it? Oh, I don't know.' A moment of doubt crossed his usually so assured face. 'If they need to, they'll get hold of you.'

I'd seen the pill bottles, and if I had, so had others who had worked in the theatre. Surely everyone at the Arcola knew Olivia was taking something. Jonas and Sarah definitely knew she was taking drugs. Abiola, too. Anyone could have helped her, it wasn't all on me.

'She was under so much pressure.' I said, looking at the cars being left behind as John drove fast.

'Yes, she was. But that's not your responsibility.' Greg reached over, placed his arm around me. I felt my shoulders ease. 'What a mess. I'm so sorry. That play was good – you were good. You've lost out here, too.'

I didn't know what to reply. It was blunt, but he was right. She had screwed it up for me. Hot tears formed in my eyes; I let them fall, glad of the release. Would this mean that I was now untouchable, unemployable? If a casting director saw me on

Spotlight, if Elle put me forward for any more jobs, all they would think about was Olivia, and her death. I felt awful for thinking it, but Greg was right. It was a mess. I needed to get away from it all, to think.

'Rebecca has a nightmare on her hands. I don't envy her,' he added, shaking his head.

I texted Elle that I was going away for a few days, that I hoped she was OK. A break was ideal – I needed to get away, get my head straight, focus about what was next for *me*. Would there be a future for me when I got back to London, after this?

Greg took my hand and we sat there, in silence with our own thoughts, as John drove past Windsor castle, industrial warehouses, identikit housing estates, and onwards, away from London, from *Poison* and from Olivia's death.

TWENTY-ONE

My forehead bounced against the car window. Outside, thick hedges and holiday cottages painted in seaside colours whizzed past. The single-lane road was narrow and winding but John drove quickly; a turn to the left and I bumped my head again.

'How long was I asleep?' I sat up, hoping I didn't have drool on my face. Greg was reading what looked like a script, heavy with black hand-written notes in the margins; he'd rolled up the sleeves of his dark blue shirt, and I could see the muscles in his forearm flex as he worked.

Greg smiled at me. 'You slept most of the way from Bristol; we're almost there. You must have been exhausted. We've just gone past Sennen Cove.'

'Is that a script?' I took a longer look at the pages as I reached forward for a bottle of water.

Greg turned the papers over and placed them on the seat beside him. 'Yes – I'm looking at it for a friend. Could be good.'

'Anything in it for me?' I tried a smile.

'Sadly, not my call. It's good, though. I think you'd like it. They want to do it in the US. How are you feeling?' He put the script in the rucksack by his feet.

I sipped water, and realised I badly needed to pee. Didn't look like places to stop here, no petrol stations. The houses were more spaced apart now, punctuated by empty, muddy fields that disappeared over the horizon. A picture-postcard church, ancient trees lining the path to the door. In places the hedges were so high, I couldn't see over the top of them, and I wondered how John felt confident to drive at such speed. What if something came the other way?

A terrace of four houses, ex-council, rendered in a grey pebbledash. A single metal swing, chipped yellow paint on the frame, just like the one we had in a garden, just the same. And then a huge barn conversion, timbers painted black, probably worth more than all four of the terraced houses together.

My phone buzzed beside me, a few text messages had popped up while I had slept – one from Ben, two from Elle, and one from Sancha. I clicked on Sancha's first:

WTF? Are you OK? Call me. So sorry to hear about Olivia. Love you. X

I know. Call you soon. I'm away a few days xx

The message took a while to send, while my phone searched for a signal. Suddenly, we turned down a narrow gravel track, which gave way to a new, smooth road, lined with perfectly spaced trees and a thin black metal fence. And then, lit by bright sunshine, a strip of gunmetal blue sea appeared on the horizon.

'Wow.' I hadn't seen the sea for quite some time; it glistened and sparkled in a way that the Thames never did.

Greg squeezed my hand. 'I love the first glimpse of the sea. Tells me I'm home.'

And just when it seemed as if we were driving towards the edge of the earth, the car stopped in a perfect circle of tarmac.

'Come on.' Greg jumped out of the car. John appeared at

my door, and opened it for me. I could see Greg disappearing out of view, heading down hidden steps. I thanked John, who nodded briefly.

'I'll get the bags – you go in, miss.'

There was nothing to see except fields in all directions with the road stretching back and out of view. I walked towards where Greg had disappeared, and down wide steps cut into the cliff edge, lined with spiky grey-green plants. Greg was typing numbers into a security panel. The house stretched out low and long, with blemish-free white walls, the flat roof planted with succulents and cacti.

I followed him into a huge open-plan living space, flooded with dazzling, natural light. A pale oak floor, glittering as the sun skimmed across it, making the floor look like sparkling wet sand.

'This is amazing.' Truly stunning, Greg's house was like something from a film. In some ways it reminded me of his flat in London, with similar sofas and a large fireplace, but homelier, art on the walls, bookshelves. As Greg walked towards the window, a section slid open smoothly, and the sound of the waves and squalling seabirds crashed in.

'I love it here.' Greg turned to look at me. I brushed his arm as I walked past and out onto the limestone terrace that stretched before me. A few leaves skittered across the stone and got caught on little piles of sand gathered at the edges. I continued onto the lawn, an impossible shade of emerald green; I felt it spring beneath my feet, each step forward effortless. And the sea, a vast expanse in front and all around me, as the cliff edge fell away to the waves below. A few more steps and it would be so easy to fall over the edge; there was nothing between me and the drop down, nothing to break the amazing, uninterrupted view – we really were right at the end of the world, as far from London as I could imagine.

'I never get bored of this view.' Greg appeared behind me, and I felt his hand reach around my waist.

'This is incredible. I can see why you love it.' Looking along the coastline, we were the only building for miles. The edges of the cliff curved and dipped, as the sea had shaped them over the centuries. 'I can't see any other houses.'

'No, it's just us here. No one has built on these cliffs for years. Too worried about erosion. We own the land around here, the most stable part. The Minack open-air theatre is just round there, but it's hidden, set down in the side of the cliff. You can see it more clearly from the jetty.'

'Is it that close? I'd love to go. I've only seen it in photographs.'

'Sure. We can walk there tomorrow if you like, or we can take the boat. I'll ask John to get it ready for us.'

'You have a boat? Are you any good at sailing?' The waves far below sounded fierce, and looked terrifying, as they crashed against the cliff face.

'Since I was a boy. Everyone learns how to sail around here. We can walk over the coastal path if you prefer. It's a beautiful walk.'

I realised that I didn't have anything suitable for walking – boots or even a warm coat, I'd left in such a rush. I hugged my arms around my body, but the wind cut through. A jumpsuit was fine for the theatre, but not down here. I felt stupid for not bringing warmer clothes with me.

Greg noticed. 'Come inside, you must be freezing out here.'

We walked back into the house, where John was unpacking groceries from two large wicker hampers. A sourdough loaf, containers of yoghurt and fruit, a box of Champagne. So posh.

'Greg, can I take a shower?' Surrounded by expensive perfection I suddenly felt grimy, crumpled from the journey, and in desperate need for the bathroom, to change my clothes and put on some make up.

Greg smiled. 'Sure. I'll show you. I'll prep some coffee while you're in there.' As he showed me down the long, narrow corridor, he said quietly: 'John will be off soon, then it will be just us.'

The shower was unbelievable – the largest I'd ever seen. It took me a while to work out how to turn it on. As the scalding hot water cascaded over my head and ran down my face and breasts, I started to feel more human. I let the water pummel my hair flat against my scalp, and knead away the knots in my shoulders. The water felt good, burning against my skin, washing away the long journey, the theatre, and the image of Olivia, lying in her dressing room, face pale, empty. I felt hot tears start to ease down my face, and I let the water wash them away.

A cool gust of air hit me as the shower door slid open, sending goose bumps across my skin, then Greg, beside me. He held me tight against his chest so the water ran over his hair, his face, and between our bodies where it could find space. His hands were firm against my hips, and he pulled me tighter, kissing me. Then we were against the wall of the shower, the edges of each tiny tile pressing into my back. Greg buried his face in my neck, as he entered me, taking my mind away from anything, letting it go blank. Afterwards, I watched him wash, removing all traces of me from his hands, chest and groin.

'I've been wanting to do that since I saw you on stage.' He ran his hand slowly down my right breast, following the curve down to my waist and hip. 'You're amazing, do you know that?'

I put one hand on his chest; I could feel his heart beating, still fast. I stepped out of the shower and wrapped myself in a thick, white robe, hanging on the wall nearby. There were two robes, side by side, and I realised, with a jolt, that the house was always ready for Greg, and for whoever he brought there with him.

. . .

I woke early the next day, and took a coffee out on to the terrace, and sipped it, overlooking the sea. In that moment, it was as if this house was all mine – I'd made it big, so famous that I could buy any house that I wanted.

But it wasn't mine. The play was cancelled. I wasn't going to make it big, get huge parts that would buy me this lifestyle. That was all a fantasy.

I drank the coffee – god, it was good, strong, rich. Maybe I needed to marry someone rich, like Sancha had, to get a lifestyle like this? Sancha and Jon had a pool in the Hamptons; she'd sent photos of her jumping in when they'd first bought the house, but I was pretty sure they didn't have a sea-view like this. She would be asleep at the moment, but I sent her a pic of the view, ready for when she woke up.

I'm ok. Staying with a friend.

It was mid-morning when Greg emerged from the bedroom. 'Good morning. Sleep OK? I always sleep so well here.' He helped himself to coffee. 'Looks like a calm day out there. You OK to go by boat?'

'Sure, if you know what you are doing. I might need to borrow a coat though, if that's OK.' We were more polite with each other in the daylight.

'Definitely! Look in the bedroom at the end of the house. Help yourself to anything you need.'

The room looked like something from the White Company catalogue, perfect white bed linen, white walls. A wardrobe that lit up when you opened the door, with neatly folded sweaters and a hanging rail packed with clothes, jackets and a couple of coats. They looked brand-new. I pulled out a cable-knit grey sweater from the top of the pile; small, far too small for Greg. Where had all these clothes come from? An ex? A dark blue padded coat with a fur-lined hood, far warmer than anything I owned. Canada Goose. I pulled that out, too. Should I ask him who these belonged to? I wasn't sure I wanted to know. Being here for a few days suited me. No need to over-complicate anything.

TWENTY-TWO

BEFORE

'Who's next? Jemima.'

'Yes, Jemima Evans.' It was strange to hear my new name said out loud. Did the drama school teacher, Messios, remember that I had a different name when I first auditioned, back in January? Maybe he did, and maybe he didn't care. When I'd got in I emailed and said I wanted to use Jemima, as a stage name, if that was OK, and no-one ever mentioned it again. The truth was I wanted to leave Gemma behind. Be someone new, better.

'Hi, everyone. I'm Jemima. From Bristol.' I smiled around the room. I wonder if they thought I'd come from the Bristol Old Vic or Redmaids – somewhere posh, exclusive. I had practised how I said Bristol, to lose the soft roll that I knew would stand out in a room of people from private school. More confident, clipped – I didn't want to be the odd one out.

Our lunch-break was in the tiny cafe space that doubled as the box office in the evenings. There were more of us than chairs, so I leaned awkwardly against a narrow ledge piled with flyers for future plays. We were watched over by framed black-and-white headshots of alumni, and I recognised three. Just last year's graduates and already famous – no pressure, then.

Some of the students took the largest table next to the grand piano and Leo, I thought he was called Leo, started to play something without sheet music, something jazzy, until he looked bored, but stayed on the piano stool, holding court. There was a space near me, a section of ledge to put lunch on, and a stool, but I watched as people glanced over and then chose other places to sit. It was day one and they'd made a decision about me already. Had I failed some sort of test – didn't I look the part?

'Do you know Gisella? I love her!' I heard screeching happiness as the mutual connections were established. 'Oh, you were at National Youth Theatre, too? When? I was the year before – it was so good...' 'Just got here from San Francisco... I'm completely exhausted, night flight...' 'Oh, I'm the black sheep of the family. My brother is the really talented one – he's at Cambridge.' I made myself look busy, eating my cold pasta salad.

'There's a pub on the corner near the British Museum. Old school, really sweet.'

'Or we can walk to Charlotte Street and find a decent bar there? Is anyone a member at the Groucho or Union?' Confident, talking over each other. Deciding where to go to celebrate the end of the first day. People gathered bags and coats; it was cold outside, already getting dark. It had been a long, mentally draining day. One of the loud, posh girls – Neema – radiated confidence and people gathered near to her, waiting for a decision to be made, knowing that it would be made with her at the heart of it. I waited, taking my time, pretend to check my phone although there wouldn't be any messages.

The students started to move towards the door, leaving me behind.

'Coming?' I heard one say. Sancha, the smiley, curvy one, paused and looked at me. I could make an excuse, say I needed to get home, to a job, or anything, but if I did that, she might not ask again.

'Sure. Yes. Thanks.' She waited for me, didn't mind that the others were already outside, and then we were walking along the road together.

'You are so good! I loved your interpretation of the text.'

I glanced at her, as we walked along. Was she being genuine?

'That's nice of you to say...'

'I'm Sancha.'

'Gemma... Jemima...' Oh hell, had she noticed my mistake?

'Jemima. Good name.'

Had she heard me say Gemma? I tried to read her face.

Sancha quickened her pace. 'Come on, let's catch up with the others, I need a drink.' She turned and grinned at me. 'I don't care what you're called. We're here to become new people, aren't we?' She grabbed my hand, and we ran to join the group.

TWENTY-THREE

NOW

Porthcurno beach came into view as we sailed around the headland, a sheltered bay of Cornish-cream sand, edged with granite cliffs. I felt a bit seasick and was glad when we stopped. Greg released the sail so it flapped gently in the breeze and then used the motor to bring us closer to the cliff, where he tied the boat to a rail. He jumped off, and I followed, walking carefully along the slimy, seaweed-covered ledge, hoping my Converses would hold their grip.

'The steps start here.' Greg bounded up narrow steps edged with gorse, oblivious to the sharp drop straight down into the sea below us. I was out of breath by the time we reached the top. He rummaged for a key in his rucksack, and then we were in.

'Welcome to, without doubt, the most beautiful theatre in the country.' We stood at the top of the Minack, looking down over the rows of seating carved into the cliff-face. The stage jutted out over the sea, like a concrete infinity pool. It was all completely open to the elements. Tropical plants edged the paths leading down to the stage, and more came into view as I followed Greg down. On my left, an actual theatre box cut into a rock face, and ahead, a Juliet balcony, ready for her famous speech. Such a magical place – it was love at first sight.

'Sometimes you can see dolphins, especially in the summer. It's as if they are drawn to the stage lights.' Greg looked so happy.

'How do people concentrate on the play?' I asked.

'Sometimes they don't. I've watched the dolphins out there many times. The actors know when a pod has swum into view as they lose the audience; they're all staring out to sea. It's part of the magic. Better than some of the plays we get here. Come on, I'll show you round.'

Greg pulled me up onto the stage and I followed him to a stone arch that perfectly framed the view over the sea. He walked to the back of the stage, where only a low stone wall stopped him from falling down onto the rocks below, and then through a doorway. Alone for a moment, I walked to the centre of the stage. I turned to look back up at the auditorium, steeper than any London theatre; the acoustics for the audience must be amazing on a perfect, still night.

These, our actors, as I foretold you,
were all spirits and are melted into air,
into thin air.
We are such stuff as dreams are made on.

I heard my words project up and away towards the back of the theatre, melting away just like the characters at the end of *The Tempest*. It had been a while since we'd done it at drama school, but the words had stayed with me. I could imagine an evening sea mist rolling in, surrounding Prospero and Miranda on stage, giving them cover to disappear from the audience as the play ends. Or maybe they would spend the evening being rained on, stage make up staying on, whatever the elements threw at it, the loyal Cornish audience watching, wrapped in raincoats and blankets. What an amazing place to perform...

I could hear waves crashing behind me, a lone seagull being buffeted by the breeze. There was nothing to protect the actors from the sea wind; the audience were more protected from the weather than you were. It would make you feel alive, acting here, at the end of the world, surrounded by nature. And Greg owned it, owned this theatre?

I followed him through the door, which, to my surprise, opened into a modern, bright dressing room, with two television screens, a long clothes rail and a glossy white shelf running the length of the room below a mirror and a strip of lights. We could have been in any contemporary theatre. I was expecting something rough, basic. One screen showed the stage where I had stood just moments before.

'It's fairly new, this bit. The actors used to get changed in a wood hut – it was very drafty.'

'Did you use to act?'

Greg laughed. 'Only as a kid. My grandma put me in all sorts. I was in *Macbeth. A Midsummer's Night's Dream.* As few lines as possible. I wasn't much good.'

'What an amazing place to perform. You were lucky.'

Greg shrugged. 'I knew you'd love it. It's incredible what my family managed to create. It would never be allowed now.' He glanced down at his watch. 'We've got about twenty minutes before Jonas gets here.' He stepped forward as if to kiss me.

I stepped back, shocked. 'Jonas? He's coming here?'

Greg looked at me, a faint line appearing on his forehead. 'I told him we were coming down to Cornwall.'

My heart was racing. 'Wait, you know Jonas? And I thought we were getting away from all of them. That it was just us.'

'Everyone knows Jonas, and he won't be here for long. Just overnight. A flying visit. Good timing, really. He's never been able to come when I asked him before.'

My head swam. The room suddenly felt very small, constricting.

'You've all had such a rough time. He's devastated by her loss, too. It's good to have a change of scene.'

Jonas, devastated? More annoyed than devastated, maybe, with all the press intrusion, loss of earnings, yes, I could see that. Maybe Greg knew another side to him.

'You've worked with him?' I asked.

'On and off. I was at Oxford with Rebecca. Met Jonas through her. He's an interesting character. I've wanted to get Sheridan Productions down here for years. They could do something amazing with this place.'

'What's wrong with it as it is?'

'It just eats money. And there is so much potential here. We could increase the capacity, bring in more professional productions, Sheridan Productions even. Mostly its am-dram stuff. My family were so resistant to change.'

'I'm not sure I'd trust someone like Jonas with your family's theatre. He seems pretty ruthless to me.' I thought again of how he was with Olivia. Of the pill bottles.

'If I only did business with nice people, Jem, I'd be screwed.' He looked at me carefully. 'He's fine. Come on, take a look around and imagine what you could do here, if you could do anything. Share those ideas with Jonas.'

It made no sense. Surely Jonas should be dealing with the cancellations, all the press? Had he just left Sarah to it? Was this why Greg had brought me here, to Cornwall? Because Greg thought I was an 'in' with Jonas and Sheridan Productions? If that was the case, he was going to be very disappointed when he realised that I meant nothing to Jonas, or Rebecca. I was just another actress, one of many.

. . .

It was like Olivia had never existed. I watched Greg and Jonas sitting on the front row of seats, drinking mugs of coffee, chatting and laughing. Jonas had hugged me as if we were best friends, had asked me with a tilt of the head how I was doing, said he'd texted me, which I was pretty sure he hadn't, and then he'd raved to Greg about Cornwall, the state of the roads, but wow! how amazing the sea views were, the clean air, the beauty of it all. No one mentioned Olivia. I sat on the edge of the stage facing them. Greg was saying he could talk to the National Theatre and see if they would come down here, if the funding was there; Jonas was saying there were small, off-West End Sheridan productions that he could bring here.

'Actors would love it, wouldn't they, Jem? You should do your Prospero for Jonas. Show him how amazing the acoustics are.' *So Greg had heard that.*

I couldn't keep it in anymore: 'We're all just sitting here, acting as if nothing has happened. Jonas – you haven't mentioned Olivia at all!' I sounded shrill.

Jonas nodded at me, looking serious, or trying to, his face concerned. 'We're all devastated by Olivia's death, Jemima. Of course I care. She had an astonishing, bright, dazzling future ahead of her. I, for one, am still processing it all.'

He got up slowly, placed his coffee cup next to Greg, stepped towards me, placed his large, manicured hands on my thighs. 'I'm thinking of you in all this, too, you know.' He glanced at Greg. 'This must be a terrible shock for you.'

I didn't buy his concern for me. 'Shouldn't you be at the Arcola? There must be so much to sort out.' I thought of Sarah and Abiola, dealing with it all, the press, the police even? Jonas could just leave. But then, I guess I had left, too.

'I'm just at the end of my phone.' Jonas looked at his hands briefly and lifted them from my legs. I could feel where he had been. He returned to his spot next to Greg, who took a sip from his coffee, clearly avoiding eye contact with me.

'To new opportunities,' Jonas added, raising his coffee mug.

'I can't believe you can just move on like that.' I could feel my heart racing. Were we all just disposable?

Jonas looked at me, not smiling. 'And what about you, Jemima? If you get a call from your agent with the next big job, will you rush back to London for the casting?'

I felt embarrassed heat rise in my neck and face, then the cool breeze across my cheeks. *Calm down, Jemima.*

I set off quickly, up the steps towards the exit, too quickly, and I was out of breath when I reached the cafe building at the top. What *would* I do if Elle called? I sat on a stone bench outside the closed visitor centre, and looked out over the theatre towards the sea and sky. Somewhere, far across the sea was Sancha. What time was it over there? I called, and after a few rings, it went to voicemail. I felt very alone.

Far below I could see Jonas and Greg walking across the stage. What did I do now? I could get on a train and go back to London. Or go and join them, act normal. See this as an opportunity. My phone buzzed in my hand. Sancha.

'Jem! Where are you? Are you OK? I've been calling you constantly.'

'Sorry, it's been so weird. Is it really early over there?'

'I'm sitting here half-naked. You don't want to know what time it is – hang on, stay right where you are, I'm just going to get my robe. I thought it must be you – I didn't want to miss you again.' I heard her open a door and a male voice, sleepy, annoyed. And then the door shut.

'Well, makes a change from him waking me up, nearly every sodding day. So, tell me. What happened, and are you OK?'

I felt my shoulders relax. 'No, not really. It was awful, Sancha. It was all so stressful. Did you see the reviews? Some were awful. And Olivia. She was a mess, and I saw her before she died and I knew she was taking something, some tablets, and I should have done something.' I had tried to do something, I'd tried to talk to Olivia, hadn't I?

'Listen. You were there to act, not be her babysitter. The papers are saying she was on opioids, had been for ages. And she had a kid – Chloe.'

'I saw a photo of her. She was really little.'

'Yep, cute kid, pics are all over the internet. With her dad now apparently, though he wasn't with Olivia anymore. He's some hotshot director, but apparently he's taking a paternity test. Can you imagine? She left such a mess behind her.'

I stared out over the sea, my face damp, cold, from the sea mist. The temperature was falling.

'I'm worried about you. Where have you been? Your text said something about going away?'

'I'm in Cornwall, staying with a friend—'

'Who do you know down there?' she interrupted.

'That director guy. Greg Trelawney. He has a place down here. I'm sure I told you.' So much had happened in such a short time.

'Greg Trelawney? How the hell did you meet him? He's a huge deal at the National.'

'We met at the bar there. That night I rang you.'

'I can't keep up!'

'Sancha, I don't know what I think of him. Not yet. I just really needed to get away.'

'Now, listen to me. I don't know what's going on there, but listen. Right now, everyone in the theatre world knows about this whole situation. Probably everyone else, too, at least anyone who follows Olivia. Right now, you need to focus on *you*. If you want to, this is your chance to get known, *really* known. I know you are freaked out, but this isn't the time to be hiding away in Cornwall.'

'You're kidding, right? If that's in any way true, they know me for the wrong reasons – not positive ones.'

'Your reviews were good. And you know what, she isn't the first person to take drugs in the theatre world, and you know it. You have done nothing wrong. Nothing.'

My mind went back to that night. How Olivia had looked at me, talked to me. So much anger in her beautiful face. The footsteps outside in the corridor. Rebecca calling for Olivia. And no reply. A fine film of rain had settled on my face and I knew my hair would be frizzing as I sat there. 'She died, Sancha. I was there.'

'Yes, I know that. It's awful, terrible. But it happened and it makes no sense you hiding away because of it.' I hadn't told her about Ed, about how he'd been with me at the casting, and at the party, and how he worked for Rebecca, too.

They all knew each other. Would Sancha feel the same if she knew about him as well? The weight of it all made my chest feel tight, breathless.

'So, Jem. Director Greg. What's he like? You still there? Can you hear me?'

Pull yourself together. I took in a deep lungful of cold air. 'Yes, I'm here, at the Minack theatre, would you believe, getting rained on. Greg's here, talking to one of Rebecca Sheridan's people.'

'What? Who? Look, stop talking to me and go and find out what they are talking about. I'm glad you're OK, I know it must have been awful. But you've worked hard to make it, harder than any of us. I know that.'

I could hear Jon now walking around in the background, and the hiss of the coffee machine. I could imagine them both in their designer kitchen, with doors out to their pool and the beautiful, sunny garden filled with citrus trees. I wondered what she had thought of the photo I'd sent of Greg's house. This wasn't the time to ask.

'You're tough, Jem, I know you are. I wish it hadn't happened, but it's the way it is. Hiding away isn't going to help you now. Listen, I'm going now, he's up. Call me later if you want to. Love you.'

Sancha might have stepped out of the acting business, but she knew what she talking about. She had seen her chance with Jon and had taken it. I wondered how she would have been if she hadn't gone to live in the USA, had stayed in London and carried on with castings. She'd have made it, I'm sure. So sexy, so charismatic. It was a waste, her playing housewife.

If she'd been at the Minack today, she would have been down there talking to Greg and Jonas, talking about plays she'd loved that might work in the open air, actors she could recommend, sharing ideas. Natural confidence had always helped Sancha fit in with any crowd, shine in any situation. I didn't have that, but I could act like I did. I tied my frizzing curls up into a knot and walked slowly down the steep steps of the Minack theatre, back to Greg and Jonas.

TWENTY-FOUR

Jonas poured a large glass of red wine, something from his favourite Napa Valley vineyard, he explained, as he passed it to me. Greg wanted to open some Cornish wine from a local vineyard, but Jonas said he didn't do white wine, and found it amusing that 'Brits even made wine'. Greg seemed to take it well, in full charming host mode. Jonas continued holding court, telling me about the sea-views at his own place in the Hamptons, and how he missed spending the long summers there, before life got super busy for him in New York. I tried to concentrate, but as long as I nodded now and then, smiled, they seemed happy enough with me.

When we returned from the Minack, a chef was busy decanting lemons and fennel from stainless steel boxes, and clearly knew his way around the place. The table was set with driftwood in the centre, candles lit, sparkling on the glassware. For four people.

'Is someone else coming?' I asked Greg as we got changed. I had brought a black linen dress with me, no idea if I would need something to go out in. As soon as I pulled it out, crumpled, I knew it was all wrong. I saw Greg glance at the dress.

'I didn't realise you'd be having a dinner party. Should have packed better... it was all so much of a rush.'

'It's just supper. Seriously. It's fine. If you want, help yourself to something from the spare room.' Greg pulled me into a hug, kissed my lips. I'd have to apply more lipstick. 'Most of the clothes in there probably haven't even been worn. My ex used to get very bored down here, and preferred shopping to sailing. I should have cleared them out, but I'm so rarely here.' Greg turned to look at himself in the mirror, and finished buttoning his thick white shirt. It just about covered his stomach; he must have bought it when thinner.

Greg's words felt more like a request rather than a suggestion. I padded down the corridor in bare feet, feeling the underfloor heating. Whoever Greg's ex had been, she had great taste. Everything in the wardrobe was incredible quality, and beautifully made, and he was right – I could see tags still on two of the dresses. Whoever had bought these clearly wasn't here in the winter; it was all very floaty and feminine, not my style at all. I pulled out a cream dress, lacy; it was almost bridal, but in a Boho way. It fit me perfectly; whoever had owned this dress must have been pretty much the same size as me. A row of shoes, one pair with tiny gemstones on the straps. A bit tight, but better than anything I had with me. I changed, and went back to Greg.

'Wow. How to make an entrance.' Greg stared just a moment too long. 'So, to answer your question, Ms Evans.' Greg started rolling up his sleeves, to show off his forearms. It seemed a bit try-hard, as if he was trying to look younger. 'Rebecca's coming. Rebecca is our extra guest.' He glanced up at me, and grinned, as if he had given me the most amazing surprise present.

'Rebecca? Sheridan? Here, in Cornwall?'

'I know! I thought you'd be pleased. This could be amazing

for me, and for you.' He almost sounded breathless with excitement.

What the hell was going on?

'Rebecca can really do something with the Minack. People will come from all over the world to see her plays here.' He smiled at me.

'I'm amazed she has time to come down here.'

Greg shrugged. '*Poison* being cancelled must have given her some spare time in her schedule. Or maybe she just needed to get away from the press attention, too. We can ask her when she gets here.'

It all felt too fast, too dizzying. Was this how it worked? If you're rich, if you've got a massive, expensive house, own a fricking *theatre*, then people want to hang out with you, talk to you about work opportunities. It was all about who you knew, wasn't it?

The real decisions were made in places like this, between old friends, people who'd met at Oxford, old connections.

I thought of the writers who'd sent in scripts to RADA who couldn't get any funding for their projects. The nepo babies who got work because Dad was famous. Stories about actors whose parents were showbiz royalty. The kids who'd appeared in their parents' films and then went on to big careers. We'd all read about people like that. Like Olivia. For so many of us it never happened, but for the Gregs of this world, it did – the contacts, the money, the opportunities came right to you. Just because of the family you were born into. The rest of us had to make our own luck.

'You look beautiful, Jemima. Perfect. I think it suits you here.' He sounded like he meant it.

Looking in the window, I thought I looked tired, my skin too pale against the cream fabric. The sea air had tangled my hair, but it sort of worked. They say that actors are people that you want to stare at, that you can't take your eyes off. Was I beautiful? Not sure anyone had said that to me before. There were plenty of actresses out there who looked better than me, I knew that. But they weren't here, were they, having dinner that evening with Rebecca Sheridan.

I'd barely spoken to Rebecca, but it felt like there was something between us. The way she'd looked at me at the press launch. But then she'd not spoken to me, really, since. Was that all in my head? She had given me that job, had chosen me – Sarah had said that. And now she was coming here, to this house, hours away from London. My chance to find out.

If Sancha was here, instead of me, she would definitely make the most of it, charming Jonas effortlessly, talking about living in The Hamptons, and who they knew in common. She would find a way to bond with Rebecca in that effortless way she always had at college, and they'd be laughing together like old friends within minutes. I could do it. I just needed to act like Sancha, like the confident girls at drama school. *Join in, laugh at jokes, ask questions. Think of it as a role, Jem.*

We were most of the way through another bottle of Jonas's red wine, out on the terrace, heated by firepits, when the wind picked up suddenly, sending leaves and sparks skittering around us. A steady popping and whooshing sound cut through the air, and Greg turned excitedly. 'She's here. I'll go.' He jogged into the house as the sound of the helicopter got louder, and then cut out.

Jonas stood up, brushed imaginary dust from his trousers. As he strolled into the kitchen, I could hear the helicopter start up again. I stood up, and waited awkwardly, like a member of staff waiting for instructions. And then Rebecca walked onto the terrace, her white shirt billowing behind her, catching in the breeze, with Jonas and Greg following close behind.

Rebecca stopped next to me, and looked out to the inky

black sea and sky. She inhaled and exhaled deeply, closing her eyes for a moment, as if breathing in the sea air would cleanse her of something. She opened her eyes and turned to look directly at me, just like she had at the press launch. 'What an incredible place. We really are miles away from everything.'

'Yes. Just the sea and stars.' I stepped towards her slightly, hoping my voice sounded louder and more confident than I felt.

'I could stand here for hours,' she said. It almost sounded like she meant with me.

Greg handed Rebecca a glass of wine. 'Thank you, Greg. Really, though, I could do with coffee. The flight was horrific.'

'Leave it with me. You two just chill here.' Chill wasn't a very Greg word – he sounded nervous, awkward. Jonas hovered to one side, like a bouncer, just in case needed for something, though what, wasn't clear.

Rebecca indicated for me to sit down near her, and she pulled a blanket off the arm of a chair and placed it over her legs. 'Jemima. I had no idea you were dating Greg. He's never mentioned you.'

'We met quite recently.'

She looked at me closely. 'What a small world. So, how are you?'

'I don't know. In shock, I think. I needed to get away...' I hadn't asked for permission before I left London. It was all such a rush. 'Should I have told you?'

'Probably.' She stretched out her legs and looked out to the sea beyond. For a few moments, the only sound was the waves crashing below us on the rocks. Rebecca sighed, and seemed to gather herself. 'I want to thank you for all that you did on *Poison*.' She glanced at Jonas. 'You were wonderful, and you must be devastated about Olivia.'

I nodded. 'I was so pleased you cast me in it.' I had to make this all seem normal. That I always hung out with top producers and directors. *Act calm*.

She turned to face me, adjusted her blanket. 'I knew you were perfect for the role.'

Should I ask her about that first casting, if she was there? I was dying to know. But then, this was hardly the time or place to make this about me.

Greg reappeared and handed her a steaming mug. I watched her wrap her long, elegant fingers around it.

'I think I remembered how you take it.'

'Ah, thank you, Greg. Perfect.'

'I wish it had all turned out differently...' I said. I thought of Olivia, the whole mess of it.

Rebecca didn't reply, just sipped her coffee, steam rising in the freezing night air.

Jonas and Greg made a big show of pulling chairs closer to us, Greg excited to see her again, "after how many years, is it, Bex?" The conversation between the three of them flowed effortlessly, talking about a new show that was going well in New York, Jonas raving about the Minack ('the dolphins!'), with bursts of laughter and over-enthusiasm, and vigorous nodding to go with everything Rebecca said. The events that had brought us all here, put aside, or not relevant. I couldn't quite tell. The wine started to blur my edges.

The chef brought out canapés, though Greg was the only one who ate them. I wasn't sure what most of them were – something orange, and something grey – and I drank more, trying to think of something intelligent to say. When would we be sitting down to dinner? The conversation turned to their plans for the Minack.

'We would have to do something about the road access. You were right to fly in, Rebecca. It's a nightmare getting here. You can give me a ride back,' Jonas said. 'And Alex in there was telling me that there is nowhere decent for anyone to stay nearby. How does it usually all work, Greg?'

'The audience come from all over Cornwall. Tourists. Some

locals. Most people just drive in for the evening. It is gridlock sometimes as they all sod off home.' Jonas was right – getting huge production trucks down those tiny roads would be a nightmare.

Jonas leaned towards Greg, legs spread wide. 'You're missing a trick, my friend. You've got so much countryside here, and doing nothing with it. You could build something really nice, a resort, somewhere for people to stay and make a weekend of it. Yurts! You need a roof too, like Wimbledon.'

Greg laughed, shook his head.

Jonas continued. 'You'd sell more tickets if people knew they weren't going to get rained on. You Brits are hilarious; if it rains in New York, we just cancel. You sit there and get soaking wet!'

I wondered if we would be heading inside soon, I knew it was cold, but I also felt warm, hot even, the red wine numbing my senses.

It must have been past ten by the time we went inside. Greg tried to wrap his arm around my waist as we walked in, and he stumbled slightly – he was drunk, too. If he wanted to make a good impression, he needed to slow down on the alcohol. So did I.

Greg made a big fuss of sitting Rebecca at the head of the table, with me at the far end, opposite her. Greg called across to Alex the chef for Champagne and, as he filled our glasses, Greg stood, put one hand on the table as if to steady himself and held up his glass.

'A toast! I look around this table and it blows my mind. Rebecca, my darling friend, thank you for finding time in your crazy schedule to hang out with us. To Jonas, for making it happen, and for your wild, brilliant ideas. To my beautiful Jemima. You look amazing. Now, I think Alex has waited long enough to get dinner on the table and is going to spoil us with some amazing food, so let's just enjoy ourselves, work talk on hold. Everyone agreed?' We all raised our glasses, and I watched Rebecca take a tiny, restrained sip.

A small plate was placed in front of me, with pale scallops set on what looked like moss and soil. I had never eaten scallops, though I'd seen them on MasterChef. They didn't look cooked. They made my stomach churn.

'What made you want to be an actor, Jemima?' *Oh god, she was talking to me.* Rebecca had turned her attention to me. Rebecca had very dark eyes. She held my gaze as I thought of what to say.

'It was the only thing I was good at.'

'Oh really?' She smiled. 'And RADA? What was it like there?'

I saw Greg lean in to focus on what she had asked.

'It was intense. Some amazing teachers, incredible... I, we, learned a lot from them.' I needed to sharpen up. I looked around for water on the table.

'Yes, they always create such interesting actors. And what were the other students like? I am sure you have some wonderful stories?' She smiled across at Greg. 'It's been such a long time since we were students.'

I really needed to answer this well, sound interesting. Sancha would make it a great story, with memorable anecdotes to bring the characters to life. I should have practiced some answers.

'They were a really interesting mix, from all around the world. Some from New York.' I looked at Jonas, to get his buy-in. 'Some I got on with, but... well, you can imagine... it was an intense group of people. Everyone had worked hard to get there.'

'Ah! Do you mean they were horribly competitive?' Rebecca smiled. 'Tell me, who was the worst?'

What did she want to hear from me? Neema sprang into my mind. Her sneering face, irritated by me being there, as if she deserved it more. Rebecca's smile was a little unnerving. She would know Neema, they had worked together. Best not to say anything. *Don't let the drink talk.*

'I only wanted to stay in touch with a couple of them at the end of it. We came from very different backgrounds...'

'You didn't like them.' Rebecca took another sip of wine. As her plate was taken away, I could see she had barely touched the food.

I was playing this wrong. I was making it sound like I didn't fit in. 'Oh, some of them were amazing. One guy, Lukas, he was fantastic. You might have seen him at the RSC? My friend Sancha, she's amazing. She lives in the Hamptons now.' I looked at Jonas again, but he wasn't giving me much back; he just sat there, observing me and Rebecca.

'How glamorous,' Rebecca replied.

'Most of them didn't like me, I think, really.' *God, why had I blurted that out?*

'Jealous?' Rebecca asked.

Jealous of me? I highly doubted that, but maybe I could work with it.

'Well, it's a competitive business.'

Greg lifted his glass. 'I think we can all agree on that.'

Rebecca tucked her glossy hair behind her ear; a diamond star at the helix of her ear sparkled in the candlelight. 'I liked your end-of-year production. You were good.'

I put my glass down. 'You saw it?'

'I try and see final-year plays if I can – it's my job.'

'I didn't know you had seen me...'

Rebecca smiled at me, and then turned to look at Alex placing new plates of food down. Swirls of vegetables on top of fish, red sauce of some kind. Must have taken him hours of work. I felt too drunk to eat it.

'Jemima was amazing in *Poison*, wasn't she, Rebecca?' Greg said clumsily, helping me out.

'I'm so glad you saw it,' she replied. 'Sadly, not many did...'

I had no idea what to say to that. I took another glug of wine.

'If we get bored after dinner,' she said, leaning towards Greg, 'perhaps Jemima will perform one of her monologues for us. From *Poison*. Or from *Electra*. That was it, wasn't it? Have I remembered correctly, Jemima? That was your end-of-year play.'

My head swam. I fumbled around for what to say. 'I'm not sure I can just do it here. I've drunk too much for a start...' The lines from Electra – could I remember any? She'd seen me in it... I was trying to process that.

Jonas spoke. 'Oh, go on, Jemima! I'm sure there is a scene you can do. You can be the after-dinner entertainment.'

I looked at my plate. I needed to eat, soak up some of the alcohol. To eat some of the red stuff, some sort of pepper and potato mash. Yellowish fish juices running into it, making an oily pattern on the plate. What was Rebecca thinking? Doing a scene from *Poison* felt all wrong. They'd all seen it – only just seen it. And without Olivia, it was too weird.

Saying no would make it a bigger deal than it was, though. They might think it was false modesty, as if what I really wanted was for them to ask me over and over, to give me more attention.

What would Sancha do? She'd laugh, just get on with it, say the lines. Get it over with. I would look like a good sport, confident, like I did this sort of thing all the time. If I didn't do it, was that a black mark against me? Something that said I was difficult to work with, one of 'those' actresses? My head was spinning.

'I've finished eating. Have you?' Rebecca looked around the table. Barely anyone had eaten.

'It's late. Maybe Jemima can perform another time. It's been one hell of a week,' Greg said.

Rebecca tilted her head to look at me. 'It's just some fun.

Please start, Jemima.' Her voice, slow, calm, familiar. Like at the casting in Soho. She was there, behind the dark window. Had she been watching me all along?

It was easier just to do it, get it done. Show that she didn't faze me. I let my shoulders relax, and took a deep, in-breath, then exhale. I pushed my chair back, made space, but didn't stand up.

'What do you want me to do?

Do you want me to scream?

Do you want me to yell?

Throw myself down on the ground?

Or do you want me to throw plates this time?

Is that what you want?'

As I spoke the lines I found myself back on the Arcola stage surrounded by darkness with just the occasional rustle to remind me that the audience were out there, watching. A white light shone in my face as I spoke slowly, asking the questions in the script, pausing at the end of each line as if expecting an answer. The lines came easily, they hadn't left me yet.

At this point it would have been Olivia's turn to speak. Would anyone mention her, think of her? I let the silence hang there. Surely we were all thinking of Olivia now. Of her lying there, dead, all life gone.

I looked straight at Rebecca. She held my gaze, unsmiling. Was that what she wanted?

'Very good,' said Greg, holding his wine glass high.

Jonas clapped twice. 'Great, Jemima. Now, Alex, is there any more of the red?'

Jonas led the conversation back to a production he was working on in New York, while Greg reached for another bottle of wine. I noticed he wasn't looking at me much tonight, his focus on Rebecca.

As the evening became night, we moved to the seating area in front of the fire. Rebecca claimed the sofa and stretched out her legs, leaving just enough space at the end for one person. Greg sat on the rug, Jonas took the armchair. I sat down at the end of the sofa, painfully aware of the tiny space between Rebecca and me. Our glasses were filled again, though I knew I didn't need or want any, and the chef left us to it, among effusive thanks from Greg.

Rebecca let her shoes fall to the floor, Manolo labels showing. As I shifted to get comfortable, my thigh brushed against her foot. I flinched away. She looked at me, then stretched towards me, placing her feet on my legs as if that was exactly where they belonged. I felt warmth flood through my body; I couldn't have moved, didn't want to move.

It was like I was watching a scene, nothing clear, the wine had made me lose my focus. Did Rebecca want me in some way? Somehow, I had always known that, right from the first casting. She'd chosen me, that's what Sarah had said, wasn't it? And now we were in the same room, finally. Greg, soaked in wine, was oblivious.

A surge of clarity, adrenaline, rushed through my body, bringing a sharp focus I recognised from those moments before you take to the stage. The two men talking loudly, trying to outdo each other about the people they knew, the places they'd been. Rebecca and I listened to them drone on, and waited.

TWENTY-FIVE

Greg fell onto the bed with all the grace of a hippo. It had been an effort to get him into the bedroom when everyone had finally stopped drinking, and the thought of trying to sleep next to him had zero appeal. I pulled off his shoes before leaving him to snore to his heart's content. I closed the door and left him to it.

'Jemima.'

I stood dead still, in the dark corridor. It wasn't a question, more a summons, her voice so assured, in control. I could pretend I hadn't heard, walk down the corridor, find the spare room, sleep alone. The morning would come round, the day would happen, and Rebecca would leave, on to her next meeting, her next project.

Aware that I'd been standing there for a few seconds, I made my decision.

The living room was lit only by the bright moon shining across the floor, casting shadows on the walls.

'It's so beautiful here,' I said, and turned to look at Rebecca standing near the window. The moonlight gave her the appearance of a marble statue.

'I came here for you, Jemima. You do know that?' she said, her voice, so in control.

'I remember you from my casting in Soho. You didn't say who you were.'

She smiled. 'Did it unnerve you?'

It had, but I wasn't going to tell her that. 'No, not really. I've been to lots of castings.'

Rebecca stepped towards me. 'I wanted to see you.' Did she mean at that first casting, or here, in Greg's house? She walked towards me.

'Greg thinks you're here to buy the Minack.'

'Oh, yes, maybe. The Minack is lovely. I do already have plenty of theatres to worry about.'

She stroked my arm, and my bare skin responded with goose bumps. 'I can't imagine the famous Rebecca Sheridan worrying about anything,' I managed.

She smiled at me. 'This is when my thoughts crowd in, late at night. When I'm on my own. But you're here now. A good distraction.' And then she kissed me, her mouth firm, insistent.

I could smell something like neroli on her skin, as well as wine and sweat. So different from Greg, more confident in what she was doing. Rebecca's fingers found my shoulder strap, and then her hand, cold, traced down my arm, slowly, taking the strap with it. I felt the dress slip against my skin and Rebecca's hand on my breast, stroking, unhurried. My heart rate responded, thudding, but in some way, I also felt removed, disconnected. Rebecca's arm around my waist, pulling me closer to her. Some part of me watched the two of us, from somewhere above, as we made our way onto the rug, where just an hour earlier Greg had sat and watched us.

Maybe I knew that if anyone else in the house was awake they could hear us, but it didn't stop me. I let her lead, her hands exploring my body with an ease that told me she had done this many times, and was used to women letting her.

Afterwards, we lay on the floor in silence, Rebecca on her side looking at me as if committing my face to memory. My pulse slowly returned to normal. All I could hear was a clock ticking somewhere in the kitchen. My dress was just out of reach and I felt cold and exposed, lying there in the dark room.

'This is how I thought you would look.' Rebecca ran her finger slowly between my breasts.

'When you saw me at RADA?'

'I knew we'd meet. There was something about you. Something raw, unpolished. So much talent.' Close up, I could see she was older than I first thought, her make up had faded. Her chest was marked with freckles, her hands lined.

'I'm freezing.' I reached over to pull a throw from the sofa, a pathetic part of me hoping the moonlight was flattering to my backside.

I wondered if I should talk about Olivia. Or mention Ed. Would that bring us together, bond us in some way? Find that connection? My mind was running through all the things we could talk about, but a part of me knew that wasn't how she worked. She was the one in control. She chose what we talked about. And when. Or maybe we just needed this, to wash our minds of what had happened before, of the horror show surrounding Olivia. I felt like reaching out to her, to touch her arm, but there was something glacial about her, something holding me back.

Something passed on Rebecca's face, as if she was reading my mind. She stood up suddenly, reached for her shirt, stepped back from me, blocking the moonlight. 'Good night, Jemima.' Moments later she was gone, leaving me alone.

I was desperate for water, really, but was grateful anyway when Greg handed me an espresso.

'Sorry – was it more comfortable on the sofa? I've been told I snore after a few glasses of wine.'

'They're right. Thanks.' I downed the scalding coffee. 'Don't worry, I got some sleep.' I had crept back into Greg's room after Rebecca had left and curled up on the sofa. A combination of the alcohol, and thoughts of what had happened, kept my mind from settling into sleep. I felt exhausted, queasy. Greg, by contrast, looked irritatingly perky. He was obviously more used to drinking a lot than I was. He was in running clothes.

'Don't tell me you are going running...' I couldn't imagine moving from the sofa right then, let alone running.

'Just got back. Twenty-minute blast along the coastal path with Jonas. Didn't feel I could say no. Crazy Americans. They are off soon. You must have been shattered – it's almost eleven.'

I dragged myself into the shower, feeling rough and nauseous. Hair up, lots of mascara and lip gloss and I just about felt ready to join the low hum of chat I could hear in the kitchen. Greg was blitzing oranges, which hurt my head, while Jonas sipped a green juice of some kind. He glanced over as I walked in. A faint smirk. 'Sleep well, Jemima?' Had he heard us last night?

Rebecca was standing with her back to me, looking over the sea, talking quietly into her phone. The breeze from the previous day had died down, leaving the palm trees lining the terrace as still and calm as if on a tropical beach. She didn't look round when I came in.

'What are your plans for today?' I asked Jonas, reaching for a banana that had been arranged along with peaches, brioche and berries on a vast white plate. Where had it all come from? Had Alex come in and done all this, before we'd got up?

'We're heading back to London as soon as the chopper arrives. I need to get another statement out about Olivia. I've got a ton of hacks to deal with. Then New York! Outta here.' Jonas looked clear-eyed and energised, clearly immune to the effects of a couple of bottles of red wine, or perhaps he hadn't drunk quite as much as I thought he had.

'Jonas said to come if we are in New York. He's hosting a Sheridan Productions party.' Greg said, through a mouthful of breakfast.

'Oh right. How lovely. When is it?' I asked, to keep the pretence going that why wouldn't I be the sort of person to fly to New York for a party, that I had the money to blow on a ticket.

'Thursday. No rest for the wicked!' Jonas drained his juice.

I broke off a piece of banana rather than sticking the whole thing in my mouth as if giving a blow job.

Jonas continued. 'We've got a great season in New York launching. So many projects at a critical point. The party will give everyone a boost just before we go batshit crazy over there.' He said 'pro-jects', with the emphasis on 'pro'. 'And no offence to you, Greg, but I miss New York coffee.'

'No offence taken. I love it, too.' Greg started to tell Jonas about a place he liked near the Ambassador Theatre that did great coffee and amazing eggs, and they traded details – *No, you really need to try this place I know...* No-one really expected me to say anything important.

'Ten minutes, Jonas.' Rebecca walked over. 'It's on the way.' She leaned across the counter, in front of me, grabbed a brioche, and then walked out of the room without saying a word.

'That's my signal. I'll get the bags,' said Jonas.

Nothing. She said nothing to me.

They left in a rush of Greg's enthusiasm and shouts of 'So great to see you', 'I'll call you'. Rebecca was on her phone again as she left, blowing a kiss to Greg, Jonas and the pilot carrying the overnight bags behind her to the waiting helicopter. I stood at the top of the steps, expecting her, willing her, to say something to me, but there was no time, or there didn't seem to be. I was completely ignored.

The helicopter blades whirred into action, throwing leaves

and debris at our legs. I kept my eyes on Rebecca's face as the helicopter started to lift. Would she look at me? Greg was saying something to me, but I couldn't hear him above the sound of the helicopter rising. *Look at me, Rebecca.*

And then, yes! A brief, momentary glance, her eyes fixed on mine. I felt her gaze as much as saw it, as the helicopter banked and turned away from the house.

'Well, that was exactly what you would call a flying visit! Can't believe they came! Amazing!' Greg led the way, back down into the house, his face so happy. He ushered me through the front door with his hand on my lower back. 'We should head back to London, too.' So soon? I thought the plan was to stay for a few days, escape everything. I guess he had got what he wanted from the trip.

He set the machine to make another coffee. 'I'm very tempted to go to that party. Aren't you? It would be an amazing guest list. Rebecca knows *everyone*.'

'Sure. Just fly to New York.'

He grinned at me. 'Why not? Anything keeping you here?' He passed me a coffee. 'I'll message John to pick us up. Can you get packed and be ready to leave soon?' Our stay in Cornwall was clearly over. 'We make a great team, you and I, Jemima. That went so well! You should come with me.'

ACT 3

TWENTY-SIX

Is it just me, or do Londoners seem to be healthier and better-dressed than the people in the rest of the UK? It must be all the cafes selling vegan, protein-packed lunches, the early morning marching they do from one tube station to another. Or maybe it's because so many come from European capital cities, where the Parisian and Italian women have thin legs, and dress only in tasteful navy, grey and black. I would spot someone from my old school a mile away in this crowd, creatures from another time and place.

Greg dropped me off outside St Pancras station at the end of a long and tedious drive back from Cornwall, where I'd had to listen to stories of his time at Oxford with Rebecca, and his plans for theatre-world domination now he was so in with her and Jonas. I doubted very much if they had talked about him that much on their journey home. I wonder if they talked about me. I promised to call him later, kissed his puppy-ish face, and walked away quickly.

. . .

Stepping onto Seagrass, I knew something wasn't right. The tarpaulin that usually covered the front deck was flapping – there was no way the movement of water would have done that. Looking back, maybe I should have called for help, got one of my boat neighbours to come inside with me, or rang Ben, who might be at the coffee van, but I didn't.

Inside, my duvet was on the floor, trampled on, filthy. The table where I had sat so many times with Mark was bent at an angle, broken, the drawers underneath pulled out. A crunch as I stood on something – my cutlery had been tipped on the floor. Clothes pulled out from underneath the bed... I could see Mark's sweater, along with a few pairs of knickers lying there, looking cheap. Over-ripe bananas, their sickly smell merging with damp, muddy footprints. It all looked so small, broken, like a child's bedroom, strewn with precious objects, favourite clothes, and then trodden on.

Whoever had broken in could have gone through my belongings in just minutes. I had so little in here. But if they had wanted to steal something, to find cash or something to sell, they were out of luck – there was nothing valuable here.

I stepped back outside onto the deck, and took a deep breath, my hands shaking. After Greg's incredible house in Cornwall, Seagrass felt so small, so confined and shoddy. I had always known narrowboats weren't that secure; you could kick in the swing doors if you really wanted to, but being moored right next to neighbours and within shouting distance of the lockkeeper's cabin had always made me feel safe, as if there was always someone to look out for you. Anyone walking onto the jetty must have been heard by someone, surely... Now I saw Seagrass for what it was – cheap and vulnerable.

Back inside, and in moments I had stuffed Mark's sweater and a few other precious things into my bag. I peeled the photographs from the ceiling above my bed: me and Mark, a photobooth strip of me and Sancha, and put those in my bag, too. I looked around on the bed, and on the floor. Where was the newspaper review? It was usually stuck next to the photo of Sancha. I looked around to see where it had fallen. It was the review from *The Stage*, about our end-of-year showcase. I'd read it so many times, late at night, lying in bed, that I knew the caption to the photo of me and Sancha off by heart.

Jemima Evans shone as Electra; a bright star with a bright future. Sancha Cottingham, as Clytemnestra.

I remembered Messios reading it out, so pleased, although that particular memory is spoiled by Neema's irritated face, behind him, as he spoke. She hadn't been mentioned at all in the review. Sancha was delighted, called me 'bright star' for days afterwards. The photo of us was amazing; I looked so alive in that picture, surrounded by the cast, doing what we all loved best. Where was it? I moved clothes, dumping them on the bed, looked again all around on the floor. Gone.

I should have thought about making Seagrass more secure, getting a better lock fitted, but I wasn't thinking, not really. I needed to get out of there, get away. As I walked up onto the canal path, I glanced over at Ben's coffee truck. He might still be open.

'Jem! Where have you been?' Ben jumped out of the side door of the coffee truck, leaving two customers waiting to place their orders. Ben grabbed me in an awkward hug, my over-stuffed bag getting in the way.

'Sorry, I just got your messages. The reception was really bad in Cornwall. They only came through when we were driving back.' Ben had always been easy to lie to.

'Cornwall? I didn't know where you were.' He looked hurt, worried.

'Sorry. I just needed to get away, clear my head.'

'Are you OK?' He looked at my bag. 'Did you just get back?'

Ben smiled then, thinking that I'd come to see him straight away.

'Yes, just got back. Oh, Ben. Someone broke into Seagrass. I can't stay there.'

'Excuse me, are you open?' A young woman with pink-tipped hair called out to Ben. She was way too old for that look. He turned with irritation. 'One minute.' She looked pissed off, and walked away.

'I'm so sorry. Poor Seagrass. You can't stay there. Come to mine, Jem. I've got space.' He reached out to touch my arm, thought better of it, pulled back. Ben's flat was miles away in Romford.

'Oh no, I can't do that to you. But thank you. That's so kind. I'm going to stay with a friend. I just came to say goodbye.' The straps of my bag were starting to cut into my shoulders.

'Really, I don't mind. You're so welcome at mine. We can fix Seagrass, get it all sorted out. You've had the craziest time. I was reading all about it.'

I shook my head. 'I can't afford rent.'

'I don't mind! That doesn't matter to me. You don't have to pay me anything.'

I could see more customers waiting near the van. Ben didn't seem to be in any rush to get back to them.

'Look, I am going to stay with a friend. Not sure when I'll be back, but thanks.'

'Which friend?' He had known me long enough to know that I didn't have many friends.

'I met him at the theatre.'

Ben nodded, and for a fleeting moment looked irritated. 'Are you just leaving Seagrass open like that? What about your stuff? It might not be safe there.'

'Not sure. I can't think straight. Can you keep an eye on it?' I wanted to get away now. Getting a little impatient. 'You'd better look after your customers.'

'I don't like this, Jem. Are you coming back to work? I do need you here.' The thought of handing out coffees to all those rich, privileged students again... No way.

I promised that I'd message him, though there was an absolute certainty in my mind that I wouldn't.

TWENTY-SEVEN

When I signed with Elle, I had lied. The agency paperwork had asked 'Do you have a passport' and I'd said yes. But I'd never needed one before. We weren't the sort of family to fly to Spain or Disneyland in the school holidays. If you get a job filming abroad, a lucrative commercial, say, or maybe even a film, then there isn't a lot of time to decide – a production company wouldn't hesitate to move on to the next actress if you couldn't travel. So, as soon as I left Elle's office, ecstatic that she had signed me, I applied for my first passport. And now I was actually going to use it. I was flying to New York! It hardly seemed possible.

Sancha had laughed at me when I said I needed to go to a photo booth to get a passport picture. She showed me how to take it on her iPhone, and then sent off the application for me, right then. I asked her, 'What are all the photo booths used for then?' So, when we were next in Brighton, she took me to a shop full of old photo booths and we had our pictures taken, her looking amazing, bright red lips, me awkward in a stupid hat. I loved that strip of photos. It was now one of my few possessions left, everything in just one bag.

I felt like a movie star arriving at Heathrow Airport. Greg's driver dropped us right outside the terminal and we breezed through the crowds, me walking fast to keep up with Greg who knew exactly where to go and what to do. My guess was I was the only person in the airport that night who had never been on a plane before; they all looked so relaxed, so bored by it all!

I felt relief that my passport worked when I copied Greg and held it down on the scanning machine. My face appeared on the screen in front of me. I looked so different now from when Sancha had taken that passport photo – better make up, better hair now, definitely. I hoped Greg wouldn't ask to look at it. The gates opened and I stepped through into departures. I was in.

Heavy, musky perfume hung in the air as walked past outlets selling Gucci, Rolex, Bottega Veneta and Bulgari; I wanted to look in all of them! Maybe try on that tasselled bag to see how it looked on me. £1200! Who bought this stuff? I could be like Julia Roberts in *Pretty Woman* – I wanted to walk on the thick carpet and ask the assistant to take the bag out of the window for me, as if I was exactly the sort of person who could afford to buy such a bag. Maybe Greg would pay for it?

'Come on, Jem. Plenty of shops in New York.'

The first-class gate had no queue, unlike the long one for economy class. A woman my age, great hair, watched as I straightened my back, held out my passport and walked past her. It felt amazing.

Turning left on the plane, we were shown to our seats across the aisle from each other. There were just six seats, the rest of the cabin designed like a hotel cocktail bar with purple velvet chairs arranged around a coffee table covered in magazines and newspapers. Didn't they slide onto the floor when the plane took off?

'Champagne, Ms Evans?' A gorgeous woman, with red lips that matched the piping on her jacket, handed me a flute. I was in total heaven, choosing the films I wanted to watch, eating delicious salmon, so pretty, covered in tiny slices of radish. Greg worked for a couple of hours, then dozed. I know I should have tried to sleep, but I was too excited – I didn't want to miss a moment of this experience.

Greg had been surprised, then sweet, when I arrived at his house the night before. My strategy to avoid too many questions ('I missed you... I think you're right, we need to make the most of this opportunity...') was to get him into the bedroom as soon as possible. He booked a flight for me to join him in New York as the sky outside the penthouse turned black, and I promised to pay him back as soon as possible. I think we both knew that I wouldn't. I was getting out of London, away from Seagrass, away from the failure of *Poison*, to New York and wherever that could take me.

I was sipping my second Negroni and flicking through the newspapers to see what shows were on Broadway when I saw her. A photo of Olivia right at the top of the page. The noise of the plane engine roared in my head.

English Actress Overdoses in Theatre
Beth Lewisohn

LONDON – Olivia Goldsmith was starring in Poison *at the Arcola theatre in London, the latest episode in her dazzling career as an actress both on stage and screen. Instead, three months after her triumph in* And Then There Were None, *Goldsmith was found dead in her dressing room.*

Oxford graduate, former model and daughter of Virginia Goldsmith, Ms. Goldsmith leaves behind four-year-old daughter Chloe. She was not married.
The Metropolitan Police Service have made an announcement to the British Press that they are investigating Ms. Goldsmith's

death. A preliminary coroner's report indicates her blood contained a high dose of benzodiazepine. A further report is expected to be made to the press.

Slowly, carefully, in case anyone was watching me, I closed the paper and tucked it back into the pile of publications on the table. When was this story going to go away? Surely it was easiest if everyone just decided that she had overdosed, and that it was a sad, desperate mistake. People committed suicide every day, didn't they, or just died – on both sides of the Atlantic.

Up here, 35,000 ft in the air, I wanted to leave that whole episode behind me. I was sad for her child, but was I going to be reminded of Olivia for the rest of my life? Surely, she wasn't the only actress to have died this year? If something had happened to me, I was damn sure she wouldn't have given me a second thought. The difference was that she was famous and I wasn't. I was just a nobody who lived on a boat in King's Cross, no kids, no tragic story here folks, move along.

I glanced over at Greg, still dozing. He hadn't mentioned her since we left Cornwall. Was that for my benefit, to not upset me? Or for his? Had Rebecca seen this? How was her team handling it all? All the negative press still coming their way. Surely someone would link this to Ed, and realise that it was two people who worked for Rebecca.

My mind was spiralling. The theatre had been packed that night, and everyone up in the bar afterwards, celebrating the play, or drinking anyway, trying to find the right words to say. Critics, directors, actors, friends of the theatre. When did they realise that something was wrong, that Olivia wasn't joining them? I hadn't gone to the party, but then, who would remember that now after all that had happened? I had been exhausted. Needed to rest after the play. I wasn't famous, no-one was expecting me at the party, it was Olivia they had been waiting for. Who had found her? And when? How long did she lie there for? Did Abiola find her? Or Rebecca? Staring out of the window, I could see that we were no longer flying over the sea, and that we were now over land, buildings, *America*. London was already far away.

I'd calmed a little by the time the cabin attendant asked me to do my seatbelt, ready for landing. Greg smiled at me, looked a little drowsy, and downed the espresso that had just been handed to him. I noticed he watched the attendant walk back to the front of the plane; I couldn't blame him, she was gorgeous.

TWENTY-EIGHT

The Paper Factory Hotel in Astoria was Instagram heaven – a red London phone box half-submerged in concrete in the entrance hall, a 1920s typewriter on the front desk and a column of stacked books, filling the foyer, spiralling all the way up to the ceiling. Greg dealt with the booking in, while I hung back looking like the stupid girlfriend. Our cases were taken away on a vintage luggage trolley, and we were shown to a lift by the phone box, with just one button marked 'Penthouse'. Greg kissed me in the lift, stopping abruptly as the doors opened. 'The Killers stayed here last week,' he told me as we stepped into the suite. It was exactly how I imagined a New York loft apartment to look – exposed brick walls, floor-to-ceiling black-framed windows and a bar in the corner, doors leading to other rooms, one showing the edge of a super-king-size bed.

'This is amazing!' I said, throwing my bag on the floor, which looked tiny in the space.

'Ours for two whole weeks. Welcome to New York.' It must have been something like four in the morning UK time, but

Greg went over to the bar and poured a whisky. How many was that on top of what he'd drunk on the plane? Part of me wanted to crash out, but I was wired from the flight, the negronis and the fact that I was here. I accepted the whisky. New York! I could hardly believe it.

Sheridan Productions had booked the whole downstairs of the hotel for the party that night, so Greg had booked the penthouse, thinking that maybe he'd be able to host an after party, if the evening went his way. It was an expensive strategy, but I was fast learning that money didn't seem to be an issue for him. Queasy with tiredness, yet pumped with adrenaline, I started to plan.

'Greg, I really need to get something decent to wear. Are you OK if I go out?' He threw himself onto the sofa, and kicked off his shoes. 'Sure. Good idea. I'm going to make some calls, work out who else is coming tonight. Make sure you find something amazing. Have fun, Ms Evans.'

The hotel's own limo dropped me right outside Bergdorf Goodman; it would have been quicker to get the subway, but the receptionist insisted it came with the suite. We had crawled slowly through Manhattan, bumper to bumper with yellow taxis, and I loved all of it. The clothes people were wearing, the pretzel stands on street corners, the glamorous shop windows, the flashes of green spaces as we drove past tiny, fenced community gardens. Berti, the driver – was I meant to tip him? – gave me a running commentary of all the key sights on our route: 'Queensboro Bridge, Trump Tower, that there is Central Park, the Met...' I pictured Carrie Bradshaw striding along these pavements (no, sidewalks, right?) in high heels, and now I was here, too, living that life!

I'd seen Bergdorf Goodman on TV; stained glass door,

chandeliers, counters filled with jewellery and perfumes. The thick mink carpet bounced as I walked over it – didn't they worry about wet, muddy shoes?

Up the escalator, and so many gorgeous clothes! An emerald halter neck dress on a black, headless dummy. I ran my fingers over the fabric, so silky and glossy. Was green with red hair too much of a cliché? $1200! That's a no, then. Racks of dresses, so much choice, to my left and right, which way to go first? A pianist in a tux at a shiny grand piano, playing New York State of Mind, tipped his head as I walked past. So cheesy, but I loved it.

A Chiara Boni dress, maybe a bit wedding-y. $750! A Rickie Freeman belted dress was very Michelle Obama. It was all so expensive. And looked a bit old for me. The smell of leather and bitter orange pumped out from the Alexandra McQueen section, a Brit among all the American designers. At the end of a rack, I saw the one. Short, dark red, and just one on display. It said size 6, which I was pretty sure was a 10 in UK sizes. $450, still way too much. I glanced around. A skinny assistant watched me from behind the till.

'Shall I take it to the changing room for you, ma'am?' Skinny appeared next to me. I followed him to the changing room, and he closed the door behind me. I stripped down, and felt the fabric glide over my hips and breasts. As I did up the zip, the corset pulled tight around me, reshaping my waist as if someone had waved a magic wand. The dress was cut so every straight man in the room would think about your body, but it was classy, too, so wouldn't piss off the women. The mirror showed a rich, expensive woman. Did they have special lighting in here that made you look better? I smiled at myself in the mirror, yep, they probably did; that's what money bought for you. I needed to show someone this dress.

Sancha picked up after just two rings; it was so nice to be in the same time zone. 'Jem! Hey, how are you? You OK?'

'Hi. You'll never guess. I'm in New York! Let me put you on FaceTime, you need to see this dress.' I held out my phone to show Sancha the dress in the mirror.

'What the actual hell? Where are you? You look amazing!'

'Bergdorf Goodman! We've got a party tonight. What do you think of this?'

'Bergdorf? Wow! Can you afford that?' For a moment I wondered if she could buy it for me, help me out. There was no way I could ask.

'I can return it after the party.'

'It's not friggin' H&M, Jem. What does it cost?'

I wondered what Rebecca would think when she saw me in this dress. 'It's not too bad. Sale. Do you like it though?' Maybe the dress was a bit much. Was red too show-off? But then, if I wanted to make an impact, I had to look the part. Make Rebecca notice me.

'It's a great dress. Now, hang on... rewind. Why the hell are you in New York?'

'It's for the Sheridan Productions' party. Got here today, this morning. I'm staying at the Paper Factory.'

'Oh wow. Because of the play? Are they transferring it?'

'It's all being discussed.' Well, that wasn't strictly true, but then, maybe it *was* being discussed? We hadn't talked about it in Cornwall, but then, it didn't mean they *weren't* talking about it. Tonight might be a chance to suggest a transfer.

'So, the party's tonight? How long you staying for? I can't keep up with you.'

'Greg has booked the hotel for two weeks. It's all been a bit of a rush. Shall we try and meet up?'

'Greg? You took my advice then! Good work. It would be amazing to meet up.' I saw her glance around her. 'I'll talk to Jon. It's quite a long drive from here. I can't just drop everything... you should have told me you were coming!'

'Ma'am, are you OK in there? Can I bring you any other

gowns?' A gentle knock on the door. How long had I been in there?

'Listen, Sancha, I've got to go. Let me know what you decide.' Sancha waved goodbye, her hand filling the screen.

TWENTY-NINE

Greg's plan was to go down to the party just after 10pm by which time I was ready to pass out with exhaustion. I should have taken a party nap, but my body clock just wouldn't let me. I lay there with my eyes closed, my mind spinning. Who would be there? Famous actors? Directors?

I scrolled the RADA WhatsApp group. Hundreds of messages, they'd all been so busy, so great at keeping in touch. Had any of them cared that I wasn't active on the group? I was surprised to see messages from Sancha on there, chatting away, saying she'd seen Josh on Netflix, everyone raving about the thriller he'd been in. Neema, with little theatre emojis around her name, with updates about filming in Spain somewhere. Had they *all* got work since we'd left? Was it just me and Sancha who'd not been busy? I couldn't resist:

> Hey! Remember me? Anyone else going to the Sheridan party tonight? Would be amazing to see y'all!

I waited, stared at my phone. Would anyone reply, or just

leave me hanging. I typed 'Jemima' underneath, in case they didn't recognise the number, didn't have me in their phones.

Oh, wow! Hi. How are you? What party?

Raoul. He'd always been OK. One of the more normal ones.

It's in New York. New season party.

Jemima!! Long time no hear. You're alive!!

And there she was. Neema. The Queen Bee of our course. She'd taken the bait, couldn't resist.

We heard about Olivia Goldsmith OMG. So sorry your play got cancelled. Sancha said.

Had she?

So devastating. She was amazing.

She really was. I worked with her on Dragonhunter.

Josh! He'd joined in the chat. He had been in *Dragonhunter*, too, though it was a small part, really, you wouldn't have recognised him if you didn't know him.

My phone pinged. A text from Sancha.

Welcome to the vipers' nest! So funny to see you on WhatsApp. Thought not your thing!

I texted back:

Going to this party soon. Exhausted!! Wish me luck

Jealous!!!

Greg passed me an espresso martini, 'to fire me up'. He glanced at my phone, so I put it down, and gave him the attention he clearly wanted. I could leave the group to chew over the fact that I was going to an industry party, and they weren't. Very satisfying.

'Let's talk through our approach for the evening. I've made a list of the shows I think they're casting for this year. There are a couple of plays that might work for you, that might warrant casting a Brit. More off-Broadway than actual Broadway, but that's not a bad thing – the critics love those shows. Talk to as many people as you can – you never know who is connected to who.' He talked at me, and I tried to take it all in. Greg's own plan was to talk to producers, to see if they wanted to bring shows over to the UK that he could co-produce, use his contacts there. I was impressed by his research – so this was how it was done.

'Do you think they might transfer *Poison*?' I asked him.

He shrugged. 'Check in with Jonas. Might be far too soon. All the heat around that. Might not want to.' He had a good point. Olivia had really tainted that whole production.

It took a lot of concealer to take away the jet-lag greyness under my eyes. Eye drops, a slick of black pen liner and three coats of mascara made me look more human. The dress was wrapped in tissue paper in its stiff cardboard bag. If I left the tags on, and tucked them inside, I should be able to return it, and just say I changed my mind. I slipped into it, and stepped out to show Greg.

'Wow! You look incredible, Jemima. That is a great dress!' Greg walked towards me and placed his hands on my waist. 'I hardly dare touch you.' *OK, good choice on the dress.*

'I hope it's the right sort of thing. I'm screwed if they're all in jeans.'

'You look perfect. Come here.' He smirked at me, a touch too schoolboy for my taste, and leaned in to kiss my neck. His hand fumbled for the zip. I stepped back, as diplomatically as I could.

'We need to go now before I crash out. I'm exhausted.'

Greg looked a little hurt but rallied, with a clipped 'Of course.'

I slipped on the gold shoes I'd brought with me – one of my best Camden buys ever, 70s style, maybe even originals, and they had never let me down. It was a pretty safe bet that someone would ask about them at the party and I'd be able to get in a line about the shoes being from London, and *Yes, I'm from London, oh, you've been? I'm an actor, worked with Rebecca, etc…*

My phone pinged. Must be Sancha again. No, it was Abiola. I felt my heart thud.

> Jemima. Hi how are you? I put your stuff from your dressing room in a box. It's at the Arcola. I'm not there anymore.

My mind whirled – what had I left in my dressing room? Nothing. Just some clothes, rehearsal clothes. Toiletries. Was there anything else? I couldn't think. My mind went back to that night, me getting flowers, they'd all be dead and brown, someone must have thrown those out by now. I couldn't think of all that now. I threw my phone on the bed – that could all wait.

Acid jazz and the sound of people talking over each other blasted us as the lift door opened into the hotel lobby. There was barely space to join them – people crowded the room and the courtyard beyond. Strobe lights danced across the ceiling, spinning out from the DJ booth. A bartender was standing at the bar, pouring out shots. I felt Greg's hand on my back and we pushed forwards, people parting as we approached, glancing at my dress, then my face. A tall woman with sleek, shiny skin, and a low-cut white dress, looked at me as we passed. Checking me out?

A waiter passed with a tray of martinis. Greg took two and gave one to me. It tasted earthy, of green olives, disgusting, but I drank it anyway. I needed something in my hand, something to do. 'Great shoes!' A short man in an orange suit, red-faced, his jacket far too hot for the party. I mouth 'thank you' back, and feel Greg press my back – I get the message – he's not worth talking to.

'Where are we going?' I shout, and Greg says something that I can't hear, and we edge past people towards a roped-off area near an upright piano doubling as another bar, with bottles of spirits lined up on top. Greg strides forwards with such confidence, and a man steps aside to open up a roped area, containing maybe twenty people? I recognise two men, so good-looking, they are almost not real, actors I'd seen on Netflix, and Greg goes straight up to them and slaps one on the arm.

And there. In the centre of the crowd, Rebecca. People arranged around her, waiting for their turn to talk to her, to get their turn in her orbit. She looks so relaxed, so polished, holding court effortlessly. Dressed in black, chic and minimalist. I've got this wrong, I don't look right for the party. My dress is too bright, gaudy, I've tried too hard. I feel my confidence ebb away.

A man in front of Rebecca, leaning in really close, trying to be heard over the music. I can see his mouth moving, but her eyes are looking away from him, over his shoulder, and then she turns to look directly at me.

'Rebecca! Amazing to see you again.' Greg pushes past me and moves to kiss Rebecca, and the man steps back neatly, as if he had always planned to end his fascinating story right at that moment.

'Greg. Welcome to New York.' Rebecca stands still and lets us walk towards her. 'And Jemima. What a double act you two are.' I see her eyes move down my body, slowly. 'You dressed up.'

'Thanks. Great party!' I take a sip from my martini, it's

almost finished, how did that happen? I should have planned what to say, I can't think of a single intelligent thing to say. Something about Cornwall?

Rebecca looks around her, as if seeing the party for the first time. 'I'm not sure who half of these people are.'

'Rebecca.' A woman pushes past me and grabs Rebecca in an awkward hug, her drink held out at an angle, so as not to spill. Rebecca smiles at her, and then looks back at me.

'Jemima. Have you met Anisha?'

The woman turns to look at me, irritated that she has to now include me in the conversation, and Rebecca takes the moment to respond to the man behind her. My stomach lurches; it's the woman with the amazing shoes from Rebecca's party in Albion Square. I recognise her at once. *Say something, Jem, act casual.* I hold out my hand, stiffly, formally.

'Jemima Evans. I think we met at a party in London.'

'Anisha Manji. Did we?' She looks puzzled. Do I look that different from just a month ago, am I that forgettable?

I didn't want to be the one who mentioned Ed, which was the link that would have made it very clear where we had met before. Her face darkened for a moment, as she made the connection. And then the perfect smile returned.

'At Rebecca's house? Oh yes. Wow, that was a shock. That guy...' She glances at Rebecca, who seems not to be listening to us. I nod, look at my glass. I look around to see if there were any waiters nearby – no joy. I reach for a bottle from top of the piano – Champagne will do nicely. As I reach over, Rebecca turns and holds out her glass. 'Thank you, Jemima. Ani – so lovely to see you again. Jonas said you were in New York.'

You could see Anisha shift into pitch mode. Her back straightens and she pauses for a beat before saying with such confidence: 'Yes! I'm producing a film about fashion week. It's going to be frickin' amazing. I have everyone in it, Stella, Jason Wu, Brandon...' Rebecca nodded. 'I'd love you to take a look,

Rebecca. Get your insights on what works, what doesn't. It could go over to Netflix.'

Rebecca turned to me. 'Ani and I were at school together, Jemima. Then university. A few years ago, now.'

'It wasn't that long ago. So many great memories...' Anisha added, smiling warmly at Rebecca.

'Not all the memories are good, Ani. I think we remember some things quite differently.'

Anisha looked slightly thrown, and then carried on. 'Well, we've all done very well for ourselves, which is amazing to see. I have to say... Jemima, you said? That dress looks incredible on you.' A smooth change of subject.

'Book in a meeting with Jonas.' Rebecca said, glancing over her shoulder. Was he here somewhere, too? Hadn't seen him yet.

'Great! I'll send you the film when it's in rushes. I think you'll love it, Bex.' Anisha air-kissed Rebecca, before apparently spotting someone across the room. Was I meant to move on now, too, my audience time with the most important person in the party over? Would she mention what happened between us at Greg's house, or should I? Ani left us, making her way effortlessly through the crowd. Leaving just Rebecca and me.

Rebecca watched her leave. 'She was a complete bitch at school. Had no time for me then. She only showed an interest when Sheridan Productions took off.'

Surprised, I replied quickly. 'I hated school. It seems a long time ago though now.'

'I'm not sure it ever leaves you, not completely. But here we are, Miss Evans. New York. Things do change.'

'Yes, they do. And look at you. The queen of all this.' My arm flew out, in a theatrical flourish. God, I looked stupid.

Rebecca leaned towards me, 'Yes, I suppose I am.'

'Drinks!' Greg appeared, butting in, with two fresh martinis. I looked from Greg to Rebecca. What could I say now, when the last time we had all been together, Rebecca and I were in his house, on his floor? He had no idea.

I blurted out, 'I met Anisha at your house. At the party.' Oh god, why had that come out? Too much alcohol, jet lag, panic.

Rebecca looked surprised. 'I don't remember you there.'

'I wasn't there long... what with...' Oh shit, I was about to say Ed. I looked around, looked at Greg, willing him to change the subject. I stumbled on.

'Are you going to stay in New York for long?' The music felt louder, and the voices around us had got louder too, so I think I shouted that.

'For now.'

Greg jumped in. 'Well, you have so much on here right now, Bex. It sounds like an incredible season for you.' I saw Rebecca's face darken a little. Did she think he was pitching for work from her too, like everyone else in the room?

'New York, the land of opportunity. Well, I'm sure you will both meet all the right people here tonight.' That sounded like my time was up.

Right on cue, one of the handsome actors stepped closer to Rebecca and she turned to talk to him, his turn for an audience. Somehow the people around Rebecca moved, shuffled and rearranged themselves around me and Greg until we were on the edge of the roped-off area, and we looked like hangers-on.

'What did you talk about? I couldn't hear it all.' Greg shouted, leaning in.

'School, weirdly. Not much.'

'Oh right. Well, she looked pleased to see you. We should hook up with her in a few days. Get dinner.' Greg looked pleased. 'Did you see Lena Dunham? Apparently she's here, but I haven't seen her. I'm pretty sure that's Richard Curtis in the courtyard. I should go and talk to him.'

'Do you know him?' I asked, as we pushed towards the

courtyard; it was easier to hear him out here, further away from the DJ booth.

'Not really. I'll play the fellow Brit abroad card. Can you look after yourself? Maybe try and talk to Rebecca again. Or find Jonas.' He kissed me briefly. I watched Greg make his way through the crowd.

'So, Jemima. It took me a while to remember you. What brings you to New York?' Anisha appeared by my side. I gave her my best smile, as if we were old friends.

'Work things. I'm an actor. I was in a play produced by Sheridan. Your film sounds great!'

Anisha looked around her, checked no-one was listening. 'It came back to me, that we met at the party, in the kitchen. That whole thing with that guy was so awful. Did the police get in touch with you?' She sipped her drink, looked at me carefully.

'No. Why, did they contact you?'

'Yes! It was horrendous. I had to go to a police station. Wait for ages. Apparently they interviewed Rebecca, too, but she's been very quiet about it all. Rumour is, she's putting the house on the market.'

'Why? Why did they interview you?'

She stared at me. 'You know he died, right? Just a few days ago. The police told me.'

I felt a chill, the nausea rising in me. 'I hadn't heard.'

Ed was gone.

'Drugs, apparently. But everyone has their own theory.' She glanced around her. 'You don't mind me talking about this, do you? I feel I can't really talk about it with many people. It's been so awful. I can't get the image of him out of my mind. Apparently, he worked for Rebecca, although she said she didn't know him really, he was quite junior. The police dragged us all in, because Rebecca gave them the guest list.'

She looked pissed off, as if how dare they? 'They made me feel like a criminal. I couldn't tell them anything, because I didn't know him and all I saw was the same as everyone else, him just lying there, outside. It was like being in *Prime Suspect* or something.'

I hadn't been on the guest list. 'They must have interviewed a lot of people.'

'Rebecca just wants it to go away. And now this with Olivia.' Anisha took a large sip from her glass.

'I'm not sure we should be talking about this here. It's Rebecca's party.' I looked around me. No one seemed interested in our conversation, but people were standing quite close to us, absorbed in their own worlds. Anisha can't have made the link to me and Olivia, or she wouldn't have mentioned it, surely? The upside of not being known, not being famous. I looked around for Greg; I needed an excuse to end this conversation. I could see him in the corner towering over Richard Curtis, who looked quite animated.

'I need to... you take care, right?' I patted her arm clumsily and left her on the steps, and made my way towards the bar, not really having a plan other than to be somewhere else. *Ed had died. Rebecca must know. Jonas must know.*

And yet, the party continued around me.

'Look, it's amazing!' I held my phone up to show Sancha the party. Music drowned out what she was trying to tell me.

'Having fun?' Another stupidly handsome man, this one with glossy grey hair pushed up in a quiff.

'Bit jet-lagged, but yes, think so.' I shouted back. I had no idea what time it was, or why I was even here still. The party had got busier and louder all around me. It seemed better to stay here, surrounded by people, than alone in the room, with my thoughts. Ed's face appeared in my mind. I tried to focus on the man. I needed another drink.

'London? By that accent?'

'You got it.' I tried out my best New York accent. I could hear something. My phone. It was still on, screen moving, Sancha talking. 'Sanch, got to go.' I pressed end call.

'Love it there! Second home to me.' He talked at me for a while, him saying he's a writer, me trying to get in that I'm an actor, probably the same conversation playing out all around the room. I hadn't heard of the things he had written, but that didn't mean he wasn't going to be the next big thing, so I played the game and acted interested. I could see Rebecca's group from where we were standing, so a useful spot to watch while I nodded in what were probably the right places.

A tall man was air-kissing Rebecca and she was giving something to someone next to her. Jonas. He was next to her, of course he was. He hadn't bothered to find me, to talk to me. I wasn't important. He was hosting the party, would be focused on the big names. The producers, the ones who had the money.

And then people started to move, and I could see Rebecca walking through the party. Towards the exit. People stopping her, trying to get to talk to her. Saying goodbye to people... The man droned on in my ear... Was she looking for me... what if she couldn't find me?

'Sorry, back in a minute,' I said, and tried to push through to get to her. Heaving with people, oblivious to me, blocking my way. The back of her head, she was moving quickly now and I guessed she had someone, probably Jonas, asking people to move out of the way for her, and I was almost near her, when I saw that she had her arm loosely around the waist of a young woman, younger than me, with thin arms and long, straightened blonde hair.

And there was Jonas, right behind Rebecca and the woman, my age, maybe younger, and he seemed to be helping them both towards the door. Always fixing things. The room seemed to go into slow-motion as I tried to make sense of my feelings. Did I want that? To be the one with Rebecca?

'I've seen that woman in something. Cute! Can't think of her name... Brit like you, I think. Rebecca always has great taste in women.'

The man has followed me, he's talking, loud, and the sound of the room rushes back into my head.

'Don't know her...' I try to reply.

I watch Rebecca, the woman and Jonas leave the hotel. The crowd seems to breathe a sigh of relief, then everyone is talking at once, the noise level rising as they discuss the most important woman in the room, and the girl who left with her. Now the party could really begin and people could relax, no longer in work mode, and with the drinks being paid for by someone else.

'What's her name?' I turn to the man to ask.

'Can't say I know, but she's brave getting involved with Rebecca.' He raised his eyebrows at me.

'What do you mean?'

'They never stick around long, she's on to the next so fast. Perk of the job, I guess.'

I didn't bother to reply, turned, pushed through the crowd, badly wanted another drink, or to get upstairs, away from all these people, this noise, these feelings.

I was just one of many to Rebecca. To her, I was nothing, just another actress. Disposable.

THIRTY

Being in New York felt like being on screen – the location, sounds and characters so familiar and memorable, and now I was part of it. If you were watching me, you'd see the exhausted though eye-catching redhead, perhaps in another life played by Audrey Fleurot, gazing out of the coffee shop window. The perfectly placed coffee cup on the window ledge, gentle rain running down the glass, blurring her face. You'd think, what's happened to her? What's her story, why is she alone, and looking so sad?

I'd slept badly, a combination of jet lag, too much alcohol, and feelings about Rebecca that I wasn't sure how to process. I had left Greg dead to the world – I needed to get out of the hotel, get some space, clear my head. Rebecca's face kept appearing while I tried to sleep. Her face when we'd had sex, lying on the floor in Greg's house. How she'd looked at me at the press launch. How she'd left the party with someone else. What should I have said or done differently? If Anisha hadn't been there, the London party would never have come up and it might have been completely different – it might have been me leaving the party with Rebecca, not that other actress. I couldn't work it out.

The door to the coffee shop kept opening and letting the chilly early morning air in. Did no one else care? I pulled my coat tighter around me.

'This for you?' the waiter asked, holding out a bowl of porridge. We used to eat Ready Brek at home. Mark would make it, and we'd add loads of syrup in thick spirals.

I ate the lumpy porridge, watching New Yorkers speed-walk past, dog walkers, a man loading saggy bags of hotel laundry into the back of a van. It reminded me of St Pancras before the commuter trains piled in, the business of getting the day going, but it also felt different and far away.

I gave myself time to finish breakfast and order a second coffee before texting Greg. Best to keep him sweet.

> Didn't want to wake you. Hope head is ok.
> Going to be a tourist for the day. XX

That should buy me some time to myself. I scrolled through the RADA WhatsApp group – so many messages, mostly from Josh and Neema, but also:

> How's the party? Anyone famous there?

> Send us photographic evidence!

> Hope you have a blast! Don't sleep with anyone
> without an Oscar!

That last one from Sancha.

I had to reply.

> So good!! AMAZING people. Paying for it now.
> My head!!

Hopefully that would make the others feel some FOMO. Would wind up Neema. It cheered me up a bit.

So, Jemima. New York. A whole day to yourself. I'd wanted to come here my whole life, and at last I was here. Maybe I could walk across Central Park, go in the Met, take a boat trip to see the Statue of Liberty. An image of Rebecca appeared in my head, lying asleep, arms around the woman from last night... I pushed that thought away.

My phone lit up, next to my empty bowl.

Guess where I am?!

Sancha. I grabbed the phone and pressed call. 'Where?' I asked, too loudly. The woman sitting along from me in the window looked up from her laptop.

'New York! Just driving over the Williamsburg Bridge.'

'What? No way! You coming here? Do you want to meet me? I'm in a cafe somewhere near Central Park, hang on...' I looked around for the name or address of the cafe and the woman next to me handed me her napkin with it printed on. 'Box Kite coffee shop. Columbus?'

'OK, no idea where that is, but I'll track your phone. On my way!' She sounded like when I'd first met her at RADA – excited and giddy. I couldn't believe she was here in New York. It had been well over a year since I'd seen her.

I killed time waiting for Sancha by reading the *New York Times* and had to order more coffee to keep my prime spot in the window. I googled Rebecca, saw the same photos again, her at the BAFTAs. A new story saying she was the frontrunner for producing the new Bond film. Wow, moving into films. Rebecca would love that. I kept scrolling. No mention anywhere of Ed's death. Strange. But a relief.

I typed in 'Olivia Goldsmith' and was shocked to see so many new links to articles about her death, including some from yesterday. Photos of her daughter appeared at the top of many of the stories, as well as comments about the risks of drug-taking, which the American press seemed to think was behind it all, with the strong implication that it was, therefore, all Olivia's fault. She was young, beautiful, British and a mother, and she had ruined her perfect story with drugs, aka 'poor choices'. One article linked to an American actress in the 90s who had also taken drugs, and then a female singer who had died, her whole career ahead of her – all young, beautiful women, perfect clickbait. All of them lumped together, women who had failed in some way, as if they had deserved their fate. I couldn't help but feel sorry for her.

Then, just as the waiter made a show of taking my empty coffee cup, Sancha burst into the cafe in a commotion of luggage not quite fitting through the door, blocking the way of a couple trying to leave. She parked a bag next to me which I knew would be right in the way of the waiter, having seen his route for the past hour or so, and grabbed me, in the strongest hug I'd experienced in a long time.

'It is *so* good to see you,' she said, holding me close.

I felt my body relax into hers, and I hugged her in return, absorbing her warmth. I'd never been a good hugger, but Sancha made it easy. I took her in, her huge, warm smile, her tired eyes.

'I was awake early with Polly, so thought might as well get going. Beat the traffic.'

Her expensive, well-cut leather jacket emphasised that she was much slimmer than I remembered.

'There's less of you,' I told her, trying to keep the surprise out of my voice.

Sancha called across at the waiter for an espresso. 'Thanks! I've been training to lose the baby weight. And the England weight.' I'd always quite liked Sancha's round body. It suited her face, suited her type.

'You looked good before! Oh, it's been too long.' It *had* been too long. She'd got married and had a baby since we graduated; what had I achieved in that time? One failed play.

'Sorry I didn't fly over to see you,' I said.

'It's OK, I know it's expensive. I guess *Poison* paid well though, as you are here now!' she said, pulling over a stool to sit down next to me.

'No not really. Greg bought the tickets. I need to pay him back.' I filled her in on where we were staying, his plans to get in with Rebecca and Jonas, the party. She drank it all in, letting me ramble on, me so excited to be able to tell someone everything that had been going on. I told her more details about the play, and what happened with Olivia. Sancha shook her head, hugged me.

'It's so awful. I'm so sorry.'

'So, how is Polly?' I knew I'd talked for too long about me.

'Oh, great! Jon's mother is with her. She's delighted, in charge of her two favourite people and me out of the way. Anyway, I don't want to talk about them... this is *my* time and god, I need it.' Sancha drained her espresso.

'How long are you here for? It's so good to see you.'

'I've got four precious days, longer, maybe, if Jon doesn't get annoyed with his mother. I really needed this. When you said you were here, well, I couldn't resist. It was too good a chance to get away.'

'Where are you staying? Do you need to drop off your bags? Our hotel isn't far.'

'Jon has a company apartment he uses for work or for shagging his secretary or something – don't look at me like that! I've got the address here somewhere. It's not being used at the moment. So he booked it for me. But also, it means he can keep an eye on me. Listen, let me get sorted, and let's spend the day together. What are your plans? Any more showbiz parties I should know about?'

I would have liked to say I had a busy day of meetings and castings, but the truth was, I didn't, and exploring with Sancha would be loads more fun than on my own.

'No plans. I want to explore. I want to go everywhere. Central Park, High Line, take a boat trip, walk along Fifth Avenue... I don't know – all of it. You're not serious about Jon, are you? The shagging bit.'

She shrugged. 'Wouldn't blame him. I'm too exhausted to shag him. No, he wouldn't dare. Anyway, today. I'm here, with you. No baby. Just us. And I want to enjoy every moment.'

I look back at that day with Sancha as magical, a perfect day. The rain lifted and we walked the whole length of the High Line under blue skies, taking in the views across the Hudson and peeking down into the designer flats. She bought us ice cream sandwiches from a pop-up stand, mine red velvet flavour, shaped like a clam. We ate lobster rolls from the food market below, and I tried not to think about how they cooked the lobsters alive.

Sancha was so happy that day, laughing, chatting about our college days, which sounded better when she talked about them. Sancha showed me photos of Polly, her cute face very like her mum, with beautiful big eyes. Their house was right near the beach in Sag Harbor, and she liked to take Polly for walks there most mornings, and there was a crowd she liked to hang out with, who met to chat about babies, dogs and exercise. They all looked perfect, with matching streaked blonde hair and pastel-coloured sweatshirts.

Was that life possible for me? I thought of me and Greg in Cornwall, walking along the beach, me with a dog and him a baby strapped to his chest. No, not my style – I had too much to get done, too much that I wanted to achieve. I threw the thought away. That was for other people.

Sancha told me stories about the RADA gang, what they'd been up to.

'I didn't know you'd stayed in touch that much.'

'Of course!' she said. 'Got to keep in with them. All good contacts. Don't be scared of them. They could be useful to you.'

It was getting dark when I said I needed to get back to the hotel, that I had plans with Greg, I'd ring her, but in truth, the jet leg was catching up with me. I also needed to be alone, to think about what to do with the time I had left in New York.

Greg was pacing the room when I got back, phone in hand.

'Did you talk much to Rebecca last night?' was his first question when I got in. 'She isn't answering my calls. I've been trying to set up a meeting.'

'She's probably still getting over the party. Taken the day off.'

Greg rubbed his forehead, as if that would erase some of the creases. 'I lost you at the party. Did you see Rebecca leave with that actress from *Passengers*?'

He looked rough, the jet lag and alcohol not suiting him either. 'It might be worth you calling her. She might pick up for you – I think you might be our secret weapon here.'

'Greg, hardly. She barely spoke to me last night – you were there.'

He turned to look at me. 'She seemed pretty into you at my house. And she's already cast you once.'

I flinched at his words. Had he heard us that night? Had Jonas or Rebecca told him something, or hinted? Surely he would have said something. He just meant us talking, surely...

Greg looked at his phone. 'I've been trying to get hold of Jonas too... no-one in their office seems to be picking up at the moment.'

'Maybe they all get a day off after a party. Don't stress about it.'

He tucked his phone into his back pocket. 'Yeah, maybe. How was your sightseeing? See anything interesting?'

'I met an old friend, Sancha. From RADA. You'd like her.'

'Oh, brilliant! An actor, too?'

'Well, she was. She's just had a baby.'

He nodded. 'What's she called?'

'Sancha Cottingham. Well, that's what she was called at RADA.' I wondered if she went by Jon's name in her mom life. I'd never asked.

'I'll look her up. Well, by all means, invite her out with us. And try Rebecca.' It didn't sound like a request.

I took a shower and looked at my limited choice of clothes. Sancha had looked incredible. Flared jeans, expensive sweater, perfectly dressed for a New York day. What did I have that was similar... My jeans were from Zara but looked OK on, though my legs were not as skinny as hers. How did she get thinner than me?

Greg was on his phone again as I left and I mouthed 'back soon'. Should I call Rebecca? No, she was definitely someone who called you, not the other way round. I turned left out of the hotel and walked. I needed to think.

THIRTY-ONE

It was cocktail hour and I got lucky with the bar I walked into. The Beekman had an old-school London-vibe, or at least the London that Americans think of, with leather bucket chairs and walls lined with books, like a gentleman's club that spies might hang out in. It was quiet, almost empty, the trendy New Yorkers obviously hanging out somewhere else, but it suited me just fine.

I ordered a Manhattan, because, why not? The bartender made a big show of making it, smiling to show his two impressive dimples to their best advantage; Sancha would have enjoyed him more than I did, and would have taken a seat at the bar, got to know him, probably would have got the drink for free, wouldn't have had to pay the stupid $18, plus service. Money was fast becoming an issue. I was on borrowed time with my cards.

I carried my drink to a quiet corner, past two men in beige jackets, squashed into their bucket seats – vintage wasn't designed for their body size. One watched as I walked past. No chance. He was old enough to be my dad.

I had such a short, impossibly short, time in New York to

make a difference to my career, to meet people. The right people. I had to give it everything I had. Elle picked up after several rings.

'Jemima! Good to hear from you. You OK?' I could hear loud voices, laughing, music in the background.

'I'm fine. Can you hear me? I'm in New York.'

'What the fuck? Why?' I'd never heard her swear before – she must have had a few drinks.

'I'm here with a friend – Greg Trelawney. We went to the Sheridan party.'

'Hang on.' I heard her move through the party, or was it a bar? Someone called her name, and then it was quiet. 'Is that better?'

'I can hear you. Have there been any interest in me at home? I mean castings? Anything in the pipeline?'

Elle was quiet at the other end for a moment. 'No. Nothing like that. Listen, god, it's so loud here. I think we just need to let the dust settle. If I send you out to a casting director, they just know you're going to bring the press interest about Olivia with you.'

'And that's a bad thing?' No answer. Could she hear me? Was there a time delay between London and New York? I spoke again anyway. 'I got great reviews. That must count for something.'

'Yes, that's true... yes, you did, and in time, I think that will work out for you.' She paused when someone came into the room, apologised loudly and left again. 'Are you OK? How long you out there for?' She was changing the subject.

'Doesn't sound like there's any reason to rush back...'

'Olivia is huge news here. Listen, you should tell me when you go away. We've had so many phone calls about you, and you weren't returning my calls. I was worried. The police rang me to talk about Olivia. They want you to get in touch.'

'Oh, do they?' I gripped the phone, tried to sound calm. The voices of the men on the next table, so loud, brash.

Why did the police want to talk to me? It was drugs, everyone would have told them. They must have tested her blood or something, too. When would this Olivia stuff all go away?

A door must have opened near Elle again, filling the phone with drum and bass and people laughing. The two men behind me, laughing. Everyone having a better time than me, getting on with their lives, and me, just sitting here, no chance of new castings, a new role. My career dead in the water.

'Elle, I need to go. Can you let me know if anything comes up? In London or over here?' I could stay longer here, couldn't I? I could rent somewhere in New York, or go and stay with Sancha? They had guest rooms, I could travel to New York for castings, help with Polly. People wouldn't think about Olivia so much over here.

'You want to go to castings in New York? How long are you staying for?' She sounded irritated. 'You need to call the police. I sent you the information.'

'I will. Sorry. Missed that.' I tried to think, panicking. 'I don't know how long I'm staying. I could stay with Sancha.'

'Oh, I remember her. Is she out there now?'

'Yes, got married, had a baby. Lives here now.'

'She was good.'

I agreed with Elle.

Sancha had signed with a big agency after graduation, but they'd dropped her when she'd moved to the US. She had been devastated. They'd had an office in New York, she thought it would be just fine, but it was different agents and they hadn't wanted that. God, would Elle drop me? I couldn't risk that. After we said goodbye, I texted Elle to thank her for her amazing support and that I'd be in touch with any updates.

I exhaled heavily. It made sense to stay out of London until the press had moved on to some other sad story. I could deal with the police when I got back. Not a lot I could tell them. I was sure they'd spoken to Sarah, Abiola, people still there, people who worked at the Arcola, who knew Olivia better than me.

The way I saw it was I had two strong options right here in New York – one was Greg, and one was Rebecca. Both knew people, had influence, and right now, in London, my options felt limited. I sat for a while, sipping my Manhattan, which actually wasn't that nice, thinking about my next move.

Greg was out when I got back to the Paper Factory, and I slept like the dead, my body finally relaxing into the time zone. He was drinking coffee on the balcony when I got up, and seemed happy enough to see me.

'Morning!' I leaned over and kissed him. Greg glanced at my breasts – OK, still interested. 'I'm going to try Rebecca today,' I lied, helping myself to a pastry covered in lime-green pistachios. There were days when me and Mark didn't get breakfast, no food in the house. If he could see me now.

Greg put his iPad down. 'I think that's a good plan. The guys were saying last night that Sheridan have loads of investment right now, so this is the perfect time to be here. They might want to invest in the Minack. Or film there.' He pulled me down onto his lap. 'Why don't you call her now and try and get her to meet us for dinner?'

My instincts told me that Rebecca was used to being in charge, calling the shots. Me calling her would make me yet another pushy actress to deal with. It didn't feel like the right thing to do but I wanted Greg to think that I was an asset. 'I'll get a shower first. Too early will seem desperate.'

I took my time in the shower, with the bathroom door firmly locked, and Greg had left for a meeting by the time I emerged, so I lay on the bed and scrolled through my messages. One from

Elle, with the numbers to call the police. Nagging me. Surely it was her job to deal with that stuff? I pressed delete.

I needed to focus. I scrolled the New York casting sites, joined one of the cheaper ones and read through what was available to women my age. So much crap out there, mostly dead-end work as extras, or mass castings that would just feed the director's ego and waste my time. So many pop-up ads for acting classes, voice coaching and movement, always trying to sell you something, to get more money out of actors. A person could spend a lifetime training to be an actor, and spend a fortune, too. This one sounded intense: 'Actors will develop a foundation from which to build themselves as actors as well as human beings.' I guess they can't promise you'll make it as an actor, so might as well try and be a more perfect human being. Bullshit.

So many people trying to make it as an actor, and so few of them would. There were only so many plays, TV shows and films to go around, and in those, so many of the parts went to the same pool of established actors. How many actors graduated from drama school each year? A thousand in the UK? Twice as many in the USA? How many actually got work as an actor, that would then pay for the course, let alone a life. Even *me*, with my training from RADA, I couldn't get a decent job. So many of these losers had no chance.

This wasn't doing my mood any good. I texted Sancha to meet up.

We had done most of SoHo, and we were in a place that Sancha had seen on Insta that she wanted to visit. It was one of those shops with only one of each thing hanging on the rail, all statement pieces, the sort of clothes you never actually saw people out in the real world wearing. A converted bank, the earnest shop assistant told Sancha. You could see where they'd ripped the panelling and plaster from the walls to reveal the brickwork, to make it look more rough than it used to be. Sancha was in the changing room, made from scaffolding and heavy, velvet curtains, trying on a Dries Van Noten dress, $300, which was completely the wrong shape for her, when my phone rang.

'Hey, Jemima, how are you?' Jonas's drawl, instantly recognisable.

I tried to sound calm. 'Hi, how are you?'

'Listen, sorry we didn't get to chat at the party. Did you have a great time?'

'Yes, thank you. It was a great party.' This was all very polite. Why was he calling me?

'So, you might be able to help me out with something. You still in New York? Greg left messages for me.'

'Yes, that's right. Still here.' I walked to the door to hear him better. A black Lamborghini with tinted windows drove past the shop slowly, blasting out a low, thudding beat. So much money in New York for the chosen few. I covered the phone with my hand, tried to focus on what Jonas was saying.

'Can we meet today at five? Sorry, it's not much notice. My assistant can send you the details.'

'Jemima!' I turned to see Sancha's head peeking out from behind the curtains. She pulled one aside in a dramatic flourish, to show me the dress and grimaced at me; the dress did look terrible. I pulled a face at her.

'Sorry, Jonas. Say that again. Can you tell me anything more?' I was sure I'd missed something. I should have stayed in, waited at the hotel. Not be in this stupid shop.

'So, I can tell her you are OK for five?' I could hear him waiting for my reply. Tell who? Rebecca?

'OK. I should be clear by then.' I didn't want to sound like I was just hanging around, doing nothing, even though I was. 'Thanks, Jonas. Will I see you later, too?' Might as well try and sound pally, although we weren't; it was all part of the game.

'Yes, I'll be there. Goodbye, darling.' He rang off.

'Who was that?' Sancha emerged from the changing room in her own clothes.

'Jonas. You know the producer I told you about? He wants to meet up later.'

'For work? Or social?'

I stared at my phone. I assumed work. If it was for work though, surely he would have got in touch with Elle and got her to handle it. It was usually agents who handled castings and meetings, but then, they did know me, and I was here in New York, and Elle wasn't. All those months of trawling through Spotlight, putting my name forward to open castings and *this* is how it worked – they just rang up the people they wanted. I was so right to be here.

'Let's get out of here and you can tell me all,' Sancha said.

We found a cafe a few doors down, and while Sancha ordered for us, I opened the messages from Jonas's assistant. A script! About twenty pages of a script. They wanted me for a casting. The title said *The Betrayal*, and there were three parts. One part was highlighted in yellow all the way through, so that must be the one I needed to prep for. The cover email didn't say much, just gave an address, time, and 'please read attachment.'

Sancha came back with two bright orange smoothies, green stripy straws sticking out of the top. 'Sorry, Sancha. They've sent a script through and I really need to head back to the hotel and prep.' I stood up ready to leave.

She put down the drinks. 'You don't have time for a smoothie?'

'They want me there at five. There's no way I'm going to know these pages by then.' I could feel panic rising in my chest. 'I'm sorry to abandon you. Are you going to carry on here? Try some dresses? Sorry.'

'Oh, that doesn't matter. This is why you are here. It's more important.' She slung her bag over her shoulder. 'I'll help you prep. I'm not doing anything. We can run through the lines like we used to.'

I tried to breathe out slowly, let the air out through my lips, to let my heart rate settle down. This was actually happening. I had a casting in New York and my best mate was going to be there to help me prep, just like we had always dreamed. It didn't feel real, but yet it was, it really was.

'Yes, that would be amazing. Shit. I can't believe it.' The hotel could probably help me print out the script or I could read it on my laptop back at the hotel; it was too small to read on my phone. Had Jonas sent it out to many people? Would there be many actresses at the casting? I wish I knew more.

'Let's get a cab to your hotel. I'll pay. Well, Jon will pay.' Sancha beamed at me. 'It's exciting, Jem. We can do this!'

Sancha swept out onto the pavement and stuck her arm out. A yellow cab pulled up moments later, just like we were in an actual film. Sitting in the back seat, I tried to enlarge the script on my phone. I was reading the lines for Emily.

As we drove along avenues of New York high rises, I googled the play. The connection was terrible, but I learned that amazing actors had done it before – Zawe Ashton and Rachel Weisz had got rave reviews; they must be looking to recast, and keep the play going, but surely they didn't want someone like me after those huge names?

Sancha didn't know either. 'You can't overthink it. It's a chance to be seen, whatever happens,' she told me, and I would have said exactly the same if she were me. My most hopeful guess was that the play suited having a Brit in the part. How many Brits did they have in New York, ready to audition? My mind spiralled trying to work out why Jonas had called me and what my chances were likely to be.

I forwarded the email to Sancha so we could read the script together, and we did our best while moving through painfully slow traffic. It felt like old times, us reading pages, talking about what the stage directions meant, trying to work out how best to say the lines. It was sparse with directions and it was all about the dialogue, bar the odd pause, where I would have to think of something to do, so I didn't stand there looking like I'd forgotten my lines. It was similar to *Poison* in some ways, intense conversations, intimate. Maybe it would then transfer back to London, and it would all come full circle, and what happened to Olivia would all be forgotten. I needed to focus, calm down.

I texted Elle on the way. Had she been in touch with Jonas and got me the casting? I was surprised when she texted straight back:

> No, not me. I'll get in touch with Sheridan.
> Excellent. Keep me posted!

It felt like the wrong way around – she was meant to tell me about castings. *You're overthinking, Jem, spiralling.* If I did get it, then Elle could take over and sort out the contract and schedule and stuff. *Your job, Jem, is to focus on the script, and make sure you get to the casting in plenty of time, as prepared as could be.* We could worry about contracts if I got the part.

We arrived at the Paper Factory to find Greg in the foyer – we had an awkward hug. Sancha and Greg stared at each other as if mythical beasts, and then Sancha's social skills kicked in and she hugged him. 'We meet at last. So good to finally meet you, Greg.'

Greg grinned at Sancha, and I noticed him glance up and down her body. Taking her in. She did look great in her black jeans, expensively faded in the right places to make her thighs look good, dark grey biker jacket and hair, perfect. Men had always liked her.

'Sancha. You've been keeping Jemima busy.'

'We've had so much to catch up on.' She grinned at me.

'Are you just back, or going out again?' I asked Greg.

'Just got back. Hope that's OK? Am I cramping your style,

girls?' We got into the elevator, a little small for three. 'I'm meeting some guys for a meeting on Upper East Side later but just need to sort a few things first.' He glanced at Sancha again. 'Do you two want to join us? Get some drinks?'

'I have a casting. Sancha's helping me with my script.'

'Oh, that's great! Today? Wow, what's it for?' I filled him in. 'Amazing work! Is that with Rebecca? She hasn't returned my call yet. Is she joining us for dinner?'

'Jonas. Not sure if she will be there.' He needed to get the hint – if Jonas or Rebecca had wanted to talk to him, they would have by now. But I also wanted him to think I was useful. The lift doors opened.

He smiled at Sancha, as he ushered her into our suite. 'You two met at drama school, right? Are you in anything at the moment?'

'Oh, I wish! I've just had a baby. But, you know... never say never.'

Greg threw his jacket onto the sofa. 'Well, I'm going to take a quick shower and leave you two to it. Break a leg, darling! I'll text you the address. See you later. Maybe we will be celebrating.' Greg beamed at us both, and disappeared into the bathroom.

'You didn't tell me he was hot!' Sancha said as she looked around the suite. 'And what a great room. He clearly has money.'

'Thanks. Glad you approve.' We settled down on the sofa to read the lines; I read Emily and Sancha read the Jack lines back to me.

The lines started to go in, like they always did. I had always been able to learn lines, right from school, and then in drama school. For some it was a drag until they could move around on the stage, getting it into the muscles, but I liked the words on the page, the patterns they created, and the space between where I could imagine the character taking shape. I ordered sandwiches from room service; nerves knotted my stomach, but I had to get something in me so I could concentrate, not let low blood sugar mess up my lines.

With an hour to go, my prep time was up. I took a shower to freshen up, get the blood flowing. My hands shook a little as I got changed into what I thought was a good look for the casting: Lululemon leggings that pulled everything in and a long grey T-shirt. Mark's sweater sat on top of my case – yes, that would be perfect. Like a warm hug from him on my way to the casting. I applied a thin layer of foundation, and painted my lips dark red. It's how I had looked at the first casting Rebecca had watched. It had worked then.

Sancha offered to go with me, keep me calm, and by the time we got to the casting room at Equity on West 46th Street, I knew I had most of the key lines and was as prepared as I could be in the time. She gave me a hug and I promised to call as soon as I'd finished.

Such a contrast to the shabby stairway in Soho where I'd been seen for *Poison*, the Equity building was so impressive – a spacious, Art Deco hallway, with a cavernous ceiling, marble floor and corridors disappearing off in all directions. It was buzzing, with two receptionists behind the welcome desk like a posh hotel, handing out neon orange clipboards to parents with young girls in tow. Spaced around the room on blue sofas, four almost-identical girls with light-brown wavy hair, waiting like pros, filling out forms, waiting to be called in. I guessed they were about nine years old. Had they decided that they wanted to act, or had the decision been made by their parents? Only one of them would get the part – I wondered how the others would cope with the rejection.

Just one other woman my age, sitting across the hall, long dark hair, earbuds in. Was she here for this too? I reported in to a receptionist, who smiled with perfect teeth, ticked something and indicated where to sit. One girl across from me, chatting happily with her mum, excited to be there, her mum leaning in to refasten a hair clip, kindly. Then a voice to my left.

'Jemima! Fancy seeing you here!'

'Neema! Wow! Amazing to see you!' I stood up, hugged Neema, our bodies brittle and unwelcoming towards each other.

'Are you here for the *Betrayal* casting, too?' I asked. If so, that surely ruined my chances.

'Yes! Just been in.' She looked a bit annoyed, then fixed a smile. 'So intense. Went OK, I think.' She had such glossy hair, so shiny. How did she get it like that? Too much make up though, for daytime.

'Oh good, well done. Do you know if they are seeing many people?'

'One before me, I think. Not sure. Who knows what they are looking for if they are seeing you and me.' I tried not to take offense – we did look completely different.

'I thought you were in London?' I asked.

'I was! But my agent got the call and, well, it's Rebecca, so here I am!' She must have heard a couple of days ago then, long before me.

'Jemima Evans?' A young guy appeared by the desk, and waved me over.

'Break a leg!' Neema called after me.

I followed him down the corridor, past film posters, adverts for Equity membership, notices about there being no place for abuse in the industry, and then we arrived at an ordinary grey office door. Neema had just been in here, and they were clearly seeing loads of people. But they wanted a Brit, right? That had to help. I'd got a part over Neema before, at RADA, so why not now.

Deep breath in, and out. Was this going to be my big break in New York? Heart banging now, I walked into the casting room.

THIRTY-TWO

'Ms Jemima Evans. Come on in.' Rebecca and Jonas sat on a sofa in the centre of the casting room. A film camera on a tripod dominated the space; a man, face obscured, behind it.

'Lovely to see you both! I'm so glad you called me in.' That came out well – confident, assured. *Smile, Jem.*

Rebecca was reading her iPad. I willed her to look up, to focus on me.

'I'm going to read through the lines with you. James is going to record.' Jonas held up the script in his hand, indicating he was ready for action. No chit-chat then, we were just going to get on with it. Of course, they had to treat me the same as every other candidate. Rebecca frowned at something I couldn't see, crossed her legs and sat up, looked at me, with a bored expression on her face.

'I'm ready.' I nodded at Jonas. He signalled to the camera man, and began to read the script:

'You're looking lovely.'

I replied: 'Really? Thank you. I'm glad to see you.'

'I saw Rachel the other day.'

'Did you? What did she look like?'

'She looked like you.' Jonas turned his page.

I glanced at Rebecca. Why wasn't she watching me? I tried to focus on Jonas. Say my lines like I'd practiced them with Sancha. It was different from my *Poison* part, a softer, livelier script. *Show them that you can do this part, too, Jem, show them your range.*

Then I heard a faint beep. From Rebecca's phone. I watched her as she tapped on the message. Smiled. She was reading a message. During my casting.

I stepped forward and raised my voice. *Look at me, Rebecca, listen to what I'm saying, right here in the room.*

We continued the script, I got through the lines. Maybe a bit rushed, a bit anxious, but OK. I became aware Jonas was speaking differently, not lines any more. 'That's great, thanks, Jemima! Thanks so much!' He turned to Rebecca. 'Do you want to run through anything else with Jemima, while she's here?'

Rebecca lifted her face and looked at me. At last, she looked at me properly. I *felt* her, her dark eyes studying me, her eyelashes long and thick, maybe naturally that way, I couldn't quite remember. Blinking slowly, perfectly winged eyeliner. She sighed, and let her arm drop next to her, the inner skin exposed, pale, against the dark sofa. I imagined running my fingernail along her flawless skin. Or biting it, like a vampire. *For god's sake, concentrate, Jemima.* She was smiling at me, as if reading my mind. She leaned forward.

'I wasn't convinced by that.' She touched her lip, as if to stop herself speaking, then tapped it lightly. A large, white opal ring glinted. I remembered us at Greg's house, her hands on my face, my mouth, inside my mouth. I swallowed.

Rebecca exhaled dramatically, and turned her hand to point at me. 'She's more desperate, you understand? That's how I see her. She's running out of chances. She needs him. Far more than he needs her.' Her lips parted, and she held my gaze, challenging me. 'You need to get that across.'

'In this scene?' Jonas asked.

Rebecca glanced at him, annoyed, or perhaps more amused. 'Of course.'

'I can try it again,' I hear myself say.

Rebecca held her hand up. 'Stop. Before you try it again, I want you to think back to a time in your life when you really wanted someone. Someone important to you. But they hurt you. Let you down.' I see a faint smirk cross her face. 'Imagine how that felt. Take your time. Then say the lines again.'

I could do this, this was no worse than drama school. It was Stanislavski method. Get into the character by imagining their backstory, all that stuff. Make it personal, somehow. Was she thinking of my time at drama school? I'd told her I didn't get on with people there, when we were in Cornwall. Did she remember that? Or was she thinking of Olivia. Yes, she'd let me down.

I was reading too much into it. It was just a prompt, trying to get me to respond to the part. To act better. The image of my mother appeared in my head, shouting, screaming at me. Mark trying to make it all right. How had that felt?

I tried to say the lines again, but my voice was tight, the air restricted. *Breathe, Jemima. Act.* I said the lines again. 'I called. I wanted to see you, but you didn't return my calls.'

Was that what Rebecca wanted to hear?

'Did you?' Jonas replied, script in hand.

'You know I did. I needed to talk to you, to see you...' Was I talking to my mother? Or to Rebecca.

I stepped forward, and shouted at her, demanding her attention. 'I tried to tell you.'

She held my look, then smiled, that beautiful, confident, sexy smile, her perfect lips. 'Much better.'

I stepped back.

'You see, Jonas? It's all in the direction.'

'I do see. Well, thank you.' He glanced at Rebecca. 'Are we

done here? OK! Well, we are seeing a few other actresses for this role, but am so glad you came in today! We'll be in touch.' Jonas put his pages on his chair and held out his hand to indicate the door.

'Thank you *so* much, Jemima.' I wanted to ask more about the play, about when it would be, but it was clear my time was up. Dismissed.

I knew, deep down, that Rebecca had used me, back at Greg's house. Just another actress, one of many. Like that girl at the party. But she had wanted me for this audition, hadn't she? Maybe that meant something. That I meant something to her. This was all part of the game, wasn't it? We were using each other. Or, was it more than that?

I left Equity and rang Sancha, my hands fumbling. Her phone rang through to voicemail. Maybe she'd gone to get a coffee, I hadn't asked. We should have made a better plan. I was desperate to talk the casting through with someone. I texted Elle.

> Went ok. They're seeing others. Not sure when I'll hear anything. Let me know if you hear. x

Good. Professional. I walked into a nearby bar, ordered a glass of the cheapest red they had, and took it to a seat in the window. Was another actress now in there, having her casting with Rebecca and Jonas? Rebecca's face kept coming back into my head. I took a large sip of the wine. That was normal. The way she was with me, the way she did castings, was normal. I should have been able to deal with it better. She liked to mess with people, not just me. Maybe that's how she got the best performances out of people. I tried to slow down, make the wine last, calm my brain, read the notices on the board next to me. There were adverts for acting classes at Equity, plays, yoga classes. Lots of actors must have come in here before or after castings; I bet this bar had seen them all.

'How did it go?'

'Sorry?'

'You had a casting? We get so many actors in here.' A man, older than me, apron tied round his waist.

'I did. You guessed right.'

'I'm an actor, too. This just keeps me going between jobs.' Of course he was. He did have a strong look, good cheekbones. Maybe he'd be great in a daytime drama, a soap, or something like that. Or maybe it was too late for him.

'I used to work in a coffee van. Done my time.'

'You're a Brit? My second one today! You're a long way from home.'

'Yep. In no rush to get back.' It must have been Neema in here before her casting. It was the perfect place to wait. Sweet guy. Would he make it as an actor? Who knew.

I checked my phone – no message from Sancha yet. But a text from Greg with a link to the bar he was in.

Bar Centrale looked like the Cheers bar on their website, a brownstone building, with a green and gold awning outside. Right in the heart of theatreland, it looked a bit touristy. About half an hour away. That was exactly what I needed. *Go out with Greg. Drink. Take your mind off the casting. Stupid acting.*

One issue – I was dressed in leggings, and looking at the photos on the bar homepage, New York women liked to dress up at night. It would take ages to get back to the hotel, and if they were already all sitting there, getting stuck into the martinis, I didn't want to wait.

'Excuse me? Are there any good clothes shops near here? Not expensive though,' I asked the bar guy.

'If you turn left out of here, there are a few places you could try. The usual places, Brandy Melville, that sort of thing. Sally's store is cool. Mix of vintage, her own stuff.'

'Sally's sounds great. Thanks so much.' I left $5 under my glass, to show that I wasn't just like all the other out-of-work actors, and left him to his cleaning. I didn't want to think how empty my bank account was.

Angel Vintage, tucked between a skateboard shop and a health food place, was thrift heaven – cocktail dresses, fur coats, leather jackets, shoes and piles of jeans arranged in order of fade.

'Hi there!' A woman, called over from behind the counter, probably Sally.

'Hi. I need a dress, for drinks. Not too flash. Or expensive. Any ideas?'

'To wear now?' She walked towards me, checked me out. 'You're a six, am I right? We need to go up for vintage though.' Her voice, deep, would be a good singer. 'Don't have that much, but there is something.'

She came back with a vintage black dress, the only decorative detail a thin, gold belt. It had a 70s vibe, and I felt the nylon crackle as I pulled it over my hair. Sally passed some black ankle boots under the curtain. A little tight, but they looked good with the dress, and would do for one night.

'You and that dress are so right for each other! I knew it. Gorgeous.' I held out my card to the machine, and was relieved when the $45 went through.

Standing outside, I tried to work out which subway station would get me there fastest. It would be cheap, but the subway map didn't make sense – nothing seemed to go where I wanted. A cab would be much easier, but the traffic stretched out in both directions, grid-locked. Which way did I need to go? Which side of the road did I need to stand on to hail a cab?

And then there she is. Arm out, yellow cab pulling in next to her.

I could call out, make it look natural, like I was just on my way somewhere. Oh, what if she thought I had been waiting for her? But this is my chance to talk to her, just us. I found myself walking fast, against the flow of people.

'Jemima.' Rebecca turned; it was as if she had sensed me near her. Her beautiful cream coat, almost touching the grimy New York street.

'Hi! I was just walking to the subway. You going home?' I sounded breathless.

'My apartment.' She looked amused. 'You got changed. Going somewhere nice?'

I glanced down at my dress. Wished I'd left my old clothes in the shop, and wasn't standing here with a plastic bag in my hand, stuffed with shoes and leggings.

'I'm meeting a friend. Greg. You know him of course! From Cornwall.' I sounded like an idiot.

Rebecca smiled. 'How lovely. Well, the dress looks good. I am sure he will appreciate it.' She opened the cab door, stepped forward.

'You could come?' I blurted out. 'See Greg, too? He would love that.'

The driver lowered the window, asked 'Where to?'

Rebecca looked at me. 'How lovely of you to offer.'

She stepped inside the car, then leaned out towards me. 'Let's discuss in the car.'

Moments later, we were moving, easing out into the flow of traffic, as I tucked the plastic bag under my legs, trying to make it disappear.

'You should have worn that dress to the casting. It suits you.' I looked down at my legs and saw how, when sitting down, the dress had crept up, and I tugged at it, trying to cover my bare thighs.

'Don't be shy, Jemima. I've seen it all before.' Rebecca looked out of the window, where lights were starting to come on, in bar windows, shop fronts, New York looking so alive, so busy.

OK, Jem, you wanted this. You got in the damn car. Say something. 'I don't feel I've spoken to you properly. Since Greg's. And at your party, you left...'

'Oh, yes.' I could see a faint smile appear.

What was I trying to achieve here? I nodded, as if replying to her, though not sure at what, or what I wanted out of this. Just try to find a connection of some kind. Now it was just the two of us.

'Greg's been trying to get hold of you.' I said, stupidly. They were old friends; why was I getting involved? It was an in, of some kind, at least.

'I'm sure he has.' She didn't give me much to go on.

'So, you finished the castings?' Sounded like I was fishing, trying to find out how many actors they were seeing. I had only meant it in a friendly way, trying to make conversation.

Rebecca turned to me, her eyes flashing with something I couldn't quite make out. Darker than I remember. She crossed her legs, her foot pointing towards me. Narrow boots that looked so new and expensive. Mine, by contrast, clearly old and cheap.

'Where are you meeting Greg?

'Bar Centrale. You know it?'

She nodded. 'My apartment is on the way. I need to go home first. It's been a very long day.'

Her apartment. The traffic hum and buzz retreated into the background, and I felt my heart thudding in my head. This was it, wasn't it. I could go to the bar, say thanks for the lift...

'OK,' I heard myself say.

Rebecca's apartment in Hell's Kitchen was homelier than I expected. Stripped wood floors, high ceilings and a curved window that framed the tree outside. It felt cosy and lived in, intimate. Rebecca zipped off her boots, leaving them in the hallway, and walked into the narrow kitchen past a large bowl of citrus waiting to be chopped up. I couldn't imagine her cooking, but the rack of kitchen utensils hanging overhead said otherwise. 'Music' she said, and something quite mellow filled the space, female vocals, almost talking, and a low bass pulsing with her.

'Drink, Jemima?'

'Yes, please. Anything.' I hovered at the end of the kitchen island, not quite sure where to put myself. I had been allowed entry to Rebecca's home, her private space. I watched her take down two glasses from overhead, select a bottle of something clear from a silver tray, then collect ice cubes from the fridge door.

'The one thing that Americans do well. Proper ice.' She popped the ice cubes into the glasses and poured over what looked like vodka. Taking a knife from a drawer nearby, she expertly peeled two long strips of lemon, and added them to the glasses, handed one to me.

'A martini, of sorts.'

The vodka burned my throat for a moment, then I felt myself relax as the alcohol hit my bloodstream. Rebecca took a sip from her glass, and looked at me, as if paused in thought.

'You look so like her,' she said, quietly.

'Like who?'

'My first girlfriend. Roisin. Your hair...'

I didn't know what I was meant to say. I sipped more vodka. 'Oh right.'

Rebecca smiled at me, and moved a little closer. 'She was an actress, too. That's how we met.'

'At drama school?' I asked, though not sure why, just trying to make some sense of this conversation.

'University. We were in productions together. She was amazing.' Rebecca put her glass down, next to the knife. 'So, Jemima. We seem to be forever in each other's paths.'

I nodded. She took the glass from my hand, placed it next to hers on the counter. Mine was almost empty, hers still full.

'I assume the reason we are here is you want the part in *Betrayal*.' She raised her eyebrows at me, and I saw her dark eyes flash with something – playful, but also slightly unnerving.

'I just thought you might want to come for a drink... with Greg...'

She smiled. 'Maybe yes, you did. Yet here we are. Just the two of us. Again.' She took my hand and we walked over to a large sofa near the window, piled with cushions, expensive, artfully arranged.

'You actresses are all the same, really. I respect that. Really I do. Your ambition. Your drive.'

Sitting beside her, I became aware that the room was cold, and I could see the tiny hairs on my thighs rise in an attempt to keep me warm.

'It's just been so weird, after *Poison*. All that happened... there.' I didn't want to say Olivia, to bring her name into this, but surely that connected us, so much had happened, in the time I had known Rebecca. I didn't know where to start. It seemed safer somehow, to talk about work. 'I just really want this, you know?'

'Yes. And you are all so beholden to producers, directors, casting agents... so much competition. I could never do it.' Rebecca reached towards me, and ran her hand through my hair, gently tucking it behind my ear. She moved her hand towards my neck, where she wrapped her palm around it, the warmth of her hand covering the cold I felt there.

'It's tough, yes.'

Rebecca placed her other hand on my leg, and moved slowly to just underneath the edge of my skirt. 'Your skin is the same. So pale. Almost blue in places.'

I could feel her watching me, studying me. What the hell

was I doing here? Greg would be sitting in the Bar Centrale, perhaps wondering where I was, if I was joining him for a drink.

Greg's house in Cornwall appeared in my mind, me and Rebecca in the dark there, on the floor as the moonlight lit our bodies. Did I want that again? My body started to respond to her touch, to her hand on my leg, but my instincts were that this was a bad idea. A very bad idea.

Olivia. Something had happened between them, surely, hadn't it? After the press event at the Arcola, but before that, probably, too. At my castings, Rebecca had clearly been messing with me, playing with me. Was that what she did, to get the best performance out of an actor? Maybe just for her own kicks. I wasn't sure I could tell any more.

And the way Rebecca had left that party with the other actress. Just suiting herself, not thinking of me in any way. But this was my chance, right? It was now just us two here. Maybe, just maybe, this was how I got the part in *Betrayal*. We had a connection between us, something that kept bringing us together. And that was it – I reminded her of her first girlfriend. That meant something.

The lines from the play repeated in my mind:

I think of you sometimes. I saw her the other day... She looked like you.

I reminded her of her first girlfriend and that was why she wanted me. It made total sense.

'I've always enjoyed watching you. Looking at you... so talented...' Rebecca murmured.

And then she was on top of me, pressing down hard onto my body, her hand inside my thighs, reaching there, touching me, kissing my neck, and my body responding, or acting, though my mind was elsewhere, watching from above. I heard a tear, a rip, as the shoulder of my dress pulled against my neck, and the seam must have torn, stupid vintage dress, so cheap.

I could see the cushions on the sofa opposite, each one slightly different from the other, but also so similar, each one lined up, one after the other.

I could smell Rebecca, her head buried into my neck, her hair against my cheek, something quite heavy, a rich, musky perfume, too strong, right in my face. I tried to push her down away from me, to give me more space to breathe. A sharp pain in my shoulder, then breast – she was biting me, leaving her mark.

Afterwards, Rebecca stood up and smoothed her hair back into position. She leaned towards me, and pulled my skirt back down, clumsily, covering one leg but not the other. I tried to make the torn shoulder of my dress meet again, but it couldn't.

'What time is Greg expecting you?' she asked brightly.

I sat up, tried to talk normally. 'Soon I think. I should go.'

'Can I call you a cab? Though it's probably quicker to just wait on the street, get one outside.' She walked briskly to the doorway, and stood there, as if ready to point me towards the exit.

'Are you coming?' I said, some strange part of me trying to make this all normal in some way.

'I don't think so. But thank you for the invitation. I have so much to do. Do say hi to Greg for me.'

I stood up, walked towards her and the door. Tried to smile. 'When do you think you will decide? About *Betrayal*?' Some part of me died, asking that question. But I had to know.

'Oh, we've pretty much decided! It's very exciting.' I watched as Rebecca placed cushions carefully back on the sofa. 'Obviously I can't say too much right now. Jonas needs to talk to the agents, get the paperwork sorted out. But I think you will be delighted, that's all I can say right now.'

She walked towards me, and kissed me on the cheek, almost gently, tenderly. 'Can I lend you a jacket? Cover that shoulder?' I glanced down at my dress and saw the tear. I couldn't go to the bar looking like this. I stood there, stupid, and then Rebecca returned, with a tiny black leather jacket, butter-soft, clearly expensive. I pulled it on, it fit me perfectly.

'It looks right on you. But return it to me sometime.'

Traffic had built up and it took ages to make my way to Bar Centrale, the cab crawling through the Manhattan rush hour, but I was grateful for the slow progress, as I tried to pin the shoulder of my dress together. Staring out at the theatre lights, dazzling in the early evening light, reflecting on the cars and pavements outside, helped to calm my spiralling brain.

Should I text Sancha? Could I tell her about this, about what had just happened? I pulled out my compact and checked my face in the mirror. I wiped the smudges of mascara from under my eyes, which helped, and applied more lipstick. *Stop shaking, hands.*

I stroked my face with the little powder sponge, and watched the red blotches on my skin fade away. *Focus on now, Jem. Look out of the window*. Queues were forming outside the theatres. So many people, each with their busy lives, each the main character in their own screenplay. Was I the star in mine? Or just the side character in Rebecca's. Maybe, just maybe, the connection we had would lead to something. To the part in *Betrayal*, to me making it in this world. It felt like my best chance, my best roll of the dice. I exhaled. Her hands on my neck, so demanding of my body. I tried to shake the image from my mind. *Look out at the theatres, Jem. Those places full of imagination and storytelling, where anything is possible.* The giant Harry Potter nest! Attached to the front of the Lyric – such a magical sight, who wouldn't want to curl up inside there and fall asleep? It had the longest queue, snaking around the building and crowding the pavement with families. The Art Deco lights of the Minskoff illuminated huge banners for *Dear Evan Hansen*. If Sancha had been with me, we might have stopped the cab, got out and tried for standby at one of the shows. The cab crawled to a stop at traffic lights, and a wave of people swarmed in front and behind us to get to their show. So many people! If we had driven forward, we would have crushed them – didn't they care?

The traffic lights changed and we surged forward. The driver turned sharply left out of the busy lane of traffic into a quieter road, passing the Samuel J Friedman Theatre, the billboard showing *The Height of the Storm*, photos of the actors blown up large in black and white, looking down on the people walking below. Behind all those fancy facades, actors were getting ready to perform, running through their warm-up, getting into costume. Directors might be giving notes, telling them what they could do to make the play sharper, a better pace. Stage managers would be checking that the backstage crew were in position, that front-of-house were by the main doors, piles of programmes ready to be sold, bars stocked with fresh ice.

I so desperately wanted to be part of it; I wanted to be on the *inside*, not out here, driving past. The actors inside all these theatres might be nervous, wired on adrenalin, but they wanted to be there more than anywhere in the world. They were the lucky ones.

There was a long queue outside Bar Centrale, contained behind a red rope barrier, with two doormen lording it up over the people at the front. If I joined the queue, it would take ages to get in, and I'd stand there looking basic, on my own. What would Sancha do? Or Rebecca. *Act confident.* I strode right up to the entrance, ignoring the irritated 'Hey, lady!' from a man near the front of the line. The doorman looked me up and down, nodded and stepped aside to let me walk straight in. *Smashed it.* It was all about how you appeared, not how you felt inside.

Loud jazz escorted me down the red-carpet steps into a basement, passing framed prints of Broadway shows and plays, photos of famous actors from years before. It was heaving downstairs, so buzzing, people crowded into the space, trying to push through, to wherever they were going.

'Can I help you?' A woman looked at her screen.

'I'm with Greg Trelawney,' I stated, an unexpected posh British accent coming out. She nodded and I followed her into the noise. Greg was easy to spot, so tall, his floppy hair in the centre of a green leather booth near the centre of the room. He looked relaxed, animated. Two men were with him, both oozing wealth and confidence – they must have tipped really well to get this table. And then I saw her. Laughing, squeezed right next to Greg, leaning into him to show how much she loved what he was saying. Sancha.

'Hello, everyone,' I said, not sure if anyone could hear me above the music, but saying it anyway. Sancha looked up at me with a start, a moment of indecision flickered across her face, then her face broke out into her usual radiant smile and she stood up, squeezing past Greg to get to me, and she pulled me into a flamboyant hug.

'You made it! Greg, move up. Guys, this is Jemima. Who we were telling you about.' The two men stood up to welcome me, their American manners immaculate. Greg patted the space next to him, put up his hand to call over a waiter.

Sancha called out to her, 'We need another glass.'

'And more Champagne,' Greg added as I slid into the booth,

Sancha going before me. Five of us, too many for the space, our thighs all pressed together, with Sancha in the middle. I felt my dress slide up as I moved along, and I tried to pull it down again, awkwardly banging my elbow into one of the men. I had a strong sense that I had disrupted their perfect set-up.

'Jemima, these two legends are Eric and Theo. Netflix. Old friends of Greg's,' Sancha said. Theo, next to me, kissed me on the cheek, lips a little too moist.

'How was the casting?' Sancha then explained to the group, without giving me time to reply, 'Jem just had a casting for a Sheridan play.'

'Sheridan Productions – impressive. What play?' That was Eric.

'*The Betrayal*. Over at the Jacobs Theatre.' Greg had been doing his homework. He handed me a glass of Champagne, and I took a sip. He turned to fill Sancha's glass, his arm running along the back of the booth behind her neck.

'Oh, amazing. We love Rebecca – we've been trying to work with her for years.'

'I think she's more theatre. Broadway. No time for us reprobates in television.' Eric smiled, relaxed. It was far more profitable at Netflix, and we all knew it.

'I thought we were meeting after the casting?' I whispered to Sancha.

She looked around the table briefly before replying: 'I'm sorry – I didn't know how long you were going to be. Greg messaged me. Thought might as well wait here for you.' When did Greg get her number?

'Yes, yes! Wise. Sorry to leave you hanging around.'

'You got changed?' Sancha asked. 'Not seen that dress before. Nice jacket.'

'How did it go, Jem?' Greg asked, leaning across Sancha to talk to me.

'Hard to know. Rebecca doesn't give much away.'

'She was there?' He looked interested. 'That has to be a promising sign.'

I almost said, 'Rebecca says hi,' but then stopped myself.

'I'm sure they loved you,' Sancha added brightly. She raised her glass. 'To Jem and may she get the part she so deserves.' The men joined in the toast. I could see the people in the booth behind us look over, wondering if we were famous, if they knew any of us from somewhere.

No. Not yet, but watch this space.

'Neema was there,' I whispered to Sancha. That felt like safer territory.

'Was she? She didn't say...'

'On WhatsApp? I guess she wouldn't, just in case she didn't get it.'

Sancha looked lost in thought, then rallied. 'Well, she is tough competition.'

I nodded.

'Maybe I should text her, get her to join us.' Sancha got her phone out.

'God, don't!' The thought of Neema here was too much. I could still remember how she made me feel at drama school, me on the outside. Let her be in that position for a change. It was me and Sancha here with Greg and his Netflix friends, not her.

'No, of course not.' Sancha nodded.

I drank, trying to forget my time in Rebecca's apartment, as the men told stories of huge budgets, actors they'd hung out with, their student days, which Sancha loved, beaming at them, laughing at their stories. I played my part, smiling in the right places, laughing at jokes when needed, but mostly I watched Sancha as she worked the table. She always had the ability to charm people; she had that knack of saying the things people wanted to hear without it sounding fake or gushing – an easy confidence that made people feel that they were in exactly the right place, with the best people, where things were happening.

I needed to absorb this, learn this skill. If I was going to make it in this industry, then I needed what she had. If I got this part, I would be here, in New York.

That easy confidence, that likeability. How did she do it? She was alert, shining eyes. She'd lean in to listen, smile widely, and then bring the conversation back to her, but careful to include others. 'Greg, I haven't had the chance to tell you about...' Even me at times. 'Jem, do you remember when we did *Lear*? A complete nightmare. I didn't understand a word! Jem was fabulous, weren't you?' I laughed along, half nodded – impossible to say anything back to that really, without sounding arrogant, me the swot, her the easy-going, relaxed one in that story.

And very beautiful in her top with skinny straps that almost threatened to slip down when she leaned towards Greg, but didn't quite. There was no mention of her baby, her life, all the real stuff. That was all far away, a parallel life on hold for the evening.

'You must be roasting in that jacket. They have a cloak-room,' Sancha whispered to me.

'I'm fine,' I lied, though I could feel the sweat pooling in my back.

No-one seemed to be bothered about ordering food and as the glasses were refilled, I felt exhaustion swim over me and the edges of the evening disappear. Could I tell Sancha about what happened with Rebecca? Some deep part of me knew the answer was no. She wouldn't understand. Chances would come her way, just as she is. She didn't need to sleep her way to the top.

I looked over at Greg. If I hadn't gone home with him from the Understudy bar, I wouldn't be sitting here in New York. That was the right call, that night. It's all about taking your chances, isn't it? I reached for the bottle of Champagne, refilled my glass and drank it down, feeling the liquid soothe my thoughts. We had very different options, and different paths to take, Sancha and I.

At some point Eric and Theo wanted to move on, and Greg made a big show about how he missed having a driver, and Theo laughed, said that he had a driver, not to worry, and made a call. I stood up, the room so loud, blurry. I fell against the squeaky leather of the booth.

'Steady! You OK?' The room tilted gently behind Sancha. She took my arm. 'Greg, I think Jem has had a long day. Do you need to get back to the hotel, sweetheart?' How much had I drunk? Too much, again.

Moments later, we are all outside, next to the red rope, where the queue of people waiting to get in had grown even longer. 'My car is almost here,' Theo said.

'Listen, Jem. I think we're going to carry on with these guys. The car will take you to the hotel. You get some rest. OK?' Greg spoke to me slowly, clearly, as if I was a young kid, or stupid. 'You look exhausted.'

A car with blacked-out windows pulled up, and then Theo was telling me his driver would drop me back at the hotel, and it was no bother at all. Sancha stood on the pavement watching, while Greg helped me get into the back, clumsily. I felt his hand just near where Rebecca had bitten my neck, sore, a little tender. Then Theo was talking to the driver, and Greg was shutting the door and I could see Sancha and Greg turn towards each other, talking, Greg taking her arm, ready to go somewhere else, as the car pulled away silently.

THIRTY-THREE

BEFORE

Mark was waiting for me on the front deck of Seagrass. I loved being able to hang out with him in London. St Pancras wasn't far from my student room, and it was so perfect – both of us in London! Far away from Bristol, and Mum, and all that we had left behind.

Daniel came out with delicious wine – expensive, probably, knowing him. Mark watched us talking, happy that his two favourite people were getting along. It was a rare balmy, perfect summer evening, and the water sparkled around us. The sound of happy people chatting, laughing, walking along the canal banks.

'Gemma. I...' Mark looked worried. 'We've got news to share with you. It's an amazing opportunity. I wanted... we *both* wanted... to tell you first.'

Mark said that Daniel had been offered a great job in Australia, starting up a new office for his company in Sydney. Daniel was now talking, filling in all the details. He was so excited about it. Mark wouldn't be able to get a work visa straightaway, but Daniel could support him while he figured something out. Daniel looked from me to Mark, and then realised that I hadn't said anything.

'I'll get some snacks. Leave you two for a mo.'

'Are you OK with this, Gem?'

I couldn't look at Mark. I focused on the water instead, the dead leaves gathering against the edge of the boat.

'Gemma. Talk to me. I can only do this if you are OK with it...'

I thought of that fourteen-year old boy in the bunk above me. How he'd dreamed of places like Australia – somewhere sunny, beautiful. The soaps we'd watched, where their lives were so perfect, full of good people, leading happy lives. The thought of him being so far away... I felt like throwing up over the side. I gripped the railing, tried to steady myself.

'Come out and stay at Christmas. We'll pay.'

'That's ages away.' I knew I sounded panicky. I tried to keep my feelings, my growing anger, under control. Feelings of fury at Daniel rose up, made my breath shallow. I fought back my tears. How dare he take my brother away? And how dare Mark let him, too? If he left me, I had no-one.

Mark moved closer to me, rested his hand on mine. 'Listen, kiddo. We haven't had it easy, you and me. But life is out there! You've got drama school, your talent, and, well, maybe this is my chance. Daniel's one of the good ones, he'll look after me, and if not... well, I'll come back. It's time we both lived. Took our opportunities. But I can't do this if you won't be OK...'

I knew then that I had to say the right thing. Summoning my best acting skills, I turned to him, my brother, my best friend in the world, and said, 'I'm happy for you. You deserve this. I'll be completely fine.'

Mark sent me photos almost daily from Sydney, and it looked amazing. Blue skies, stunning views, waterside brunches with groups of good-looking men, all sun-kissed. I could hardly bear to look at them. Why would he ever want to come back from all that?

They asked me to live on Seagrass while they were away, and it suited me. Daniel didn't ask for any rent – 'just look after her for me'. I knew he felt guilty about taking Mark away, and maybe it made him feel better, giving me somewhere to live. Working at the coffee van brought in enough cash to pay for food and tube fares. It was kind of Daniel to let me live on his boat, I knew that deep down. But I couldn't forgive him for taking Mark.

I barely recognised Daniel's voice when he rang me, early one afternoon, when I had just finished a movement workshop at college. He sounded so far away, so distant, so strange. I remember standing outside RADA on Malet Street, facing the student union of the university opposite. A woman, about my age, with dark hair dyed blue at the ends, was waiting for someone. They arrived for her – her parents? Sensible coats and shoes for walking around London, delighted to see their daughter, probably about to take her out for dinner somewhere, to hear all about how she was getting on. She didn't even look that pleased to see them as they hugged her.

I knew Daniel was talking, but I couldn't take it in. A crash? A car crash? Daniel was repeating himself, trying to make me listen. But it didn't make sense. And then it hit me with a sickening rush of hot blood. Mark was dead.

Mark was dead? No, that wasn't right. Daniel was speaking again, telling me that Mark had been in a car. Then he was crying and I couldn't understand what he was saying. There was a young woman. And now Daniel was in a hospital for some reason. But why?

I felt the ground dissolve beneath my feet and I slid to the pavement, my hand trying to grip the step behind me. All I could take in was that Mark was gone. Somewhere, miles away across the ocean, he was gone. My wonderful, kind, caring brother – obliterated, leaving a terrible gap that would never be filled.

I looked at the family now walking away, all together. Arms around each other, the daughter between the parents. She had no idea what she had.

I looked at the phone in my hand. Now I understood. I was on my own now. Completely on my own.

THIRTY-FOUR

NOW

Greg wasn't in the room when I woke up, my head pounding, sun streaming in. I drank a glass of stale water from his side of the bed. No messages from Sancha or Greg. Where had Greg slept? I rang down to reception, and breakfast arrived ten minutes later. I drank coffee, ate carbs and tried to think. He must be with Sancha. No, more likely staying with one of his friends, couldn't be bothered to travel over the river, too far. Maybe all four had gone to Sancha's apartment, carried on drinking, he'd crashed over, they were all still asleep, though it was late morning. Was I meant to feel jealous? What did I want from Greg, anyway? He had more than served a purpose – he'd got me here. Got me away from London. He could have come in the car with me back to the hotel, but he'd chosen not to. He preferred Sancha, who wouldn't... Her confidence, her way with those men. She was much better at all that than I was, the charm, the making people feel good. If anything, I realised, what I felt was relief. I was used to having to do things myself, alone.

I stretched out in the vast bed. Maybe it was going to be OK. Here I was in New York. I'd been to a casting with one of the world's top producers. If I did get the play, I was sorted, could rent somewhere, stay here in New York. Maybe Sheridan Productions arranged that sort of thing for their actors, so I could be near the theatre at all times. Elle would help me sort it all out. My mind was spinning, working hard. Maybe Rebecca would choose me for *Betrayal* – she'd chosen me for *Poison* after all. It was her style to be cool, not show Jonas what I meant to her, surely. It was all so close I could taste it. If I *did* get the play... just one phone call could make my whole future change. Me, here, in New York, making it *at last*. I just had to keep things moving along until they made a decision.

I texted Sancha.

Morning. Great night! You ok?

I thought about calling Elle to see if any news, but it was too soon. She would tell me if there was news. I just needed to stay busy. Stay on side with Greg, stay in this hotel as long as possible, save money where I could. No reply from Sancha yet. I knew I needed to get out of this hotel room, walk, clear my head, make some plans. Plans that would work for *me*.

Anyone who trained at RADA has heard of Julliard. I was curious to see the world-famous drama school that had turned out stars like Adam Driver and Jessica Chastain. Messios told us in Year 1 that students could swap with someone at Juilliard, do a year in New York, which sounded incredible – the chance to train on Broadway! But the cost was terrifying and I hadn't applied.

Standing outside, you wouldn't know it was a drama school. Modern, loads of glass, it looked more like an office block used by some IT company. The only clue to what was inside were the beautiful people hanging around: Lycra legs, great cheekbones, so confident in their right to be there. Two women, deep in conversation, I tagged behind them closely and followed through the slow-closing security gate, and found myself in a vast, light-filled atrium, with colourful sofas filled with people. So much activity and purpose! Everyone had somewhere to be, or someone to talk to. I joined the queue for coffee, for something to do, and tried to take it all in. TV screens showed the room names where lectures were happening, classes in 'Classical Ballet 1' and showtimes for a play that was on that evening. Swisher, more impressive than RADA, it was typically American – bigger and richer.

I took my coffee out to a grass slope overlooking a concrete pond – if that had been in London it would have had rubbish floating in it – and chose a spot among the clusters of students. I pretty much blended in; possibly a student, maybe even a lecturer. A muscley man in shorts sat with his legs splayed out almost in box splits, his friend reading from what looked like a script. They all had so much confidence, so much presence.

One pale, skeletal woman sat with her headphones on, ignoring those around her, or being ignored? That was more like me during my student days. Trying to look like she didn't care.

All this talent around me, every single one of these people wanted to make it in the performing world. So many new faces, full of talent and enthusiasm... Would they stay so friendly with each other when they found themselves up against each other at castings? Would box-split man still be so happy when his mate got the part in the Broadway musical and he didn't? Did Julliard train students how to cope with failure, to handle rejection, or was that not the message they wanted to convey – it was success at all costs.

I had beaten hundreds of others to get into RADA, just like the people here had to get into Juilliard. New blood being churned out each year, ready to take my place. Two women walked past and found a space on the lawn just in front of me, choosing a rare sunny patch. One threw her jacket on the grass and they both sat on it, close together. Like we used to.

You alive?

I texted Sancha again.

Shall I come to you? Check out the apartment?!

Was she ignoring me? The two friends in front of me were laughing, looking at something on a phone. So close. Dots appeared on my phone. Sancha was replying.

Just got up! Sure! Bring food.

THIRTY-FIVE

BEFORE

'The fees are overdue, Jemima. Can you make an appointment with the bursar to make a plan? There are schemes that can help.' The email from Messios was kind enough, I guess, but did he really think I hadn't already tried everything? £6,000 was nothing to them, nothing. I bet one of their former students, a famous one, earned that in one day on a film – they should pay it back, to help people like me out. I'd asked the bursar. I had told him about my brother, how he used to pay some of the fees, and he was gone.

He tilted his head to one side, didn't ask for details. Suggested I get a job. Like I hadn't already! The coffee van shifts barely covered food and basics – it didn't get anywhere close to paying fees. Rehearsals were every night in term time; when was I meant to work more? He had no idea – everyone else here had parents who just transferred the money. He said I could apply for a hardship grant for next year, but this year's fees needed to be paid. Sorry.

There was no way Mum would have that sort of money. Could Daniel help? We'd barely spoken since my brother died.

I left the room, fighting back tears. I couldn't drop out, that was unthinkable.

Actors didn't usually hang out with the people from the production course. Mostly because we were always rehearsing, but the truth was the other acting students didn't think they were important. I didn't like treating people like that. Ed was leaving at the same time I was, and we joked about getting stuck in the door. He said he was going for a drink with his friends, did I want to come along? And I said yes, because I didn't want to be the asshole acting student who didn't hang out with production.

On the way to the pub, Ed told me he wanted to be a director, and thought this was a way in. He had a part-time job at one of the West End theatres, helping backstage doing something, because RADA didn't expect them to work every night. I told him I wished I could do that, I was so broke.

He bought the drinks that night. There were others there at the beginning, but they eventually drifted off, or had it been really late? I couldn't remember. I told him I might need to leave RADA.

'You can't! You're so talented!' He looked genuinely horrified at the thought.

'I'm behind on the fees. Just a term. It's so humiliating.'

'Can't your parents help?'

I shook my head. 'Don't have those sorts of parents.'

'This industry is so shit. It's only for the rich people, really. Who else can afford it? It's not like you're even guaranteed work at the end of it!'

I agreed, felt heard. He was so like me. Not like most of the acting students.

We walked towards the station together. I felt light-headed, relaxed, all that wine, not enough food.

'Stay at mine, if you like? It's near.'

I'd asked for it in a way, hadn't I? I barely knew him and I was here in his flat. At home, he seemed different, somehow. The kindness he'd shown me in the pub, the understanding, seemed to ebb away, and he looked sharper, more focused. His flatmate wasn't there – away for the weekend. We were so close to RADA. It had been easier to stay here than go back to Seagrass, and I felt so sleepy, woozy even. Exhausted from it all. I wanted to sleep, to lie on the sofa, curl up, rest.

After a while, I felt him on top of me but wasn't sure how he had got there. I'd been lying on the sofa, and then he was next to me, on top of me. He pulled at his belt, grunting as he shifted his weight onto one arm, fumbled at his zip. I felt the cool air on my skin. Was that my leg, why wasn't I wearing my dress? No, I was... my dress was tight, bunched up around my chest, where he must have pushed it up. His hand was inside my bra, the elastic strap digging into my shoulder. I couldn't move, my arms dead beside me, his body pinning me down. I was sure someone said 'no' – had it been me? The voice sounded so far away and weak. His face, buried in my neck – a sour smell, sweat – and him pushing, and entering me, and I felt sick and distant, like I was watching.

I woke up and Ed wasn't there. I felt hungover, woozy. Aching. Sitting up, the flat was eerily quiet. I drank some water and started to pull on my clothes. I really wanted to get home. And then it hit me. A dull ache between my legs. Ed had raped me.

'Someone likes you.' Sancha grinned at me. It was the next day, and we were putting our costumes in the bin dump after our dress rehearsal. Ed was standing in the corridor, watching. Was he waiting for me?

'There's always a fan.' I grimaced. Should I tell her? I didn't want to relive it.

'Get used to it!' Sancha's phone rang and she indicated that she would see me outside.

Ed took his moment. 'Hey, that was amazing! It's really coming together.'

I glanced around. We were the only two left in the corridor.

He continued, 'Do you want to come for a drink? Or are you meeting the other actors? They left earlier. Not sure where they're going.'

'They're waiting for me.' I pulled on my coat, made it clear I was leaving.

'Come back to mine instead. Pick up where we left off?' He took a step closer to me, briefly looked around.

'I don't think—'

'Did you get the money OK?'

I must have looked confused.

'I sent you some money. You said you needed it.'

What?

'I don't understand.'

'Your bag was on the floor. It was easy. I transferred you some money... for your fees.'

He went through my bag? When I was crashed out on his sofa.

'Think of it as a loan. You can pay me back when you get famous, right?'

I fumbled my phone and clicked on the bank app. Usually the numbers showed in red. There it was, £1,000. He'd sent me £1,000. It wouldn't cover all my fees, but it could buy me some time. *No, that's insanity.*

'I'm sending it back.' I tried to work out how, what button to press, but my hands shook. I looked down the corridor to where Sancha had gone.

'Ah, but you don't want to.' Ed took a step towards me,

placed his hand on the wall, just behind my head. 'Keep it, Jem.' He smirked at me. 'It's a lot of money for one night, though. We could make this a regular thing...'

He looked around him. 'How about now? I've always wanted to see inside there.' He glanced at the women's dressing room.

And then he was pulling my arm, trying to get me inside, which I knew was empty, soundproof, and no-one was due back here tonight as class was long over.

'No!' With a surge of strength, I was clear, running down the corridor. Pushing the heavy door, I was outside, my pulse racing, people walking past on the busy London street, where anyone could see us and he would leave me alone.

THIRTY-SIX

NOW

Sancha was staying in one of those brownstone buildings with wide stone steps up to the front door like Carrie in *Sex and the City*. She opened the door in a silk kimono covered in orange goldfish; she looked gratifyingly hungover, grey shadows under her eyes, hair flat.

'Late night?' I asked, following her up marble stairs, my hand gliding up the polished banister. The apartment opened into a grand sitting room, high ceilings, ornate fireplace. 'Wow, this is amazing.'

'Jon is paid well. God knows what he does, but it's very useful.' She picked up a coffee cup from the kitchen counter and drained it. 'Did you buy food? I feel so rough.'

I handed her the paper bag. Sancha threw herself on the sofa and pulled out a pastry. 'Thanks. Probably should be eating something carb-free, but sod it.' I glanced around the flat. There was no sign that Greg or the others had stayed here, it was so tidy, untouched.

'It's quite a change from your old flat in London.'

'What a shithole that was.' She chewed, flakes falling onto

the sofa. 'So, news... I've got a pass. I'm staying here a few more days. Jon's fine with it.'

'Oh wow! That's great. That's good of him.'

'It won't bother him at all. His mother will look after Polly. He'll barely notice I'm not there.' She glanced down at her phone.

'What time did you get in?' I asked.

'Too late. Or early, I guess! Three-ish? Those boys like to party.' Such an American phrase. She glanced up at me. 'You got back OK?'

'Yes, fine. I could get used to the driver thing. Greg didn't come back though.' I watched for her reaction. Her face gave nothing away.

'I left them to it. Must have stayed with one of the guys.' She crumpled up the paper bag and got up to go into the kitchen area. She poured out two glasses of green juice of some kind. 'Tastes disgusting but probably good for us. Rehydrate.'

So she hadn't slept with him? 'What are you doing today? We could hang out. If you're not too hungover.' We still had whole areas of New York to explore, so many places to see. I wanted to take a boat trip out to the Statue of Liberty. Anything to take my mind off the casting until I heard one way or the other.

'I've got a couple of things I need to sort out. Might need to leave the sightseeing. Is that OK? Sorry. Didn't sleep enough. Is that OK with you?

'Yes of course.' It had taken me forty minutes to get to her apartment.

'When do you think you'll hear about the play?' Sancha asked me, sipping her juice with a puckered face.

'Ah, I don't know. I guess Elle will call me, if they need to see me again. I mean, they do know me. Rebecca's chosen me for *Poison*, so maybe they won't need to see me again. They might just decide.'

'That's so true. They do know you. Yes, that will be a factor.' Sancha put her glass in the dishwasher, then reached towards me for mine. Tidying up, wanting me to go?

'While you're in the city, shall we go and see a show? Let's just go tonight and see where we can get in. Some last-minute cheap tickets,' I suggested.

'I would love that. Why don't you see what's on? I'll pay. No need to be up in the gods.'

I felt slightly offended – for all she knew, I had money from *Poison*, or from working. Though I didn't, to be fair.

'We can go halves,' I offered, hoping that it wouldn't mean paying a fortune when I would have been OK up in the circle. If she paid though, it would mean we could get better seats, in the stalls probably. Just go with it, Jem, enjoy that she has money. Anything to take my mind off waiting for news.

'Not tonight though. Tomorrow? Text me about availability, yeah? Now, I really need to get in the shower.' That was clearly my cue to leave.

I left Sancha's apartment, and walked, and kept walking past the subway station, a feeling of irritation growing inside me. It had taken me ages to get to her apartment. I could have tagged along with her today, or just hung out in the room if she had emails to do, or whatever. Maybe she just wanted to get back to bed. Was she meeting up with Greg, or one of his friends? I was spiralling. *Snap out of it. You are going to meet up soon, tomorrow, go and see a show. Don't be needy, clingy.*

Not sure what to do with myself, with a whole day ahead, there felt like too many options – I badly needed a distraction. Working with Rebecca... it would change *everything*.

I sat on a wall outside a tiny green space labelled 'community garden' and made a call.

'Elle? It's Jemima.'

'Jemima. Hello again.'

'Hi. Yes. Sorry, is it early? I wondered if you had heard anything about *Betrayal* yet?' There was a pause at the end of the line. Was everyone getting sick of me?

'I did call them for you. One of the assistants said that they are seeing a couple more people before making a decision.' She paused a while. A man walked his tiny dog into the garden.

'When they called you in, I was very hopeful. I couldn't find the casting on Spotlight, so they are only calling in people they know. That's a good thing. You were pleased with how it went, weren't you?'

'They auditioned someone from my old drama school. She must have flown over for it. Can you call them, and say I'm really interested?'

I could almost hear Elle thinking, considering what to reply at the other end of the line, thousands of miles away across the ocean. That agent thing they do where they are choosing their words carefully. That's never a good sign.

'To be honest with you, I did try calling Jonas. He didn't take my call, but then, if they are still seeing people, he won't want to get into a discussion with me. It's a big play, it makes sense for them to call in lots of actors. You've done *extremely* well to get seen for it. And, it's not a no. Don't forget that. This all takes time. It might still go your way.'

'OK, I get it.' I didn't have time to hang around in New York, waiting for more castings. Greg wouldn't stay in New York forever and I couldn't afford to stay here myself. I thought about the actor in the coffee shop. Maybe I could work there? But that felt like a failure.

'Is the Olivia thing a problem for me?' I felt I had to ask.

Maybe I really could stay with Sancha in the Hamptons and commute if I got an audition. Would Jon let me stay? Their house was massive, wasn't it?

'I'm not sure. Yes, in the short term. But working for

Rebecca does bring its benefits. It depends how it all plays out over the next few weeks. People might not connect you to that... honestly, I don't know.'

I was paying her to know. Well, ten per cent anyway.

'Elle. Do you remember when we were out on that balcony? Back in London.'

'Oh yes, of course.' She seemed relieved that I'd changed the direction of conversation.

'I got the sense that you weren't sure about Rebecca. It felt, looking back, like you were warning me? About her?'

A pause at the end of the line. 'That's a bit strong. Rebecca has a reputation, yes, not always a great one... but you've worked for her now, you got on fine. Are you worried about something?'

'Not sure.' This was my moment. 'I don't know... it makes me wonder. Her castings are just... so weird.'

Silence at the end of the line. What was my aim here?

'Has she made a move on you?' Elle asked, awkwardly – it sounded like she really didn't want to hear the answer.

'Rebecca and Olivia... there was something between them.' I thought of Rebecca on that awful night, looking for Olivia. Had anyone else known that Rebecca had left the bar and gone to look for Olivia? Abiola might have noticed, or perhaps Sarah. Sarah noticed everything. But I was the only one downstairs near the dressing rooms.

'There was something going on that night... when Olivia died. I don't know what...' I let my voice trail off, let Elle start to catch up.

'Jemima. Listen. I'm not sure exactly what you are saying. This really is best left to the police. Are you OK out there?'

Did she think I was losing it?

Elle continued. 'Be careful, mindful, who you talk to. Rebecca isn't someone you want to piss off.'

'I'm not gossiping... I didn't mean...'

'You know this industry, Jemima. Gossip travels fast.'

Silence, as we both tried to work out what to say. Then Elle spoke, a shift in tone, cheerful, professional. 'Look, I need to jump on another call. Sorry, it's so busy here. I'll be in touch if I hear anything. You can always talk to my assistant, too.'

I filled the day exploring on my own, walking for hours around Central Park, queuing for the Guggenheim, taking photos of the John Lennon memorial, though I wasn't a massive fan of the Beatles. When I got tired of walking, I checked my phone, scanned online castings. There were a lot of casting calls for music videos that didn't seem to pay very much. One for a crowd scene filming next week in Queens; they needed extras and the pay was $85 for what I knew would be a very long, boring day. What was that in pounds? £50? It was a joke; I could earn more working for Ben back at the coffee van.

I read the RADA WhatsApp group – Neema hadn't said a word about her casting, or that she was in New York. She was keeping her cards very close to her chest. So that was how they all did it – act like friends but keep casting info very quiet. Heaven forbid she would have to tell them she got rejected, didn't get a part.

I wanted another coffee but couldn't justify the stupid price, so I just sat there in the park. I needed to know *something*.

Nothing to lose. I texted Sarah. She might know what was happening with *Betrayal* – she was on the inside, after all.

Hey. How's things. I'm in New York!!

I wondered if she'd reply, and how long it would take. We hadn't been in touch since *Poison* got cancelled.

I scrolled the Sheridan Productions social media for news – there was no mention of *Betrayal* yet, no adverts, no tickets on sale.

I clicked on the link to their website and found a map showing their office location. It wasn't *that* far away. What did I have to lose?

50th Street looked like the nearest subway station to the Sheridan Productions office. It might be a total waste of time, just an admin office, but it was all I could think of to do. Maybe I could hang out in a cafe nearby and Rebecca or Jonas would come out, maybe to get lunch, if they didn't have assistants to do that, and we would chat and it would all feel quite natural, and one of them would tell me how it was going, what the delay was. I could tell them just how much I wanted this. That I would give it everything. Would they be there? I knew, in a way, that it was madness, but I didn't know what else to do. It gave me a sense of purpose, of taking matters into my own hands. Like I always had to do.

Emerging from 50th Street, it felt like being in the heart of New York. Tower blocks sky-high above me, blocking out any light, and the street heaving with traffic and people. I tried to get the map on my phone, work out which direction to go in. A man banged into me, shouted 'Stupid place to stand!' Dickhead.

I took the next right. Sheridan Productions wasn't far, just along this road, though it looked like a really long road, with numbers into the thousands. I felt a sense of purpose, exhilarated to be in this vibrant city. If I saw Rebecca or Jonas, it would make sense, they might even be pleased to see me. And there it was. Sheridan Productions. Across the road, a doorway that you wouldn't really notice if you were just walking past, on your way to the theatre, to meet friends, or wherever. Rebecca's office.

Now I was here, what *was* my plan? Should I go over there, press the buzzer and just go up? See if Rebecca would see me? Surely they had receptionists whose entire job was to keep actors out of the way, while people like Rebecca got on with important business. But she knew me. Her face when we were together in Cornwall, her hands caressing my body. I reminded her of her old girlfriend. I *wasn't* just any other actor. I looked up and down the road; maybe I should buy a coffee to take in to her, like we were old friends.

And then I saw her, walking on the other side of the road.

Sancha.

Wearing a beautiful coat I hadn't seen before, her thick hair piled on top of her head, looking gorgeous, so confident. A man, smiling, letting this dazzling person past on the pavement. I stood, rigid to the spot.

And then she saw me, standing opposite her. Frozen for a split second, she made as if to walk away, but then a woman pushing a buggy got in her way, and she stood still, as if not sure which way to go, and I found myself moving, as if floating, and then I was standing in front of her, a car sounding its horn, angry that I'd walked across the road right in front of it. Why was she here?

'Jem! What are you doing here?' Sancha stepped back away from me, but the pavement was narrow and there was nowhere to go.

'No. Why are *you* here?' I asked, my voice sounding weirdly far away, as if someone else was saying it. She looked around her.

'I've got a meeting. Sorry. I'm a bit late. I need to go.' She made to walk away.

'A meeting? Where?'

'Sheridan Productions.' She looked around again, so awkward, so eager to get away from me. To get away from *me*. Her friend. Her closest friend.

'What for? You didn't say...'

'I didn't... there was no point telling you. I didn't expect...'

Her face uncomfortable, eyes looking past me, hoping for someone to give her an excuse to get away.

'Tell me what?'

'It's just a meeting, Jem. About a potential job.'

'You could have told me that. I tell you everything.' I'd only seen her that morning. Just a few hours ago.

She laughed at that, snorted almost. Not attractive. 'Do you? Do you tell me everything? I don't think so. Going to Cornwall? Coming to New York. Hanging out with Olivia Goldsmith. Hardly, Jemima! You don't tell me anything at all.'

'I do! You know everything about me.'

'Oh, bullshit. You don't give away *anything*. Your family... your past. So mysterious. I don't know you. Not really. None of us do. Only what you choose to show.' She pulled her bag higher on her shoulder and looked along the pavement toward the office. Just a few steps away. 'It's always about you, isn't it? All about what *you* want, Jemima.'

'That's not true.' Where had this outburst come from? Her *anger* towards me.

Sancha turned and walked. I stood still, rooted to the spot, no idea what else to say.

She hovered outside the door to Sheridan Productions. 'I got the part, OK? There's no easy way to tell you. I've got a meeting with Rebecca.' A wave of cold flooded over me.

'What part?'

'It's only an understudy part. No big deal. It wasn't worth telling you because if I didn't get it you would have been pissed off with me, and for no reason.'

I was aware of a car behind me, too close.

'You're in the road, Jem. Get out of the way. You could get hurt. Look, don't make this a bigger deal than it is.'

A bus horn blared, the noise of the street, the traffic, people, loud, crashed into my head. Swirling around me. Noise, so much noise.

'My part? In *Betrayal*?' How was that even possible?

A woman, standing, staring at me. Because someone is screaming. And that person is me. 'That part was *mine*.' The woman crossed the road, to get away from me. 'That part was *mine*. You helped *me* learn the lines. You wouldn't have even known about it if it wasn't for me.'

Sancha looked around her, horrified that people were now clearly watching us, watching the scene developing.

'Calm down, Jemima. I need to go.'

I ran towards her, grabbed her arm. 'No. You knew what that part meant to me. You don't even *need* it. You have Jon, you have Polly. I have *nothing*.'

Her face, almost snarling at me. 'Well, now that's not exactly true, is it? You have Greg, or you did at least.' She looked bitter, a half-smile forming. 'If they'd wanted you for the part, you would have got it. I was right for it. Rebecca says so. It's how it goes, and you know that. It's just the business.'

'Since when did you even want to audition? I thought you didn't want to act anymore!' I shouted at her.

'When did I ever say that? I trained, too, you know. Just 'cos I've had a baby doesn't mean everything else ends. Shout at me if you like. I get it. You're disappointed, angry with me. But you *know* this business. If the part was yours, really yours, they wouldn't have seen anyone else. They saw Neema, too, right? It could have gone to her. I'm *really* good at acting – of course I still want to do it. If you were a friend to *me*, you'd know that. Support *me*.' Her face was so red, so angry, it was just pouring out of her. How long had she been holding all this in?

'I was sick of it. I was always the character part, wasn't I? The fat one. Never the leading lady. Well, not anymore. I'm sorry it hurts you, but I want this, too.' Her face softened, just for a moment. 'You'll get another part, one that's right for you.'

She had to be kidding me. I laughed then. I was meant to feel sorry for her? To support her in this?

'You tell yourself what you want, Sancha, but you know you would never had got that part if you hadn't known me. You know that.'

A man appeared, right next to me, right in my space, expecting me to move out of *his* way, when I was stood here. 'Fuck off!' I screamed at him. He scuttled away, stepping into the road to get past us.

I look back at Sancha. '*That's* why you came isn't it? That's why you came to New York? I thought you wanted to see me, but you came because you thought it would help you? You didn't want to see me at all.'

Sancha looked at me, face blank, and I realised, looking at her beautiful face, that yes, of course, that was what she had thought. This had been her plan all along, and it had all worked out perfectly, even better than hoped. She had the perfect family, the husband who supported her, who put her up in the gorgeous apartment and this had gone her way, too. And she *was* right for the part. She was the more talented one, the one who could charm anyone, get her way. Always get her way.

'You need to get over it, Jemima. It isn't personal. This business is never personal. I need this, too.'

She walked into the Sheridan Productions office, leaving me standing there, left behind.

THIRTY-SEVEN

Years of friendship, or what I thought of as friendship, over. Sancha had taken in everything I'd told her, about the part, about Jonas, Greg and Rebecca, and used the information for her own benefit. For herself.

I thought of her face outside the Sheridan Production offices, the way she'd looked at me when she'd told me. It was if she had won something, and that I was the loser.

I walked and walked, tried to think, to calm down, fighting back tears. Angry, so angry, raging at what she had done. *To me.* Skyscraper buildings around me, overwhelming, crowding in on me, telling me that I didn't fit in here, I didn't belong.

Greg was on the phone when I made it back to the hotel, hours later. I threw myself onto the bed, and lay there staring at the ceiling. Every time I thought of Sancha, anger would well up inside me, fierce hatred at what she had done to me. Betrayal in every way. I thumped the bed with my fists, the thick duvet absorbing my blows, not satisfying at all. I wanted to hurt my hands, feel the pain, get it out of my body. Hurt her. But how?

I rolled onto my front and grabbed my phone. The RADA WhatsApp group had been busy as usual. I typed:

Well done Sancha!! Getting the part in Betrayal. So PROUD of you hun!!

Within seconds there were bouncing dots from Neema as she decided what to reply. Ha! See how the group handled that one. Would Neema say that she had been up for the part? Be angry at Sancha? More dots. When was Neema going to say anything.

Josh

Amazing!! Let us know dates, I'll try and see you!

Leo

OMG! Such great news! Do you know Zawe? I'll send you her number. She'll have tips!!!

More dots from Neema. Then nothing. She was usually the most talkative on there. Her silence was deafening. Good. That meant she was angry with Sancha. I threw the phone across the bed. That would have to do for now. But it didn't feel like enough.

A reply from Sarah to my text message!

New York, how fabulous. Abiola was trying to reach you. Hope you ok. Have the police been in touch?

I rolled onto my front and typed my reply:

It must be SO early there! No. Sorry, just going into a casting!! Hope you ok too.

I put my phone in my bag, didn't want to continue that

conversation right now. A gentle knock on the door. Greg walked in, ran his hands through his hair.

'Hey, how you doing?' Was he trying to sound more American?

'Fine.'

Greg was pacing the room. 'Listen, Jemima. Oh, this is awkward...' He rubbed his head.

I sat up. 'OK.' I was listening now.

'I'll just say it – I'm not sure this is working, you and me.'

For a moment, I was lost for words. 'What do you mean?' I managed.

'I don't want to be an asshole. I mean, we get on well, don't we, you and I....' He grinned, sheepishly, reminding me of when we first met in the Understudy bar.

'I wasn't sure how long I'd be here, and now, well I'm thinking of staying a while longer. I just thought... if you have friends here, Sancha maybe, you said you knew lots of people in New York? Maybe you could stay with them? With her. I don't know.' He genuinely looked confused. Did he want me to reassure him? To tell him that I cared for him? He didn't want that surely.

No, he wanted me gone. Why? What had changed? Maybe he could see me for what I was – nothing special, another wannabe actor, just one of many. I couldn't even be angry with him, not really. Others had been far worse to me. He owed me nothing. Greg stood up, glanced at the door.

'Shall I go now?' Oh my god. I looked at my stuff, scattered around the room, clothes heaped on the chair in the corner. Where was I meant to go?

'No rush. Really. I'm expecting someone, though. I mean, in your own time... I wasn't expecting you back...'

'Who?' Did he want me out of the way?

A buzzing sound, and Greg walked to the door. 'That's her.'

I had a horrid, sinking feeling. Who was he talking about?

Sancha? Sancha had got on so well with Greg, was so confident, so great with his friends, and would fit in with his world so much more than I did. Was she coming here?

I followed him out of the bedroom, and as Greg waited for the lift doors to open, I sensed who it was immediately, her presence making itself felt. She stepped into the room, and looked around, surveying and assessing this intimate space. Rebecca walked forward and kissed Greg, her hand on his arm. 'Hello, darling.'

And then she turned her focus to me. 'Well, here we all are. How lovely to see you, Jemima. Again.' Rebecca walked towards me, her boots making a sharp tapping sound on the concrete floor. 'You look lovely, Jemima. A little tired though.' She threw her bag onto the sofa.

'I didn't know you were coming here.' I said stupidly.

Rebecca smiled. 'I doubt Greg tells you everything he gets up to.'

Greg walked over to the drinks tray, and poured two whiskeys. He handed one to Rebecca and sipped from the other. Clearly he had no plans to pour one for me. He expected me to leave.

'You gave the part to Sancha.' I knew I was on borrowed time, and I wanted answers.

Rebecca sipped her whisky. 'This is very good, Greg. American or Scottish?'

'American.' Greg looked from Rebecca to me, as if waiting for instructions.

I looked from one to the other. Both so confident in who they were, in the power they had. Greg, with his wealth, his contacts, his own *theatre*, for fuck's sake. Born into the business. Everything just handed to him, so effortless. Rebecca, with her power over others, them all so desperate to be part of her world.

People like Ed and Olivia were disposable. People like me. We meant nothing to Rebecca and Greg, and all the people in the industry exactly like them.

I was nothing to them. Nothing. Just another actress. One of so many. They had used me, enjoyed me, and now my time in their spotlight was up.

It was a small, shabby room, with a noisy air-conditioning unit right outside the window, but it was cheap, available and had a lock on the door. I dumped my stuff on the bed. That stupid Bergstrom bag, the red dress, peaking out, reminding me of how it hadn't worked out for me. The room would do until I could figure out what next. I'd been relieved when Greg's credit card had worked at reception. I'd used it to pay for room service a few days ago, and somehow it had found its way into my bag, just in case. I hadn't really planned to use it. He had so many in his wallet, I doubt he'd even notice that this one had gone. I didn't feel bad about it now. It would buy me a few days here to think, to work out what I was going to do next.

I pulled out my laptop and typed in Rebecca's and Greg's names. There were loads of articles from *The Stage*, from their individual projects over the years, but nothing really of them both together. I lay there, thinking. Had Rebecca told Greg what had happened between us, at his house? Memories of that night spun around in my mind. Is that why he had wanted me to leave? What had Rebecca said to him? She must have told him that I hadn't got the *Betrayal* part. Had Greg had any influence on that decision?

I clicked on photos of Rebecca and scrolled through, the years erasing from her face with each image going back through the years, though she always looked glossy, polished, beautiful. So many actors with her, so many famous faces she had known over the years.

I typed in Greg, Anisha and Rebecca. They had been at university, right? Something might come up. And there it was, an old photograph. Greg looked so different – so slim, hair still long, so carefree and relaxed. Being a student suited him. They looked, what, early twenties? I wouldn't have recognised Anisha – she looked plain, serious, hair scraped back. Maybe that was the role she was playing, or perhaps she just hadn't cared so much about looks back then. And in the middle of the group, Rebecca. I clicked on the photo, tried to enlarge it, which blurred it, annoyingly. She had the same confident look, challenging anyone looking at her. She looked older than the others around her, or maybe just more confident, more presence. The clothes looked like costumes, yes, it was definitely a show. Something Shakespearean? No caption but it must have been a university production, it looked amateurish, low budget. I didn't recognise the others in the photo, so they hadn't stayed in the business, but that's normal – loads of people do drama at university and don't stay with it.

Then something catches my eye. Just to the edge, crouching forward, as if about to step forward, her face makes my heart jolt. The photo is black and white, but there's something about her, something familiar. I can't see if her hair is red, but yes, she has my colouring, pale skin, freckles, a similar jaw. Is this the girlfriend Rebecca mentioned to me? I can see a resemblance. I want to take a screenshot of it and send it to Sancha, ask for her opinion – she *does* look like me, doesn't she? We do look similar. Where is she now?

And now Sancha is part of their exclusive group. She is the one they have chosen to be in *Betrayal*. Not me. If Sancha had wanted to pursue acting again, then why did she have to do it using *my* part. She knew how much I need it.

It was time for me to take back some control.

THIRTY-EIGHT

I watch Sancha bounce down the steps, and walk past, oblivious to me sitting across the street from her apartment. She looks great, so happy. I find myself following her, a distance apart. Down into the subway station, she passes through the spiral metal gate and it clangs behind her. It's heaving with people down here, roasting hot, peak commuter time, all the bodies squashed together in their coats, emitting heat. I bet she regrets not getting an Uber. I follow her on to the train and stand right at the end of the carriage. I don't need to worry about her getting off before me because I know where we we're headed – right back into the heart of theatreland.

I follow her to the theatre stage door, where only the chosen few are allowed. Rehearsals. It couldn't be more perfect.

A quick glance around as if she thought anyone would be watching her, perhaps someone hoping to get an autograph? Did she think she was famous already? Did she think she had to hide from paparazzi? Perhaps she senses that I am near.

A tall man runs to reach her as the door opens. He beams at her amazing cheekbones, a perfect face like a Ralph Lauren model. Holding the door open for Sancha, making a bit more of it than is really needed, and then they are both inside, and the door closes firmly behind them.

I walk into the foyer as if going to the box office to buy a ticket, a return for tonight's show, perhaps. Every theatre has a box office, even though most people buy tickets online. It's sweetly old-fashioned, really. Chances are the person behind the window won't bother to look as I walk past, if I look purposeful. Thin black jacket, leggings, cap, I look like I work here, so I walk straight to the door leading to the stalls, and no-one stops me.

I'm inside the auditorium – it's empty, just rows after rows of red velvet seating. Completely dark except for the ghost light on the stage. There's no-one watching me take the three steps on to the stage. I glance out at the stalls, and can imagine a packed house, the audience all watching me, waiting for me to speak my lines, to perform.

I walk into the wings. There's a clipboard on the floor, so I pick it up – it will help me look the part – and I walk backstage into the bowels of the theatre. A young woman, hair scraped back, is kneeling on the floor, separating a pile of cables like thick snakes, and she looks up at me and smiles, as if she thinks she should know who I am. Probably an intern or someone, because she carries on with what she is doing and doesn't say a word.

I go down the narrow corridor to the dressing rooms. Sancha has always liked to be early for rehearsals – she's so eager to please – so it's quiet with no-one around. Which dressing room is she in? I'm almost at the end of the corridor now, far away from the stage, which just shows how the theatre world rank understudies. But, hey, she'll get paid just sitting in her room, even if she never goes on. The money will be nothing to Sancha, but it would have been everything to me.

Ah! Here's her name on the door, written in felt tip on printer paper, and slid into the compartment. A bit tacky, Sancha. I'd have got someone to print mine, at the very least. I can hear voices, two people? Sancha. Yes, but with someone? I pause a moment. No, she's going over her lines. That's fine.

I step inside. It's a tiny room, with a mirror filling the wall opposite, a single strip of lights illuminating her face from above, casting unflattering shadows down onto her. How is she meant to get her make up right with that lighting? There is only one chair, and Sancha is sitting there, phone in her hand, and she turns when she sees me. The room reminds me of Olivia's dressing room in the Arcola.

I recognise the smell of tuberose, coming from a Jo Malone candle, or is it wild fig? Sancha always liked expensive candles; she couldn't bear the smell of chemicals, anything fake.

'What are you doing here?' she says. I close the door behind me. There's barely room for both of us in there, and I can feel every inch of the space between us. Sancha looks pale. Have I shocked her?

'I came to see you.'

'I'm working. I need to rehearse with one of the cast in a minute. I can't believe you just turned up here. Who let you in?' She sounds annoyed.

'So, how is it being the understudy?' She flinches slightly, before regaining her composure.

'I prefer alternate.' She glances at me. 'OK, understudy. But I might cover some of the midweeks. Give Zawe a break. It's a very demanding play.' She glances at the door. 'Why are you here, Jemima? Greg said he thought you'd gone back to London.'

'No. I'm still here. So, you're in touch with Greg.'

She turns to look in her mirror, pulls a powder compact out from a make up bag. I recognise it! She had the very same one when we were at RADA. We bought the same ones, I thought it was very sophisticated, padding at your nose to take away the shine. In that moment, I feel such a rush of affection for Sancha, for all that we have been to each other. I can see her hands shake a little as she takes out the little sponge, loads it with powder. She's nervous. Good.

'I need to get ready. You should have texted me.' She sighs, impatient, irritated, a little too theatrically.

'Did you sleep with Greg?' It became so clear to me in that moment that of course she had. After drinks that night. That's why he wanted me out of his hotel. Had she?

'Sod off, Jemima.'

I move to sit on the edge of the shelf in front of the mirror, close to Sancha, my thigh close to her arm. My thigh almost exactly twice the size of her arm, strange really.

She glanced at me. 'I have no interest in Greg.'

'Rebecca, then?'

She turned and looked at me, something falling into place. 'Oh, I see. *You* did. You slept with Rebecca! And it still didn't get you the part.' A half-smile crept onto her face. 'You *did* work hard for this part, didn't you? Get over it, Jem. She chose *me*. And now, you really need to go. I'm working.'

It was like I was watching a film, or a television drama, something on after 9pm, when all the children are meant to be tucked up in bed. I felt as if I was watching from somewhere high up, somewhere in the corner of the room, as if through a tiny camera lens, tracking me.

Thoughts ran through my mind, as if watching flashbacks at the start of a new episode: the two of us walking along the river by the National Theatre, the white lights in the trees above us, shining down on us, like the stars we were surely going to be. At RADA, Sancha watching me in rehearsals, smiling, encouraging – the popular, talented Sancha, who was so great that she could afford to be friends with the girl that no-one else was interested in. But she'd used me, in the end, to make her own way in this business, hadn't she?

It was so easy to place my hands around her neck. Her skin so warm and soft. My fingers strong, gripping tightly. I had got so strong now, it would be effortless, really, to crush the shouting out of Sancha. To make her stop yelling at me, to stop grabbing at me. I watched her face get redder, as if she was really angry with me, then paler, as the blood drained away, as if her heart knew that my hands were winning, no air could get to where it was so desperately needed.

I felt a strange sadness as I watched her, her eyes staring at me in disbelief. Had she trusted me, after all? That was a surprise, a little awkward. Had we ever really trusted each other? Did anyone in this business?

Sancha had everything; a beautiful daughter, a husband, a home. She hadn't needed this job like I had. She reminded me so much of Olivia. Olivia hadn't thought about me when she had taken those drugs, how it would affect her performance and ruin the play. She hadn't cared that it would ruin my opportunity, *my* big chance. She hadn't thought about her lovely, beautiful daughter, waiting for her at home. What was it with these mothers? Both Sancha and Olivia had put themselves before their children, left them to fend for themselves while they went in search of adulation. Like my own mother... unable to think of anyone but herself.

And then I looked at her, at Sancha's beautiful face. I stepped back, found myself pressed against the wall of the dressing room. I hear Sancha try and stand up, her chair scrape back, as she moves, desperate to get away from me.

'Get out...' she tries to shout.

And I realise in that moment that all my anger towards her is wrong. So wrong. Sancha isn't to blame. Not for all of it, for all my rage, my anger.

'Sorry, so sorry.' I step towards her, reach out to her. Her hands are up, forming a barrier between us.

'It's all got to me. The part. Rebecca. You getting it. It's too much.' I'm crying now, hot tears filling my eyes, spilling down my face. She's looking at me, and I can just about make out through the filmy tears, that she is trying to work out what to say.

'I wanted it. I wanted it so much...' I say, the words catching in my throat, as they leave me. 'I went to see Rebecca and she said this part was mine. Made me believe that...'

Sancha is looking at me carefully, breathing calmly, working out what to say. She leans back on her dressing table and reaches for a bottle of water. 'You got that part in *Poison*. You were hanging out at the Minack with Rebecca, Greg... I was stuck at home. Doing nothing. Nothing with my talent.'

She drinks the water, taking that moment to regain her composure. 'This isn't all about *you*, Jemima.' I see her hand is shaking slightly. She is looking at the door. For an escape? Willing me to leave?

Moments later I am outside in the corridor, stumbling along, trying to find the way I had come. Past closed doors, where actors were tucked away, one in each cell, like little wasps murmuring over their lines, ready for action. The air is so stale in here, so claustrophobic. At the end, a double red door, neon lights shouting 'Exit Stage Door'.

Then I am outside gasping for air, leaning against the wall, trying to process what I had just done, what had just happened. People looking at me, wondering who I am. Look away, people – I'm just another nobody, along with the hundreds of other hopefuls and wannabees in New York, waiting for their moment. Don't look at me, nothing to see here.

As my heart rate slows down, and my breath starts to calm, one image appeared in my mind. As clear as anything.

Rebecca. It was Rebecca who had done this to me, to me

and Sancha. It was her, right from the beginning, wasn't it? That casting... letting Ed do that to me in the Arcola? What happened to Olivia. Then choosing Sancha and not me for this part. All of it went back to her.

Rebecca had all the power, was pulling all the strings, playing with all of us – me, Sancha, Greg, Sarah, all of us. The thoughts spiralled around and around in my mind. It all came back to her. To Rebecca.

THIRTY-NINE

Standing on the stage, before you are revealed to the audience, is the most amazing place to be. I can hear the audience taking their seats, asking to get past, talking about if there's time to get another drink before the play starts. Not long now. I exhale, slowly, counting to ten, as we had been trained to do before every performance. I smooth down my dress, though it doesn't really need it.

It's opening night, so everyone who is anyone in the New York theatre scene is here. I can see so many famous faces, actors who I've seen on TV – a Rebecca Sheridan play is a big deal and everyone wants to see this new cast. I can see Greg just ahead of me in the stalls, but then he would be here, wouldn't he? If it's a Rebecca show, then he is here, part of the circus.

Rebecca must be here somewhere. Will she be watching from the wings, or from the back of the auditorium, or maybe somewhere central in the stalls, where the view is best. She will want to watch it, to see how the play is when it is performed in front of an audience. A play doesn't really exist until an audience watches it. Until then, we are just people messing around, playing make-believe.

Just minutes before the play is due to start, and the atmosphere in the auditorium is electric. The audience can already see the stage – it's lit dark blood orange, almost red. It's very clever. The furniture and props on stage are also orange, which saturates everything in the colour. The stage is raked and everything tilts inwards, drawing your eye into the centre, making the stage feel claustrophobic, focused. Lighting pulses, waiting for the action to start. It's like looking inside a strange, weird womb.

And then I can hear the audience getting louder, all talking at once, excited about something, and I look to the right of the stalls, where a group is now standing up, shifting, moving aside to make way for someone. And of course, it's her.

Rebecca has arrived, just seconds before the play is due to start. She is gliding along the row of seats, effortlessly, smiling at those she passes, leaning in to kiss one man, another leaning forward to give her arm a squeeze, all telling her that yes, she is the one they have come to see really, that she is the star turn here. To show their support for her, so she, in turn, will support them when the time comes, whether they are directors, casting agents, actors... It's a gang, a clique, and she is surrounded by her adoring fans. She won't see me, I'm too far back, just off to the side, but I am watching her.

A flash of blinding white light from around the proscenium arch, and there is Sancha, standing in the centre of the stage. I feel a surge of excitement for her. And she does look amazing. So confident, like she does truly belong there. Her first professional role since we graduated. I stare at her face and suspect that I am the only one who really knows what she is feeling right now. That mixture of nervous tension and exhilaration. Trusting that the muscle memory will kick in and the lines will come, and you will be able to lose yourself in the part and make the audience suspend belief for the time that you have them captive.

I wonder if Jon is here somewhere? It was all so last minute, with Zawe not able to go on.

I had been lucky to get this ticket really, a standby. I'd had to queue up for returns, but because I was on my own I got in, leaving the couples who'd tried out of luck. Sancha had messaged the WhatsApp group with so much excitement:

> I'm going on!! Zawe's ill. They talked about postponing opening, but it's going ahead!! Aghh! Wish me luck!!!

I don't think she expected any of us to turn up at such short notice, more just boasting really, but as I was still here in New York, why not? Neema had replied saying she would try, but hadn't updated on that.

I had thought about telling Sancha I was in the theatre, about texting to say, 'Break a leg'. The memory of us in her dressing room and what had happened between us... my mind went to the image of my hands around her neck. But I had to come tonight.

I thought back to the two of us at RADA. How she was on stage – she was an electric performer. We had so much history. I had to be here for her big moment, her debut.

And to see if she was better than me in this role, too.

It's over. I make my way out to the foyer with the rest of the audience, and stand there as the building empties. Should I go to the stage door? Try and find Sancha? I look around, try to see where Rebecca has gone. Will she be backstage too, to see her cast?

'You OK?' a short woman with an iPad asks me. I glance around, a stream of audience members are leaving the theatre, pouring onto the street. Some hang about, waiting for something.

'I'm not sure,' I reply, truthfully.

She glances at her iPad. 'Are you press?'

I guess that me being on my own marks me out in some way. I turn on my best British accent. '*The Stage*'.

'Ah! British! Amazing!' She looks at her iPad again. 'I can't see...' She looks confused bless her. She's even younger than me.

'It was all very last minute. We aren't always in New York. But you have so many Brits in this cast.' I use my very best RP accent – one thing I had mastered at RADA.

She nods. 'You've come out the wrong way. If you go back through that door, head to the stairs, the after party is up on the terrace.'

'Lovely. Thanks so much.'

A loud buzz of excited chatter tells me that I have found the right place. A DJ plays near the bar, and on the far side of the room, a terrace, open out to the night sky. The girl on the door is surrounded, overwhelmed by guests, and I just walk past, taking a drink from an almost identical girl holding a silver tray. No-one asks me who I am, or checks for a press pass or anything, and with a glass in hand I look completely at home. I'm in.

Loud voices, all trying to talk over each other. Somewhere here there must be Sancha, Rebecca and who knows who else. Journalists, directors, casting agents. A new Rebecca play is a big thing. What are they all talking about? I think of Zawe, who was meant to be the star of the play. Is anyone talking about her, on this press night? Sancha really does get all the luck.

I make my way around the edges of the room, wondering who I might spot. I reach the far side, and step out onto the terrace. It's freezing cold out here, so I find myself pretty much alone, apart from two men at the far end, vaping. I peer over the edge. We are so high up, and the view beyond is spectacular. I can just about glimpse the Hudson, through the skyscrapers, glittering beyond. Traffic below, horns blaring, everyone going about their hectic lives. I think back to that balcony at Rebecca's, and Ed. How he'd looked at me, how he'd talked about me. I find myself smiling, thinking back to that night. He had got what he deserved.

I walk back into the party, wondering what my next move will be.

'Jemima! Here you are, in real life.' Jon. He had made it from the Hamptons. Had he any idea what had gone on, in the last few weeks? He seemed OK to talk to me. Sancha can't have told him about what had happened in her dressing room.

'Oh, hi, Jon! Amazing to see you! Wasn't she good!'

'So good. I am so proud of her.' He looks like he had just come from an office, too smart and uptight in his suit for this theatre crowd. 'Sancha didn't say you were coming. All these years you never made it over to the States, and now here you are!'

'Things change.'

'She's so lucky to get the press night,' Jon continued. 'Really bad luck for Zawe. Food poisoning. Apparently she was really supportive about it. Sancha was so nervous.'

'Oh, yes. Really unusual. I wonder if Zawe will be OK for tomorrow.'

'Don't know. I hope so! It will be a nightmare if Sancha is on all the time. Polly really misses her.'

I look at him. 'She'll need to be here, as the understudy though. Just in case.'

'Every night? I don't think so.'

Did he not understand? I wondered what Sancha had said to him. Really, she did need to be in New York for the length of the show, in case Zawe couldn't do it, even last minute. Understudies need to be in the theatre in case something happens right until curtain up. I'd even heard of them going on mid-show. In London recently, the star had fainted in the second act and the understudy had gone on to finish the play. That was all part of the job. Didn't sound like Sancha had explained that part to Jon.

'Sancha was amazing, wasn't she?' I tried to bring the conversation back to safer ground, before I could move away from him. I glanced over his shoulder.

'Oh, for sure. Though I just see her as Sancha, you know what I mean? Hard to think of her as someone else. The whole acting thing – well, it's still just her, isn't it?' He grinned at me, his boyish face not really doing the job for me.

I nod, not sure what to reply.

Had Sancha been good? It was hard to tell. I would have played it differently. In some ways, she was a bit *obvious* in the role. But then, that's the issue with being the understudy – you don't get enough time to rehearse. Or perhaps the role wasn't right for her. I wonder if Rebecca was now seeing that, too. Maybe she was thinking that I would have been better, after all.

I hear a loud, confident American voice. Jonas. Holding court near the bar. I can just about make out his face, surrounded by people, the tallest of the group.

'Excuse me. So sorry. Have to talk to...' I make my way towards Jonas. I have nothing to lose by talking to him, playing the game. Just act confident, like you have so many parts coming up, so many opportunities, and you are just saying hi to an old friend. Or is it more like picking a scab, trying to find out what's underneath.

'Jemima.' I turn and see Greg.

'Hi.' We hadn't spoken since I'd left the hotel. Really, what was there to say?

'Enjoy the play?' he asks, glancing awkwardly around me.

'It was amazing! So good.'

'Greg. Are you going to introduce us?' a woman says, with more volume than you would expect from such a short, narrow person. Posh American. Swishy hair. Too blow-dried to be fashionable.

'Yes, yes, sure! Jemima, this is Stephanie.' She holds out her hand for me to what, shake? Her skinny, under-nourished arm looked like you could snap it.

'Lovely to meet you!' I reply, doing a great job of appearing interested. So, who was Stephanie? A date? An old work friend? I found that I really didn't care. Good luck to him.

'I need to talk to...' I beam and let the words get lost in the loud babble around me, and I was sure Greg was as relieved as I was, when I moved on.

Jonas is still talking when I reach him. Does he ever let anyone else get a word in? I take a deep breath, ease back my shoulders and let out a loud, 'Jonas! Darling!' as I reach around his waist to hug him towards me, just as if we were *such* close friends.

His face falls, just for a split second, and then, 'Oh! Hello there!' He laughs loudly, styling it out. 'Everyone – this is Jemima. An actress. Over from London.'

Two men lean in to kiss me, happy to include a pretty woman in their circle for just a moment or two. Makes the old men look good.

'Jonas, can I get a very quick word with you?' I pull him gently away from the group and not wanting to seem like a dick, he comes with me. We stand just to one side, and I notice that he moves me slightly, so his large frame blocks me from anyone tempted to listen in. He clearly wants this to be a short conversation.

'Surprised to see you here,' he says.

'Are you? Sancha and I are old friends. I thought you knew that.'

He lightly shook his head – he didn't know? Or didn't want to talk about it.

'She said she was going on tonight, so here I am!'

'Amazing,' he replies, his enthusiasm not quite reaching his eyes.

'Last time I saw you was at the casting. I thought I was in with a good shot of this!'

'I can't really discuss the casting process with you, Jemima. I'm sure you understand that.'

I nod. 'The casting process. That's one way of putting it. I guess that's just how Rebecca does things. And you go along with it.'

I thought back to that night in Cornwall, when I'd performed for them all, Jonas just watching. Happy to go along with whatever she wanted, and whoever she wanted. Escorting that actress out of the party at the Paper Factory. He was used to making things happen for Rebecca.

This was my moment, and I wasn't sure if I would get another.

'Jonas, what happened to Olivia? You knew, didn't you? That she was taking drugs of some kind.'

He looks around him, then looks straight at me, annoyed. 'This is a night for celebration.' He starts to walk away from me, so I place my hand on his arm.

'Don't. I can talk very loudly, if I need to. I am sure the whole room would love to know what we're talking about.' I hold his gaze.

'It was an accident.'

'Was it, though? You knew she was taking drugs. Something wasn't right. Did you help her? Did Rebecca?' He looks around him, as if expecting someone to help him out here. 'Did *you* supply her with something?'

Jonas leans towards me, his face now close to mine, his voice clipped, trying to remain in control. 'You bringing this up because you didn't get this role? Is that it?' He sneers, his perfect teeth look so fake against his old face.

'You could have given this to me. To make up for *Poison* and what happened in London. You called *me* in!' I felt I had nothing to lose, saying this to him.

'Rebecca doesn't want you,' he snaps at me.

'And you just do anything she wants, don't you? You know Rebecca was there that night, when Olivia died. In the theatre.'

'Everyone was there, Jemima. We were all there, you included.'

'I heard her. Rebecca. She was looking for Olivia.'

'What are you saying?' He looks at me, focused at last.

'Rebecca was more involved than I think we realise. Or do you know more than you are letting on...'

He looks shocked, then composes himself. He glances around to check no one is listening to us.

I had his attention. 'You know all sorts of things about her, don't you?' I wanted to rile him, get him thinking.

He takes a sip from his drink and tries to look relaxed.

'Olivia made her own choices. There's no conspiracy here, Jemima. Just people who really don't know what they are taking on when they get into this business. Stupid people. Weak people.' He grips my arm, tightly. 'Move on.'

He turns and walks back to his clique, with a loud 'Hey!', and they envelop him back into their circle.

I stand there, letting the adrenalin subside. Maybe it would come to nothing, but I had planted that seed.

Jonas got paid well, enjoyed this life of parties, of power, and to access that, his job was to fit in with what Rebecca wanted. But if people started to question Rebecca's behaviour, how long would that last? Had he known that Rebecca was there the night Olivia died – maybe even with her? Did that worry him at all? When would people start asking questions about him, too.

I badly needed another drink – something short and strong would do. The bartender was working hard at the far end, so I stood there waiting for my turn, not important enough to be seen fast. Still no sign of Sancha. How long would it take her to remove the worst of the stage make up, get changed and get up here from the theatre? How would she act when she saw me? Ignore me, I guess, and instead focus on the Sheridan Productions people, her colleagues, Jon, those who would be waiting to praise her.

I rubbed my arm, where Jonas had squeezed it. After what had happened in the dressing room, she might even make a scene, demand that I leave. But Jon hadn't said anything, so surely she hadn't told him about what had happened. I wondered why.

I lean onto the bar and try to catch the bartender's attention. A glimpse of sequins, someone waving at me. Right at the end of the bar, giving me a wave, Anisha. She looks so glamorous – flawless make up, glowing skin in a barely-there dress. She leans over and catches the arm of the bartender and signals in my direction. He is straight over, and takes my order. I smile 'thank you' back at her, but she is already talking to someone who looks far more important. Back to hustling to get her film made.

The vodka has the desired effect, relaxing me, softening the edges of the evening. *So, here's the plan, Jem. See Sancha, say well done. Leave it so that maybe, just maybe, she will get in touch with me some time, and that maybe in the future we can be friends again.* But if she doesn't want that, then could I really blame her? But that isn't the main reason I came tonight.

I become aware that the DJ has cut the music, and people are turning to face in one direction.

The main players have arrived. I see Rebecca, about to step onto a small, raised platform at the far end of the room. Jonas is right there, beside her, Sancha just behind him. I make my way forward, pushing through the crowd. I find myself in front of the tiny stage, focused on her, on Rebecca.

With a start, she notices me, then glances at Jonas, indicates for him to send me away. And then he hesitates, pauses and steps back. He isn't quite as sure anymore. Good. He glances at me.

I take my moment. Step forward, right up close to Rebecca.

'Why did you treat me like you did? Is it all just a game to you?'

Rebecca looks around to see if anyone is listening. I know I don't have long.

'You made me think that part was mine.'

She smiles at me, and runs her hand slowly up her arm, and I can almost feel the goose bumps.

'This isn't the time or place, Jemima.'

'This seems like the perfect time to me.'

'It's Sancha's moment.' Rebecca looks around her, as if looking for Sancha. 'I am sure you don't want to ruin this for her. Now, excuse me. My audience is waiting for me.' She moves away from me, about to step onto the stage.

I reach for her, hold her arm. She looks at me, irritated. Looking around her, for someone to make this irritation go away. We both realise that Jonas has moved away, is no longer by her side. The last thing she wants is a scene, right here, with all the theatre press watching. We are both aware that people are starting to listen in.

She steps close towards me, that incredible voice, now so close to my face.

'You know, you really do look like her. It's lovely in some ways, and also, a little unsettling.'

I feel like everything has been building to this scene, but I really hadn't understood the role I was playing. I wait for Rebecca to say her next line.

'I couldn't believe it when I saw you at your end-of-term

show. You look so like her when she was young. The same hair, anyone can see that. But it was something else. The way you looked... as if you were looking at me, right at me, challenging me in some way.' She smiles, at some distant memory. 'Like she did. We were very different really, very different backgrounds. But she had such a spark about her. So much hunger for life! I recognised that in you, when I first saw you... I've been interested in your career ever since.'

Rebecca continued.

'She was so excited when she got the chance to act in a play in Australia. I didn't want her to go. We'd only just got together. I said I'd get her work in the UK, there was no need to go, she should stay with me...' I see a shadow move across her face, a sadness I had never seen before in Rebecca, always so confident, assured.

'It was just a small play really – the one in Australia. *Poison*, of course.'

My mind was trying to keep up.

'I wanted to do that play for her, it was my way of remembering her, of honouring her. It had to be perfect. Getting Olivia was so key. I wanted it to be amazing, special, convince all the best people to see it, to get incredible reviews. Which she would have got. And you. You had to be in it – you are so alike...'

I could see people gathering nearby, one of the other actors from the play was standing next to us. People were expecting a speech and I could sense people were starting to get restless, curious. The audience was building.

Rebecca continued talking, but I wasn't sure if she was talking at me, or just remembering.

'I flew out there to see Roisin. To surprise her. In her first play.' I look around, wondering who can hear this. People hovering nearby, listening in. Rebecca didn't seem to register them.

'But it had been cancelled, and I couldn't find her. I went to the theatre, and it was closed, no reason given. And then, when I heard... It took hours for me to find out. Her parents didn't know about me. Roisin hadn't told them about us. Didn't think they would take it well. So, I only heard about it, hanging around the theatre, that she'd died. Can you believe that?' She shakes her head.

Then Rebecca looks at me, stares at me. Her eyes so dark, all the affection she'd been talking about, gone in an instant. 'And it was your brother who killed her.'

I step back, try to steady myself.

'I don't understand.'

She laughs then, lifting her head to look out at the party around us.

'Your brother. He killed her. Your brother was driving the car that... she was in his car.'

My legs go weak. I look around wildly. Rebecca steps closer towards me and I step back, almost to the edge of the stage.

'He fell asleep at the wheel, or got distracted. They don't know.'

No, that can't be right. Not Mark. He was always such a careful driver. Though he didn't drive that much in London, who did? She had to be wrong.

'When I saw you at drama school, you looked so like her. I couldn't believe my eyes. I had to find out more about you. It's amazing how every little story stays online forever, isn't it? You getting into RADA made your local newspaper. Your drama teacher was so proud of you. As did the story about your brother dying. Same name. Same school...'

Rebecca looks increasingly manic as she speaks, her eyes searching my face for some sort of understanding of what she was telling me.

'I couldn't believe it. How you and I had been brought together. We were meant to meet.'

I just stand there, trying to take it all in. Why hasn't she told me all this before? There have been so many chances.

'You see, he stole everything from me. The one person I loved. I could see it so clearly when I met you. It was like Roisin sent you to me.'

This made no sense. I didn't know about the woman in the car, with Mark. Or maybe they hadn't told me... Mum, Daniel... To protect me? Or maybe I hadn't been able to take it in. My perfect brother. Nothing made sense anymore.

It feels like the music had died down, or is Rebecca's voice louder, or is it all just in my head. *She hates me, because of my brother*. I look around wildly, and can see people staring. Someone is recording this, on their phone.

'It wasn't me... it wasn't my fault,' I hear myself shout, and I am not sure what I am referring to. People are staring, looking at me, looking at Rebecca.

And then Sancha is there beside me, and the crowd parts to let us through, all the time staring, watching, and she pulls me with her, and then we are by the door.

Sancha stops dead in front of me. 'Why the hell are you here?'

'I wanted to see you in the play.'

'You need to leave.'

'I'm sorry... so sorry. This should have been different for us.'

I looked over to where Rebecca is standing, she's loud, angry, shouting at people. 'Rebecca told me that my brother killed someone. Someone she loved...'

'What? Is that true?'

I rub my face, try to make sense of it all. 'I don't know. I didn't want to know... yes, it might be true.' I had avoided Daniel when he tried to talk to me about it all, cut him off. I blamed him for taking my brother away, and it was easier for us both not to talk, to avoid each other, to live our separate, damaged lives.

Sancha is trying to talk to me. 'I can't have you here. Not after... Jon's here.'

'I know. We talked.'

Sancha looks around, panicked. 'Don't try anything here. What you did to me—'

I looked at her, calmly. 'It's a room full of people, Sancha. What could I possibly do?'

She takes a step back from me and smooths her dress. She is the star here tonight, and there's no way she wants a scene. I can see her gather herself, her thoughts. She looks at me, calmly. *Well, she is an actress.*

'You never said what happened to your brother. So, he killed someone. You're messed up, Jemima.'

'None of this is my fault. Rebecca hates me. Wants to punish me.'

And then I watch the slow realisation on her face. 'Wait, do you mean...? Is this why she cast *me*?' We look at each other, trying to work it all out. 'To get at *you*?'

We look over to where Rebecca is standing, because there is noise, and commotion and something happening that we can't quite make out. I can see Jonas is there, and a man I don't recognise, and I can only guess at what they could be saying to her. She is shouting something, and people are watching her, and talking about her, and it almost looks like she is being taken somewhere, towards a side room, and the man is... who? Someone she works with? Security? Another woman has her phone out, and is recording it all. The room is watching Rebecca, taking it all in.

Time for me to leave. Sancha has her face turned away from me, watching Rebecca, no doubt trying to work out what this means for her.

I lean towards her, and kiss her lightly on the cheek, and I wonder for a moment, if we will see each other again.

And then I'm on the stairs, red velvet carpet under my feet, almost running down the sweeping staircase, and I'm out of there. Show over.

I am outside the hotel, people streaming past. I walk along 42nd Street, taking in the theatres, the blaring, gaudy adverts for musicals, plays, concerts – life is all around me. I stop eventually, overlooking the Hudson River. So vast in its grimy darkness, so deep and full of secrets, it reminds me of the Thames, and far away, of Seagrass and home.

So my story has brought me here. It started in London, at that first casting, or I thought it had, but it really started years before, with a talented red-haired actress, about to make her debut, somewhere far away, her dreams about to come true. I think of her now, the woman in the photo, the one who looked like me. She had her dreams, and they have been taken from her.

I think about my brother, too. Two people with their whole lives in front of them, and the pointless waste of all that potential. And how that had brought me here, to Rebecca, to New York, and here.

I try to make sense of it all. Of everything I've done.

Roisin had been in the car with my beloved brother that night. I wondered if Roisin and Mark had been working on the play together, or had been travelling back from a party. Mark was so kind, maybe he had offered her a ride. But why wasn't Daniel with them? Why had it been just the two of them in the car? Perhaps there was more between Mark and Roisin than we would ever know. Or maybe it was just something that happened, oil on the road, a fault in the car, something that caught his eye. He would never have wanted to hurt anyone.

Whatever it was, it had brought me to here, and this moment of realisation how anything can change in a split second, and the ripple effect of that, years later. I could ask Daniel, but I haven't been in touch for a long time, and maybe part of me doesn't really want to know.

I watch a ferry go past, packed with people staring back at me. A little girl waves at me, her face so sweet, so full of innocence and hope. Around me, skyscrapers full of people, going about their busy lives.

All these people in the world, and I thought I would be the special one? The one to make it, to get that admiration, success, stardom, to be *somebody*. This industry, *this stupid industry*, where adults get paid to pretend, to act out stories and play make-believe, with people desperate to be in it, at any price. This script had started years ago, and we were the ones who got to play out the final scenes.

I think back to Ed and Olivia. Gone. Would any of it ever be traced back to me? It all felt so far away, so unreal, far away in London.

Ed had been such a creep towards me – treated me like a prostitute, or tried to. The way he'd spoken about me to the other guy at that party. Like I deserved to be talked about like that!

It had been so easy, he was close to the balcony edge anyway. It was more that I didn't help him when I saw he was unsteady... rather than push him, exactly. The relief I felt when I walked away from that party. Oh my goodness, it was the most delicious feeling. No one noticed me. I wasn't important, noticed, recognised. I had done the world a favour, getting rid of that one. He'd brought it upon himself. Lying there, the blood pooling around his head, he looked so still and peaceful, no longer a threat to anyone.

And Olivia. That was harder, but then, once you've seen one person die, it's easier the second time. She was so out of it, anyway, I just helped her along. Just slipped into her room, saw the pills. She *knew* how important this play was to me. So I took her favourite scarf and put it over her mouth and nose... it was so quick, really. They had all treated me so badly at the Arcola, hadn't thought of me at all. I'd had enough of people treating me like that. Thinking about it, I eased her out of her pain, helped her to leave her worries behind. It was a real shame about the play though – perhaps I should learn to control my temper a little, going forward. An understandable mistake, given the pressure I was under. And one more actress out of the game can only help. There is so much competition for parts.

Had I planted enough seeds to link it all to Rebecca, I mused? Surely the focus would all be on her, now, and Sheridan Productions. In some ways Ed and Olivia died because of this industry, the pressures it places on you. The competition, the judgement...

No one would think of me, just another actress, one of so many. I wasn't the star here – no one was looking at me.

When I go home, and speak to the police, I can tell them about the stress everyone was under, how Rebecca treats people. How she treats actresses. So many people had witnessed that, or experienced that, over the years, people will be only too willing to share their negative stories about her. I can mention, just casually, that Rebecca was there in the corridor when Olivia died, and they can make of that what they will. Jonas knows she was there, too. And Sarah. They know Rebecca left the Arcola bar, around the time Olivia died. They are smart – they will be thinking about that. A room full of people will notice that Rebecca wasn't there for a short while.

If the police talk to me, I have my lines all ready. I am really good at acting, that much I do know. I can be really convincing.

Rebecca chose the wrong actress to play games with. That's her all over – she sees us as desperate, easy to dominate, easy to control. So pathetically grateful for any work that comes our way, that we'll put up with anything. But I've had years to prepare. I've been a victim before, and I've had enough of it. It's all so strangely liberating. I've got away with murder, so who knows what I could handle next? No director, producer, actor or agent will intimidate me now.

I stand up, roll my shoulders back, and take in a deep breath, just as we've been trained to do.

Ready for my next act.

A LETTER FROM THE AUTHOR

Dear reader,

Huge thanks for reading *Someone Like You*. I hope you were hooked on Jemima's journey. If you want to join other readers in hearing all about my new releases and bonus content, you can sign up here:

www.stormpublishing.co/becky-alexander

If you enjoyed this book and could spare a few moments to leave a review that would be hugely appreciated. Even a short review can make all the difference in encouraging a reader to discover my books for the first time. Thank you so much!

I have always loved going to the theatre. Sitting there, in the audience, you get to escape from the real world for a couple of hours, and to experience other people's amazing creativity and storytelling. If you haven't been to the theatre for a while, go – there is so much incredible talent out there.

But I have never wanted to be an actor. Being an actor has always seemed incredibly brave to me – how do they learn all those lines, and what if something goes wrong? What if ticket sales are bad, or the reviews are terrible? Not to mention the expensive training, the auditions, the rejections... It's a wonder anyone does it at all, but I am glad that they do.

I was curious to get inside the mind of an actor, and to explore why someone might want to be on the stage. Because it's fun and makes them feel alive? To bring people together, to share stories, and bring joy? Or is there a deeper need, perhaps to be admired, become famous? I enjoyed creating Jemima, and putting her into this high-pressure world. Thank you for reading about her.

I am grateful to all the real-life actors who shared their experiences with me. You know who you are, and your secrets are (almost) safe with me.

Thanks again for being part of this amazing journey with me and I hope you'll stay in touch – I have so many more stories and ideas to entertain you with!

Becky Alexander

 x.com/beckyalex_books

 instagram.com/packedwithgoodthings

ACKNOWLEDGEMENTS

Writing *Someone Like You* has been a long process. Writers out there, please take heart!

I first had the idea for this novel at a Lucy Cavendish writing course – it was my first trip away on my own for a very long time, and the chance to get away, listen to authors, meet other budding writers and try some creative writing was priceless.

Many months later I enrolled on a short course at City University with Caroline Green. She taught our small group about structure, plot and thrillers, and was so generous with her time and support. Especially thanks to Karen Richardson and Will Finch for early reading, train chats and accountability.

A terrible first draft and many months later, I knew I needed more help. My beloved Grandma May gave me some money just before my fiftieth birthday, and I spent it on a Curtis Brown writing course. Charlotte Mendelson and my talented course mates showed me how to write and edit a novel. Thanks to Emily, Ally Zetterberg, Roisin O'Donnell, Abi Graham, Madelon Fleminger, Fabian Foley, Sam Robertson, Jenni Lieberman, Aoi Matsushima, Joyce Dvorak, Sarah Ball Moore, Natasha Dandavati, Lindsay West and Sean Bennett. I list the group by name as some already have novels out, and there are more on the way – do look out for them.

Thanks to Dave Baker for his insight into the London police world. I am glad to hear you are writing your own book about your new life in the countryside.

A huge thank you to OVO theatre company in St Albans, for letting me watch a rehearsal for *Macbeth*. I urge you to go and see one of their productions in the St Albans Roman Theatre – it is one of the most spectacular theatres in the world. They also perform at the Minack, which you have just read about. OVO are an incredible, talented company of people, and nothing like the characters in my novel.

Partly for research, and also to face my fear of public speaking, I joined the adult acting classes run by Best Theatre Arts, and found a brilliant group of people to hang out with. Thanks especially to Lisa Schulberg and Catherine Lomax for showing us what fun acting can be.

Thank you to Nick Hern Books for allowing me to quote from *Poison* by Liselot Vekemans. It's a great play – do go and see it if you can.

Charlie Campbell rang me as soon as I sent him *Someone Like You*, and likened it to one of his favourite novels. He has championed this book all the way, at the same time as launching Greyhound Literary and raising a young family – thank you for all your hard work! Thank you to Kathryn Taussig at Storm for showing me, with great tact and author care, what needed to change, and giving me time to do that. Thank you to Liz Hurst for her excellent editing skills.

Thanks to Sancha and Jemima for lending me their names. Jem, we miss you x

And to my family and friends for hearing all my early ideas, and reading those rough drafts. Steve, Isabel, Polly, Katie and Vicky – thank you x

Printed in Great Britain
by Amazon

36519076R00189